AMONG THE WONDERFUL

A Novel

STACY CARLSON

STEERFORTH PRESS
Hanover, New Hampshire

For information about permission to
reproduce selections from this book, write to:

Steerforth Press L.L.C.
45 Lyme Road, Suite 208, Hanover, NH 03755

Earlier versions of chapter seven and eight
were previously published in *Inkwell* Magazine.

Library of Congress Cataloging-in-Publication Data:
Carlson, Stacy.
Among the wonderful : a novel / Stacy Carlson. -- 1st ed.
    p. cm.
ISBN 978-1-58642-184-7 (alk. paper)
1. Barnum's American Museum--Fiction. 2. Barnum, P. T. (Phineas
Taylor), 1810-1891--Fiction. 3. Curiosities and
wonders--Fiction. 4. New York (N.Y.)--History--1775-1865--
Fiction. I. Title.
PS3603.A75327A83 2011
813'.6--dc22

                                    2011015162

ISBN 978-1-58642-201-1

This novel is a work of fiction. Names, characters,
places and incidents are either the products of the
author's imagination or used fictitiously.

1 3 5 7 9 10 8 6 4 2

FIRST PAPERBACK EDITION

For Jason and Djuna

Prologue
Ana's Passage

The water below did not surge or recoil. It neither splashed — not from where I could see — nor frothed. No current swept it along the coast and no moon pulled it to tides. I watched the slow rolling of this gray syrup while the steamer *North Shore* pushed thickly on, seeming to labor more than water should demand.

"Shh. Look!" The deckside breeze carried an exaggerated female whisper directly to my ear. "Right there. I *told* you!"

I did not look. I clenched the railing, aware that I could rip it free of its stanchions and hurl it toward this noise, this intrusion. Were my hours, days, years of being gazed upon not enough to earn me a moment's privacy? Rage flooded back, filling the contours gouged last night by Mr. Ramsay (I will never say his Christian name again) shouting after me as I left Toronto once and for all. But I would not wheel around and claw the air. I would not throw the benches arranged so tidily on the steamer's top deck. I would not give that whispered voice the satisfaction. Instead I peered into the water.

No delicate creatures inhabited these depths. The only fish alive down there scooted blindly above a muddy carpet, skin flaking, jaws filtering stagnant water in search of wormy food. I ignored the brightness of the sky and the mindless tumble of gulls. I perceived the eyes of the two women boring through my back. I was sure they discussed their strange luck that I should be here for them to behold.

I imagined the water sucking me down to a place untroubled by any pulse. Gravity, that appalling master of the body, loosened its grip for once. My preposterous heft sloughed away and I drifted, deliciously weightless. In one swift motion I could be there. I willed Lake Ontario to yield more of this perverse solace even as my mind clamped tight around it: Drowning, indeed. What a ridiculous notion.

"Look! Look!" the women cried again, their bleats barely distinguishable from the gulls.

I turned, then, and there I was, reflected in their small, astonished faces and their delicate gasps. I straightened to my full height and cooled the rage with your words, with what you'd told me, Mother, time after time: *You are a mirror held up in front of other people, Ana, which reflects their truest selves.* But if that is so, then truly all humanity is an abomination.

"Look! There it is!" And then I saw that they were pointing past me. "America."

She was right: It was there on the horizon — a drowsy leviathan drawing closer every moment, casting its hungry eyes across the waters.

Ark of the City

One

They had discarded the egret. And strangely, the lynx. As he approached the building Guillaudeu observed that someone had draped a burlap sack around the wild cat and left it on the sidewalk. But the covering had half fallen away, exposing taut feline shoulders poised for attack. Inside the museum the lynx had inspired awe among the visitors. But against this new backdrop of street refuse, and in the bold morning light, the specimen had the look of a bleached housecat enchanted by a ball of dust.

Until very recently, the changes had all been to the exterior of the building. The brick façade had disappeared under layers of whitewash and teams of men had painted oval portraits across the face of the structure, depicting everything from elephants to the Annunciation. They had even rebuilt the balcony, and judging from the crowds that now filled it, this narrow promenade over Broadway was as entertaining as the museum's contents, if not more so.

Guillaudeu did not appreciate the new owner's gaudy taste. He averted his eyes from the huge transparency at the museum entrance that bore the smiling, bare-breasted image of the museum's most recent acquisition: a mermaid. In his irritated mind, he shuffled through the myriad upsets in routine that had occurred since that scoundrel had taken ownership of the museum: the new exhibits, the theater, the rooftop restaurant, and on each floor an army of concessionaires. The whole place was a roiling mess.

He watched three men leave the building. One carried the white-faced ibis by the neck. The others struggled at each end of a reindeer. He did not betray even a hint of displeasure, though he felt an urgent desire to snatch back the ibis.

The first visitors of the day formed a line outside the ticket window, and a vendor was selling them hot corn and coffee. Guillaudeu continued into the entrance hall, pushing through the inner door just behind a man and his young daughter.

"A Chinaman pulled her up in a net!" the girl sang out as she skipped ahead of her father. "She's got hair mixed with seaweed and a necklace of pearls!"

The man hurried as the girl bounded up the first steps of the great marble stairway that led to the exhibits. She had holes in her stockings, and her father moved stiffly in a worn oilcloth coat.

Guillaudeu walked past the door to his own office; like the patrons, he had business on the second floor before the day's true work began.

"Here, Margaret. This way!" the father called.

"I can almost *see* her." The girl's voice was frantic as she approached the exhibit.

Guillaudeu heard a shriek but he did not stop. He was already well aware that the desiccated horror the girl now beheld was nothing like the siren depicted on the transparency hanging outside the museum, and it was certainly nothing like the image she had coveted in her mind. When he glanced toward them, the father was making the sign of the Cross. Guillaudeu hurried around the corner without meeting his eye.

His footsteps echoed as he walked across the portrait gallery where the blank faces of monarchs and presidents added their gazes to the empty air. At the far end he turned left into Gallery Three. He found the sloth in its handsome pergola, sleeping high in the crook of a dead tree trunk. It squatted with its long arms folded around its legs and sunlight from the gallery's high windows warming its back.

Guillaudeu had hoped that by now a proper naturalist

would have been hired; he resented the amount of his time that had been wasted worrying over the museum's newest inhabitants.

"You're an odd sort of fellow," said Guillaudeu to the lump of gray-brown fur that acted as if sleeping in a museum were the thing one was born to do. With one hand Guillaudeu clutched a small parcel wrapped in newspaper and with the other he twisted the end of his mustache, which, though his hair was white, remained the color of cinnamon. The creature was in precisely the same place as when Guillaudeu had visited the pergola the previous afternoon.

In an absurdly languorous movement the sloth raised its head. It lifted its arm and soundlessly scratched its armpit. Then the animal directed its attention toward the ceiling.

"How can an animal never come down to the ground?" Guillaudeu was unaccustomed to analyzing animal behavior, never having had to account for it during his thirty-eight years as a taxidermist. "Who wants a sloth in a museum anyway?"

He located the key to the pergola in his waistcoat pocket. He unlocked it and unwrapped his parcel, which contained half a cabbage. He pulled apart the outer leaves and placed the vegetable in the sloth's tin bowl, which still held the two uneaten carrots and several brown lettuce leaves of yesterday's meal. The creature now appeared to be gazing out the window, where the diffuse light of a March morning brightened.

Guillaudeu descended the marble stairway against an incoming tide of people. Shoulders bumped him. The feather of a woman's hat brushed across his neck and he swatted it away. The crowd's excited murmur gave him a bitter sense of constriction. At the bottom of the stairs he turned left, out of the throng, and passed through a door marked NO ADMITTANCE into a corridor with one closed door at the end. Guillaudeu would take up the matter of the sloth with the new proprietor.

Phineas T. Barnum had inherited Guillaudeu, along with the museum's collection of mounted specimens, from John

Scudder, the museum's original owner. Scudder had been Guillaudeu's benefactor, professional mentor, and closest friend. He still could not bear to think of his old companion signing over both of their lives' work to a man like Barnum. He had made a point of avoiding Scudder ever since the older man had relinquished the title to the collection.

Guillaudeu had spoken with Barnum only twice. In the first conversation Barnum praised the museum's taxidermy displays and assured Guillaudeu that his services were invaluable to any natural history enterprise. But he then proceeded to reinvent the museum. *To add interest,* he had said during their second conversation, while men hoisted the first of the transparencies outside. *Anything outdated must be expunged!* Guillaudeu half expected to be thrown out himself.

He was increasingly upset as strangers delivered more and more live animals to the museum. The creatures arrived in a racket of squeals; there was even a man who arrived at the door to Guillaudeu's office with a one-eyed eagle tethered to his wrist. As he made his daily rounds among the specimens, he now looked closely to make sure no new creature was pacing or swimming in a cage that had sprung up unbeknownst to him. As he dusted and fumigated, he looked twice at specimens he had mounted himself: Was that a twitch of the head? Did the crane shift its weight from one leg to the other? He came to dread his peripheral vision.

He considered looking for employment elsewhere, but he could not bear the thought of leaving behind his menagerie of specimens, which now numbered close to one thousand creatures, despite the loss of the lynx, the egret, the ibis, and others.

He banged on the door to Barnum's office. No answer. He leaned his head briefly against the door frame and thought he heard something rustle on the other side. "Where are you?" he whispered. He knocked again, but no one came.

Guillaudeu made his way back to the entry hall with an uneasy feeling. The incoming crowd was almost impenetrable and he pushed himself against it to reach the door of his office, which was across from the ticket booth just inside the main doors. Once he was safely inside he moved to the opposite end of his cluttered workroom, past the piles of crates that had been arriving steadily and delivered, unfortunately, to his door.

He paused before the skin of the owl, *Asio flammeus,* which hung, splay-winged, from hooks in the wall. The skull-less hood of its head remained erect above the pinned wings. He ran a finger along the banded brown primary feathers. It had taken him several days to identify the bird. He'd bought it at an auction and knew it came from arctic Norway, but its tags contained nothing legible except the words BOG OWL. It had taken careful study and verification from three different sources to characterize it as a short-eared owl. Now the specimen embodied this taxonomic victory and was thus endeared to the taxidermist. The poisoned varnish on the bill and feet was completely dry, and he examined the owl's soles to ensure that the incisions that had drawn out the tendons had not damaged the appearance of the specimen. They had not. Poised at the threshold of his work, about to dive into its infinite solace, he turned away.

"It's not my job to take care of live animals!" he irritably told no one. "That's not why I'm here! I'm not responsible for observing a godforsaken *sloth.* How should I know what it eats? You'll have to find someone else to be your stable hand, Mr. Barnum." He slouched into his chair. In an attempt to banish the sloth's dolorous visage from his mind, he picked up the current issue of the University of Edinburgh's *Scientific Journal.*

Guillaudeu's hero, the French anatomist Baron Georges Cuvier, had published a discourse titled *On the Revolutionary Upheavals on the Surface of the Globe,* which the journal had excerpted. Cuvier described long periods of equilibrium on earth, during which whole kingdoms of plants and animals flourished. These epochs, though, ended in cataclysms of fire or flood. Out of the rubble of the old age would arise entirely new creatures to crawl and fly across the globe until the next apocalypse consumed them. As he read these words, Guillaudeu's mind filled with the image of a massive cyclone of wind and lightning ripping up forests and carving great wounds in the earth. He had the uncomfortable sensation that Cuvier's theory explained more than just an ancient scenario: A dark whirlwind, he realized, had struck the museum in the form of Phineas T. Barnum.

Two

Guillaudeu pushed handfuls of excelsior into the varnished rib cage and bound it tightly with strips of linen. He replaced the owl's spinal column with a stout iron wire and strung on the bird's bleached vertebrae. Below this manufactured spine, a ball of bound excelsior became the new pelvic girdle, and he cut and sharpened the ends of two wires before slipping them through the incisions in the soles of the feet and upward inside the feathered legs. He used even heavier wire for the wings, since he wanted the specimen's ultimate pose to reflect the last moments before flight, wings uplifted.

He worked slowly, with precision and confidence. The rushing flood of visitors outside his office no longer bothered him. He recast each curve of musculature into shape and coaxed the emptied skin into what he believed was an essential new form. To Guillaudeu the scraping and stretching of leather, the briny, bloody, and alchemical tasks, each and every resinous and oily step in this metamorphosis was work that came with thrilling repercussions: What other process allowed people to come this close, so intimately close, to nature's meticulous designs?

His palette of chopped tow, powders, poisonous liquors, knives, brushes, and wires was spread out around him, each restoring ingredient within his reach and endowed, to his mind, with a numinous quality. There was no problem of anatomy, decomposition, or tanning that he could not solve. He worked single-mindedly, with a sense of duty that approached faith. Although he would never describe his joy as religious (he had never been a believer), his exultation burned like a glowing iron wire running all through him.

As he threaded a sturdy needle with catgut, Guillaudeu was interrupted by a violent knock on his door. The sound made two tiny golden monkeys, who had appeared at his doorstep the day before and who were extremely difficult to catch, leap from the bookshelf, where they'd been sleeping, and run back into their burlap-lined crate.

A large man wearing a dark blue suit, with slicked hair and one eyebrow slightly raised, stood at the door holding an ebony cane. His impatient, slightly theatrical posture made Guillaudeu instantly uncomfortable.

"Good morning?" Guillaudeu ventured, his mind still entirely with the owl and the delicate operation of securing its skin to its new architecture. With his broad face and tiny, close-set black eyes, Guillaudeu observed, the man resembled the American badger, *Taxidea taxus*.

"I'm looking for Mr. Barnum."

"Oh."

"Is he here?"

"Certainly not. Barnum has never set foot in my office."

The man looked past Guillaudeu into the room, as if Barnum were hiding among the crates inside.

"I am Mr. Archer," the man declared.

"I see." The name meant nothing to Guillaudeu.

"I am in need of an office. Barnum assured me I would be accommodated."

"You're an employee?"

The man seemed perturbed. "I am Mr. Ar-cher," he repeated, tapping his cane on the ground to match the two syllables of his name. "Formerly of the *Herald* and *The New York Sun*?"

"Ah! Mr. Archer. Yes, I'd forgotten you were to arrive today." Guillaudeu had never heard of Mr. Archer, but it would do no good to say so.

"I had expected to be met at the door. I have my things."

Mr. Archer pointed with his cane. "They're unloading it all now."

"I see. Well, come in."

Guillaudeu settled Mr. Archer into a chair and hovered near him. "Mr. Barnum is actually not in the building at the moment."

"Then who is running the museum, *at the moment?*"

"Well." Guillaudeu leaned against his desk. "I'm not sure how to answer that question."

"What do you mean, Mr. —"

"Guillaudeu."

"Mr. Guillaudeu. In what way is that question a challenge to you? Who is running this museum?"

"Well, the theater staff runs the performances; certainly the custodians and ticket-takers manage themselves . . ."

Mr. Archer stared at Guillaudeu as if the taxidermist had just told him there were pelicans on the moon. Guillaudeu continued: "The managing chef runs the restaurant and sees to the concession stands. And the exhibits themselves need no supervision. With exceptions, of course. But I tend to those. We're expecting some kind of naturalist, someone other than myself to look after the new . . . menagerie."

"I see." Mr. Archer peered again at the office. Bookcases lined one side of the windowless den, and a small reading desk was pushed up against the wall. Chips of petrified wood fallen from the larger museum pieces had found their way to the bookshelves, along with various specimens: a few mice, a robin, a tattered hare. These were duplicates of the specimens in the galleries, too damaged or old for public display. All along the opposite wall, tools hung from hooks in an assortment of sizes, from the tiny silver brain spoon to rib clamps the size and shape of a wolf trap. The worktable was the center of this panorama, displaying its array of tools and the owl spread out, half clothed in its skin. Underneath the table were shelves of jars, metal canisters, and clay pots. There were bottles of alcohol, ether, cornmeal for absorbing a specimen's natural oils, bags of excelsior, hide-curing salt, glass eyes in brown, yellow, and even blue (for certain New World nocturnal species). As Mr. Archer swiveled in the chair to take it all in, Guillaudeu saw it as this stranger might: as if a great tide had left surf-blown piles of flotsam.

"Your wife?" Mr. Archer pointed to the framed likeness on the wall. Guillaudeu's throat filled with an awful bile that he quickly swallowed.

"Celia," he said weakly, not permitting his eyes to meet his, or hers.

"Well then," Archer tapped his cane on the floor. "About my office?"

Guillaudeu cleared his throat. "Given the museum's rate of growth in recent months, organization is sometimes difficult. Regrettably."

Mr. Archer gave a short nod. "I wouldn't have guessed organization to be the underlying principle here."

"I suppose not," Guillaudeu replied. He did not like the man's tone, and he still had no idea how Mr. Archer fit into the scheme of the museum.

"Sir," Mr. Archer said as he brushed a few golden hairs from his trouser leg. "Where is my office? I'd like to get settled."

"If you will excuse me, sir, I will research that detail." Guillaudeu ran across the hall to the ticket window. "William. Have you heard of a Mr. Archer?"

"Archer?" William was an elderly Irishman with tufted eyebrows and a wandering eye. He had worked for John Scudder for many years and remained a reliable nexus of information of all kinds. He continued to take coins from the hands of incoming visitors. "Isn't that the ad man? The fellow from the papers?"

"Is it? What's he doing here?"

"Barnum hired him."

"Do you know where his office might be?"

William laughed, half looking at Guillaudeu for the first time. "Who knows? Not much room down here. I haven't heard anything about it. But since you're here, I had a complaint from a patron yesterday that you'll want to know about."

William paused to take admission from an elderly woman wearing a coat made from the pelt of *Pagophilus groenlandicus.*

"Apparently some kind of bull on the fourth floor has some worms. In the eye area."

"What!"

William chuckled.

"The fourth floor? That must be the wildebeest. But that seems highly unlikely, since I've fumigated —"

"I'm just the messenger, Emile. If I hear anything about this Archer, I'll make sure you're the first to know."

Guillaudeu reluctantly returned to the office. He'd have to go up there straightaway. Worms! Maggots, surely. Guillaudeu's embarrassment flared.

Mr. Archer had retreated to a corner and held his cane out as if he were about to engage in swordplay. The burlap sack moved. A monkey peeked out.

"They're harmless. They're much like you" — immediately he realized that it was an unsuccessful analogy — "because they're waiting for their permanent habitat, you see. See? *Leontopithecus rosalia* —"

Mr. Archer was unmoved by the monkeys' Latin name, but as if in response the tiny creatures darted out of the sheltering bag and disappeared between the crates littering the floor.

"As you can see, Mr. Archer, the museum functions rather on its own terms. Information doesn't always make it to every corner of the building. Your office" — Guillaudeu could think of no better way to put it —"does not exist. Yet. The museum has undergone so much transformation in recent months that the other offices are still full of ladders, equipment, building apparatuses. Apparati, rather. You get my meaning."

"This is ridiculous! I left the *Sun* for this?" He waved his cane.

Guillaudeu shrugged weakly.

"What do you propose as to my accommodations?"

Guillaudeu's instinct was to escort Mr. Archer straight out the door and proceed with his day as if they'd never met. Out of discomfort and an irrational and ill-fated desire to end their conversation at all costs, he offered a second choice.

"We could clear out these crates and set you up in here on a purely temporary basis."

Mr. Archer paced back toward Guillaudeu, who fought an urge to dive under his desk. The man was clearly accustomed to having his way. Mr. Archer seemed to be fuming, or so Guillaudeu supposed from the fish-like opening and closing of his mouth.

"Will these louse-infested creatures stay?" He gestured toward the burlap sack.

"We'll see what we can do. There are many such . . . specimens in need of a cage."

Mr. Archer stomped out to direct the unloading of his carriage.

Guillaudeu broke up empty crates and carried the piles of wood and papers to the curb. He moved the unopened packages that he could lift to his side of the room, all the while silently enraged that he had made such a careless offer of hospitality. Mr. Archer's valet and Guillaudeu then carried a large oak desk into the office while Mr. Archer stood by to make sure the desk was not scratched in the process.

"This will have to do," Mr. Archer muttered. "The rest can wait until I have my own office."

After the two men eyed each other for a moment, Guillaudeu retreated. He watched Mr. Archer pull a sheaf of white paper from a box and set it in front of him on his table. He primped the papers, squaring the stack so each leaf lay aligned with the next. He pulled a pencil from his waistcoat pocket and put it on the table.

Guillaudeu picked up one of the crates that had been sitting in the office for days. He'd been receiving everything from African artifacts to monkeys, and he pried the lid off the package warily. He dug through the packing material and finally pulled out a wrapped bundle.

"Mr. Guillaudeu, I'm curious about something." Mr. Archer held up a sheet of paper. "I have a letter from Mr. Barnum here, describing my duties."

"I see." Guillaudeu began to unwrap the bundle.

"Of course I fully understand the advertising bit. I've worked in the papers for years, as you know."

"Quite right."

"But there's a whole other element, you see. To my job here."

"Oh?"

"Yes. 'Illuminating the exhibits,' Mr. Barnum says. 'With Historical, Scientific, and Astonishing Facts.'"

"Yes, it seems like more descriptions and explanation would help visitors," Guillaudeu said.

The final layers of wrapping fell away from the bundle and Guillaudeu put a small mounted specimen on the desk. He then jumped back as if the creature had spoken.

"I see," Archer continued. "But then he mentions something I can't understand: *The Representatives of the Wonderful.* What or who are they? What does he mean by this?"

But Guillaudeu neither comprehended nor even heard Mr. Archer's query. He tugged his mustache and then grabbed the crate, searching for a return address. He tore through the packing material.

"What on earth is happening over there? Did you hear my question?"

"This is unthinkable . . . definitely impossible!"

"Good gracious, sir." Mr. Archer rose from his seat. "I don't see that there is cause for such a loss of composure, no matter what it is."

Guillaudeu looked at him. "Have you ever seen anything like this?"

The stuffed animal specimen was only a foot long. The creature had a dense coat of smooth brown fur fading to brassy blond at its belly. Its head was round, with no discernible ears and tiny black eyes.

"Look. Its tail is like a beaver's," Guillaudeu whispered, picking up the specimen. "But rounded, and short! And its feet. They are fully webbed, but these long claws . . . look at them!"

Mr. Archer by this time was standing next to him, arms folded across his chest. "Obviously someone's a humbug, Mr. Guillaudeu. Look at its beak. There's nothing natural about its beak. What would you call that, anyway?"

"It seems to be cartilaginous. It has nostrils just here." Guillaudeu brushed the top of the animal's broad fleshy muzzle. "It appears to have part of a spoonbill's beak attached to it. Perhaps with an epoxy of some kind?" Guillaudeu searched the creature's face. "If it's manufactured it was done by a master."

"You mean you think it may be real?" Mr. Archer scoffed, his chin jutting.

"That's difficult to say. Even the mermaid was so well made it was hard to say for sure."

"You must be joking, monsieur. China has been manufacturing mermaids for centuries! Men are born into the mermaid business over there." Mr. Archer took the creature in his hands. "Its tail does seem quite real, though, doesn't it?"

"See." Guillaudeu pointed. "It has a coat like a seal, with longer hair on the outside and a sort of downy layer near the skin. This animal lives in the water. At least part of the time."

Guillaudeu pawed around in the crate, finally discovering a crumpled sheet of stationery. "Thank goodness. A letter." He held it up.

Mr. Archer cradled the creature in the crook of his arm. "Well?"

"*Dear Mr. Barnum: here is* Ornithorhynchus anatinus. A-ha! Let's see . . . bird . . . snout. Duck-like snout."

"Not terribly helpful."

"*I can scarcely believe I'm parting with it, but your price was too generous to pass up. So here she is, all the way from Botany Bay. I know she will draw a crowd, even in New York. Yours, V.*"

"Who is 'V'?" Mr. Archer handed the specimen back to Guillaudeu.

"I don't know."

"Is it real?"

"I don't know."

Guillaudeu examined the junction between the specimen's bill and its skull. He could see no stray stitches or gloss of adhesive. It seemed to have an entirely natural transition from fur to flesh. "I don't know." He turned the animal over. "I see no mammaries. If it is a she, as 'V' suggests, there should be mammaries. If it's a mammal."

"How could it be anything else? Look at her fur." Mr. Archer brushed a finger along the animal's back. "It certainly is soft."

"It's not a reptile. And it certainly is not a bird."

"The tail seems to be a bit scaly. What an extraordinary tail."

"How could it *be*?" Guillaudeu looked at the ad man.

Mr. Archer raised his eyebrows. "You're the naturalist, Mr. Guillaudeu, not me."

"Taxidermist." Guillaudeu sat down in his chair.

Mr. Archer picked up *Ornithorhynchus anatinus.* "People will pay to see it, I'm quite sure." He walked back to his desk, petting the specimen. "I would pay to see it, wouldn't you?"

"But we don't know what it really is."

"That is true, but is that a relevant question, Mr. Guillaudeu? Is that truly the correct question to ask *here,* of all places? I'm not sure Mr. Barnum gave me that impression."

"Well —"

"I don't think so." And Mr. Archer, now sitting at his desk with the creature in front of him, licked the tip of his right forefinger and swept a leaf of paper off the stack. After rubbing his hands together and glancing at Guillaudeu, he tapped the tip of his pencil seven times against the page and began to write.

Guillaudeu pulled down the third volume of Cuvier's *Illustrated Natural History.* This book provided Guillaudeu with not only an encyclopedic survey of the planet's creatures but also what he considered the necessary philosophical context for his studies. In one essay Cuvier stated: *It is only really in one's study that one can roam freely throughout the universe, and for that, a different sort of courage is needed, courage which comes from unlimited devotion to the truth, courage which does not allow its possessor to leave a subject until, by observation and connected thought, he has illuminated it with every ray of light possible.*

Guillaudeu had been following the debates between field naturalists and sedentary scholars of nature. The field naturalists embodied, in his opinion, a sort of base recklessness in their travels, haphazardly bringing home natural objects from all over the globe without knowing anything about them or taking the time to place them in a proper taxonomic context. The sedentary naturalists like Cuvier, though less traveled than the field-goers, were repositories of knowledge and applied that knowledge to each specimen in the solitude of their offices. Being an anatomist, Cuvier shared, Guillaudeu felt certain, his own love of close, meticulous study of the internal structures of animals. Knowing that an important man of natural philosophy agreed with Guillaudeu's own ideas strengthened his resolve. It was an added benefit that both he and Cuvier were French by birth. He flipped through pages of engravings. No duck-like bird snout. He pulled the index off the shelf. Nothing.

He paced the length of the office. He stared at the brown creature on Mr. Archer's desk, which stared right back at him, defying the implausibility of its own existence. He stroked the animal's back. He looked again at the small curved claws, the webs of leather in between. No artist, however masterful, could have created this from bird and beaver parts. But where was the proof? He returned to his desk and again flipped through the book, passing pages of beetles and pages of birds. His desire to find the little creature safely documented by Cuvier was more urgent than he would have liked to admit. An ominous sense grew in the back of his mind that the boundaries of Cuvier's world were not as fixed as his elevated language and four-color lithographs implied.

"There we go," Mr. Archer said, swiveling in his chair. "A first draft."

"Already?"

"Would you like to hear it?"

Guillaudeu wished to be left alone, but Mr. Archer waved the sheet with a grand gesture.

"This is what will bring them in, monsieur. They'll come in droves. I can get it to the press tonight, and it will be in the papers tomorrow."

"I wouldn't say droves."

Mr. Archer held the paper daintily. *"Don't miss your chance to see the Astounding Antipodean Anomaly! For the first time in History, behold a creature that defies Scientific Explanation! Bear witness to the Enchanting Ornithorhyno. Half reptile, half bird, you will be struck speechless by this curious creature. Observe a lost strand of Creation! Participate in Scientific History! Leave it to Phineas T. Barnum to bring you the very substance of Science, or is it God's idea of a joke? Barnum's American Museum, open seven days a week from eight in the morning to ten at night, on the corner of Broadway and Ann. Only twenty-five cents to see all!"*

Mr. Archer stood motionless for a moment, and then moved toward his desk. But he managed only a few steps before a tiny golden monkey jumped out from somewhere and landed on his head.

Three

The night had chilled uncomfortably; Guillaudeu shivered in his thin coat, standing in the shadow of the building where he lived. Across the street, the grocer, Saul, watched him from between two pyramids of yellow apples. Guillaudeu affixed his gaze to the brass door handle three feet away, but he could not move.

Ever since his wife died there, he had been unable to enter his apartment without making at least two passes around the block. Even then he often stood just as he did now, poised on the threshold with his thoughts clouding over.

There was pity in the furtive eyes of his neighbors as he circled his home, and this night was no exception. He looked over his shoulder at Saul, who gave a barely discernible shrug before disappearing behind the apples. Finally Guillaudeu raised his arm, inserted the key, and propelled himself inside.

Death smells of pumpkins. After five months, the sweet, foul odor that had lingered in the apartment was certainly gone, but Guillaudeu was sure it had permanently destroyed his olfactory apparatus, if not his deepest core. As he climbed the narrow stairs to the second floor, he knew he would always remember that smell as he approached this place. His nose would always be testing the air: Is it gone yet? Is it truly gone? Could imagination alone conjure the stench? As time passed, he became certain that it did. The ever-rising bile was evidence. Or did he actually smell a far less dreadful scent

22

and he was just twisting it in his mind? The grocery was right across the street, after all, and given his profession he was never far from dead things, the shreds of rot.

After she died, he sold all the furniture in the parlor. To pay for the burial, he told himself. But he surely did not have to sell the drapes for that, or every single lace tablecloth that she'd acquired over the years. The truth was that once he started, he couldn't stop himself; it had felt profoundly right to him as he watched the heavy uncomfortable chairs, flowered rugs, and countless stools with their embroidered cushions disappear. Now that it was all gone and the parlor was empty except for his tall bookcases and their contents, the situation was better. The world, especially the museum, was crowded enough; this domestic emptiness soothed him. He had no plans to replace anything.

The disease had colonized Celia's body and after two days of symptoms they both knew she would die. The only question left was whether it would be in a day, two, or just a few more hours. Actions were reduced to pathetic details: She could no longer bear to be moved, so Guillaudeu propped her up on every cushion he could find. By lifting his wife off the bed's surface onto pillows, he was able to fit the chamber pot beneath her. He emptied it every half hour, turning his face away from the viscous, white-flecked fluid. Cholera was an efficient assassin. It drained its victims quickly, and without fanfare ferried them across the divide.

On the fourth afternoon of her illness Guillaudeu was stirring the bitters in the kitchen when he heard her half-choked breath. This is her last breath! Is this her last breath? She is gone! But he found her reading the newspaper. She was laughing.

"Emile," she croaked. "This is too funny."

She had vomited in such large quantities that her lips and chin were rashed and flaking. Beneath the skin, her flesh seemed to have been scraped away from the inside; he'd never seen the contour of her cheek and jawbone in such sharp relief. He almost did not recognize her, and her laughter, framed by this ghastly appearance and her white hair tangled by too many hours on the pillow, transformed her even more.

"What is it?"

"It says here that five hundred and seventy-six people have died in the last two days."

Guillaudeu took the newspaper gently from her hands.

"Right here in Manhattan." She turned her head slightly toward the window. She looked between the brick buildings up to the smoke-gray sky.

"I cannot distinguish myself even in my own death," she announced. "My existence will be swept away. It will sink unremarkably. No children. No great works. Nothing to set me apart from five hundred and seventy-five other forgettable souls! The newspaper will not even have room for my obituary." She laughed softly. The strange mask of her face swiveled toward him. "I've upset you."

"It's all right." He braced himself, but could not keep his hand from shaking as he offered her the tea. "You know how the papers exaggerate. And you have brightened so many lives," he continued. His voice sounded odd. "How can you say those things?"

But he knew how she could. Guillaudeu sat on the edge of the makeshift bed. The skin had wrinkled terribly on each of her fingers, and Guillaudeu wondered if the nausea he felt while he clasped them was simply a reaction — or could it be the first sign of his own demise? But he remained well. It was a fact that added its own kind of delirium to those days: What kind of order did this world contain if he tended to a sick and contagious person, yet remained well? Randomness was not something Guillaudeu was built to appreciate.

The tap on the door surprised them both; the doctor was not scheduled to arrive for several hours yet. Guillaudeu went to answer it in his socks.

The caved-in appearance of the man at the threshold revealed that he, too, had been struck. He clutched at the door frame, peering beyond Guillaudeu with distracted, half-sunk eyes. The man's dark beard was matted with spittle or worse.

He was tall but he bent forward with one arm clutching his abdomen.

"I must see her," the man whispered.

"You've come to the wrong place, sir." Guillaudeu glanced out into the corridor behind the man. "I'm sorry. You should get to a hospital. Do you need a carriage?"

"Joseph?" Her hoarse voice reached the men with surprising force.

"Celia!" The man swung his head frantically. "Emile. Please."

Guillaudeu took a step back, confused. The man lurched past, leaving Guillaudeu in his malodorous wake.

It was not until he followed the man into the parlor and discovered the stranger's head resting on his wife's bosom and her shriveled arms clasping him about the neck that he understood that this was her lover. He observed that had she not been dehydrated of all her body's liquids, his wife would now be crying the first tears of her illness.

Guillaudeu leaned on the sideboard. Her disease had forced everything from his brain, even as it let his body live; all past and present disintegrated, disappearing like his wife's flesh with only the thinnest membrane holding together the tatters. He had become an automaton, and now he felt only the dimmest flicker of feeling. So this was the lover.

He imagined her walking arm in arm with this man just as she now appeared: emaciated, her skin pulled too tightly around her skull, hanging loosely from her chin. Wearing the rags of the grave. Of course it would not have been that way. But he could see nothing but their skeletal hands entwined.

He could not conjure the outrage that might have been appropriate in any other circumstance. He had known this man existed, after all, that he was somewhere in the city. It was strange to finally see his face, although certainly this ravaged caricature was a poor impression of the original. He felt a peculiar satisfaction, even now, in being able to clarify and catalog what had for so long been obscure. He did not

feel anything that approached sadness. He was puzzled, horrified, relieved, and tired. His only certainty was that they
would die, and that his own life was in a precarious flux.

The best he could do was to give Joseph a cup of bitters.
He offered to help the man off with his jacket. He gently
wrapped his wife's lover in a quilt. The man would not meet
his eyes.

When the doctor arrived, Guillaudeu simply said: *Now
there are two.* The exhausted physician required no further
explanation.

For another full night and day Guillaudeu tended to them
as best he could, propping Joseph up as he had done with
Celia. He wiped away sputum and vomit and emptied their
pots. While the invalids slept, he crept into the room and
watched them lying side by side like a monstrous pair of still-
born twins whose gray skin met with the light only to il-
luminate death. Each time he left the room he was drawn
back almost immediately by the force of his curiosity: How
many glimpses of the world were left to them, how many
breaths? Halfway through the second night she died. Guillaudeu moved her carefully to her bedroom and then tended
to her lover for eleven more hours. When Joseph, too, finally shuddered out of the world, Guillaudeu rushed from
the apartment down two flights of stairs and burst into a
cold, bright morning. He felt as if *he* were the ghost, emerging from one life and hovering at the threshold of the next.

Four

To Guillaudeu's dismay Mr. Archer had made himself quite comfortable in the office, even commandeering Guillaudeu's leather reading chair. As far as he could see, Mr. Archer spent most of the day reading newspapers. This did not particularly bother Guillaudeu, but Mr. Archer tended to exclaim over the day's news rather loudly, and rather often. Worse, he did not care for clearing the papers away once he finished with them. Mr. Archer had been in the office just four days, but for Guillaudeu, who was accustomed to entire weeks of comfortable silence, this was far too long.

"They say Barnum's back in New York," Guillaudeu said. He was arranging the short-eared owl in its final position, sponging soda water carefully onto its plumage to eradicate any residual bloodstains. "He's gathering some of the staff for lunch today in the Aerial Garden. He may be able to clear up the matter of your office."

"That's strange. I heard he was still abroad."

"Abroad? I thought he had been traveling down the eastern seaboard," said Guillaudeu. How could Archer know things that he did not?

Mr. Archer abruptly turned toward him. "Would you show me around the museum?"

"Show you around," Guillaudeu echoed. "Why?"

"If Barnum is indeed back from his travels, and I am to speak to him with any intelligence, I should be familiar with his work."

"It's not really his work. He's only just arrived here. And haven't you walked around at all?"

"I couldn't be bothered." Mr. Archer dismissed the idea with his hand. "It's too tedious. I would rather have your explanations of the exhibits as accompaniment. That would make all those trips up and down the stairs worthwhile."

"I can give you half an hour," said Guillaudeu. "No more than that."

"Excellent," Mr. Archer replied, rising from his seat.

The taxidermist looked over at *Ornithorhyncus anatinus*, where it sat next to the open pages of Cuvier. He had wanted to spend the rest of the morning scrutinizing the specimen and the afternoon mixing resin, linseed oil, and ink into the putty that would form the short-eared owl's new eye sockets. But more and more often, the museum required that he serve its interest, on its own terms. Or maybe the specimens were simply becoming more challenging. And demanding. Especially the ones with canes.

"I don't know if we want to start here, Mr. Archer," Guillaudeu called down the hall when he saw where the ad man was going. "I would really prefer —" But Mr. Archer continued straight past the marble stairway to a set of doors at the far end of the ground-level hall.

"But the waxworks! Surely, with the crowd it draws!" Mr. Archer was already swinging open the door. "The *Herald* said it was the most impressive new exhibit here. Ah, yes. Here we are." The men started along the path made by a narrow red rug stretching the length of the dark, wood-paneled gallery. On either side velvet cords ran through brass pedestal guides to keep visitors in the appropriate realm. Guillaudeu hated the wax gallery.

"I've always been fond of wax dioramas," Mr. Archer continued. "Because I'm not always in the mood for statuary, you know. Sculpture has such a conceit. But here" — he waved his cane dangerously — "here the sculptures wear real shoes. You see this? I've got a chair just like that at home." He stopped to read the placard. "John Milton, yes indeed. He did have good taste in chairs. Ha!"

"I just . . . I don't mean to be rude but I cannot bear to be in here. I may have to continue upstairs."

"Why, Mr. Guillaudeu? What do you mean?"

"I practice taxidermy, as you know. I'm concerned with rebuilding a sort of . . . *anima*. Not that a mounted creature comes close to its living essence, of course, but I'm interested in a certain grace. The way I see it, whoever created these wax figures was not interested in any sort of . . . vitality. See here, for example: Milton's eyes. He's not looking down at his writing desk, though he's got a quill in his hand. He's not ruminating into the distance. His gaze, in fact, is so askance that he seems to be —"

"My dear sir!" Mr. Archer interrupted. "Milton was blind! Of course he's not looking at anything. But look at this one! THE INTEMPERATE FAMILY." This unfortunate group was gathered around a rough-hewn table. The unkempt patriarch bent over a jug, while his youngest children cried with empty bowls in front of them. They passed Petrarch, Aristotle, and Queen Victoria.

"This one's the worst," Guillaudeu said as they passed the scene of Judas' betrayal. "Let's proceed." He pulled his key ring from his waistcoat pocket. "The small stairwell ahead of us doesn't open to the public until noon. We can access all floors up to the rooftop garden. Shall we move on?"

Mr. Archer paused in the doorway. "Mr. Guillaudeu, if I may interject. I wonder if we might focus our tour less on your animals and more on . . . how shall we say . . . the humanoid elements of Barnum's collection? I've heard about automatons, you see. And —"

"Yes, all right," Guillaudeu interrupted as they climbed the stairs. Too often visitors passed over the work of the taxidermist simply because they assumed that an animal specimen was less worthy of their scrutiny than some overembellished and underfunctional machine. He hadn't expected the ad man to be any different, but still it disappointed him.

The wide halls and high-ceilinged galleries of the second floor clattered with visitors. The building's layout allowed people to flow into each floor's main galleries from the wide landing that surrounded the central marble stairway. Patrons could also walk from one gallery to the next through arched portals, with smaller doors scattered throughout that detoured into smaller annexes. Some of the annexes then led into additional hallways, which in turn led to even smaller salons. It had taken a long time for Guillaudeu to memorize each floor's idiosyncratic layout. The second floor was fairly easy, with its nine main galleries and several annexes. The third floor had more numerous, but smaller, galleries and no annexes at all. The fourth floor had so many annexes, salons, and narrow connecting hallways that people always got lost; there were more directional signs on the fourth floor than anywhere else in the museum. The fifth floor had six larger galleries and that was all. As the two men reached the second floor, they observed whole families congregated around the hot- and cold-drink concessionaires. Children rested on benches, and couples strolled and loitered among the exhibits.

Even Guillaudeu understood that Barnum had improved the museum's general atmosphere. Shortly after his arrival, the new owner had instructed workers to remove the faded velvet draperies that Scudder had hung across the building's high windows. True, the curtains had protected specimens and other objects from damage by the sun, but they had also created a funereal gloom that could not have been good for business. The windows had been scrubbed; a few had even been opened. Apart from an occasional house sparrow flitting into the building and smashing itself against a glass cabinet, Guillaudeu could find no fault with the sunlit galleries.

But despite the steeply angled light that accentuated his specimens and the cheerful atmosphere, the museum's visitors unsettled Guillaudeu severely. They always had, even before Barnum's advent. Too often the crowd surged up with no warning, bumping into him, crowding him, and emitting a disconcerting roar. But just as he would begin to panic, to feel himself drowning, it faded away in the hiss of a retreating skirt, leaving him feeling foolish.

"Barnum calls this one an Egyptian priest," Guillaudeu said. They were approaching a waist-high vitrine in Gallery Two. The figure inside the cabinet lay on a bed of crumbling wood. "By the name of Pa-Ib."

"Oh, good! A mummy." Mr. Archer leaned over the case. "Although he looks more like a heap of dried apples."

"They claim he's a two-thousand-year-old priest. In my opinion, without the accoutrements that would have accompanied him to the grave, it's difficult to say what kind of man he was."

"If only he could sit up and talk, eh?" Mr. Archer tapped his cane lightly against the glass. "Wake up, sir!"

"Or if only we could count the number of nightmares he's caused."

Mr. Archer turned. "What?"

"Among the children." Guillaudeu pointed to one little boy staring at the mummy as if he'd been hypnotized.

"I'm surprised Barnum doesn't have Joice Heth in here," Mr. Archer said. "That would seem an appropriate finale to his first enterprise in the show business, wouldn't you agree? Displaying her mummified remains to the paying public?"

Guillaudeu cringed. "Advertising Joice Heth as one hundred and sixty-six years old was an act of the crudest deception."

"That's the least of it, Mr. Guillaudeu. Deception was quite the least of it, let me assure you," said Mr. Archer. "Barnum made enemies during the Joice Heth debacle that will last him a lifetime! Half the staff at the *Herald,* including Bennett himself, and even some at the *Sun* are set on seeing Barnum a broken and — what's worse — a *broke* man. But I must concede that his allies in the business are also strong."

"And what is your opinion of Mr. Barnum?"

"My opinion? I hardly see the relevance of that. You might as well ask me my opinion of the wind."

Mr. Archer passed two carpenters building a tall wooden booth of some kind and stopped next to the stone blocks imported from the Giant's Causeway. He bent down to look into a case of fossils.

"Ah," said Guillaudeu. "This one is part of Scudder's original collection. *Homo diluvii testis.* Man who witnessed the flood."

"Preserved in stone?"

"Just his imprint. The bones are long gone."

"But look." Mr. Archer squatted in front of the case. "His skull is far too small. Where are his hands, his arms? The way the stone's grain dips, you really can't be sure what you're looking at, can you?"

"You said it earlier, Mr. Archer: We're not so sure that's the right question to ask, when faced with such a thing, are we?"

There was a crowd in front of Cornelia, the gray dog in Gallery Four who operated a sewing machine using a custom-made set of foot pedals. It was the first time Guillaudeu had seen her at work, and he watched as she guided a piece of blue muslin through the machine with her muzzle. The placard beside her said that she had come from Italy, but Guillaudeu had heard from William the ticket-man that Barnum found her in the back room of a tavern in the Bowery. By the look of the dog's keeper, whose sharp features resembled *Vulpes vulpes,* Guillaudeu believed the story. The keeper tipped his oily top hat and exposed his toothless gums in what might have been a smile. The man's hand was obscured by a tangle of black, vine-like tattoos. Guillaudeu hurried back to his companion.

"You must explain this to me." The ad man led Guillaudeu past shelves of idolatrous objects: carved totems, the feathered rattle, white masks of cured leather ringed with feathers. He stopped in front of a cabinet that held a tall glass jar.

"I know," Guillaudeu intoned. "I find it terribly inappropriate."

"It's a human arm," Mr. Archer observed.

"Yes," Guillaudeu sighed. "It is."

"Why or how did it come to be here?" Mr. Archer whispered. "It looks quite old, really. Quite disgusting."

"Yes. Tom Trouble's arm. Apparently he was a pirate. A devilish prowler of equatorial seas, as they say."

"But how did . . . he lose it? And how did it end up here?"

"Perhaps this is one of the exhibits Barnum was referring to when he hired you, Mr. Archer. To provide such stories. Facts. Or whatever you want to call the explanation."

Mr. Archer straightened up. He laughed. He swiveled his head toward the clamoring crowd. "Of course! I should have known!" He poked his cane into the air, his laughs ringing out. Guillaudeu backed away from him. "That gives me a splendid idea." He wiped his eyes with a canary-yellow silk handkerchief and scrutinized Tom Trouble's arm. "Yes, indeed. This place is turning out to be rather amusing after all, Mr. Guillaudeu. I'm going back to our office. I want to get started. The rest of the museum can wait."

With a headache blooming at his temple, Guillaudeu watched the crowd envelop *Homo malaccus:* man with a cane.

Five

The small orb, with its emerald-and-indigo pattern of continent and sea, hung against a painted firmament. Guillaudeu did not mind this diminutive view of earth, although this exhibit had caused a ripple of controversy when Scudder unveiled it. Nor was he bothered by what the rendering made obvious: Any notion of the heft and volume of the highest mountain range, or the deepest oceanic trench, was a simple illusion. The planet hung without an anchor, free and unprotected in the void, susceptible to cosmic forces of which man could never conceive.

The only thing that unnerved Guillaudeu in this vista was the tiny sailing ship dangling alongside earth, positioned by a delicate filament as if it had caught a trade wind straight out into the universe and then wheeled around to take a good look homeward. Behind the ship, on whose stern was the name USS *Happenstance*, Guillaudeu's line of sight seemed to be aimed at the whole scene as if he, or any observer, was the very force, massive and unknowable, that could annihilate the planet and man's futile though doggedly consistent attempt to conquer it.

To view this scene, Guillaudeu had discovered when he first peered through the brass viewer labeled SCIPIO'S DREAM, was to take part in a strange charade: Here the whole earthly world was represented, including humanity itself, but the whole vista encompassed no more than a foot of space within a single room of a labyrinthine museum that was just one building on a quadrant of buildings making up one block in one neighborhood in a city on a small island in the —

"What's this?" A familiar voice accompanied a quick tap on his shoulder.

Guillaudeu pulled away from the brass viewer to find Edie Scudder with her hands on her hips. "Just a shell of the former man, eh?" She smiled.

"What are you doing here?" In his sudden elation, the paradox of Scipio's Dream spun off into the ether.

"I received an invitation from Mr. Barnum to join his staff for lunch today."

Edie's wiry brown hair fell loose around her shoulders despite the fashion of the day. She wore a fitted velvet jacket and cobalt-blue skirt, though there was a streak of tar along the hem. Edie spent most days near the ships and had picked up everything from tattoos to foul language. She had long ago learned to censor herself with Guillaudeu, and now she patted him on the back and hooked her arm through his.

"You look tired."

"I've become the keeper of a squealing menagerie."

She laughed, and several museum visitors turned their heads. Guillaudeu had always hoped that Edie, John Scudder's only child and a natural businesswoman, would take over the management of the collection when the time came. But her interest was shipping, and as unlikely as it seemed she was proving very successful at it.

"It's not funny," he said. Her lightheartedness suddenly made his disappear. "On Thursday a man delivered three parrots to the kitchen instead of my office. By the time I got there, they were already on their way to the restaurant: The chef had wrung their necks and plucked them."

Edie laughed harder.

"It was *not* funny. I've got to do something."

"Barnum's got big ideas, Emile." Edie looked around the crowded Cosmorama salon. "And it looks like they're working."

"But some division must be made between the specimens and the living. It's simply not right to stumble upon a live serpent when you think you're in a room full of stuffed ducks, for God's sake."

Edie hooted again and slapped him lightly on the arm. "That's *not* right, is it? Not acceptable at all."

They moved among the Cosmoramas, now and then peering into the viewers at some exotic miniaturized scene. Guillaudeu did not explain that Barnum's lack of organization was quickly eroding the integrity of the taxonomic principles on which Edie's own father had built the museum, and to which Guillaudeu fervently adhered. To see the specimens shoved to the side or disappear entirely would kill him, he was certain. The prospect was harder to bear than the disappearance of his wife, as unnatural as that might be. These disappearances were erasing him. And so he hated Edie's good humor about Barnum, but since he loved Edie, ruining it would not be worth the risk that she might leave.

Edie rarely came here anymore. She was twenty years his junior, which made her approaching thirty-five. But when he looked at her, Guillaudeu saw each stratum of her girlhood. His life enveloped hers; he'd been in her father's employ since the day she was born.

She used to confide in Guillaudeu as he worked across from her. She was the only person to ever share his worktable. Opposite whatever specimen he stretched, scraped, or sewed, she would carefully spread her own work. Sometimes it was a tray of shells she organized, sometimes a box of agates. Sometimes it was schoolwork and sometimes it was her own sketches, kept safe in a notebook that he had given her on her seventh birthday.

His affection for Edie was never paternal. Even then, when she was seven and he was twenty-seven, he regarded her with a combination of delight and impatience. If only she could grow up faster, or he could go backward to meet her on equal ground. He hung back during her adolescence, watching periods of bravado give way to interminable solitary walks in her father's galleries. She still told him things during this period, about her friends and the places she'd visited. She told him what she would not tell her father, and yet he still waited.

He had endured several periods of romantic longing, the first during Edie's fifteenth year. He considered this a natural evolution; it was a love that opened its arms wide to the child he had known. He considered his feelings respectful, reverential. He had believed it would not be long before they reached their final and permanent mode of relating, as lifelong companions. But in that peculiar way that lives diverge as sharply and decisively as an incision, soon after her twenty-third birthday Edie eloped with a naval captain. When her outraged father told him the news, Guillaudeu felt as if lightning had ignited every atom in his body. The gap between them, always wider than he would have liked, snapped open once and for all. What else could he do but swallow his hope that they would marry? Within the year he had married Celia, the daughter of his favorite bookseller.

Two years later Edie's naval captain deserted her. Neither Edie nor her father ever discussed the matter with Guillaudeu, and eventually he and Edie reached what would become their permanent relationship: more like uncle and niece than he would have hoped, but still a great comfort to him through the years. With her arm through his, Guillaudeu could not imagine life without her sharp eye and her hardheadedness to flex against.

Moving from viewer to viewer, Guillaudeu half expected to find a replica of the museum as he'd first known it. During the building's construction, John Scudder had asked Guillaudeu for advice about the dimensions of galleries and necessary precautions for optimizing space for the larger animal specimens. They had been discussing the construction of the new building for three years while Scudder raised funds. Guillaudeu had accompanied Scudder and Mr. Olmsted, the financier, on a trip to the Westchester quarries to pick out marble for the stairwell and façade. He had been among the first men to set foot in the finished building and that experience had been one of the highlights of his career. He could still conjure the fragrance of newly hewn lumber filling the air as he walked through the main entrance for the first time and then up the great marble stairwell, cut smooth and straight as the very path to heaven. The ceilings of the main galleries stood at thirty feet, and though the place lacked altars or stained glass, it felt like a grand church. It was a perfect home for his specimens.

It had taken him almost two months to move the collection from the almshouse building and arrange the mounted animals across the five floors of the museum. He set the specimens in their carefully chosen places, making sure the snowy egret's knifelike beak was poised exactly as it would have been in life, hovering above the water, waiting for the moment of its prey's fatal mistake. Setting up the museum for Scudder had been the most pleasurable work of his life and now, as he stared at a tiny guardsman outside a balsa Tower of London, he couldn't believe so many years had passed.

One Cosmorama revealed a model of a cobbled street, with tiny carved carriages hitched to delicate wooden horses. On the far side of this street stood streetlamps the size of matchsticks, and a few trees meticulously sculpted with minuscule paper leaves. A river flowed in a fluttering of mesh blown by a tiny fan on a hidden belt. Just beyond the river rose Notre Dame, its apostles carved under a magnifying glass. Each beveled buttress lay flush along the cathedral. The figures of saints leaned, as they did in reality, almost suicidal on the precipice. The sculptor had even added pigeons to a few of the saints' shoulders.

Among Guillaudeu's only surviving memories of the city of his birth were the smell of bread in his father's bakery and certain tender feelings toward rivers that he re-experienced every time he saw the Hudson. He looked on the Cosmorama not with a sense of home, but with the feeling that the view, in wood and tiny plaster bricks, had successfully replaced any other memory he might have of the real city. He found it comforting, this sturdy little Paris. If only we could look in on the world like this, he thought, and find everything fixed in its proper place.

Edie led Guillaudeu out of the viewing salon up into the main fourth-floor galleries. There was a new exhibit, in a case built in the style of all the vitrines of the museum, with wood moldings carved in various designs, but this case did not contain shelves. It was filled with water, and in the water were twenty little creatures that seemed to glide and float on springs. Their tails were coiled like fiddleheads below them, and they maintained themselves relatively upright. The specimens of *Hippocampus zosterae* had arrived just two days earlier, and Guillaudeu had been all over town until he found a Chinese mercantile on Third Avenue that sold tiny dried shrimp, which the swimming creatures darted after and inhaled with gusto. The strange, feathery fish drifted up and down, sometimes twining their tails around one another like schoolchildren holding hands and generally addressing the world with a kissing motion.

"Look at them," said Edie. "Where are they from?"

"Who knows?" Guillaudeu tried to remain annoyed.

"How does he get seawater in here?"

"That was one of the first things he did. We all wondered why, but he built a pipe to the harbor right away."

"Must've cost a fortune. And how does he pump the water?"

Guillaudeu shrugged. "He must have bribed the aldermen. The octopus was the first to arrive. It's in Gallery Fourteen, but I think I'll have to move it."

"Is it near your stuffed ducks?" Edie laughed.

"Oh, stop! Please, Edie. These are serious problems, and not just taxonomic. When your father ran the place, I was invited to every important auction in the city. The zoological societies, hunting clubs, every respectable private collector, and all the government expedition companies. I had access to all the specimens coming into the city. I thought I might even have been close to receiving an invitation from the Lyceum."

"You want to join the Lyceum of Natural History?"

"Yes! I would like nothing better. Just think of the camaraderie, the exchange of ideas. But now" — Guillaudeu was embarrassed by his own sputtering tone — "now it's all wrong."

"I can't imagine you don't get invitations anymore, Emile. You've been here for so long; you know everyone in your field. I can't believe the Lyceum hasn't contacted you."

"I still get some invitations, not as many as before, and not from the Lyceum. But now I'm too embarrassed to go anywhere."

"Why?"

"Because Mr. Barnum has decided to publicly ridicule this museum! He is soliciting animal specimens from the general public. He put advertisements in the papers."

"Why would he target the public?"

"Let me describe it this way: Yesterday an elderly servant showed up at my office with the corpse of some kind of spotted cat. It was larger than a housecat, about the size of a raccoon, and wrapped in a sack. Ultimately I determined it was *Felis yagouaroundi,* from South America. The man told me that his mistress had received the cat as a gift, from a friend who had just returned from a government expedition to the Amazon. Exotic pets are common in certain circles, you know. And those pets very often die. I soon discovered that Barnum has offered a small sum for each creature. It's a low practice, completely illegitimate. It's awful, really. And the cat was far too decomposed to mount."

Edie took his arm again. "I'm sorry, Emile."

They soon reached the electric eel, safely pickled in its jar as it had been for twenty years.

"Hello, old friend," Edie whispered.

"Indeed."

They regarded the eel.

"Emile. My father misses you. Why won't you go to him?"

Guillaudeu kept his eyes on the eel. Patches of its skin had begun to dissolve into slimy filaments. He had embalmed the creature twenty-one years ago. He still remembered slipping it into the jar of alcohol, sitting at his desk in the old alms-house building where they displayed the collection in the years before Scudder had built the museum.

"You'd best leave that subject be," Guillaudeu said softly. He saw Scudder's broad, bearlike face as it had appeared during their last conversation, in which the old man had justified his decision to dismember his own, not to mention Guillaudeu's, life's work. *The character of natural philosophy is shifting,* the old man had insisted, his jowls trembling. *The arrogance and impossibility of encyclopedic knowledge is obvious. The new age of Science is dawning, Emile. The great outstretching of our minds to invisible realms. We must accept it or else we'll grow as dusty as this collection!*

Guillaudeu had argued valiantly. The public, he insisted, will always hunger for knowledge of the natural order of creation, of nature's unique catalog. Where else can an American citizen examine a Chinese water deer or a bin-turang, except at Scudder's Museum? Scudder had blinked at him and laughed, shaking his head. It was at that point that Guillaudeu stormed from Scudder's study. Now he did not want Edie to know that her father's betrayal had been total; he'd vowed to never to speak to Scudder again.

"I know you miss him, Emile. Why don't you find new work? This place is bothering you so much now. I can see how it's wearing on you. And we've been so worried about you since Celia died. We don't understand why you have not leaned on us in this —"

"I won't discuss it. Shall we go on, or must we part here?"

Edie straightened and took a step away from Guillaudeu. "Why are you so disagreeable? If I didn't know you so well, I'd think you actually wanted me to leave you."

He allowed her to take his arm and lead him away from the eel.

The truth was that he would not let Edie see that he was relieved, now that Celia was no longer hovering in the cor-ners of his life. He and Celia had not known the intimacies of marriage for a very long time. Thankfully, they hadn't wasted their lives fighting. They had reached an adequate stasis. It was not what either of them had hoped when they married, but it was a kind of equilibrium. Celia at least had been very comfortable, if not satisfied, in the contours of their life; he had never acknowledged her lover, and over the years she had stopped complaining about the consuming nature of his work. But he could never share this with Edie because even though all of it was true, he was afraid she would perceive each detail of the history as proof that his marriage had been simply a sustained act of cowardice.

In the next gallery they encountered a family who stood transfixed in front of a new exhibit.

"Automatons," Guillaudeu observed drily.

"It sounds like a hundred music boxes!" said Edie, staring at the tiny metal spools. Within a large frame, delicate machinery moved on a series of metal cogs, cylinders, and sliding rods. Attached at eye level to the metal framework was a wax head, complete with glossy black ringlets. At regular intervals the talking machine's "face" grew animated, the jaw dropped open, and mechanized "words" came out of her mouth.

"The time it must have taken to make this," Edie added. "It's hard to imagine."

"I find I can't even look at its face," replied Guillaudeu. "It gives me horrible chills."

"I've heard a certain instrument, from Africa, I think, with a similar plunking sound," said Edie.

"There's something profoundly diabolical," Guillaudeu continued, "about a machine with a human face. It's not meant to exist."

"I want to see the roof, Emile. Will you take me?"

Scudder had never opened the roof to the public. *It's a liability*, he'd said. Naturally, it was the first place Barnum wanted to go after he bought the museum. Barnum, twenty-five years younger than Guillaudeu and fueled by disconcerting confidence, had walked onto the roof, raised his arms as if about to conjure a storm, and slowly rotated, taking in the view of the buildings and the harbor. *My Ark of the city,* he proclaimed.

The vast rooftop held a miniature English garden with potted laurels and even a patch of grass, planted on a raised pedestal, that framed the view of the harbor. Along the southern edge was a promenade, complete with inlaid brick, balloon vendors, and scattered stone and wooden benches. Even now, in the cold beginning of spring, groups of visitors walked the periphery, weaving among bedecked flagpoles and leaving puffs of white breath in their wakes. The restaurant spread northward from the midpoint of the roof. Most of the patrons had moved their chairs close to the freestanding stoves placed throughout the restaurant on cooler days, and waiters moved between them and the large kitchen on the northern edge. But as Guillaudeu and Edie emerged from the stairwell, what caught their eyes was a crowd gathered near the center of the garden, pressing its collective nose against a huge new wrought-iron cage.

When they approached, Edie read the placard aloud: "THE HAPPY FAMILY?"

A coyote paced the length of the cage, picking its way around three ground squirrels sitting on their hind legs. A peregrine falcon with tattered tail feathers hunched on the ground, and mice scurried near its feet. A housecat sat in the corner like a loaf of bread, the coyote not even looking at it as it paced. A dead forked tree leaned against one side of the cage where a corn snake lay asleep like a pile of yellow rope. Above the snake was a mottled gray owl.

"Look!" In front of them, a little girl called to her mother. "The dog doesn't eat the cat!" She laughed and pointed.

Guillaudeu could not interpret Edie's fixed smile. "Nature did not intend this," he said ominously.

"Where'd he buy it?"

"From someone who apparently found perverting nature a fine entertainment. They've been trained out of their own natures." Guillaudeu watched the coyote gliding the length of the cage. It turned like a swimmer, barely brushing the corner with his tail. The dog watched the people looking in. The children squealed at the falcon and the mouse.

Edie read the inscription on a brass plaque. "THE DIVINE PLEASURE SAW TO IT THAT THERE WAS A GREAT PEACE AMONG THE ANIMALS; THE LION DID NOT HURT THE UNICORN, NOR THE FALCON THE DOVE. Touché, Barnum."

Guillaudeu looked away.

"Maybe you're the one being presumptuous, monsieur," Edie said, stepping back from the cage. "We all play God now and then, even you. Especially you, my dear."

"Edith, really. That's not true."

"Just think about what this place is, Emile. It's not a natural history museum anymore."

"But what is it?"

"That" — she was laughing again — "I couldn't tell you. But the children are smiling, and so am I."

As they approached the group of employees sitting at a large table near the edge of the restaurant, Edie ran ahead to embrace William the ticket-man and his nephew, Gideon. Guillaudeu introduced her to the new theater manager, Mr. Forsythe, who sat among four uniformed ushers. Mr. Archer was nowhere in sight. At the far end of the table was a newcomer, an odd-looking man of slight build in a dusty suit coat and three days' growth on his chin. This man avoided looking anyone in the eye and introduced himself as Thomas Willoughby.

"Thomas Willoughby?" Edie gasped. "The pianist?"

Mr. Willoughby visibly shrank. His brown-black hair floated at least three inches above his forehead.

"The one who used to play at Mason Hall?" Edie continued, incredulous.

"Unfortunately, the same," Mr. Willoughby murmured.

"Mr. Barnum's set to have him lead a band on the balcony," William added.

"Well," said Edie, regaining her composure. She addressed the assembled group. "How do you all like the new museum?"

"I like it just fine," said William, taking out his watch and

checking the time. "We had a record number of visitors yesterday, and it's going to just keep getting better."

"Have some wine, Emile." Edie poured them both a glass,
and raised hers. "To the Happy Family."

A wind flicked the red and blue flags on their poles and set
the rooftop trees rustling. A hat flew into the air and a group
of children chased it until it sailed beyond the edge of the
museum. Another surge lifted the corner of the tablecloth,
upsetting two wineglasses and blowing Guillaudeu's napkin
off his lap and away. They waited for Barnum, but Barnum
did not appear.

Six

"I'm surprised Mr. Willoughby is still in New York," Edie whispered to Guillaudeu. After the meal they had left the others, and they now strolled along the promenade. A high railing protected museum visitors from vertigo. It was pleasant, Guillaudeu admitted; though windy and unusually cold, March was proving to be particularly bright.

"I thought he'd left town after what happened. I've never seen anything like it."

"Like what? I've never heard his name before."

"Oh, you've never heard of anyone, Emile. Thomas Willoughby's a brilliant musician! Celebrated in London and Vienna. Solo performances every week at Mason Hall. I was there with Rosemary Timm. You remember her, don't you? Mr. Willoughby had been praised in all the papers as a phenomenon not to be missed. Well, we just happened to go to the performance during which he became . . . *unhinged*, as they said in the papers."

"That makes it sound as if his skull opened up like a treasure chest."

"He was finishing Beethoven's Piano Sonata Number Thirty-one and positively *soaring*, Emile. When all at once he leapt to his feet. His stool toppled and slid across the stage. At first we thought that in his fervor he had transported himself somewhere far away from Mason Hall and the movement of his body had separated from the music. Perhaps that was the case. I don't know. He continued to play for a few moments, and we could see he was staring into the piano's innards some feet in front of him. And then he climbed right over the keyboard and up into the piano."

"You're joking." Guillaudeu looked back to the table where Thomas Willoughby huddled alone with a glass of wine.

"His left knee hit the lowest notes and his right shoe hit the highest. The audience! You should have heard us gasp. Then he was plucking the strings inside the piano with his rump in the air!" Edie laughed, covering her mouth. "It was spectacular, Emile. Two men rushed in from offstage and picked him up by the waistband."

"Did he resist?"

"Not exactly. But he was fixated on the instrument the whole time, his arms stretched out, playing the air, until he disappeared from view. Needless to say, we gave him a standing ovation. All his scheduled performances were canceled after that. He disappeared —"

"Until now." Guillaudeu finished.

"Barnum must have hired him for the publicity his reputation would bring."

"And here we are, playing his game." They stopped by the railing.

Guillaudeu peered down at the people far below. He noted myriad worlds brushing past one another, and the randomness of it made him ill.

Looking away, Guillaudeu snapped open his watch.

"I think he's crazy," Edie murmured. "But even if he is, he's not dangerous. I'm certain of that. Just look at him. Why don't you invite him down with you, Emile. I want to stay up here, but I can see you're ready to return to your office."

Edie let go of his arm and straightened the collar of his shirt. He observed sadness in her eyes, but to acknowledge it would make it worse and Guillaudeu could not bear to do that.

"Yes, I'd best get back."

"Invite Thomas Willoughby to go down with you. He looks so forlorn over there by himself."

"All right. For you." Guillaudeu gave her a little bow and said good-bye.

Thomas Willoughby appeared to appreciate the gesture and followed Guillaudeu into the stairwell with barely a word. But on the landing outside the door to the fifth-floor galleries, the pianist stopped.

"What's in there?"

"That door is usually locked," Guillaudeu replied. His mind was already on the final positioning of the short-eared owl. It would complete his collection of Old World owls, and he was restless to place this one among them.

When he bought the collection, Barnum had closed the fifth floor to the public, and rumors were circulating among the staff about what he was building. William the ticket-man was certain it would be a jungle. People would open the door, he said, only to be engulfed by vines. Birds would live in the branches of huge living trees, and a tiny river would coast through the galleries operated by a system of pumps and drains. Guillaudeu had tried to keep away from the rumors; refusing to participate in the speculations was his one small protest against Barnum's new regime. But now the door's padlock hung open on its latch.

"What is that sound?" Thomas leaned toward the door. "What *is* that?"

"What sound? I don't hear anything."

"Listen." Thomas held up his hand.

There was a small hammer tapping, and a louder creak, like an old door, and then a quick pull of saw teeth zipping wood grain. A very small saw, maybe.

"Somebody's building something in there," Thomas whispered.

"I don't think so. Oh, yes, now I hear it." From inside came a series of snapping clicks and a whistling sigh that slid down the musical scale.

"I want to see what's making that sound," Thomas said. "It

sounds . . . *strange.*" He pushed open the door, and Guillaudeu followed him into a vast open space.

"Dear God," Guillaudeu whispered. "He's knocked out the gallery walls."

Barnum had removed half of the interior walls that had originally divided the fifth floor into six galleries. Guillaudeu now stood in an open space the size of three galleries. He turned in a circle, absorbing the new dimensions of a space he had known so well over the years. There were the two groups of three high windows, and new yellow stripes along the floor where the walls used to be. Scudder had displayed geological models on this floor: the eruption of Vesuvius, a diorama of the Noachian flood. The largest specimens had been up here, too: the polar bear, the cameleopard. Now there was a new wall that bisected the floor, a pile of tools in one corner, a ladder leaning against the wall, and a single tipped-over chair.

"He just went ahead and did it. He destroyed it." Guillaudeu's eyes glazed for a moment. His rage did not overwhelm him, but he was conscious of its searing flame licking up out of the crevices of his mind. He remained as composed as possible.

As he took a few more steps into the room, Guillaudeu finally comprehended the single structure in the middle of it: a cylinder, at least forty feet in diameter and seven feet high, with a Portland cement base and wide wooden staves bound by metal rims. It appeared to be a gigantic barrel.

Thomas was now standing with his ear to this structure. "Are they building something inside of there? Hello?" They heard the sawing sound again. A series of mechanical clicks and a high-pitched creak came from the barrel, then the tapping hammer. Thomas closed his eyes as Guillaudeu approached the tank. Listening. Clicks; a yawning yap, another disappointed whistle descending the scale. A whoosh of breath.

"It's full of water," Thomas whispered. "It sounds like horn players clearing their instruments." The pianist opened his eyes. "Let's see what it is." They heard a whirring trill, a bleat. Thomas ran to the far side of the gallery and returned with the ladder.

The tempo of the clicking increased. Thomas scurried up the ladder, and although it was a rickety perch, Guillaudeu managed to follow him, peeking over the top of the tank from a few rungs below, clinging to the edge of the tank for support.

Cutting through the water was the chalk-white ridged back of a creature swimming in tight circles. So smooth was its motion that it barely broke the water into waves, even though its body was ten feet long and moving fast. The animal stopped in front of the two openmouthed men, raised its bulbous head, and chirped.

"What in the world is that?" Thomas whispered.

Guillaudeu stared at the circling animal. *"Delphinapterus leucas."*

"I've never seen anything so . . . white. And it's tiny, for a whale."

"I've never seen anything so preposterous!" Guillaudeu's voice rose. "What does Barnum think he's doing?"

"How did it get here?" Thomas was still whispering.

"Barnum has people coming and going at all hours of the day and night. He doesn't tell anybody what he's doing." Guillaudeu was barking his words and glaring at the whale. "We don't even know where he is, for God's sake. Who will take care of this . . . monstrosity! Where is the placard to tell visitors how this whale fits into an exhibit, and into the natural order?"

"Do you hear that? It's making the most extraordinary sounds," Thomas murmured.

"He hasn't informed me of what he's done!" Guillaudeu's voice broke.

"Look! Look how it swims! It's frightening to be so close to it, don't you think? Perhaps it's harmless."

"I don't care!" Guillaudeu shouted. "I am appalled! How did he get it up here? That's one thing I'd like to know, Mr.

Willoughby. But more than that, what I'd really like to know is *why* is it here? Why?"

As he watched the whale swim in circles, Guillaudeu became aware of a different emotion forming on the heels of his dread. If Barnum could produce a whale that twittered like a canary on the top floor of the museum, why in the world should Guillaudeu feel so compelled to explain it? Barnum had accomplished an almost magical feat; the evidence swam in circles just below him. But instead of melting into admiration, or even respect, or at least acceptance, Guillaudeu's rage flared to such a degree that in order not to be swept entirely away he clung to it harder than ever: The whale was an abomination, an embarrassment to all known rules of scientific exhibition and curatorship.

"Excuse me, gentlemen." The tone of this new, feminine voice gave Guillaudeu the impression that its owner had been standing there for more than a few seconds.

"I am aware that the museum is considered primarily a place of entertainment. And that, indeed, it contains objects, such as this beluga whale, that are here specifically to entertain you."

Guillaudeu stumbled to extricate himself from what he now saw was a schoolboyish position on the ladder. The woman below him appeared to be particularly large-boned, with a plain, doughy face, a pronounced double chin, and small dark eyes under a broad forehead. She had emerged from a door built into the new wall on the far side of the gallery.

"But as you may or may not know" — the woman continued — "the museum has recently acquired a different function."

As he returned to the ground, Guillaudeu discovered there was another reason for the woman's formidable tone. She was close to eight feet tall. Thomas Willoughby remained frozen at the top of the ladder.

"This floor has become something of a hotel." The giantess waved her hand toward the newly built wall and the open door from which she had come. "There are museum employ-ees living in apartments up here, myself included. I'm here to request that you kindly refrain from conducting shout-ing matches while you're visiting the fifth floor. The whale makes quite enough noise as it is."

She Stands Up Again

Seven

I had to laugh at the room, with its too-small chair and an oval mirror hung the height of my chest. It was a new room nested inside an old building, with a drift of sawdust in one corner and sap pearling from the walls. A window, thankfully, but not facing Broadway. And the ridiculous bed, like a toy to me.

It's a bed like any other. I knew it would break from the moment I saw it, so why did I even lie down? I can hear your voice even now. I can see the three of us in the kitchen by the stove, all of us laughing, you into your hands, me with no sound, and he with his mouth hanging open. We were still unsure: How had it happened? Where did I get it? What would happen next? I could touch my hand to the ceiling. Mornings, I woke with my legs hanging farther off the edge of the bed, my bones already a network of pain. You said if the bed's too short, just take off the footboard! We used it for kindling. I will do the same thing here.

You would grab me by the waist with no warning, as if there was some urgency to your message, as if I didn't have my whole life to understand what you said, to learn and hate your lesson again and again. *You're a mirror, Ana, for people to see themselves.* And he would come up saying, *Be prepared. Think ahead. Have what you will need.* As if we control the world with foresight. As if you would have me believe the whole thing was planned. *Do not look for yourself in others, Ana. But they will see themselves in you.* I wanted to lunge out and take both of you in my arms. Already I was big enough to do that, big enough to know you were afraid for me. Here is the hammer and there is the bed. I am prepared. I have what I will need.

You would stand here, your eyes alight, peering up at me, proud that I don't depend on the world for sustenance or for answers. But look at me. Just look. I am alone in this ridiculous room with a hammer in my hand, talking to my dead mother about broken things.

I could do nothing about the bed. I used crates to hold up the foot, but I knew it would crash down again. I had spent the day in alternating bouts of energy, unpacking, pacing, and fuming. Both my jars of sea salts had broken among my clothes so I could not even soak my feet. The train journey from Rochester had rattled my spine to such an extent that I felt each vertebra was about to pull free of the others. Sitting was no relief, nor was lying down, even if the bed had not broken. Dull reverberations echoed through the halls of my body. Doors slammed into my nerves, windows crashed together in gritty bone-gratings. Thank God my crates of Cocadiel's Remedy hadn't broken during the journey. I broke the seal on one of the cobalt bottles and held it between my thumb and forefinger to drink the bitter tonic.

At times throughout the day I doubted my decision to work without a manager. But each time this thought fluttered up, I experienced the subsequent, undeniable certainty that the way I had chosen was the only way I could proceed. At least with my career and my sanity, my life, intact. There was another way forward, the one that the sluggish waters of Lake Ontario had offered. But for now I continued to work. I busied myself with some triviality before the memory of my recent debacle, the events that had led me to Barnum's museum, could wedge itself into view. I could do things differently now, I reassured myself. But what, exactly? I was in business for myself only, with no one taking away what I earned. But what changes would I make?

I was saved from this paradox by a crisp knock at my door. When I opened it, I beheld a familiar sight: a woman, her prodigious eyebrows furrowed, standing with her hands on her hips. There is always a hirsute woman, whether you join a one-wagon show or the most grandiose collection of exotica. This one had her beard coiled neatly in a net that hung by loops from her ears.

"Please tell me you play whist," she said.

"I do, as a matter of fact."

"Then life is bearable."

She extended a hand covered in long black hairs. "I'm Maud Kraike."

Maud was forty years old and wound tight as a fiddle string. In the two minutes I spent talking with her she insisted we'd been in a show together seven years earlier in Halifax, and that I'd worn a medieval princess costume with a conical, veil-draped hat. I had no recollection of this, but it could have been true. She had arrived from Niblo's Garden two weeks earlier, and despite the energetic recitation of her past, it held nothing new for either one of us. We did not need proof that our lives ran closely parallel.

"We still need a fourth. I got Mr. Olrick. But the Chinaman will never do. Never play whist with a Chinaman."

"I see," I said, not seeing at all. I was suddenly weary. Or, more likely, I had returned, after a short lapse, to the fact that I'd been weary for quite a long while.

When Maud had gone I lay down on the collapsed bed, propping my feet on a crate. My spine relaxed slightly, and I closed my eyes, hoping to fall asleep before it found its next complaint.

You came to me every night, before I left you. Before you left me. You leaned over me before I slept. You stroked my face with the back of your hand. *Ana,* you said. *Ana. We named you for Anastasia, your grandmother. And do you know why, what your name means?* Why? What? Tell me. *It means She Stands Up Again.*

Eight

In Jones' Medicine Show they put me in a bizarre patchwork of furs over a chiton and girdle. They gave me a wooden shield and a helmet and called me Athena. More recently, during my time with Mr. Ramsay, he nearly always embellished me in some manner, usually with a high ladies' top hat with a wedge of lace draped across the brim. Near the end of my tenure with him he instructed me to wear a horrible costume that he had made at his own expense: a girl's picnic dress, all yellow daisies, ribbons, and a white lace pinafore. *A walking juxtaposition*, he said. As if I wasn't one already.

There would be no costume here. The taxidermist had delivered a letter from Barnum addressed to me. No costume, he said. Unless I wanted one. *Wanted* one. But speaking with the audience was part of my contract. The letter included no details about advertisement, when to expect my pay, and nothing about merchandise. Near the bottom of the page, though, one stipulation: *For between three and five hours each day, Miss Swift will stroll among the visitors. For the remainder, there will be a booth in Gallery Three on the second floor.* His intention was to surprise the crowd with an exhibit outside its case. *I will disconcert them first, and subsequently please them.*

There would be no costume and so in the morning I put on my blue ombré dress and the gray shawl over my shoulders. A mist from the harbor gave the impression of frost, but the morning was strangely warm, much warmer than March at home. I tidied my hair in the small oval mirror. What will they see? Shoulders wider than their fathers'. Strides wider than they can jump. A hand strong enough to lift them off the ground, big enough to encircle their necks. Breasts they will imagine when they get home. A face. Yes, up there, what about the face? As white and expressionless as fog.

I picked up my bottle of Cocadiel's Remedy from the small table and drank deeply.

By the time I had walked across the beluga gallery and down the many flights of stairs, the remedy had numbed the revolting pain in my legs, lightening my burden in its usual way.

At nine in the morning a sizable crowd already roamed the halls. I walked as slowly as I could bear. If I was to walk for three hours I needed a slow rhythm to sustain me. Also new shoes. In the past my manager would arrange for a cobbler to visit me. I worried over how I would find one in the city. I feigned a charitable countenance, entered the portrait gallery, and listened as conversations trailed off in my wake.

The very tall, like the very beautiful, become accustomed to a certain range of response from those around them. Whereas the beautiful woman maneuvers in an arena of unprovoked deference, envy, illusion, and lechery, I remain mostly surrounded by the many incarnations of fear. I am an amusement in the marketplace, but delight is not usually the emotion I provoke. There is only one element of my work that has remained interesting to me over time, and that is the infinitely variable expression of surprise.

A majority of people respond to my presence in familiar ways: a widening of the eyes, of course, and the related eyebrow movement; an audible intake of breath (I have never seen an exhale in these instances) that may or may not become a vocalization; some stutter in bodily movement, most often stopping completely or backing up, and occasionally an actual leap backward.

Apart from these generalities, the average member of the public has one or two involuntary responses that, frankly, would surprise them if they could see them as I do. In Halifax

I encountered a lady who, when she saw me as Athena, began to violently pull her own hair and did not stop until her escort shielded her from my sight. One fellow seemed to take no notice of me at all. But as he stood with the others looking into my booth he suffered a delayed reaction: He crossed his left leg tightly over his right and leaned forward, twisted as a pretzel, as if he was overcome with the need to urinate, pointing at me while his hat toppled off his head.

And then there's my favorite kind of surprise. It is that instance when a person tries his hardest not to show a change in expression at all. This particular, temporary flatness in the eye and stiffening of the neck may be the only symptoms, but they are enough to give him away. I find this response strangely heartbreaking: as if by denying a reaction he is denying reality itself in a small, futile attempt at self-protection in an uncertain world. Then there are always the yelps, the clutching at friends' hands, the jump back, the handclap, the run away, the simple laugh, the blush, the hoot, the faint, and the horror.

I passed a group of three friends lounging on benches. They seemed accustomed to the portrait gallery, as if they met often there. The men — boys, really, they must not be older than twenty — wore wool frock coats and striped vests, one with a brown umbrella for a cane. This one stood with one leg propped on the bench, leaning over his knee with his hat tipped slightly over his forehead. His friend, skinny and red-haired, produced peanuts from one vest pocket, shelled and ate them, and deposited the shells in his other pocket.

The woman sat on another bench. She wore a pale coffee-and-cream-colored dress and cape and spoke excitedly to the boys. She was so caught up in the conversation that she'd failed to notice that one of her slippers had slid off her foot. It was as if they hovered around a table in their parlor instead of a wooden bench in a museum. None of them saw me when I passed. How could they not see me?

"He's just wrong if he thinks he can stop it using the city government," the girl with the fallen slipper was saying. "Just wrong."

"Are you back on Mayor Harper, Bitsy? Why don't you find something else to talk about?" This from the one with the umbrella.

"Because he's about to fail at the job, and he's had it for only two weeks."

I slowed down. They *must* see me by now. They did not.

"He wants to stop liquor and immigration using the same method, and it's simply not going to work. It's insulting," the woman huffed. "A Temperance man, for Christ's sake. That's not what this city needs. Doesn't he know that a public ban will —"

"Are you saying the Irish are like whiskey?" said the one eating peanuts.

"I'm simply saying that if Harper *encourages* the dismissal of immigrant labor, the only thing it's going to cause are riots and more illegal —"

"The only thing that'll stop the Irish is cholera," said the peanut-eater. They laughed.

"Cholera didn't stop you, did it, Colin?" the other boy said.

"No, sir. I wasn't going back to Dublin just because of some trifling disease, was I?"

I stole looks over my shoulder as I walked farther on but the friends had not looked up. Now I was disappointed, and angry at myself for it. I paced down the other side of the gallery, where two raggedy children squealed and pointed at me.

"The only reason Colin didn't lose his job" — the boy was waving his umbrella as I approached them again — "is because he already had money. Harper doesn't care where you were born, as long as you've got it."

"I don't care what you say. This platform will never —" and then, finally, they saw me. "Well! At least someone can see the portraits they've hung up so high," said the woman.

The boy with the umbrella straightened, off guard for only an instant before he tipped his hat and gave a little bow. "Good morning, miss."

I nodded, suddenly overcome. By what? Something that

made the natural distance between us stretch threefold. I tried to smile. Was this simple shyness, the same thing I would feel if I could look them straight in the eye?

"You weren't here last Saturday, were you?" the boy went on. I shook my head. "You do work here, miss?"

"Yes. I've just arrived." All of them nodded. I took a step back. "From Canada."

"We *adore* Canada," said the woman. "I'm Elizabeth Crawford. Welcome to New York."

"Thank you."

I said my name and wanted to say more but I blushed like a girl. Why? For what? I could easily have stopped, asked or told them something. Anything. Easily. Instead, I was grateful for my assigned task and I moved on.

Nine

After three hours I returned to my room. No one was monitoring my movements, so who would care if I left the public sphere for a while, to rest a little and then take my lunch? I had the annoying sensation that someone *was* observing me as I made my rounds, but this was the result, undoubtedly, of the myriad eyes of museum visitors.

When I reached the hall on the fifth floor, I saw an open door two doors beyond mine. It wouldn't kill me to be neighborly, would it?

It was a bigger apartment than mine, and a carpet with a distracting geometric design dominated it. Several suitcases filled with clothes were strewn about the place. I wondered what would appear as a feminine voice grew louder, but the woman who appeared from a small adjoining room appeared normal on first glance. She stopped when she saw me. She had never seen someone as tall as me. How could she be here, moving into *this* museum, and still be surprised? We looked at each other. Her mouth opened slightly. Her eyes: *How dare you frighten me?* She didn't speak.

"I'm Ana Swift." I held my ground. People find my hands monstrous and I never offer to touch others, so I kept them at my sides.

We were the same age. Hers was a narrow face, smooth and curved like a cake of soap worn down in the middle. Eyes set high and close under trembling black curls. A small mouth my presence had soured.

"Are you a new one? You must be." The woman didn't come closer. "They're coming like a *plague,* for goodness' sake." Her eyes darted uncontrollably. Behind her were full bookcases and velvet chairs. They appeared to have been living there for some time, and yet there was no outward sign of her purpose in a museum of curiosities, unless she was an acrobat or had another invisible talent. But she didn't have that look about her. She was a woman with *things:* tablecloths, porcelain, and a portrait on the wall. "They didn't tell me this would happen."

"That what would happen?"

"Mama —" A girl with a ridiculous blue satin bow around her head entered the room behind the woman. "Oh!" Eyes widening, hand rising to her mouth.

"They're still arriving," the woman murmured. But the girl rushed forward, tripping over her own feet and quickly regaining balance.

"I'm Caroline." Breathless, the girl craned up.

"Ana Swift." The girl was as tall as my waist, probably ten or twelve years old.

"I'm so glad to meet you." The girl gave a little bow. "Where did you come from?"

"Pictou, Nova Scotia, originally."

"Would you like to sit down?" Caroline waved at the tiny chairs.

Her mother took a step forward as if to stop her, but the girl gave her a stern look, and she wilted. Now the woman was not only unsettled by my presence but also embarrassed to be following her child's example. "Well, yes. Do come in. I'm Mrs. Charity Barnum."

The chair was not sturdy enough; I sat on the edge of the love seat, supporting myself partially with my legs. It is my usual custom in these situations to ensure that my full weight never rests on other people's furniture. Mrs. Barnum went for tea, and Caroline sat across from me.

"You're very tall." The girl walked to the chair I'd rejected and sat down primly.

"Oh, you can do better than that, can't you?"

She swung her legs delightedly. She seemed no different from other children, with her bold, somewhat refreshing manner. I meet at least as many children as adults and I've come to depend on them to simply blurt out one of several variations on the sentence Caroline had just uttered.

"It must be strange. There are two others. Tall, like you. One's from China. They live next door to each other, down the hall. The two last rooms. They arrived on the very same day. Tuesday, I think it was. But it was the first time they'd met."

"Mr. Barnum is your father?"

"Yes. We moved into the museum a month ago, but Mother refuses to unpack her things." Caroline gestured to the suitcases with her foot. "We couldn't keep our apartment."

"Why not?"

Caroline leaned toward me. "My sister's sick," she whispered, her smile fading as she pointed to the back room. "In there. It costs *money*. My mother" — she leaned forward even more — "is going to have another baby. But Papa is going to come back with a lot of money."

Mrs. Barnum returned with a pot of tea and cups. Shakily, she set down the tray and sat down herself.

"Well," she said. She glanced somewhere below my collarbone before looking at her lap.

"I just arrived." The decent thing was to try, for just a few minutes. You're always over my shoulder, Mother. *They will see themselves in you.* But do they see something good? Something that they want to see?

Caroline poured the tea. "The best time to see the museum is at night when everyone's gone. That's the very best."

"Hush, Caroline."

We sat in silence. How long could Mrs. Barnum bear it, this stillness with me in the middle of it? Caroline had handed me a teacup and saucer. I had not taken a sip and did not intend to. The teacup was absurd in my hands. I was not working. I would not entertain them.

No one broke the silence and within it I awakened from a

certain fogginess of mind. I do not know how long I'd been in it. There's been a haze ever since they put you in the ground, Mother, but this is different. Maybe it's that sense of half belonging that I feel in a place like this. The emotion facilitates a certain stability, a certain focus of intention that makes me look up suddenly, wanting to have something, like a hobby or a pet. But it's a strange deception, the idea of a community of anomalies. The feeling crumbles when I examine it. No, this feeling must be a simpler vigor, perhaps chemical in nature, born in the silence between Mrs. Barnum, glaring from behind her tea, and me. I came awake when the silence stretched on too long. I felt no need to fill it but I knew Mrs. Barnum did. I didn't need to do *anything*. She didn't expect me to behave normally. Just as Father said long ago, although by that time he wouldn't meet my eyes: *You're lucky, Ana. People will pay to see you and you don't have to do a damned thing.*

Suddenly these small people, this typically sized room, these things mattered. Not to me personally, perhaps, but they mattered because this is where life had delivered me, and from this point I must function. This woman's husband was paying me more than anyone ever had. Paying me to be here and show myself. In two weeks I would send the money home to Father. Maybe he would visit me. Perhaps I'd have a place with a carpet, with a bookcase full of books.

Finally the two of them cocked their heads toward the back room, toward a child's high voice. "Who is it, Mama? Caroline, who's there?"

Both of them jumped up. Caroline went to her sister.

"She has a fever . . . I don't know. We'll leave this place very, very soon. The draftiness, you know. It's not right. It's very bad for us. For the girls."

"I hope she recovers soon." Small talk doesn't suit me. "When will your husband return?" If I could get that information from the woman the visit would be worthwhile.

Mrs. Barnum did not take well to this question, either; she rose and turned on one small heel. "Soon, very, very soon . . . I'm sorry, Miss Swift, this . . . *place* is wearing on my nerves." She offered me a pained expression as she raised her hand toward the door.

"No apology is necessary," I said. I arose, not without dramatic intentions, I'm afraid. I towered above her. "I won't keep you any longer."

Mrs. Barnum could not manage more than a short nod as she ushered me out.

But as I stood at the bleak window of my room, contemplating the bricks of the neighboring building and the small injustice at having no control over whose lives adjoined my own, I heard children's footsteps in the hall. I was not surprised when they stopped outside my door. After all, I hadn't said good-bye to Caroline.

"Miss Swift, are you in there?" Caroline chose to announce herself not by knocking but whisper-shouting at the closed door.

"Come in if you'd like."

The girl peeped in, still with the absurd silk bow flopping over her forehead. A good round face. And then another little face below hers, this one pale with tiny gray crescents under its eyes and tight curls bobbing up.

"This is Helen."

"Would you like to come in?" Momentarily shy, Caroline nudged her sister. Helen walked a little unsteadily, a four-year-old in a high-collared nightgown and woolen socks. Caroline followed.

Helen came close. "I didn't get to meet you."

"Here's our chance."

"We didn't have any proper visitors up here," Caroline said. "Until all of you began to arrive. We *adore* visitors." Caroline had appropriated a sophisticate's manner of speaking and aped it perfectly. It was not difficult to imagine her picking it up from Mrs. Barnum, although it was quite impossible to imagine the children's dour mother *adoring* anything. "But where are the rest of your things?"

"These are all my things."

"Five crates and a bag?" Caroline pointed at them.

"Yes."

Caroline strolled to the foot of the bed.

"It broke," I admitted.

"Yes. And these crates are making it crooked. What is this?" She read the labels on the crates. "Cocadiel."

"Medicine." I showed her the bottle.

"Are you sick?" Caroline looked at me skeptically.

"I'm sick," Helen confided.

"No, just prone to aches and pains." I smiled at the understatement.

The girls perched together on the chair, with Helen looking up at me with glassy eyes. They let out little oohs and snorts of delight as I pulled my things from the crates to show them. Gabardine skirts and a crinoline they could make into a tent. They hid behind my spoonbusk corset. Helen reached for my leather gloves. She held one in both her hands before fitting it on her head like a cap. The fingers fell down over her eyes. We sat together until Charity Barnum called them back. Children being the strange creatures they are, they each gave me a kiss, demanded one in return, and asked to be lifted up to the ceiling before they left.

Ten

If I hadn't caught a flicker of movement out of the corner of my eye, and if I hadn't wondered what that movement was, I never would have stopped in that gallery on my way back to my booth, and I would have missed the show entirely. This one was smaller than the other galleries, a foyer for the theater and empty of visitors. It didn't need a giantess. I reached the doorway and the flash of red movement turned into an usher, emerging from the theater doors. He set out a sign on a metal stand: TODAY'S PERFORMANCE, THE HUMAN CALCULATOR, WILL COMMENCE AT TWELVE NOON.

For the second time in one day I was invisible. The usher, in his brass-buttoned tailcoat and close-fitting cylindrical cap, propped open the doors leading to the museum's theater. He disappeared, only to reappear and straighten the sign. This man tended to his task with a singular concentration; he did not even notice the giant standing in the doorway. I was about to turn away when the usher began to perform.

He positioned himself beside the theater door, facing away from me now. He straightened his jacket and hat in a some-what exaggerated manner. Then he began to react to a great crowd of imagined people. He smiled. He gestured. He murmured words to the invisibles that I could not make out. I took a step back but I did not leave. There was a charm in what he did. He stepped kindly aside for an invisible guest, even extending his arm to assist what perhaps he saw as an elderly matron bound for the show. His gestures communicated gentle concern as he pantomimed his duties; something in the slight hunch of his shoulders. He bowed and nodded continuously. The only time he ignored his patrons was when he took a moment to rearrange his shirt cuffs and adjust his cap.

He didn't see me, so he performed for no audience. Even when, as I imagined would soon be the case, an actual audience filled his theater, it would not acknowledge him. Patrons would accept his courtesies without a thought, and yet here was this flushed performer with an embarrassing eagerness; he emanated a weird hope that even I, to whom hope was usually an uneasy abstraction, could actually feel. I wanted to look away from him, but I was entranced. Here was an optimist. They should put *him* in a cage.

As if by categorizing him I had somehow broken his concentration, the usher looked up, mid-gesture. His gaze swerved directly to mine. Because he was an employee of the museum and someone I would meet again, I decided to speak. As I approached, the usher, who was certainly taken aback not only to be observed but to be observed by me, gave me one of the most common surprised expressions. His face then deepened to a blush that matched his uniform. He recovered slightly, adjusted his lapel, and concluded his reaction by surprising me: He grinned.

"I'm not deranged, if that's what you're wondering."

"Not at all. I had the impression you were . . . practicing."

"Yes." The usher blushed again. I thought he was young, maybe twenty-five, but the bright spots on his hairless cheeks gave him the air of a schoolchild. He had waxed the ends of his wispy mustache, and the resulting comedy could not have been what he intended.

His eyes darted up to my face again. He cocked his head, eyes squinting.

"Are you one of the . . ." Don't say *exhibits*, Optimist. "Residents of the fifth floor? They told us to expect new faces and we've . . . all of the ushers, I mean . . . have been wondering."

"Yes."

"And you're working now?"

"I am assigned to stroll through the galleries."

"You're just walking around the museum?" The usher took a gleeful look over his shoulder as if we were fooling everyone.

"It's a good strategy, actually. I've noticed some people think I'm a visitor, like them. I should really carry a handbag and wear a hat."

"I see."

"But after a few seconds they usually talk among themselves and seem to decide I am not an innocent, though very tall, bystander."

"They realize that you must be . . . what you really are."

"Yes."

"I am Samuel Beebe."

He lifted his cap to reveal a high, square forehead. Someone had cut his curly fawn-colored hair into a triangular shape, with two ledges of curls at his ears that narrowed to a rounded apex on his crown. His eyebrows were perfectly straight lines and his eyes brown and round. It was the kind of face that would ask a worried question and then relieve you of answering with a foolish grin.

"Ana Swift."

"Mr. Forsythe told us about the apartments on the fifth floor. Are there many? We're not allowed to go up there. They told us to expect new people, whole groups of people. Employees. Performers. But Mr. Barnum has been out of touch, at least with Mr. Forsythe. Everybody's worried about the new employees getting lost . . . before they even find their way here. Lost in the city before they even —"

"Surely Barnum has provided for them."

"Did he provide for you?"

"I suppose he did, yes."

"Then he probably has. He most possibly has. He generally does." Beebe's sentences crowded one another before trailing away. He gazed up at me, still with a querying expression.

"Where did *you* come from?" I deflected the conversation from returning to the subject of me.

71

"Oh, not far. I'm from Bethel Parish, Connecticut. This is better for me. A better type of feeling. Much more exciting, of course. In my experience. Which is much different from yours, if I may venture to guess."

"You may."

Beebe layered his words and phrases so recklessly I was tempted to retreat from him altogether, despite his pleasing features and somewhat winning manner. Strategies of avoidance and repetition usually annoyed me, but I was certain this Beebe was not conscious of any strategy.

"The performance begins thirty-five minutes from now, Miss Swift. I must prepare." Again he gestured, this time toward the theater. "In there. May I venture . . . do you take meals in the Aerial Garden and Perpetual Fair?"

"Is that the roof?"

"The same."

"I do."

"Well, then."

I didn't see how this concluded our conversation, but Beebe ducked and bowed away, finally giving me a little wave as he disappeared through the theater doors. I enjoyed his exit but did not return his wave.

I continued through galleries, past pockets of visitors looking at the things they had paid to examine, myself included. I observed a tinge of pleasure as I replayed those moments when Beebe had cocked his head and squinted up at me, as if the sun shone brightly to my back. I enjoyed the sensation as long as I could before I scorned my hunger for it. Why did Beebe's display attract, not repel, me? I wondered if the fact that I, certainly one of God's more jaded creatures, had warmed to his innocence was one of the world's more wicked jokes or one of its greatest gifts.

I found my half-built booth adorned only with two carpenters nailing up its sides. The booth had not yet been painted. No façade provided color or interest, and only my name was sketched in pencil onto the wooden frame. I quite liked it this way. I passed my hand along the empty front counter. I would need a new set of lithograph portraits and a new True Life History to sell. This was a good location, near the balcony so I could at least see the sky and receive the breeze. I surveyed the view: Glass cabinets lined the opposite wall, a mummy lay in the center of the gallery, two stuffed gazelles stood in the corner, poised as if they would leap through the balcony doors and out over Broadway.

The problem of my True Life History had bothered me since my arrival. I hadn't brought any copies of my old one, an absurdly gothic melodrama that recounted my "early life" in the remote Hebrides, where I was apparently raised by a clan of druids whose tendency to use me as a centerpiece for cultic invocations partially accounted for my stature. Mr. Ramsay had spent days composing it, and the pamphlet sold well. The public must have souvenirs, and fabricated accounts of my origin seemed to please them very much.

There had been other True Life Histories before the Hebrides story, a new one every year or every time I changed managers. The only one I was ever particularly fond of was the first. The manager who wrote it was not an educated man, but he owned a copy of Tabart's *Jack and the Bean-Stalk* and decided to invent me as the ogress in his own interpretation of the fairy tale. She was an awful character; he dressed me in rags and a yarn wig. My props included a hen and golden egg, a small harp, and, when he was available, a dwarf who agreeably played the boy Jack in our crude skit.

What new story would I now invent? I had never written a True Life History myself and I had to come up with something before my booth was finished. But the prospect of writing it irritated me in the extreme; it gave me the feeling that *I* was falling for some kind of prank, even though I knew it was those who would part with their money for the pages who were the fools. I recalled a History from several years ago in which I was cast as Anoo, a mighty South American Amazon. Despite its premise, the story lacked verve. Perhaps I could reuse it, this time embellishing it with details recently brought back with the latest expedition to Surinam.

"Will you join us on the balcony?" Elizabeth Crawford had appeared below me, and I was grateful for the distraction.

Miss Crawford and her friends now had a dozen little girls with them, and two nuns. "These are children from the Sacred Heart Girls' Home. We sponsor a monthly outing for them, and today's their lucky day!" Miss Crawford smiled down at the girl she held by the hand, whose eyes had grown to the size of chestnuts as she beheld me. "Come with us," she urged.

I followed them out of doors, wondering if by doing so I was no longer officially working. On the other hand, my presence on the balcony might lure more business from the street.

The day was cold and bright; a group of twenty people was already gathered at the railing. The street rushed below in a jarring confusion of colors and noise, with a particular commotion coming down from the north. In one corner of the balcony, a man was playing a harpsichord, accompanied by a fiddler and an ophecleide player. They all had the look of street hawkers, in fingerless gloves and threadbare coats buttoned up to their chins. Miss Crawford and her orphans pressed against the iron railing near me. Up the street a carriage drawn by two white horses came into view. Accompanying it was a crowd of at least a hundred people. I noticed four men come out of the museum below us, each carrying a stack of handbills. Two men stayed on the museum-side of Broadway and two crossed the street. They waited for the carriage and the crowd to arrive.

"Is it a parade?" I asked.

"Yes, it is," Miss Crawford answered, shaking her head. "I doubt you have this kind of parade in Canada, though."

A lone figure could now be seen standing in the open carriage, wearing a white tailcoat and hat. He waved to the crowd and wore a strange smile that raised the hairs on my neck. The crowd cheered. All the little orphans laughed and clapped their hands. In an alarming gesture, the musicians on the balcony began a dirge. On an organ the tune might have carried some weight, but the harpsichord transformed it into a farce.

Miss Crawford saw my confusion. "It's a gallows parade."
She used the same tone a resigned schoolmarm would use to
correct a child.

"Who pays for it?" And who, I wondered, gave you that
ludicrous white hat, Prisoner?

On the street below us, the four men from the museum
passed out handbills, and soon the brochures floated high
above the crowd. Miss Crawford's friend with the umbrella
snatched one from the air.

"The police commissioner," whispered Miss Crawford,
smiling. "Isn't it *awful*?"

"Yes. Yes, it is. What did he do?"

"Who?"

"Him. The one to be hanged."

"Who knows. Something horrible."

The dirge had become frantic. The pianist was banging on
the harpsichord harder than ever, and I recognized him as
the man who had been with the taxidermist at the whale's
tank. The wind had reddened his cheeks and set his hair
askew. He resembled a desperate beggar. As he played he did
not take his eyes off the horde below us on the street. Barnum should be more careful whom he hired.

The man in the funeral carriage looked over his shoulder
to acknowledge the museum visitors with a kind of salute. In
an hour, Prisoner, you will be far from this world.

I find it is these moments, when the world displays its corruption so perfectly as to reach the sublime, that are the most
difficult to bear.

Eleven

It will surprise no one that boredom is the greatest, the most contagious evil in the show business. When it overtakes a talker or a showman, the audience is lost. It is the same with a performer, except that in my experience, given time, a bored performer is less likely than a showman to change her occupation. Instead we devise strategies for enduring it.

At the beginning of my career I was sunk in melancholy. No action was required of me to fulfill my role as a display, and so I lost great pockets of time when it simply wasn't efficient to remain attentive to my surroundings. At first my mind went in circles around the absurdity of my profession and the endless sequence of ridiculous faces and exclamations people made at me. This was exhausting, of course, so I developed a method wherein I simply put myself on a repeating loop of smile, nod, fold hands, acknowledge the audience, turn, unfold hands, nod, smile. Thus separated from my surroundings, I peered into my own cabinets of memory and examined everything I found. The problem, though, was that after I had done this (and I spent many months at it) it was done. Through excessive repetition, I petrified my own life. Images of my home and my family lost all interest, even to me, the only person to whom they shouldn't. That was what depressed me. So as an antidote, I attempted to reanimate memory through conversation with the dead or those otherwise lost to me.

During my first week in Barnum's American Museum, I

familiarized myself with the mummy and the rest of the collection in my gallery. I was grateful that my booth, still under construction, was near the balcony and the band, because the pianist played exquisitely. If he had not, the location would probably have been unbearable. I grew accustomed to eating my meals on the roof; the chef was gracious to all the performers and supplied me with unlimited hot water for soaking my feet. He even gave me a metal basin big enough to immerse both my legs up to the knees.

"It doesn't fit in the ovens," he said. "It's useless to me. Take it."

On my sixth day of work, I met the pianist formally. He appeared as disheveled as he had been during the gallows parade, with a thin, white-flecked beard on his chin. He was a perpetually startled sort of man, vaguely ill equipped for the roughness of the world around him. His close-set eyes darted all around as he introduced himself as Thomas Willoughby, and then awkwardly asked my permission to visit the beluga whale on the fifth floor.

"My permission?" I laughed. "Do I look like Phineas T. Barnum to you?"

"I've been waiting to ask him, but apparently he is still away. I thought, since you lived up there . . . maybe there are no visitors allowed. I wouldn't want to intrude."

"Go ahead! I don't care. You might want to ask the Indians, though. They're sharing the gallery with the whale."

"You think it really might be all right?" Thomas looked directly at me for the first time. His hair appeared to suffer from excessive static electricity; it floated like an undersea plant. "It really is an extraordinary beast," he asserted before striding back toward the balcony.

After a week of walking among the museum visitors in Barnum's establishment, and standing in my stall, I settled into my usual patterns. I passed into the mental arena where I live much of my life, where one figure, emerging from the dusk of memory, dissolves into another and the doorway of my childhood home in Pictou, Nova Scotia, could lead to my old room above the saloon in Montreal. The only continuous thread in this tapestry was the certainty that I will continue to be the abhorrence that I've always been.

One afternoon near the end of my second week of work, I was lulled by the coy repetitions of a sonata breezing in from the balcony. My mind conjured an image of Beebe the usher, and I could not keep away his inevitable shadow-selves, the spectral composite of Men, collected over the course of my thirty-four years into one ringing echo, which then arose in my mind.

Out of this mnemonic throng, my father emerged first: On one side, he stands over me as I sit reading on the hearth. He gives me his tired smile and hands me the rabbit-skin gloves he spent all Sunday stitching. He can no longer look me in the eye. *You could build a barn with all the books you've read.* And there he is again, walking away from our house with the first promoter who came to our door. Unfortunately, he did not walk far enough away to hide his outstretched palm and the money that filled it.

Close behind my father came the boys from my childhood, but they are a short and expected story leading directly to the slingshot-flung rock that left a scar on my right shoulder blade. I can't remember their faces and now I tend to think of them not as people but as a small, strong force behind my joy at leaving home seventeen years ago.

The next apparition came forward dusting off his lapel and straightening his cravat. He was old enough to be Beebe's father, I shuddered to think. I'd long ago given up trying to stop the encounters among the figments of my mind. If I had, they would insist on returning to the fore until they made the connection they wanted. So I let Mr. Ramsay, hawk-nosed and elegant in his rimless spectacles, approach Beebe and, as I knew he would, straighten the younger man's usher's cap.

Mr. Ramsay, who had been my manager until one month ago, made a home for me in his Yorkville row house, where he lived with his elderly aunt. He gave me the largest bedroom, even had a bed custom-made. I had become accustomed to an itinerant life, moving from hotel to hotel and town to town, so I loved that room. His own bedroom was next to mine; we even had an adjoining closet, though he took great pains to demonstrate that his access door had been nailed shut. *For peace of mind,* he said.

Mr. Ramsay also shifted me from an exotic mode of presentation to what he called an ennobled one. Instead of Athena the Goddess, or Anoo, the South American Amazon, I became Anabelina Swann, Countess of the Hebrides. Mr. Ramsay taught me to mimic a unique derivation of the British accent, and he told me stories of the Hebrides Isles, where exceedingly fine wool and tea were made. He even obtained samples of these products and put them for sale after my performances. He had a silk gown and a fine wool shawl made for me, and I performed recitations not only of my local history but of English poetry as well. The ennobled mode, said Mr. Ramsay, is not at the whim of whatever scientific exploration happens to be the fashion. American Anglophilia, he declared, will never wane.

Unsurprisingly, I grew smug and comfortable in my new role. Months of reciting Donne and Shakespeare lifted my spirit. I enjoyed a period of singular scorn: for my audiences, for other performers. As embarrassing as it now is, through repetition and perhaps isolation, I began to believe my fabricated history.

Each evening Mr. Ramsay and I sat late in his library, drinking sherry and discussing the day's audience or the industry's latest trends. *It is always best,* he said, with his spectacles reflecting the fireplace glow, *to take advantage of people's aspirations. To amplify their own desire to move up in the world.* The show business wasn't about the mystery of unknown lands; it was about the mysteries of the known elite. Our evenings together in the velvet-draped library seemed to belong to a different world, a world in which I loved poetry and spoke fervently of it while Mr. Ramsay nodded his head and gazed into the fire, or at me.

At the end of these evenings I ascended to my room, with Mr. Ramsay waiting courteously until I was safely shut in before he made his way up. Then I would listen while he opened drawers, lifted out his pajamas, I imagined, setting his spectacles on the nightstand and unbuttoning his clothes. After a few months I had determined to see all of this for myself.

I recited Shakespeare's sonnets. I lingered at the end of the evening, complaining that the nights were so long. It did not take much for him to see my intention. I allowed him to accompany me up the stairs, then to kiss my hand.

"You are the most introspective woman I've ever met," he said as we stood on the landing outside our two bedroom doors.

"But this does not surprise you, surely?"

"No. But observing you awakens a certain desire," he said, taking a step closer. "To bring you outside of yourself, to give you, of all people, a sense of wonder. But the only way I can imagine to accomplish this," he went on, removing his spectacles and putting them in his waistcoat pocket, "is by a purely conventional, although admittedly ancient and successful, mode."

"Oh?" I didn't want him to lose his nerve, so I slouched my spine, which brought my height down a few inches.

"The body, Ana. Through the body."

He achieved this goal with the first touch of his lips against my collarbone. I was not a stranger to physical intimacy; there had been a gymnast, and then a tall boy from Cooper's Medicine Show. But aquiline Mr. Ramsay, with his solemn, graceful manner and his velvety library, made my heart rise with a delicious new expectation.

"You can't know, Ana," he murmured, his lips moving across my décolletage, "the effect you have on the men who see you."

"I know very well the effect. Imagine if I were beautiful."

I led him into my room and sat on the edge of my bed. He kissed me, and I relished how his prodigious nose pressed against mine. He began to unhook the buttons down the side of my dress.

"Why did you take the mirror down from the wall, Ana?"

"Do you really need to ask?"

"I didn't know you disliked the sight of yourself."

"It's not that. It just reminds me that I ought to charge myself admission. That's not right, is it?"

"No, no, it's not. Come here." He slid his hands inside the dress and felt the smooth, hot cotton of my shift. I helped him off with his coat. I wanted to see him out of it, and out of the pointed collar, out of his sleeves. Then we were laughing and gawking, him at my broad expanses, I at his narrow waist, his chest covered in white down. With his shiny pate and regal nose he struck me as a newly hatched bird, flailing in the nest, trying to fathom the size of its mother.

Next morning we smiled into our tea, trying to pay attention to his aunt's comments on the morning newspaper. Mr. Ramsay had not stayed long in my room; we did not expose ourselves fully, or otherwise overreach our fragile intimacy. But that evening I went to bed early, and he tapped on the door. When he came in, he stopped long enough to hang the large, gilt-framed mirror back on the wall.

"I want you to appreciate your own beauty, Ana."

He was so adamant that I indulged him. And soon he was in the bed with me, navigating the folds of my nightgown. I discovered that my hands could almost encircle his waist, and if he moved up far enough to kiss my lips, his feet would tickle my knees. He discovered ways in which I was five times stronger than he; he discovered my breasts, and groaned and suckled and his taut, curved penis poked my belly like a stick.

The next night we grew bolder. He wanted me to see myself as he did. He left two lamps burning and maneuvered me so that we could see ourselves in the gilt mirror. He lifted my nightgown over my head and I lay naked. I did not tell him that this display excited only him; I had seen myself a thousand times, of course. He leaned over the bed to caress me, running his hands up and down my legs, across my belly, dipping his head to kiss my neck, my arms, my lips.

"Now you," I whispered, reaching for his shirt buttons. But he wouldn't let me.

"Not yet," he said, and continued running his hands all

over me, no doubt feeling me soften. I closed my eyes. He put a hand on each of my knees and slowly spread my legs apart. And then, from very close by, from somewhere just behind my right shoulder, someone coughed. It wasn't me; I was sure of that. And when I looked at Mr. Ramsay, he was already horrified, staring back at me. I leapt up from the bed and lunged for my nightgown. Holding it in front of me, I turned in the direction of the sound and saw a shadow move underneath the closet door and I flung it open. Inside, a man with a terrible look on his face was just getting to his feet. He was dressed in a fashionable suit, a wealthy man. He stumbled backward with his hands up in front of his chest. He made no sound as he disappeared into the closet. I saw a small hole cut into the door about four inches from the bottom. An eyehole. I followed the man, pushing past my dresses in the closet, and emerged in Mr. Ramsay's room. The man was already gone. I stood there, holding my night-gown to cover my front, looking at Mr. Ramsay's small bu-reau, where a basin, pitcher, and shaving brush sat neatly on a linen cloth next to a small pile of bent nails.

"Ana —" Mr. Ramsay came in through the proper door. Like the man in the closet, he held his hands out as if to stop me, though I had not moved. "Let me —"

"How much?"

"Ana, just —"

"How much?" I turned on him.

"Really, Ana. If I thought you would —" In two steps I had him by the arm. My nightgown fell to the ground. I took hold of his other arm and I lifted him into the air. His head hit my chest and I lifted him higher, shaking him now. I let my hands slide up to his neck. I could kill him easily. "How much money did he pay?" I jerked him from one side to the other. His eyes nearly popped out of his head and I wished they would.

"One hundred dollars," he whispered.

I lifted him so high he was level with my face. "You hung that mirror just right, didn't you? Probably before I even moved in."

He grew redder and redder in the face, opening and closing his mouth, and uselessly prying at my hands.

I let him drop to the ground, where he crumpled. "I'll be gone by morning." I was already thinking of a steamer and the gray syrupy waters of Ontario widening the gulf between us, and the possibility of my body sinking into a place with no more breath, no more me, ever. Or else New York. "You can leave the one hundred dollars on the table in the library for me."

Twelve

I entered the world an average size; my mother, a missionary's wife, held me easily in her arms on the deck of the ship that carried us to the jungled shore of South America, which was to be our home for as long as the Lord willed it. Safely under God's wing, we had no idea what terrors we'd soon encounter, and what black magic would be incanted upon us.

Or perhaps:

My father guided my mother down the gangway onto the rough-hewn pier that led into the jungle with one arm around her shoulders and the other gently touching her heavy belly. They were relieved that the baby had not arrived on the ship; little did they know that this gestation would be the longest the world had ever known; the birth of such a monstrous baby would be so gruesome that my father, the most devout soul in South America, would lose his faith in God. At my mother's funeral he gave me to the black nurse who had attended the birth-murder. It was she whom I would call mother, and, after the mission burned and my father's head rotted on a wooden stake beside the ruins of his church, it was with her that I fled to my second life in the jungles of Surinam.

Horror sells, but maybe this was too much? I put down my pencil and rubbed my eyes. I should just hire someone to write it. I could speak to Barnum's ad man. What was his name? He could recommend someone, and I would be rid of this terrible task. The True Life History nagged at me incessantly. Without a story, however full it was of nonsense, I was just an oversized body on display.

I sat on the north edge of the rooftop garden, half hidden in the shadow of the kitchen. Under low clouds that threatened rain, about a hundred museum patrons wandered the rooftop promenade. An umbrella vendor would soon appear, and some of the restaurant staff had already started to unfold one of the large tents that could stand over a section of tables. A crowd had gathered around a white-suited juggler wearing a harlequin mask, whom I could tell was a woman. She juggled well; her seven gold balls cascaded in a perfect circle. She was probably French. I scanned her audience, wondering if she worked with a disguised accomplice who gently robbed the enchanted crowd.

My first act on earth was to destroy my mother. By the time I could read I knew that most of literature's lessons and pleasures did not apply to me. By the time I reached Womanhood, my punishment was fully realized: I was eight feet tall.

A shadow crept over my paper, and I covered the scrawl with my arm.

"May I?" Thomas Willoughby, slouching and spectacularly unkempt, gestured to the seat next to mine.

"By all means. I'm just waiting for my lunch to arrive."

Thomas sat heavily and crossed his grubby hands in front of him. "What are you writing, a letter?"

"Just a story to sell at my booth. About my so-called origins."

"Fabricated?"

"Of course. But I'm tired of it." I folded the paper and placed it under my water glass. "Tell me something about your origins, Thomas. Did your parents set you aside at birth to become a prodigy, or were you driven to it by some mysterious, possibly divine force?"

"Nothing like that." Thomas Willoughby smiled. I had heard that he was widely known in Europe some years ago, and even here in New York, quite recently. I still had no idea why he was working for Barnum.

"I didn't start playing until I was eleven, which is quite late. I would never have come to it on my own. One of our neighbors played, and it was because of her that I learned.

Mrs. Corbett." Thomas smiled coyly and tapped his fingers on the edge of the table. It appeared that he was feigning shyness, which made me smile.

Above us, the overcast thickened. Museum visitors strolled among the flagpoles and potted trees, their shawls wrapped tight and jackets buttoned against the breeze that wanted to blow their hats toward the harbor.

"My mother and father didn't own a piano. Neither did Mrs. Corbett, actually. I would meet her at the church. She was a widow. I was in love with her."

"Of course." With his rabbity nervousness, I wouldn't have taken Thomas for a storyteller. Two plates of chicken salad arrived for us.

"A widow, but still young," I goaded.

"Not very young."

"But pretty."

"Not so pretty. I adored her! She paced the church while I played. We were the only two people in existence. You know how it is."

I did not.

"As if the church were some kind of ship and we were far from land! She would stop me in the middle of a movement and shout my name. 'Thomas! Do you hear? Ludwig called that C minor chord *Fate knocking on the door!*' She referred to composers by first name. By the time I was fourteen, she had stopped playing the piano herself."

"Because your skill had far exceeded hers."

"Yes. But she remained my teacher. She read things to me. Biographies. I was fourteen. I wanted to go home with her. She started giving me different, more powerful music. Music that held both love and grief. Primeval, we called it."

Thomas was staring at the horizon with a bit of chicken grease shining on his chin.

"Good Lord, Thomas. You're waxing quite poetical now."

"I was in love with her, Ana. Surely you understand that!"

That I would know what it meant to be in love was not a fair assumption, but I kept quiet.

"She sent me away."

"No!" I suppressed my laugh because Thomas looked so crestfallen in the retelling.

"She had written to Leopold Heinrich in London. A famous teacher. I don't know what she did to convince him to take me. I was so much older than his other pupils. But he invited me to his school."

"But not before you declared your love?"

Thomas shook his head. "I did not. During our last lesson she sat next to me on the bench. She said, 'Counterpoint, Thomas, is two melodic lines diverging and intersecting. It's how harmony is made. Think of it as a conversation of two voices, both contained by the piano.' The way she said it to me . . . I can't explain." He was positively dreamy. "The next day I climbed into a carriage and never returned."

"You never saw her again?" I set my wineglass down; a few crimson drops spilled onto the tablecloth. "How excruciating."

"I spent twelve years in Europe, and then came here, to Manhattan. That was ten years ago now. But long before that, my mother told me Mrs. Corbett had moved away." Thomas finished his tale with a flourish. "Gone."

I did not trust myself to open my mouth; I was afraid I would mock him, and that would be cruel. I could not tell if the pianist regarded his love story as melodrama, so I commiserated while we finished our cake, and it wasn't until I returned to my booth and subsequently heard three hours of a continuous fugue that I determined he did not.

Maud had found a fourth for the whist table in Mrs. Martinetti, eldest of the Martinetti family of acrobats. The ten-person Martinetti family, the Marvelous Monarchs of the Air, performed in the theater twice daily wearing orange-and-black winged costumes. They drew a huge crowd, mostly Italian immigrants, for every one of their shows. Out of everything in Barnum's museum, I was sure the Martinettis made him the most money.

Though her furniture was not substantial, Maud's room

was an Aladdin's cave of richly patterned rugs and tapestries draped upon every surface. The table was made of two stacked trunks and lit by several standing lamps pulled close.

"Ana, come in. Everyone else is here," Maud said when I appeared. I ducked under the frame and closed the door. Mrs. Martinetti looked more like a grandmother than an acrobat, apparently proving that the two occupations were not mutually exclusive. She perched on the edge of her seat, preposterous next to Mr. Olrick, the Austrian Giant, who immediately rose to greet me.

"Miss Swift, good evening. We've not yet had the pleasure of acquaintance." His voice held no trace of an accent. "I met the other giant last night, the Chinese fellow. I wondered when I would have the pleasure of meeting you."

"Mr. Olrick," I returned. I suppose I could not ignore him forever. "I didn't know there was a third giant in the museum. That's an awful lot, don't you think?"

"No one sees him very much. He stays shut up in his room," said Maud.

Mr. Olrick had a pleasant enough face: a softened rectangle creased at all corners. His lips were entirely obscured by a mustache of unfortunate proportions. A trademark, perhaps. He wore some kind of military uniform. I enjoyed the touch of an equal-sized hand for a moment, and even imagined what it would feel like against my cheek, gently, or else roughly clasped in passion. I could make a fortune if I married a giant publicly, of course. I despised the idea, just as I despised other giants, especially the men who must see me (as I also see them, however fleetingly) as a potential lover. Why is it assumed that I belong with others of my kind? Why double something that is already enormous? No thank you, I will stay firmly away.

"We were discussing this rain," said Maud. She gestured me toward a less-than-substantial chair. "But now we can dispense with trivialities and get down to the business at hand. Mr. Olrick has limited experience —"

Mr. Olrick huffed. "I'm sure I can hold my own, my dear."

"Ana, I've paired you with Mrs. Martinetti, whose skills we have not yet determined, as she does not have English."

"Fine." I rested gingerly on the seat across from Mrs. Martinetti.

"Ana, will you oblige us with the first deal?" Maud picked up the deck, which was emblazoned with a gold-and-scarlet coat of arms. The cards gave a satisfying snap and hiss as I shuffled. Mrs. Martinetti cut the deck and I dealt out the hands, turning the last card face up.

"Diamonds trump," I announced and the game began. Maud led with the queen. Mrs. Martinetti followed with a three, and Olrick quickly played the king.

"Mr. Olrick!" Maud gasped. "Have you played this game before?"

"Well, yes," he sputtered, reddening. "But it has been some time."

"You do realize that I am your partner?"

"Yes, of course. Ah, I see my mistake now. I apologize."

I finished the trick with a five. Olrick led the next with a nine.

"Actually I haven't played since my convalescence." He directed this remark to me as I won the trick with the ten. "My mother and I had eleven months together, while I waited for my bones to strengthen."

Of course he had to bring up his *convalescence*.

"We played all kinds of card games, and then in the evening when my brother and father were home, we played whist."

"You were ill?" Maud played the ten of hearts.

"Some giants" — I interjected, with a clear inflection of boredom — "have a period of time, usually around the age of twelve, when the skeleton grows faster than the body can support. I'm surprised you haven't heard this story before, Maud."

Olrick continued to prattle about his virtuous mother nursing him into Monsterhood, and of course I remembered my own bed rest, but I would die before mentioning it aloud.

A full year flat on my back was nothing to share with others, a full year longing to peel myself out of the thick skin coat that fit less and less as the weeks marched on. People from town sent crate after crate of books, and I read them all and asked for more. One day my mother came home with a set of three volumes wrapped carefully in a sackcloth with the corners folded like an envelope. She handed them over and stood there, her eyes boring holes into me with an expression I didn't want to understand.

The Giant in History and Literature. I never did find out from whom those books came or what it took to procure them. But for good or ill, the Titans became my great-grandfathers, roaming the earth to make war with the gods. Goliath. Gilgamesh. From behind the misty curtain, Ohya and Hahya stepped out of the centuries as my distant sisters. But in the second volume, on page one hundred and seventeen, a hateful prophecy was delivered: *Through time it has been observed that Giants seldom, if ever, live to see their fortieth year. Earthly forces pull their organs to premature deterioration; their frames, though massive, are brittle and precarious, not meant to bear the weight with which they have been endowed.*

At first, still trapped in bed, I masked my horror with noble thoughts: As an example of this ancient and powerful race, I must gracefully bear this strange sentence. Rise above, so to speak, the inevitability of this verdict.

But when you came into the room, Mother, with a cup of broth steaming in your hand, you rushed to me. *What ails you, daughter?* My thin veil of dignity instantly dissolved to tears. You pulled the book from my hand. You took the whole set away, as if that could erase what I had already read. As if my aching bones, each throbbing step, each time I massaged a leg or shoulder or saw myself reflected in a window was not a reminder that my body is nothing but a death cage.

Mrs. Martinetti proved an attentive player but not much of a partner, since she barely looked up from her hand and never uttered a sound. We played on, with Maud and Olrick taking the next two tricks.

"Which war was it, where you fought, Mr. Olrick?" I couldn't help myself, though I knew it was cruel. "I see a nice row of medals on your lapel."

"Well." Olrick reddened again. "The truth is, none." He paused to play the four of clubs. "This is a costume."

"Ah, a costume," I agreed.

"You see, my clothes, and all of my belongings, were lost somewhere en route from Chicago. If it had happened in the past, my manager would have taken care of the arrangements for a tailor. But Mr. Barnum has been unresponsive to my predicament. It was only yesterday I found the name of a tailor, so it will be another week, he said, at least, before I have something else to wear. Until then, I'll just have to feel silly in this." He was clearly embarrassed. I let him take the next trick, as reparation.

"You know what I've been wondering." Maud leaned in and lowered her voice. "Ever since I saw them — or him — I've been suspicious. The conjoined twins. Have you met them yet?" We hadn't.

"They live next door." Maud nodded in the direction. "Ever since I saw them, something has rubbed me the wrong way. A certain awkwardness in their movement."

"Well," said Olrick. "Given their condition that's hardly surprising, isn't it? Are they conjoined at the usual place?"

"Yes, but that's just it. Usually conjoined twins are quite graceful. They move as naturally as we do. They don't know any different. But these two, they seem . . . clumsy. And they fight."

"What's wrong with that?" said Olrick

"I'm just saying, it wouldn't be the first time I've seen a gaff."

"A gaff couldn't have made it past Barnum's scouts, Maud." I had seen two or three instances of a relatively ordinary person impersonating an oddity over the years, and I'd always wondered at their motivation. There had been a dog-faced boy who actually attached his fur with epoxy. My mind always drew a blank when I considered what might drive a normal person into the life of a performer of that sort.

"And one of them would have to be deformed already. How could they move like that if each of them had two normal legs?"

"It wouldn't be the first time, is all I'm saying." Maud took the next trick with the ace of diamonds. "That makes a game. I believe Mr. Olrick and I have made two points."

Mrs. Martinetti silently and sternly dealt the next hand, and we had taken two tricks before Charity Barnum glided into the room without knocking.

I hadn't seen Mrs. Barnum since I visited her apartment. She wore the same dark dress with a thick lace collar, and her pale hands clasped at her waist. She walked to the center of the room and stopped, swiveling her smooth and oddly boneless-looking face toward each of us, one after another. She even opened her mouth slightly, and a frightened look came over her, as if she had just realized she did not know how to speak. She bore a striking resemblance to the automaton on the fourth floor.

"Mrs. Barnum!" Maud rose. "I thought you would never accept my invitation, so I filled the fourth seat." She gestured helplessly at Mrs. Martinetti.

Olrick jumped up, looking vaguely relieved. "Madame, please. Please, sit. You may take my place."

Mrs. Barnum glided to the chair and sat down. She picked up Olrick's discarded hand. Her hands shook terribly.

"Mrs. Barnum, is something the matter?"

"Are you unwell?" Maud leaned forward.

Mrs. Barnum put down the cards and tried to steady one hand with the trembling other. "I'm afraid . . ." She looked into the eyes of Mrs. Martinetti. "She's been so ill, my daughter. I thought it would be all right, but" — Mrs. Barnum turned in her chair to look at the hallway, now shaking uncontrollably — "I think she's not. She appears to be . . ." Her jaw hung open as if she were waiting for the last word to emerge of its own accord. She pointed out the door. "She's in there."

Olrick went to find a watchman while we followed Mrs. Barnum to her apartment. The rain pounded against the windows. Mrs. Barnum led us into the small nook of a room behind the kitchen. Helen lay on the narrow bed, her blankets flung back as if she'd dreamed her way out of them. Damp tangles were stuck to her forehead, and Mrs. Martinetti went to the bed and peered into the girl's half-closed eyes. I expected her to still be alive. Mrs. Martinetti felt the girl's forehead, then her wrist. I waited for Helen to cringe, to flick her hand away from the old woman's grasp. Instead Mrs. Martinetti snatched her hand away from the child. *"Morto."*

Maud put an arm around Mrs. Barnum.

"I didn't think it would be so fast," Mrs. Barnum said, her voice high, piercing. "I thought I could call the doctor in the morning."

"You couldn't have known," Maud whispered. Mrs. Martinetti pulled the blanket up over the child, and Mrs. Barnum leaned heavily against Maud. I watched the lump of Helen's covered head for a toss, an awakening. She was dead, though, of course.

"Mrs. Barnum?" A watchman in a dripping overcoat appeared in the doorway with Olrick behind him. When she saw this man, Mrs. Barnum jerked herself away from Maud and nearly tumbled into his arms. "Thank God someone has arrived. Have you found a doctor?"

"We've sent two men out, ma'am. They should be back shortly."

"Thank you." Mrs. Barnum turned from her new position, held up by the watchman, and appeared to see us for the first time. A bearded woman, two giants, an elderly acrobat, and a dead daughter.

Maud moved toward the watchman. "You won't need a doctor, sir. She's —"

"Get out!" Mrs. Barnum shrieked, waving her arm toward Maud. "All of you!" Only the watchman was startled by Mrs. Barnum's outburst. We filed out of the room. As we crossed the living room, Caroline emerged bleary-eyed from the other bedroom in a wrinkled blue flannel nightgown. "What's happening, Ana?"

"All of you . . . people. Just get out!" Mrs. Barnum's voice held the slick edge of delirium. Caroline froze as she heard it.

"Well if this doesn't get Barnum back to the museum," hissed Maud in the hallway, "I will certainly doubt his humanity." She paused before going into her room: "At least now he'll finally pay us."

Back in my room, I could not sleep. I listened to the hooves and the mostly drunken voices rising from Broadway. A child had died; the fact itself was oppressive. I considered going for a walk. What better time than now, when I would be a phantom among night-walkers: transients, nocturnal workers, people perhaps more accustomed to strange sights in the darkness. But they would flinch when they saw me, and strip me of the dark's camouflage. And where would I go from there? The idea of leaving the museum had only a fleeting appeal that dissolved in these details. What was the point of going? Instead, I got out of bed, lit a candle, and took up my pen.

Nature seems to have no fixed standard by which to fashion and shape her works, and though we are compelled to believe in a design, to the careless observer every living thing seems to come and go by chance.

Certainly no visitor to the museum would pay money to read the words of a philosophizing giantess, especially on the subject of "careless observers" whose association with the reader would be clear. Frustration stilled my hand, as it did every time I thought of writing a True Life History. But my booth would be finished tomorrow. I had to sell something. I needed the revenue. I forced myself to continue.

The truth is that Nature's design contains every extreme and variety, and everyone must fashion intuitively in her mind a standard of comparison, based upon her own experience. When she finds something outside the limits of that standard, she at once views it as a curiosity, and her mind is chained with astonishment.

But if we follow one of these anomalies all the way back to her genesis (and I don't mean Genesis 6:4) we do not find her breaking out of an egg, or, like a golem, bursting from the bowels of the earth. We find her kneeling by her father's side in the village of Pictou-by-

the-sea. She is a homely but spirited girl of unequivocally average stature, untangling nets in anticipation of mackerel season.

Why not? Why couldn't the True Life History begin in Pictou?

At first my father thought my gasps were a simple ploy; the day was fragrant with blossoms and he knew I would rather be out among them instead of working on the nets. But real pain cannot be faked and it spread, filling every socket and cavity, ricocheting off the slats of my rib cage, the agony flowing down each appendage and up my neck to explode as brightly murderous rosettes in my brain.

I awoke in my bed, where I remained for the next eleven months, the pain my intimate companion. To the bewilderment of my parents, I grew at a rate of one and a half inches per month. Finally my body stabilized enough for me to stand. I looked down with exuberant joy upon my mother's neatly parted scalp and the upturned face of my father, as if I were ascending to heaven. I reached down and lifted them both into my arms. Releasing them, I ducked under the door frame. I gulped delicious, frozen air into my huge lungs and marveled at the miracle of God's will. I strode away from the farm, crunching through old snow, leaving monstrous footprints behind.

Exhilarated, I paused. It surely could have happened this way, if only I had cultivated that first bloom of incredulous pride that had, in fact, faded so quickly. That story had been one possibility.

Finally my body stabilized enough for me to stand. As I rose to my new height, I recognized gravity as my mortal adversary, my body as a tomb that I was forced to pilot through the years. Instead of living out my allotted time under the added weight of the world's stare, I waited until midnight and left the farmhouse. I found the nets laid out in the field and dragged one down the hill to the sea. In my father's boat I rowed myself to the mouth of the bay. The current then carried the boat out farther, while I wrapped myself tightly in the net and strung on as many weights as there were in the boat. My final thought was to curse the steady moonlight as it illuminated my plunge into the frigid sea.

This was an account that would never sell, but it was one that I had imagined many, many times. It deserved to be recorded in this True Life History.

Finally my body stabilized enough for me to stand. The first thing I saw from my new perspective was a crowd of people from town gathered outside my house. They wanted me to touch the hands of their sick relatives, to heal them. It was then that I realized how eagerly people believed in nonsense. We built a booth in our yard and charged people ten cents to see me. We made enough money in three years to buy a new boat. One day a man with strange eyes wearing a violet waistcoat appeared. I did not refuse his offer, and under his guardianship I traveled to Halifax and began my career as the only professional Giantess in the world.

Lusus Naturae

Thirteen

Guillaudeu pretended to study Cuvier's treatise on *Pongo pyg-maeus*. Supposedly, he was searching for clues to explain why the museum's wispy-haired red ape refused to eat. The creature's voluntary starvation was a problem: Its ribs poked out in a most unbecoming manner and the visitors were notic-ing. But Guillaudeu's show of flipping through Cuvier's thick pages was just that. He absolutely could not concentrate on anything other than the unfortunate situation in which he now found himself: Mr. Archer would not move out. The ad man was pacing around the office with the end of his pencil stuck in his mouth.

"But surely" — Guillaudeu began in a renewed, but still evasive, effort — "surely a *writer,* an artist such as yourself, needs quiet, needs . . . solitude to work."

"Artist! You can't be serious." Mr. Archer laughed as he always did, from the belly, with his shoulders shrugging up-ward and his head bobbing as if he had no control over his body. "I am anything but an artist, Monsieur Guillaudeu." He continued to pace.

"But why would you want to stay here, with the speci-mens . . . and me?"

"It's true that the stench of your glues and preservatives are disagreeable," Mr. Archer considered, giving Guillaudeu a flash of hope. "But this location is perfect. I can peek out at everyone who comes and goes. I may even have a window built, just here, looking out to the entry hall" — Mr. Archer pointed to the board-and-batten wall — "it will allow me to see every face that passes into the museum. Last Saturday, Commodore Vanderbilt reserved the entire rooftop restaurant for a late-evening soiree and if I hadn't been right here, in this very spot, I wouldn't have even heard about it. I would be a fool to lock myself up in some attic somewhere and miss all the excitement."

"The office we found for you is on the second floor, Mr. Archer, with a clear view over the balcony to Broadway. You would have an even better view from up there."

"Nonsense! I'll have nothing to do with it. If anything, monsieur, *you* should move. After all, nothing about your work necessitates your proximity to actual people."

"I have been in this office for sixteen years, sir, ever since they hung the door on its hinges. I designed this room for my work and I will not be crowded out. Now, if you will excuse me." Guillaudeu walked stiffly to his bookshelf and pulled out the sixth volume of Cuvier. "Unlike some I could name, I have work to do."

"And so do I!" snapped Mr. Archer. "Work that concerns the very breath of history!"

"Are you referring to the penny papers to which you swear your devotion?" Guillaudeu huffed. Mr. Archer did not reply, which infuriated Guillaudeu all the more. Barnum's takeover of the museum was one thing, but to allow this Archer, this . . . spinner of lies, to infiltrate his domain was one injustice too many!

The ad man halted his perambulation. "You never mention your wife. I find that odd."

Guillaudeu's hand froze over page eighty-three, wherein Cuvier described the orang-outang's frugivorous habits.

"I don't see how that's relevant."

"What a lovely gown she's wearing in this portrait. She seems to be a lady of taste."

"And that surprises you?"

"I didn't say that."

"She's dead." The words fell like stones from his mouth. "Cholera."

Guillaudeu did not turn to face the ad man and barely heard his ornate, though stilted, apology. Instead his ears rang with the word that had plagued him since he was a child, a word he chased from his mind by whatever means necessary, but that kept coming back, time and again. In its two syllables lay the explanation of his life: *orphan*. That he was well into middle age, and it was his wife who had most recently died, made no difference.

Before Celia became too weak to walk, Guillaudeu had returned from the pharmacist one afternoon to find her standing in the parlor wearing her bridal ensemble. The disease had eaten away so much of her body that she could fit into the gown again. The look on her face was ghoulish glee, and her jeweled bracelets tinkled against one another as she adjusted the cascading lace veil around her jutting shoulders.

When she saw him, she attempted to curtsy. "It's my last chance to wear them, dear."

"I cannot bear it," he'd whispered as she petted the mesh that framed her face.

She turned on him. "*You* cannot bear it?" Her laugh turned into a violent cough and she sat heavily back on the daybed. That may have been the last time in her life that she stood.

Guillaudeu's hand shook as he traced his finger down the columns of Cuvier's text. He stood up, unable to remain in the same room with Mr. Archer, or Celia's portrait. Edie Scudder was expecting him for lunch in an hour. He would go early. He retrieved his hat and coat from the rack and walked out without so much as a nod.

He slipped into the shifting horde on Broadway, his eyes on the sidewalk in front of him. A warm wind tunneled around him, and Guillaudeu proceeded with one hand anchoring his hat and the other gesturing wildly for a cabriolet. He crowded out the image of his dead wife with the image of the museum's new proprietor. I must speak with him, Guillaudeu decided. It had been four days since Barnum's daughter died and all the museum employees were looking over their shoulders, expecting Barnum to appear at any moment.

Seated in the small carriage, safely away from the pushing crowd, Guillaudeu's head filled with the points he would make during his conversation with Barnum: *People want to understand how nature works,* he imagined himself saying. *The museum's visitors are interested in the* organization *of nature, the model that becomes visible through correct classification. There is a place for spectacle,* Guillaudeu would concede, *but it must be within the larger paradigm of nature's elegant order.* That's why it was an abomination to put the tropical snake specimens in the same gallery as the common ducks, while the Floridian alligator crouched alone near the theater door. People love the patterns in nature, he would say. There lies harmony, and they want to be a part of it . . . as they were *meant* to be, not merely walking through a jumble of chaos. He pictured Barnum tilting his head, half closing his eyes as he realized the truth. If Barnum understood, and made certain concessions, including the restoration of his office to its former solitude, then Guillaudeu would stay. If he did not, Guillaudeu was no longer interested in the museum or its contents. It would probably be in the papers: *Museum's Original Taxidermist Scorns Barnum, Leaves Post After Thirty-five Years!*

The sharp, smoky odor of pine tar grew more pungent as the carriage approached the warehouses on Front Street. He climbed down and paid the driver. Edie would give him ideas about how to show Barnum the problems he faced if he continued to run his museum like the back room of a saloon. He dodged two men struggling with a giant cedar crate. He continued south for half a block before ducking into the cool doorway of Scudder & Williams. He ran up the plank stairs two at a time. Barnum could be back at the museum tomorrow, he thought. He envisioned Barnum confiding in him: *I've been concerned over the direction the museum seems to be going, my friend. Thank goodness you're here.* Barnum would clap him on the back and invite him to dine at his private table in the Aerial Garden. *Museum Taxidermist Rises to Assistant Manager!*

There was someone with Edie in her office. Guillaudeu took a seat on the bench in the empty foyer. The building had been constructed out of the same cedar planks as ships, and the wide beams emitted a faintly spicy breath into the quiet room. Guillaudeu leaned forward with his hat on his knee. The museum was headed toward disaster unless it changed course. He knew that much. Either bankruptcy, because people would lose patience and stop coming, or some other disaster, which Barnum would recklessly sail toward at full speed unless someone warned him.

"Of course," Edie's impatient voice reached Guillaudeu. "I know Captain Morehouse. I will speak to him —"

"Yes," a man's voice interrupted. "Find out if there's anything special we should know."

"I think that's all, Mr. Sim. Good afternoon." Mr. Sim, a thin man in a dark blue cutaway coat, walked swiftly past Guillaudeu down to the street.

As Guillaudeu walked in, Edie was leaning over a ledger, scribbling audibly with a mother-of-pearl pen he recognized as her father's. The heavy curtains of her large office were drawn against the glare of water-reflected light, and the dark room held a swampy stagnation. His friend, sitting at the center of a pool of yellow lamplight, did not hear him enter.

Suddenly Guillaudeu was paralyzed, unable to breach the invisible wall separating him from Edie. It was not an unfamiliar feeling. The sudden panic overcame him periodically, as if he'd slipped behind a veil into invisibility. He stared at Edie, hoping to attract her attention through a force of will. He considered tossing his hat onto her desk to get her attention. How foolish! Then all at once he perceived a human figure, almost lost in the dim corner of the room beyond Edie's right shoulder. The figure shifted its weight from one foot to the other.

"Good heavens!" His hand clamped down, crushing his hat brim. He heard Edie's pen tear through paper.

"Emile, God damn you! Are you trying to kill me?" She jerked up, her raised eyebrows lost under the low-hanging bird's nest of her hair. "I've ruined my page." She glanced over her shoulder and then down.

"I'm early," Guillaudeu admitted, peering into the darkness, trying to make out more than the silhouette of a human form. "Who in God's name is that?"

"A recent immigrant." She gestured at the figure. "He arrived this morning on the *Contessa*. A British ship. I'm probably going to have to track Captain Morehouse down at one of the whorehouses on the hook if I want to speak to him." Edie closed the ledger. "I hate doing that." She beckoned to the silhouette, which moved slightly.

The figure, which turned into a man, was clearly wearing someone else's clothes and appeared to have been wearing them for a very long time. The wool pants hanging off his body had weathered to an obscure shade and were ragged at the hem. He wore an unbuttoned and much-too-large shirt of the same indeterminate color. He carried a bundle on his back, secured to his shoulders by a length of rough-hewn rope. His skin was darker than most of the Africans Guillaudeu had seen, and it appeared slightly dusty. Like old shoes, Guillaudeu thought. Creased like the boots worn by a soldier for the length of a war. *Homo scorteus:* man made from leather. But aren't we all, he mused.

The man's tufted brown-black hair stuck mostly straight up, with the ends bleached to a brassy blond. He could have been forty or sixty years old. He was as tall as Guillaudeu's chest and he kept his eyes pointed at the ground. The man bore all the traces of someone who lived outdoors: flattened, callused feet, tough skin, and an obvious disregard for clothing.

"A tribesman," Guillaudeu concluded. "He must be cold."

"He won't wear anything we give him."

"Where is he from?" He studied the geography of the man's face.

"I told you, he came off the *Contessa*. From the colonies somewhere. His origin doesn't really concern me."

"I wanted to talk with you, Edie. About the museum."

"Oh?" She pulled out a different ledger and scanned its thick leaves.

"I've had just about enough of Barnum."

"Has he returned to New York? Oh good, here it is." Edie's finger stopped on the page. She copied something from the ledger onto a loose square of paper.

"No. Well, maybe," said Guillaudeu. The tribesman stood silently across the room, barely seeming to breathe but disrupting Guillaudeu's train of thought. "Why is this man in your office, Edie? This isn't your usual type of cargo."

"It's funny you should ask, Emile, because you and the tribesman are heading in the same direction. He belongs to your museum."

Edie handed Guillaudeu the paper she'd been writing on. "Here's the note Barnum instructed me to send with this type of acquisition."

"What?" He took the paper from her. "Are you *working* for Barnum?"

"It's mutually beneficial. A few weeks ago he sent a couple of his own men down here to look for interesting cargo coming off the ships. But the ships' crews wouldn't tell them anything about what came ashore." Edie smiled. "These captains like to trade with people they know. So he came to me."

"I can't believe you're doing this. After everything your father worked for at the museum. After everything *I've* worked for!"

"Why are you riding the high horse, Emile? Barnum is paying me a very respectable sum for this service, and I intend to provide it. He's been nothing but fair and honest about what he's after."

"And what might that be?" Guillaudeu noticed his voice rising higher, tighter. "Because that's what I've been wanting to know."

"Exotic objects. Natural anomalies, anything to spook people or make them curious."

"And this tribesman qualifies?"

"Read it for yourself," Edie said with a shrug. "I'm not going to refuse a good contract, Emile, no matter who it's with. And I can guarantee Barnum operates under the same philosophy."

"That's not philosophy," Guillaudeu seethed. He read the note in his hand: *Please welcome the newest Representative of the Wonderful.*

How could Edie have come to this? His hand trembled as he put on his hat.

"I cannot bear it," he said, his voice catching pathetically in his throat. "First your father, and now you? Abandoning all respect for nature's innate order, ignoring the legacy of your family business, not to mention my own life's work? I can't —" He stared at her familiar, beloved face and felt nothing but anger. "I don't know what to say, except good-bye."

"Emile!"

He had already left her office and had started down the stairs.

"Emile, you must take him with you! Make sure he gets to the museum!"

Guillaudeu did not look at the tribesman as they marched up Broad Street. Groups of men crowded around them on their way to warehouses, ships, or one of the taverns scattered around the shipping district. Edie Scudder, Barnum's employee. Guillaudeu fumed. Hadn't she learned anything, growing up among the great collections, visiting the Peales in Baltimore, even the British Museum? One would think the organizational principles supporting the exhibits would have left at least a vestigial mark on her. He quickened his pace in a half-conscious attempt at losing the man who followed him. She is nothing but a simple opportunist, with no thought for the integrity of science.

He was reminded of the day after John Scudder signed away the museum. Guillaudeu had arrived for work, expecting Edie to appear as she always did to manage the accounts. He had waited all morning. An accountant arrived after lunch and informed him that Edie had hired him. Edie herself, Guillaudeu found out, was signing a rental agreement on her new office at the port. As if she had been *waiting* for an opportunity to leave him!

As they started up Broadway, he glanced behind and saw that the tribesman was keeping up effortlessly but looking neither left nor right; he ignored the first city he'd ever set foot in.

Guillaudeu walked straight past the door to his office, but not before Mr. Archer leaned into the hallway. "Did you pick up a friend, monsieur? Or will you cure his hide and stuff him?"

Guillaudeu marched on, through the waxworks gallery, to which the tribesman paid no attention whatsoever. They ascended the back stairwell, passing several groups of museum visitors. Unlike the people on the street, these citizens gasped when they saw the tribesman. They continued up, past the entrance to the second floor, where the twelve o'clock show in the theater had drawn a crowd that extended all the way to the landing.

The huge fifth-floor gallery was now occupied by a group of Indians who crowded around the beluga whale's tank, standing on chairs and the ladder to peer over the side at the singing creature. Guillaudeu walked quickly across the hall to the door to the apartments. Which one did the giantess inhabit? He thought it was the second on the right. He felt sure that the giantess would know what to do with the man. Was it Miss Smith? Swanson?

But the giantess was not in her room. Of course. She's working. The tribesman stood behind him, looking at the floor or somewhere thereabouts, with one arm kinked behind his body to support the bundle on his back.

"Well, let's see if we can find you somewhere to stay. Do you understand me?"

The other man made no indication.

Guillaudeu found a small empty room at the end of the hallway.

"I don't know if this one is spoken for, but why don't you take it for now." Guillaudeu walked to the window and surveyed the brick wall outside. "This will do, I suppose. I'll let someone know you're here." Guillaudeu did not know whom he would notify. He would at least tell William, the ticket-man.

The tribesman stayed in the doorway.

"Well. Here you are, then. Barnum will be back soon, so they say. Until then, please eat your meals with the other performers on the roof. There's a restaurant up there." Guillaudeu pointed a finger toward the ceiling.

"Well, good-bye." He squeezed past the man, whose body exuded the deepest musk. As he passed back through the gallery, the Indians erupted into laughter over the beluga's antics.

When he returned to the office, Guillaudeu ignored Mr. Archer. He went straight to Cuvier's *Natural History* and flipped through the index until he found the volume concerned with the races of man. It was a slimmer volume than the others, and Guillaudeu could not recall ever opening it before.

Of the Mongolians, Cuvier pointed out: *The religion of these benighted tribes is that of the Dalai Lama, in which the people are held under the entire subjection of priests and jugglers.* Guillaudeu snorted. Jugglers?

Yes, he was quite certain that he'd never ventured into the ethnological chapters. He'd had no need to consult the anatomist on the behaviors of man. He knew Cuvier to be scientifically scrupulous and often playful in his descriptions of the lower kingdoms. He'd always enjoyed these touches of humor. And yes, several of the snakes cataloged here had downright ominous descriptions. But this scornful tone was new.

He scanned sections on Batu Pigmies, Saharan giants, Esquimaux, and the Aborigines of the American continent.

He was momentarily satisfied when he found an etching that perfectly illustrated the tribesman's facial structure, his tufted hair, and even the deeply creased face: *The tribes of Australia have already been noted for their ignorance, their wretchedness, as well as their moral and intellectual debasement. Their tribes are not numerous, have little communication with each other, and are sunk into a state of almost hopeless barbarism.*

Perplexed, he verified that Cuvier was the sole author of the text; the frontispiece even contained the anatomist's elegant declaration that the study of nature was the study of

God's Divine Plan. Guillaudeu stared at the image of the Australian tribesman. For Cuvier, could the races of man lie somewhere outside the realm of nature? Could this be possible? Didn't God's Plan include everything that crept, swam, flew, *and* walked upon the earth? How could Cuvier rationally say otherwise?

The degradations on the page were evidence of a fatal clouding of scientific observation. It was a betrayal so sudden and thorough that Guillaudeu's impulse was to tear out the pages and pretend he'd never seen them.

Cuvier had ignored the fundamental principle of scientific observation. Including one's emotional conclusions and personal judgment in a scientific manual was an offense of the highest degree. Published under a different title, in a book devoted to such things, Cuvier's thoughts on primitive man would be legitimate, but this? He stared at the pages of his beloved volume, no longer reading but unable to turn away from the columns of type that had provided him shelter, structure, and guidance. Was nothing in this world reliable? Would his abandonment be complete? His erasure total? Guillaudeu was glad that Archer, absorbed in his own entertainments, did not see him slowly close the book.

He gathered the volume in his arms and left the office. For once, the obnoxious surge of the crowded entry hall had no effect on him. He walked quickly through the waxworks gallery, but instead of going upstairs using the back stairwell, he unlocked the small door next to it and descended all the way to the cellar of the museum.

He hadn't been down there for years, ever since he'd had to bring the black bear specimen down to the furnace. It had become infested by moth eggs, and the only way to avoid a widespread danger to the collection was to bake the eggs off the bear's fur using the furnace's heat.

A new sound clanged and hummed from some dark region. He found matches on the stone ledge and lit the single dusty lamp where it hung on a hook at the bottom of the stairs. He held it before him as if he now entered a dark forest. He walked toward the sound until he came to an old metal door with a brand-new lock hanging from the latch. The banging and whirring was so loud, the door vibrated. There was a machine at work on the other side, and after a few moments of standing in the lamp's weak light, his brain rattling thoroughly, he realized that it was the work of this machine that kept the beluga alive. What else could it be but the pump he'd heard the staff whispering about, that Barnum had built to bring harbor water all the way to the fifth floor?

He went to the farthest corner of the dingy room and wrapped Cuvier in an oily rag he found on the dirt floor under his feet. A deep crack branched in the wall of the building's foundation; he shoved Cuvier inside at the widest point, at the height of his chest. Guillaudeu wiped his forehead with one trembling hand: *By God, here's where you belong.*

The tribesman sits in the corner of his room at the top of the museum, unable to stop the persistent rocking motion that upsets his balance when he moves and also when he tries to be still. He rests his head against the wall. In his body he holds eight months of the sea's constant pulling. Each time he closes his eyes he returns to the hull of the ship.

In the beginning he was sick: first with grief, then with scurvy, and finally with boredom. He spent each night deafened by the sound of one hundred and fifty snoring men and each day dazed by their kicks, wishing first to kill and then to die. He clung to, and soon lost, the patterns of land and life that had guided him for fifty years: the shadow of the stone cliffs lengthening over the grasslands during dry seasons and shading the mirrored floodwater in the wet; hot wind blowing from the south, the people with their faces turned into it, eyes closed, smiling.

In the hull he floated day after day, adrift upon the deepest, most terrible fluid. He felt the vast distance of compressed, liquid space beneath him and clenched his fists, enraged to be gliding over the back of this abyssal enemy. He held tight to memories of stone and flame, the crackle of the fire just there, proving all was as it should be as he slept in the home place with his ear to the ground. As the ship went on, the water washed it all away: The dry earth of the home place turned to thick mud, to silt, and finally melted into a swift-flowing river overrunning its bed, drowning the hearth flame, the sustaining fire. The substance and source of life was dissolving, disappearing into a terrible sea, the great eraser.

He did not believe he would live, and for a time he was not living at all, just lying in filth and tilting darkness. It was only when a man tried to take the small bundle he kept tied to his chest that he remembered he was alive. He fought the man. After that it was two months before he heard the sound of birds and considered the possibility that he might walk upon the earth again.

Fourteen

In the blue dark of earliest morning, shadows wavered across the far wall of Guillaudeu's bedroom like reflections of water cast sideways. His wife sat straight-backed at the foot of the bed. He struggled to focus his eyes while she mumbled, her face obscured by a ribboned bonnet. With both hands, she rooted around in a basket, first pulling out a newspaper and then a small pumpkin. Every few seconds she stopped her mumbling to listen, head cocked to the side. Guillaudeu held his breath, frozen, until she resumed her search.

He lifted the covers and stood up. He took a step toward her. She cocked her head again, listening, but did not turn. With a thrill of anticipation, Guillaudeu dipped his hand into the pocket of his waistcoat. He pulled out his coiled measuring tape. In response, his wife held her arm straight out to the side. She still did not turn her head to look at him. Guillaudeu walked to her and measured the arm, not allowing his own hand to touch her wrist or her shoulder. Twenty and a half inches. I must remember. Must remember. He felt around in his other pocket for his pencil, but what he pulled out was a wriggling worm. He jerked it away. He knelt and rummaged among her skirts until he felt her legs. He found her patella and stretched the measuring cord down to her ankle. Seventeen inches exactly. She rose to her feet and he measured on, femur to humerus. Depth of body. Height at shoulder. She stood still with perfectly straight posture, which made his work easier.

The scene changed: Celia now lay upon the bed, her face still obscured by some unnatural shadow. He stood over her, rubbing his hands together. He would need more arsenic, much more salt, human glass eyes, and pounds of excelsior. He found the scalpel in his left waistcoat pocket. He reached out and sliced through the layer of lace at her collar.

Once she lay flayed from her clothing, her skin, webbed with veins and sagging in most places, was so delicate, like crumpled tissue. He would need all his skill to handle it. He stepped back from his wife's prone body.

Before making the first incision, he must clearly visualize the finished specimen. It was this decisive view of the ultimate goal that led him unwavering from the messy beginning all the way through to the finished specimen. So he imagined Celia in her various familiar poses: behind her father's bookselling counter with ringlets around her shoulders and that notebook she always had open in front of her, for her poetry. Celia turning toward the door as he returned from work, her smile and her calm or amused gaze. Celia asleep beside him all those years, even when she spent her afternoons with another man. Celia frowning at him over something or another, there always seemed to be something. Celia in the pale first throes of cholera. The images flashed before him faster and faster, and he could not alight on one long enough to consider it as her final position before another took its place. Faster and faster they came: Celia lying down with her head resting on a pillow stained with vomit. Celia as he first saw her, among the stacks of shelves in the bookshop. Celia turning away from him in disgust, halfway through their marriage. Celia in his office at the museum, holding her nose. Celia.

His wife rose slowly from the worktable. The pieces of her dress swung from her arms as she got to her feet. She now regarded him from inside the moldering bonnet. Hers was the face of Barnum's hollow-eyed mermaid: papery gray skin framing empty eye sockets. A wasp emerged from one of them and buzzed straight toward his face. He awoke instantly, hands over his eyes and a fly bumping against the bedroom window. He jumped out of bed as if it were an open grave.

Fifteen

A lone sparrow perched on the glittering branch of the chandelier. It hopped a few paces, perhaps looking for food, and set the crystal ornaments swinging. It flew to the elaborately carved molding at the intersection of the theater's walls and ceiling, hoping for better hunting there. But it stayed for only a moment before winging back across the gallery, this time alighting on the stage curtain, where it delivered a significant streak of white excrement.

Like the pit embedded in a gigantic fruit, the new theater was at the center of the museum. Before Barnum built it, the space had been a much smaller and plainer lecture hall. Education was important to John Scudder, and he had scheduled weekly presentations in the hall on topics that ranged from roses to osteology. It was during a lecture on the latter subject that Guillaudeu first heard the famous story of the brash young Cuvier, who declared that he could determine a creature's entire skeletal structure by examining a single bone. There were reports from visiting natural philosophers, and demonstrations given by botanists who had returned from abroad with strange potted specimens and the remnants of New World fevers. The lecture hall had been one of Guillaudeu's favorite places: In its straight-backed chairs he had traveled the world.

Barnum had raised the lecture hall's ceiling a full story by demolishing three galleries on the third floor. He removed walls and added columns and support beams. This remarkable architectural feat became known throughout the city, and the museum staff had discussed it for weeks. Despite the reports, however, Guillaudeu had been reluctant to visit the new space. He held on to the idea of the old lecture hall even as crowds hurried past his office, bound for the new matinee performances. As a result of this delusion, he was not prepared for what he saw when he filed in, as instructed, with the rest of the museum employees.

The theater shimmered in layers of gilt and filigree. A newly built balcony hung over a sea of black velvet chairs, and the walls, covered in ivory damask, reflected globules of light from the chandelier. It was like being inside a monstrous jewel box, Guillaudeu imagined. He was uncomfortable and distracted by the dozens of employees he had never seen before, and by the way the theater contrasted so sharply with the academic décor of the rest of the museum. When he lost sight of the sparrow, he took a seat as quickly as he could. So quickly, in fact, that he sat directly behind the giantess and had to move over two seats just to see beyond her colossal shoulders.

Guillaudeu had not given Barnum's human exhibits much thought. His path did not often cross with theirs, and he hoped the episode with the Australian tribesman was the single exception to this rule. He had never watched the acrobats, or observed any of the others in their booths or on the various stages where they showed themselves. As he watched the giantess lean down across a ridiculous distance to speak with the woman next to her, he could not help but think that these oddities belonged in the saloons, or at Niblo's Garden. Such entertainment was properly displayed in the evening, under dim lighting, with the accompaniment of a jigger of whiskey and no pretense of educational merit.

But the tribesman. He wanted to alert one of them to his presence, and the giantess was the only one he knew by name.

"Miss Swift?" he offered.

Both women turned. He froze at the sight of the outlandish beard on the smaller woman's face.

"I . . . ," he stuttered, averting his eyes. He had not seen her before. He wondered what else might be living on the fifth floor.

"Well?" said the giantess.

But the house lights had begun to dim. Voices around them grew momentarily louder as people finished their conversations and then hushed.

"There's a man —" Guillaudeu blurted, shrugging helplessly and looking up at the chandelier. The hirsute woman laughed at him and both women turned away. From the wings, someone yanked open the curtain.

The stage was a careful replica of a museum gallery, with rows of paintings high on the walls and cabinets scattered across the broad space. A group of visitors strolled across the stage, laughing at specimens and gawking appropriately. Whoever set it up had moved the mounted polar bear onstage, complete with its velvet guard rope. The players ambled forward and a man disentangled himself from the arm of a companion. A cheer went up.

It had been two months since Guillaudeu had seen the museum's owner, but Barnum seemed younger than he remembered. Round-cheeked and curly-haired, in a crimson vest and dark blue coat, he looked nothing like the small portrait that hung in the museum's entryway. He was more like an overgrown boy than an entrepreneur. Barnum stepped to the front of the stage and opened wide his arms as if to take his employees to his breast.

"Since the day my American Museum opened its doors, fifty thousand people have visited us. Word of it has traveled around the globe, confirming that this institution is on its way to becoming an international destination for entertainment and education!

"And so the first thing I'd like to say is thank you." Barnum extended his arms. Sections of the audience, mostly the restaurant and custodial staff, applauded.

"As some of you know, I have just visited our great southern states, where news of the museum has already proliferated. The reason for this trip, as you might have read in the papers, was an extraordinary young man, whose destiny is great indeed, and intertwined with that of this museological enterprise. I now present this young man to you, the General himself! My personal prodigy: Tom Thumb."

Barnum backed up. He stopped next to a glass cabinet that held, Guillaudeu now realized, a very small human being wearing a very large hat. With a flourish, Barnum opened the cabinet and the dwarf leapt out. He wore what appeared to be a pair of long underwear, high black boots, and a cutaway coat with a banner draped around one shoulder. The boy strutted across the stage, kicking up his tiny legs with each step, pausing to execute a sharp quarter turn toward the audience. He gave an exaggerated salute.

"Soldiers of my Old Guard: I bid you farewell!" Thumb's voice was loud, confident, and discordantly young. He stalked across the stage. "For twenty years I have constantly accompanied you on the road to honor and glory!" he yelled. "In these latter times, as in the days of our prosperity, you have invariably been models of courage and fidelity."

Oh God, not Napoleon. Guillaudeu sank lower in his chair. Here was a parody in miniature of the man for whom Guillaudeu's father had been killed, his family destroyed. The memory spawned the familiar chain of images that had worn deep ruts in Guillaudeu's mind and now swept him away from the dwarf's recital: that night, so long ago, how the rain had turned the cobble to onyx as he walked behind his mother, who carried his infant sister, Adèle was her name, in her arms and looked neither right nor left; the way she turned from him with her hand raised to the door of someone's cousin, the second mate on a ship; the rough paper she handed him with the name of someone in America, an address on Cortlandt Street; her whispered voice near the river: *Where you land, I'll find you.* And finally, the spiraling realization that the slip of paper had fallen from his pocket somewhere, blown into the river, or even back onto the cobble near his mother's feet, the folded paper catching her attention like a fluttering moth; she is bending down to catch it and realizing that all of her intention was not enough to keep him safe. Had she followed? Had his sister lived? Forty-eight years later Guillaudeu still did not know, but it was not for lack of searching the faces of old women on the street. Years ago he had stopped calculating her age.

Applause for the dwarf subsided and Barnum took the stage again. "My friends, there are those in this great city who would destroy us. Already I've read articles in some of our . . . well, not our most respected papers, but papers I know well. These articles describe the American Museum as a den of sin! A nest of immorality where bawdy entertainments are played to drunken crowds. There are quotes from our new mayor, the *honorable* James Harper, vowing to root out the vipers at the heart of our establishment! He says we are no different from the back rooms of the Bowery saloons. Says we are those who would sell idols at the door of the temple! I read these things, friends, and I laugh! I laugh because we are an establishment devoted to the enlightenment of men. Amusement, too, but of a kind that the ancient philosophers would call nature's sense of humor, *Lusus naturae*. And who are we if we cannot laugh at ourselves? There is no vice in that! Just ask Ashmole, Tradescant, Kircher, and all the others preserved by history who collected and displayed the wonders of our world! I might add that the gentleman virtuoso Ferdinando Cospi employed a dwarf as museum guide in Italy two hundred years ago!

"As an antidote to these accusations, I have hired these men" — Barnum stepped to the side, making way for three figures who now appeared at the back of the stage and walked toward the audience — "to add Scientific Authority to selected exhibits and performances. Please welcome the Professors Wilson, Chatterton, and Stokes."

Guillaudeu leaned forward in his seat. *Professors?*

"Beginning Monday, these learned men will present Scientific explanations of exhibits such as the Human Calculator and the Aztec Royals." The professors waved and Barnum gave a small bow. "Please welcome them to the fold." And as the curtain fell around him he gave a final shout: "Onward!"

Guillaudeu struggled to retain his composure as he was jostled in the riptide of people leaving the theater. He felt that his growing excitement could carry him above the heads of everyone, that his relief in seeing these new professors would float him gently up to the gorgeous ceiling. He waited for the crowd to thin.

Finally, he would have someone to talk with about the problems facing the museum! He could show them the *Ornithorhyncus anatinus,* the sloth, all the anomalous creatures, and they could come up with a taxonomy. They would eat together, they would cultivate a certain strain of their own humor about the museum, in which Guillaudeu's worries would become manageable, communal. Barnum had finally, of his own accord, realized that a museum without scientific organization was useless to the public and an abomination to history.

When the theater was empty, Guillaudeu climbed onstage. The museum set, which had looked so real from his seat, was made from painted cloth, paper, and spindly planks. His footsteps echoed as he walked into the wings.

"Hello? Are you still here?" Guillaudeu continued past costumed mannequins and various musical instruments arranged on chairs. He heard men's laughter coming from one of the dressing rooms. "Professors?"

A door opened and one of the men, Guillaudeu thought it was Chatterton, poked his head out. "Who is it?"

Guillaudeu stepped into the brightly lit room, where the other two men sat on overstuffed chairs. They each held a tulip-shaped glass filled with crimson liquid. "I'm so pleased to meet all of you. I'm Emile Guillaudeu. Perhaps Barnum mentioned me?"

"Perhaps." Professor Chatterton looked to his companions. "Do you boys recall?" One of the others shook his head. Was it Wilson? The third man simply stared at Guillaudeu with a vague smile.

"I'm the taxidermist. I worked for John Scudder here in the museum before Barnum came. Lately I seem to have taken up the duties of Menagerie Attendant. I'm so glad you're finally here. I need guidance with various issues, not the least of which is developing an underlying philosophic principle for this collection. It is growing, as I'm sure Barnum explained, at an unsettling rate."

The three professors looked at one another. Guillaudeu could see something like alarm in their eyes. "Oh, don't worry," he continued. "With the three of you, and my particular experience here, we should be able to make short work of it. I'm just glad you're here."

"Well, we're glad to be here, too." Chatterton seemed to be the spokesman. The other two remained quiet, and Stokes appeared to be laughing into his hand. "But there's something you should probably know."

Suddenly Guillaudeu thought he would lose his job. These professors were surely more qualified than he for the monumental task that lay ahead.

"We've been hired by Mr. Barnum to infuse the museum with Scientific Authority, as he says. In fact, though, we are actors by trade. I thought he would have told at least some of his staff. We are here to give the *illusion*, so to speak, of science."

Sixteen

Guillaudeu banged on Barnum's door. No one answered. Recklessly, he turned the latch and the door slid open, revealing Phineas T. Barnum sitting at his desk reading the New Testament.

"Monsieur Guillaudeu, is the museum on fire?"

The stage had dwarfed Barnum, but now he reminded Guillaudeu of the men he'd seen lifting crates of cargo off ships at the South Street port. He had a strangely graceful bearing, like a hound on point. Jerky, perfectly attuned. Not quite leonine, was he, but what? What does a griffin look like?

Barnum leaned forward and Guillaudeu fought the urge to recoil. "No fire."

"Then sit down, please."

He obeyed. Barnum looked at him curiously.

"You know" — Barnum swiveled in his chair toward the window — "when I moved to New York, I had no money. I was living in a pitiful room in a neighborhood I don't even like to name. By luck I found an excellent job almost immediately." He shook his head. "I became a salesman. I sold the one thing you can always count on people buying."

"Food?"

"Bibles." Barnum tapped the book in front of him. "Bibles, my friend."

Barnum rose from his desk and pivoted around his chair,

still staring out the window. "Do you remember the story of Peter Cooper?"

"No."

"When the B and O Railroad opened up, Peter Cooper moved to Baltimore and bought up a whole lot of land near where the rails were going in. He speculated that the rail works would boost the value. He started digging, draining swamps, thinking of building a hotel. And he hit iron. Iron ore. Exactly what the railroad needed! So he set up a forge and started selling rails to the B and O. But lo and behold, the railroad ran into financial trouble. They didn't have a good enough engine to run these new distances. The value of the company started to drop. So Peter Cooper said he'd build them an engine himself."

Shaking his head, Barnum turned to Guillaudeu.

The taxidermist found he could not respond.

"And he did! He did. He built a little steam engine in his barn and hobbled it up to some old wheels and musket barrels. It ran eighteen miles an hour. When they unveiled it people bought B and O bonds so fast the railroad didn't know what to do with all the capital. This museum is my iron ore, you see. I had nothing when I got here except a hunch. You know what Cooper called his little steam engine? The Tom Thumb.

"My point is that I can provide what the people want. But sometimes, I'm finding out, the people don't yet know that they want it. My job is to show them. That's what this museum is all about."

"Show them what, exactly?"

"A few months ago one fellow, a journalist, wrote that my museum was a great hive. To him, all the people streaming in and out were like honeybees. But I'll tell you, a hive is all symmetry, uniformity! Not so with my enterprise. The purpose of a hive, after all, is the same as a factory: to create order. This museum's effect is the opposite: to baffle. And listen to this: Another man wrote that it was like a Chinese puzzle. That was in the *Herald* a few weeks ago. He was a little closer with that one because the museum has untold layers, like the puzzle, and it contains elements of suspense and surprise. But again the symbol falls short because this museum is always changing! There is no innermost layer. A Chinese puzzle may delight us by revealing smaller and smaller interlocking worlds, but the museum offers the opposite: The deeper you go, the smaller you feel because the wonders you encounter grow greater and greater."

Barnum gestured upward as if addressing the brick and wood of his building.

"How would you define it, then?" Guillaudeu ventured.

"*Omne ignotum pro mirifico,*" he murmured. "Most metaphors I've heard are too simple for this place. Too limited in meaning."

Barnum tapped the Bible on his desk. "That's exactly where the whole thing becomes rather interesting. Are you a religious man? Right here, in the book of Matthew, we meet Jesus, of course. This Jesus is a teacher. He stands on the mountain. He gives us a sermon. Commandments. Instructions for living. Now let me ask you a question: Can you imagine the number of eyes in that audience that must have glazed over? Because who in the world likes to be told exactly how to live or the parameters of what is possible? To me, it is a strategy that ensures only resentment and boredom.

"But in Mark's story it is not Jesus' words that instruct us. This Jesus never even confirms that he is really Jesus! He relies on something better to convey his message, something inherently compelling: mystery itself. And public performances, of course: healings and exorcisms, wine from water, all that sort of thing. This Jesus gives you an opportunity to live through the experience of puzzlement yourself. Each individual is invited to rely on his own experience of life to figure out what it all means. *That* is the foundation on which I built this enterprise. Walking through these halls, people encounter nothing but mystery. They interpret what they see according to the patterns of their own lives and relate it to the larger pattern of our city, of the world. So to answer the question, How do I define this place? I give you this: I never will. It is true that I will hire people to do it. That is the way of our time. But just as in this book, there are many authors; interpretation is infinite. And so mystery lives."

Seventeen

Guillaudeu walked away from Barnum's office holding his breath, feeling as if he were underwater, not remembering how he'd responded to Barnum's monologue, or how he had extricated himself in the end, only that he wanted to go home. He emerged from the back hall into the crowded public entryway where the river of museum visitors flowed thickly from William's ticket booth to the marble stairway. The crowd chattered and formed small whirlpools: families, elderly gentlemen, young girls wearing feathered and silk hats, graceful or tattered dresses. A hive, he'd said. A puzzle. A steam engine. But it's not a puzzle, because there is no solution; the farther in you go, the greater the mystery. He pushed his way against the current of the incoming crowd and burst onto the street gasping for air.

In City Hall Park birds perched in the maples. Real birds. Robins. *Turdus migratorius,* going about the usual business of building a nest, following the natural law of seasons. Girls pushed carts down the street. These vendors operated under the same natural laws, gathering clams according to the tide, buying corn from people who plucked the ears under a harvest moon. He looked back but the museum was no longer visible through the trees. He continued up Broadway. Produce, picked from gardens. Fruit from orchards. These people lived their lives without a thought for Chinese puzzles and museums of deception and perverted nature. These streets operate under the universal laws of survival, honest livelihood, and praise of nature's inviolate order. He turned onto Franklin Street. He said hello to Saul and bought an apple. He ignored three small boys squatting on the sidewalk throwing dice.

Fitting his key into the lock of the building door, his stomach queased. He could stand to be in the apartment, but only if he did not allow himself to think. He could sleep at night, if he did not allow himself to dream. He could work at the museum, if he resisted the changes Barnum engendered. He leaned against the closed door. He felt that he could not go on, but he wanted more than anything to sleep so he pushed ahead, enduring the flickering memory of his dead wife in the shadows.

In the bedroom, he lay down his coat and hat and took off his shoes. He went to the kitchen and started water boiling in the small kettle. He sliced the apple. He unwrapped some cheese from the icebox, and in a few minutes he poured the tea and sat down.

Professors! What fools Barnum had made of them all. And all the hundreds of Guillaudeu's specimens, the result of a life's work, now possessed by a false museum and subject to the whim of a madman. He could not bear to think of the animals for long because his mind imbued them with the energy of a trapped herd, charging and hedging in a desperate attempt to outrun a wildfire.

Lusus naturae. The words came suddenly to him as he lay on his back in his cold bed. Nature's sense of humor. Guillaudeu stared through the blue night at the ceiling. But wasn't humankind itself nature's greatest joke? Created, apparently, in the image of the Divine, man could perceive, even conjure, the weightiest questions: What is the meaning of a life's work? What is the correct path through this crooked world? But unlike the Creator, whose Divine omniscience leads to decisive, righteous action, man can never answer his own questions with certainty. Guillaudeu lay pondering this for some time in the dark before he realized that no good would come of such an inquiry. He shut his eyes tightly, but his mind had awakened fully. Sleep was no longer possible.

In his socks he stood before the wooden case of books in what used to be his parlor. He regarded them as beloved companions and ran his index finger along the spines, which raised a tiny plume of dust. He sneezed. His finger stopped on a slim volume, *Miscellaneous Tracts Relating to Natural History, Husbandry, and Physick.* Edie Scudder had given him the book for his birthday countless years ago. It contained, among other essays, Linnaeus' famous inaugural speech, given to the students at Uppsala. Guillaudeu had read only the opening paragraphs before discarding the book; he'd not been interested in an oration "On the Necessity of Traveling in One's Own Country." But now, partly out of regret for his quarrel with Edie, and partly out of genuine desire for distraction, he pulled the book smoothly from the shelf. He walked into the kitchen, sat at the window, and lit a candle to read by.

All human knowledge is built on two foundations: reason and experience. We must confess, indeed, that the business of reasoning may be carried on with equal success at our desks, supposing we have an opportunity of conversing with men truly learned. But it is experience, that sovereign mistress, without which a physician ought to be ashamed to open his lips. Experience ought to go first; reasoning should follow. Experience ought to be animated with reason in all physical affairs; without this she is void of order, void of energy, void of life. On the other hand, reason without experience can do nothing, being nothing but the mere dreams, phantasms, and meteors of ingenious men who abuse their time.

Linnaeus' words stung. Guillaudeu considered himself anything but an explorer. Any of his own accumulations of knowledge, scientific or otherwise, had been gleaned only in his workrooms, from the bodies of his specimens and his books. Surely this was not the ethereal, impotent specter of Reason that Linnaeus described, or was it? The imagined disapproval of the great taxonomist's ghost burned Guillaudeu's pride, but as he read on, the figure of Carl Linnaeus emerged as more and more amiable. Yes, he tramped the mountains of the northernmost reaches of the European continent, but his aim (and it was obsessive) was to *name*. To create order from chaos. To incorporate species into his newly created but robust taxonomy. Venturing into the unknown, he procured the evidence for the greatest system science would ever see. As he read, Guillaudeu gradually stopped comparing elements of his own life unfavorably with those of Linnaeus. Tales of rugged Lapland, the forests of Dalecarlia, and the groves of Gothland engulfed him. They were journeys into places so strange and magical to the ear that he could hardly believe that to Linnaeus, they were simply travels in his own country. Even as his eyes blurred and his head nodded closer to the page, he followed Linnaeus through field and valley.

Eighteen

He awoke to the shouts of men as they unloaded crates in front of Saul's grocery. He'd fallen asleep at the table with his arms folded across the pages of Linnaeus. Groggy, he closed the book and stared for a while out the window at the men, all three of them barrel-chested and laughing. Saul appeared, wearing the apron Guillaudeu had never seen him without. The grocer looked up at the sky, marking the advent of another day on Franklin Street.

Guillaudeu rose stiffly, working the knot out of his neck, and went to the bedroom. In the back of his wardrobe he found his old canvas satchel, its buckles tarnished with disuse. He traded his twill trousers for thicker ones. From a drawer he pulled a woolen undershirt and a scarf, which he folded into the satchel. Back in the kitchen, from the icebox, he put a wedge of cheese wrapped in newspaper, two apples, half a pound of smoked sausage wrapped in paper, and a loaf of bread into the satchel. He turned in a circle, thinking of what else he might need. He had no idea. Panic rose in him, spraying the inside of his head with sparks. He ignored it. He put Linnaeus in the satchel. He looked down. The shoes he wore, the same old brown leather Spencers he wore to work, were his most comfortable. He had no others more suited. From his bureau drawer he removed what money he had, folding the bills and funneling the coins into a leather purse that had been Scudder's, and putting that in the inside pocket of his overcoat. How did he come to have that purse? He could not remember his own history. He buckled the satchel and put on his tweed cap. Later, he would think of a hundred other things he should have brought, but as he left his home it felt deliciously simple. Hoist the satchel onto his shoulder, turn the key, turn away.

Standing on the corner of Franklin and Broadway that early in the morning, all the carriages and people moved southward as he had done every day for many years. He watched twenty horse-drawn coaches pass by, two omnibuses, and several carriageless riders. Hundreds of bobbing hats and ladies' shawled or bonneted heads walked downtown, toward the museum, where an office full of his own work waited for him to take it up again. Indeed, he leaned southward, his body starting on its customary track, his mind pushing at the threshold of his daily duties: Which specimens needed care? Did the old cameleopard need extensive hide repair, or was it just getting too old to display? Guillaudeu had noticed it was losing pieces of its coat. He'd need to fumigate it somehow, but how would he —

Guillaudeu walked straight across Broadway, keeping his eyes fixed on Franklin Street sneaking narrowly eastward as if behind Broadway's back. He was nearly struck by a hackney cab but he didn't notice. All he felt was fear as he resisted the undertow that would drag him toward the museum. But when he emerged on the other side of Franklin he was suddenly bathed in the light that fell between buildings and he smiled, his face contorting out of its usual creases and angles as he walked into the unknown.

Nineteen

Guillaudeu harbored just two memories of his first day on New York Island. Unlike the predictable images evoked by the Cosmorama salon's sturdy miniature Paris, these memories shimmered and dissolved; they shape-shifted across the years, and although it wasn't terribly often that Guillaudeu thought of them, when he did his interpretations inevitably included speculation and unrequited doubt.

He did not remember disembarking from the massive sailing ship that had carried him across the sea. Much later he knew it must have been on one of the piers near Fulton Street. Of the man from the ship who led him into the city, out of kindness or some other motive he did not know, he recalled only the man's squeezing grip on his hand. It was daytime, he remembered that, and he was very small. Perhaps the man had been a sailor, home after his long voyage. Or he could have been headed to a tavern for the evening, and would return to the ship to sleep.

They must have walked north up Pearl Street, because they ended up deep in the Points, maybe near Cross and Orange. Now, white-haired, with his satchel over his shoulder, and propelled by some obscure but certain need, Guillaudeu walked boldly toward that intersection.

During the years that Guillaudeu had lived in New York, the Points had blossomed into their bloodiest five-petaled glory. The district's filth now had international standing, and the whole place was buoyed by its own feral pride, which would have easily deflected Guillaudeu had he not been determined to see a certain building that now revealed itself farther down the block. If Linnaeus could scale mountains, he told himself, then surely an old man could walk another half a block.

This was the only part of the city that had been rebuilt with timber after the great fire, and not by the most skilled carpenters, judging by the precarious angles of some roofs and doorways. There were grocers on every corner, but he saw no sign of food in their windows. Men with faces shadowed by wide-brimmed hats brushed past him, and he heard the hum of voices coming from inside shacks and clapboard warehouses.

The building was still there. Its unmistakable brick façade, notched in the Dutch style, loomed. Guillaudeu stood before it, searching the building for the word that had left the indelible memory, but the sign was long gone.

But I'm not an orphan! He had screamed when he saw the wooden sign swinging lightly on its two hooks. The word was in English, but the French was similar enough that he knew. The man tightened his grip on Guillaudeu's small hand. That man could have been laughing, or his eyes could have been resigned, even sad. As the two of them stood there, a woman rose inside the building and moved toward the worn door. She was silhouetted by small lamps that hung on sconces behind her. This was all he saw before he wriggled around, twisting his captor's arm and flailing against him.

"It's better than nothing," the man whispered in French as Guillaudeu writhed against him. He finally bit the man's hand and ran.

Now he stepped closer to the old brick orphanage. Its two wide windows were glassless holes. The front porch was missing planks and the awning was held by untrustworthy supports. With the sense that he was testing fate, or at least trespassing upon the sacrosanct boundary of memory, he walked up the steps to the narrow porch. The boarded-up door and wooden windowsills were burned to charcoal along their edges. After the fire, the city had rebuilt itself so dizzyingly quickly that husks like this were rare artifacts. He ran a finger along the vertical edge of one window.

"That's just about far enough, son." The growl could have come from the walls themselves; there was something singed, both fallen and constant, in it. "Just be on your way."

"I mean no harm," Guillaudeu said weakly.

"But you bring it anyway, don't you?"

A man disengaged himself from the shadows.

"Scared people bring harm. Usually upon themselves."

The man's bright blue eyes gleamed from under thick black brows. With those eyes, his rounded features, and full gray beard, in another life he could have played the part of Irving's Saint Nicholas. But here, in a decrepit cloak that he had pulled aside to display a handle-less blade at his belt, the man's potentially jovial face instead seemed to mock credulity itself.

"I know this place," Guillaudeu said softly, aware that he was in danger but strangely calm. Could he have grown into a man like this if the circumstance of his arrival to this country had shifted ever so subtly? For a moment he reeled in the chaos of the world: Everyone, without exception, is simply an accumulation of choice and chance; each president, each pauper, each Phineas T. Barnum. And chance, it seemed to him, appeared more often than choice. He was a puppet in someone else's hand.

"Well I live here now," said the man in the shadows.

"How do you know I'm scared?"

"How you move. Your eyes. I smelled it as soon as I saw you."

"I hadn't noticed. I was feeling rather *good* today."

The man laughed, never taking his eyes off Guillaudeu's face. "Oh, you hadn't, had you? You were feeling good, you say?"

Guillaudeu clutched his satchel.

"I don't want anything you've got, son. It's just better for me if no one saw you standing there talking to nobody. Go on back where you came from."

As a boy fleeing this spot, he'd cut through a narrow passageway somewhere near where he now trotted away from the bearded man. He'd run for blocks, recklessly shouting to any French-speaking person who might have been near. He was thoroughly ignored by everyone on the street, and he'd run until he came upon the thing that had contaminated his dreams for years, the second memory of his first day in New York. In a muddy lot behind a hive of tenements he beheld a mottled monster, with dots for eyes and a double row of protruding, fingerlike teats on its belly, some of which were raw and bleeding. The animal was almost his height, its chapped pink areas marginalized by evil-looking black splotches. It was a terrible, gargantuan pig chewing dripping garbage, and its belly and snout were coated with refuse. Frozen in terror, he watched as the creature shat a pressurized stream of filth onto its own hind legs. The image would never leave him, this foul minotaur lurking just around the next corner, the guardian of this new city. When he could move again, he had run back to the brick orphanage and knocked on the door.

Twenty

As he hurried out of the Points, Guillaudeu was bumped and jostled on the crowded sidewalk. Men in ragged hats spat on the ground and filthy children scurried at the edge of the street. He dared not look back, but he felt someone following him. It wasn't that he heard footsteps that paused or accelerated with his, but he felt pushed from behind by a steady, unmistakable force. Perhaps it was his fear; apparently he exuded it so clearly it was palpable. He slowed to a brisk walk once he passed Broome. *I smelled it,* the man had said. Of course he'd been scared. He hadn't been back to the orphanage in forty-five years. But the man had been referring to something else, something deeper. And then he felt something like gratitude toward the man. Why? For having the decency to point out something that must be obvious to everyone who knew him, but of which, he, himself, had been ignorant. His excitement at being away from the apartment and away from the museum returned. He was confident he would not be harmed, even by whatever was following him. He turned up Prince and shot a quick look backward over his shoulder. Apart from two men standing outside a run-down coffeehouse and a stringy dog sniffing the gutter, the street was empty.

At Broadway, Guillaudeu watched people board an omnibus. The long, glossy carriage had crimson curtains in the windows; inside, he knew, were comfortable benches with matching red cushions. From where he now stood it was a ten-minute ride to the museum. He watched the driver latch the doors behind the last customer and leap into position behind the four horses. It would be even faster by cabriolet, he thought. Feeling eyes staring at his back, he plunged off the curb and again resisted the street's southward current.

In Washington Square he sat down on a bench to rest his feet. He rubbed his hands through his thin hair, smoothing it as best he could, and then fussed with the ends of his mustache. He stretched out his legs. To the west, a number of students emerged from a university building to lounge in the park. Children threw rubber balls and chased one another on the grass while their mothers stood together like hens. The morning clouds were lifting and the sun — Guillaudeu now closed his eyes and faced it — warmed him. Spring is finally here. Even a taxidermist must go into the field at certain times, and it really should be in spring. It was good.

He turned suddenly, opening his eyes and craning his head to search along the park's periphery. Some distance away, a couple faced away from him on a bench. He scanned the pedestrians walking across the park, but no one looked suspicious. A copper-colored dog sat panting under a tree, and beyond it, on the sidewalk outside the east entrance to the park, someone peddled apples and newspapers.

Ahead of him, people streamed up Fifth Avenue toward 14th Street. In the distance their shapes disappeared into haloes of sunlight. North. He would go into that sunlight. He hoisted himself up, shouldered his bag, and walked on the cobbled path to the northern park gate. He looked back once and saw that the dog had risen from its place in the shade and was following him at a lope. He stopped. The stringy dog stopped but kept its eyes on him as it delicately sniffed a clump of clover.

"A-ha!" Guillaudeu laughed. "The culprit. What did I do to deserve this attention?" When he moved, the dog moved. When he stopped, so did the dog. It would not come closer, but remained fixed on following him. In tandem, they started up Fifth Avenue.

Above 14th Street half the buildings on the broad, tree-shaded avenue appeared to be under construction or undergoing major renovation. The line of sight that he remembered, which included a great swathe of sky above wide-shuttered brick houses, was gone. These new buildings were four, sometimes five stories tall, and so narrow they made the older homes look like startled bullfrogs. Workmen climbed scaffolding to attach wooden embellishments and dainty cupolas to the roofs. An older home that Guillaudeu remembered as being quite pretty was being dismantled, its brick salvaged by a man in rags with a mule-drawn cart. He passed a new house of painted brick with a steeply pitched roof and miniature gothic spires attached, ridiculously, at every possible apex. This is how the city breathes, he told himself. The fire, seven years ago, was its deepest breath, and it blew the rich out of downtown and scattered them here and northward, where they used what imagination they could muster — certainly money was the more plentiful resource — to build a new generation of the city. Each block contained at least three new houses, sitting shoulder-to-shoulder with their older neighbors. This is the way of the city, he thought. The world.

The dog ambled silently behind him with its nose to the ground, weaving in between gates and stoops, sometimes tracking into open construction areas, private property. Once, it appeared behind him chewing something, with a pleased look in its eye. Good for you, he thought. You can survive anywhere. He tried whistling but emitted only a pathetic hiss. He laughed. When was the last time he had whistled? He tried again, this time managing the miniaturized sound of a winter storm. Finally he squeaked out a recognizable series of notes, but the dog had not noticed.

He was distracted enough by the construction and the dog that he didn't quite anticipate how quickly he would arrive at the corner of 19th Street. After all, usually when he traveled this way he was riding in a carriage.

He crept to the corner and looked down the street at John Scudder's imposing Federal-style home, with its two pillars made, he knew, from the same Westchester marble as the museum's main stairwell. He knew that inside the door lay the same cobalt, black, and brown Arabian rug that he remembered from all the years of walking over it to Scudder's study, wondering where in the house Edie was. When he inhaled, Guillaudeu smelled the leather and pipe smoke that Scudder always emanated. Home. A home, one of his homes.

He wouldn't have survived a week at that Points orphanage, and thankfully the women running it recognized that right away and sent him uptown. He was well dressed, French, and tremendously frightened. A perfect example of who could be successfully saved by the reform societies, and so he was sent up to the boys' boardinghouse where he'd be seen by the right people. It was a holding place for suitable apprentices, house servants, and even the occasional adopted son of the wealthy, or seemingly wealthy, class. Choice and chance. Again, mostly chance.

He wandered toward the old house, which was flanked on one side by an almost identical twin, and on the other by a strange new edifice, painted an ostentatious yellow and displaying the same gaudy moldings as several others he'd seen. How many times he'd grasped that worn iron gate handle and wondered when Edie'd last touched it, or thought of what he'd learn that day about curing hides or mold making in Scudder's sunlit laboratory. Just the memory of that work gave him such a feeling of alignment with the world that he smiled.

He didn't see the figure at the window until it was too late; the figure had already smiled back. John Scudder was paler than the last time Guillaudeu had seen him, which made his thick black eyebrows, under the fine white hair, even blacker, and his lips, stretched in greeting, an almost grotesque red. Was it a phantom? Scudder disappeared from the window. Guillaudeu took a step back. He couldn't see Scudder right now! This day, which had started with his defiance on Broadway only two hours ago, could not narrow so soon into familiarity. He was just now shaking loose the old binds, he realized. Too soon! The door above him creaked open. Even the creak was familiar. Scudder's visage appeared again, and this time his too-red mouth opened to speak.

"No!" Guillaudeu let the word fall from his lips to the ground at Scudder's feet as he ran away. The dog, who had been behind him, was now in front, leaping ahead of him and barking.

"Emile!" Scudder's voice was strong, magnetic. "Emile, come back! Why are you running? Where are you going?"

At the corner Guillaudeu looked back. There was Scudder at his own gate, shuffling onto the sidewalk after him. And then, nightmarishly, tripping over his own feet. The old man fell to his knees. Guillaudeu ran from him, raising a hand to his mouth. He had not run in years, maybe a decade, and it felt dangerous. His bones were brittle. He was not a man of action. Tears sprang to the corners of his eyes and cooled as he ran. *I can smell it on you.* He kept his blurry sights on the lean coppery streak of a dog who bounded ahead toward the orchards of Murray Hill.

After running only a few minutes, he limped and could not catch his breath. He slowed to a lopsided walk. There was a cramp in his abdomen, and the biggest toe of his left foot throbbed from jamming into the end of his shoe. Scudder would be all right, he told himself. How old would he be now? I hadn't *wanted* to be seen, he thought childishly. He couldn't see the dog anymore, and this made him sadder than the glimpse of Scudder falling down.

The sun had broken entirely free of clouds and washed him in that undiluted glare that one feels only in the harsh beginning of spring. But the city that the sun now illuminated was completely foreign. The few handsomely dressed pedestrians on this stretch of Fifth Avenue seemed unaware that they walked upon cobble that had been dirt . . . only yesterday, wasn't it? When had they gone to the tavern on Murray Hill? Could it have been a year ago? Celia had insisted on the trip, so it must have been two, even three? He remembered coming home from the museum to her sly smile. She'd told him there was an exhibit of specimens in Murray Hill, a private collection. Once they'd boarded a carriage and ridden it out of the city she gaily confessed that there was no exhibit, just a beautiful summer evening.

"We can dine in the open air! I can smell orchard grass on the breeze already, can't you, Emile? It feels good to leave the city."

She was wearing her orange coat, the one he'd never liked. She had been happy, almost girlish, though the hair that sprang loose from under her hat was already showing silver. Absurdly late, he regretted the scowl he'd given her in response.

As he walked, Guillaudeu became more and more perplexed. All around him arose amplified versions of the steeply spired and gaudy houses he'd seen below Scudder's. He passed a massive brick edifice boasting twin turrets and too-wide shutters that flanked each window like exaggerated eyelashes. The next building was blindingly white and designed to emulate a Greek temple, complete with Corinthian columns and an ornate cornice that included a frieze sculpted in low relief, depicting a nude woman bent over an open trunk that emanated the glow of riches. Or all the ills of the world, Guillaudeu thought. What had the city become? Where was it going? As he walked north he passed house after house in these astonishing styles. None of them, he felt certain, had been there a year ago.

Sitting by the iron gate of one of the mansions, the dog waited for him.

"You're still around, eh?" He was glad to see it. He opened his satchel and tore off some of the bread he'd packed. "It's not the heartiest fare, but I've got some sausage, too, for later." He knelt near the dog, who daintily rose to its feet and leaned toward him, sniffing. It would not come closer, so he tossed it the bread. The dog caught it in its jaws and lowered its front end, stretching out its forelegs. When Guillaudeu started walking, the dog backed away, but he noticed that as he went, it followed him at a closer distance than before.

All along these new blocks, stone foundations emerged from the earth. They resembled ruins, he thought, except for the masons bending over them, placing brick after brick, layer upon layer, creating this new city. He shivered. The entire block was under construction. A couple of apple trees stood in the midst of upturned dirt. Had they been part of the orchards he remembered? Murray Hill was just ahead, and he saw its greenery with relief.

In the next block only one house stood, and it looked like it had been there for ages. A wooden farmhouse, but now surrounded by the diggings for new construction. Strangely, the cobble was smooth under his feet. New. But ahead he saw the end of it.

He stepped off the last cobblestones onto packed and dusty earth. In the distance was a bend in the road, where the track disappeared between two grassy slopes. All his life, he could duck into a grocery, a cobbler, a restaurant, at any given moment that he walked the street. The ease, the brisk efficiency, and the people, everywhere people, had simply been the way things were, the point to work from. The bend in the road struck him as vaguely menacing after so many years lived in the sharp angles and straightaways of the city, but it also pulled him strongly. Behind him, the dog whined.

"Come on, then. Let's go!" He stopped and waved the dog along. The creature stood at the edge of the pavement, sniffing the air and growling. Guillaudeu returned to it, but as he approached the dog kept its distance.

"For heaven's sake. I'm your friend!" Guillaudeu called. "Can't you see that?"

He wanted it for company, but the dog would not leave the cobbled street. He tossed it some more bread and a bit of the cheese, but the dog would not be bribed. When he finally set off northward, the unmoving dog barked after him. Looking back, just before he disappeared around the bend, the dog was still there, pacing the line where the city ended.

She Stands Up Again

Twenty-one

Maud was babbling about the gaff again. All morning I'd been posing for the lithographer's sketch artist and my neck hurt. After the sitting, I had given the lithographer's assistant the pages to publish for my True Life History pamphlet. It would encompass only six pages, but instead of the jungles of Surinam, the setting was our old farmhouse in Nova Scotia. It was a crude sketch, but it was true. Would it sell? Was it ridiculous? These thoughts distracted me, and if I'd known Maud would be so talkative I wouldn't have stopped at her booth on my way up to the roof for lunch.

"I'm just not certain whom I should report it to. Straight to Barnum? Maybe one of the scouts? I *would* like him to know I was the one to discover it."

"Why are you making so much out of this?"

"It's a fraud, Ana. It doesn't belong here." Maud coiled her beard into a braid as she huffed up the stairs beside me.

"Them, Maud. Them, not 'it.'"

"Last night *they* woke me up. I swear. I never heard conjoined twins make so much noise. And I heard definitive evidence: *two* sets of footsteps."

"How can you be sure?"

"Because I heard it."

"Why do you care so much?"

"Because it's not *real*."

"You don't seem to have a problem with the mermaid. Or that wretched pickled arm."

145

"The arm is real."

"Of course it's not."

"This is different."

"I don't see how."

The rooftop garden was bright and quiet. Voices seemed to fly away in the wind, which was an agreeable effect. Barnum had never designated a separate area for employees. It was an oversight, certainly, but no one complained. There was a group of five tables slightly apart from the rest of the restaurant where the employees usually gathered. Thomas sat at one of them. He waved when he saw me and I could see his feet tapping the floor.

"Ah, your friend the nervous pianist. Shall we join them?" Maud walked toward them. "Who's that he's talking to, an usher?"

I recognized Beebe's curly ledge of hair. He'd taken his little red hat off and had his sleeves rolled up to his elbows. The two of them looked so much like schoolboys that I smiled. I had seen Beebe three times since we met. Twice he was strolling through the galleries. He consumed the museum exactly as it was designed to be consumed: staring for minutes in front of the catoptric room, shaking his head as he passed the small horn extracted from a woman's forehead in Italy. He represented the quintessential customer, but somehow it did not repulse me.

"Miss Swift. Miss Kraike. Please, sit down." Thomas and Beebe rose, and Beebe bowed slightly.

"We should have brought our sun hats," Maud said to the men, extending her hand to Beebe. "I don't believe we've met." They were introduced and we sat with the cold April sun in our eyes. Thomas ordered lemonade.

"We were just discussing the Human Calculator," said Beebe, smiling a bit too eagerly. "And how it is that he can solve such . . . extravagant mathematical formulas entirely in his head."

"I was just saying that it couldn't be possible," Thomas said. "He must have a system of codes, perhaps through gestures, or even voice inflection, to communicate with the professor moderating the show. I've heard that's a common practice."

I would have been more interested in their conversation if they had been speculating on the shapes of the passing clouds. The weather, the meal, anything other than opinions about the contents of the museum.

"He has a sickness of the mind," Maud corrected. "Ah, good. Our soup is coming."

"What do you mean?" This from Beebe, the Innocent.

"Part of his brain is diseased, which allows him to calculate numbers at an abnormally fast rate."

"Seems like a good sickness to have," said Thomas. "Useful."

"Except that he has some rather strange habits," said Beebe. "He clutches things, spoons, mostly, while he's on-stage. His pockets are full of them. And he doesn't seem to ever stop moving."

A man set bowls of chowder before us.

"You know who is the strangest of all? Who gives me chills every time I think about him?" Maud paused for a dramatic scoop of chowder. "Tom Thumb."

"What?" said Thomas. "He's just a little boy!"

"I find him fascinating," volunteered Beebe.

"He's terrifying," Maud declared. "Think about how young he is."

"But there are other children," I added. I didn't know where Maud was going with her argument and I felt an urge to undermine her confidence. "The albino twins are here. There's a Martinetti child younger than Thumb."

"But they have their parents here. I heard from one of the bookkeepers that the parents gave him up. My point is, can you imagine if the only life you'll ever know is here?"

"Sometimes I feel that way," I said.

"But you had the farm, and your family. Thumb will know only Barnum. Horrifying."

"I didn't take you for a sentimentalist, Maud." Her words chilled me. Not because I pitied Thumb; it was my own life that I suddenly abhorred.

"Our sanity is in our perspective. I participate in this way of life for a specific reason: money. But this will be the entire scope of his life, where he looks for all types of sustenance."

"Like Caligula in the Roman army," Thomas murmured.

"How is Thumb so different from us, Maud?" It seemed to me that her argument was based on a false pretense. "You're speaking from the luxury of your particular situation. You could shave your face and walk outside into anonymity."

"Why don't you?" Thomas blurted.

"That's none of your business," she snapped. "But Ana, you've experienced normal life with your family. It's in you somewhere. He won't have that, ever."

"He won't be with Barnum forever, surely?" Beebe interjected.

"But by the time he's done he's not fit for society. He'll be done for."

In the silence that followed, Mr. Olrick lumbered into the restaurant from the stairwell.

"Oh, look!" Maud was about to raise her hand in greeting. "He's still wearing that military suit."

"Maud, please. Don't call him over." I could not stand the thought of the forced formality, the implied camaraderie, of having another giant at the table. Don't make me a fool, Maud.

Maud shrugged and lowered her hand. "I don't see what you have against him. Oh, no!" Maud suddenly became very intent on her soup. "It's Mr. Archer," she whispered. "He's coming this way."

I looked over my shoulder just in time to see Archer, in a black overcoat and hat, overtake the towering Olrick, who was walking uncertainly toward our table. Archer reached us first, and that was enough to dissuade Olrick from following. He went instead to an empty table on the other side of the restaurant.

"Ah, yes. Good. Just the people I wanted to find." The ad man took a chair from another table and squeezed between Maud and me. "I've just seen an interesting sight. Hello, Mr.

Willoughby." He nodded toward Thomas and ignored Beebe completely.

"I'm hoping you can help shed some light on a certain matter. You see, I was just working in my office, and I happened to observe Mrs. Charity Barnum and her little girl leaving the museum. With numerous trunks and boxes." Mr. Archer looked back and forth between Maud and me. "It looked like they were moving out."

"I'd forgotten that was going to be today," I said. I had wanted to say good-bye to Caroline. To Charity even. "Are they gone?"

"Yes," Mr. Archer went on. "They packed all of their luggage on one cart and disappeared into a carriage. I'm wondering if you could help me understand . . . I'll put it simply: What's going on?"

"The Barnums lived here?" Beebe furrowed his delicate brow.

"I never saw *him* on the fifth floor," said Maud. "But Charity and the girls did."

"The youngest daughter died, Mr. Archer." I lowered my voice. "Here. In the museum."

"And you were there." Mr. Archer leaned in. "What happened?"

I told him the story of Mrs. Barnum's strange entrance to the whist game, and the whole scene that followed.

"She was already dead when you got there?"

"Yes. There was no doctor present," Maud chimed in. "I tried to get one of the Indians to come to the bedside. Once in Philadelphia, we had an Indian who could treat fever. I thought it couldn't hurt, but the Indian wouldn't come."

"So it was you, and you, Miss Swift. Who else was there?"

"Only Mrs. Martinetti. And Mr. Olrick. That one, there." I pointed.

"That's a terrible shame." Mr. Archer shook his head. "Truly awful. Now I understand why they left in such a hurry. Do you know where they will go?"

"Mrs. Barnum was not in the habit of confiding in us," I said. Archer was already eyeing Olrick. He rose to leave.

"Well, thank you, ladies, for filling me in on the details. I'm much obliged."

Archer took his leave and made his way to Mr. Olrick's table.

"Did you see the advertisement he wrote in yesterday's *Atlas*?" Beebe asked, tipping his bowl for the last of his soup. "There were so many adjectives you could hardly keep track of what it was you were reading about. I didn't know we had a sewing dog."

"Cornelia," said Thomas. "Remarkable animal."

"Mr. Olrick really is a nice person," Maud said, watching the two men at the other table. "No matter what you say, Ana. Quite self-conscious, really. Almost humble."

"He's just embarrassed because he's been wearing that suit for two weeks." The waiter served us plates of beef and steaming carrots. "But the truth is, I've become tired of pretending that giants really have anything in common. And Olrick is so nervous."

"Perhaps his awkwardness belies his true feelings," Thomas suggested.

"We're both tall. That doesn't mean we're linked by fate," I spat. "I don't believe that similarities, especially on the physical level, are the basis for friendship. I have a hard time believing that you might think so, Maud. "

"Yes," said Beebe. "It's often the unlikely couple who turn out to be the most well suited."

"Unlikely. I'll drink to that!" Maud said, lifting her lemonade. "I like to be reminded of my late husband, the unlikeliest of all."

"You had a husband?" I could not hide my surprise.

Thomas asked, "Was he a performer?"

"Of course. But not made to last long in this world."

We drank lemonade and amused ourselves with observing ladies' hats, absurdly festooned with ostrich feathers, taxidermied doves, even flags, and all solemnly worn by the female museum patrons strolling the rooftop promenade.

That evening I returned to my apartment with a basin of steaming water to soak my feet. I found a note outside my door from Caroline Barnum. I set down the basin. *Dear Miss Swift. We are leaving. Papa has found us a new house. It is not near the museum. It is in Connecticut. But Papa says I will visit often because the Happy Family will miss me. Do you think animals miss things? I think they must. I'm sure I will see you very soon. Goodbye. Your Humble Servant, Caroline Barnum.* My humble servant. Where in the world had she learned that?

"Miss Swift?" Beebe walked down the hall toward me as I picked up the water. It was strange to see him here, among the apartments, and he appeared a bit nervous about it as well. "I hope I'm not intruding."

"Not at all, Mr. Beebe."

The steam had flushed my face and dampened my hair.

"I was just going to ask, and forgive the presumption, if you would care to join me for an evening away from the museum."

"You mean there is a world outside the museum?" I said.

His face clouded for a moment before he smiled. "There is indeed, Miss Swift. A world of wonders."

"I've heard it's quite pleasant to be amazed by something wonderful."

"Well, good. Tomorrow night, then?" He took a few steps back, still facing me, and tipped his hat. "Shall I meet you at the entrance at seven o'clock?"

"Seven o'clock." I wanted to say something else, something graceful. Instead, I allowed him to open my door so I could maneuver the basin and myself inside. Unlikely, indeed.

When I stepped out in the morning, Maud was waiting for me in the hall. She held out a morning edition of the *Sun,* opened to the amusements page. She pointed to a headline: *P. T. Barnum's Daughter Dies in His American Museum, in the Company of Human Anomalies.* Mr. Archer hadn't even bothered to use a pseudonym in the byline. I could not believe our naïveté.

Twenty-two

I hadn't left the museum in thirty-five days. It wasn't so different outside, except that I wasn't getting paid for provoking disturbances. The only relief was that I no longer had to wear a charitable countenance toward the passersby. I stood outside the museum entrance, my back against the marble façade, concerned that perhaps Mr. Archer had seen me since his office was just inside the main door. But surely a giantess dining with an usher wouldn't be newsworthy, even to him.

Visitors streamed in for the evening performances, and Broadway was lit up like a stage. Somewhere above my head Thomas' band emitted an insistent sonatina. I was too warm in my good gray shawl, but I kept it on. I was outside, after all. Outside. Does the street, the city, change me? Or do I change the street? This incessant dialogue between seeing and being seen exhausted and sustained me. Where was Beebe? I did not tell Maud I was leaving; she would have discouraged it. *Barnum,* she told me, *doesn't like us to leave without telling him.* But Barnum was gone again. People said he was in Europe. Some even said California, but I didn't believe that.

"Miss Swift!" Beebe dodged carriages across Broadway toward me. "Miss Swift. Good evening."

I extended my hand. You've greased down your hair rather strangely, Beebe.

"Have you been waiting?"

"Only a few minutes." I had never seen him without the scarlet uniform and the little red hat in his hand or on his head. He wore a dark blue frockcoat now, and even from my vantage point, which was rather more distant than average, I saw that it was shiny at the elbows and ragged at the lapel.

"I trust you are well." He took a step back from me, but his eagerness flew forward. So eager, for what? You've shaved that feeble mustache, thank goodness. Do you have a sister, Beebe, or a mother advising you?

"Quite. Shall we proceed?"

"It's a lovely night." Thankfully, he did not extend his arm. We started down Broadway. I focused my gaze above the passing faces turning toward me like heliotropes toward the sun. He was poor. Of course he was. Is that flush in your cheek embarrassment at suddenly being a spectacle (perhaps for the first time in your life) or is it simply a consequence of keeping pace with me? Even the blacking couldn't conceal the worn-out leather at the toe of his shoes. People exclaimed and whispered around us. Was it ever different from this? It was always the same, even in the distant past of my girlhood. The only difference is that when I was young I had known everyone who whispered. It was true there was a certain headiness on the streets here, from the sheer number of strangers packed into a small area. A claustrophobic freedom.

Beebe pointed out places familiar to him: the barber, a tiny establishment with a rusted sign; a public tavern, of a decent sort, he said. By the time we'd walked three blocks my heels felt as if nails were punching up through them, piercing the flesh all the way to my hips. Unfortunately, I was not made to roam the earth. If I had been, if my body were sturdy and strong, I would be somewhere in the forests of Nova Scotia, living on wild foods, traveling with the seasons to keep up with my appetite. I suppose I could still go there, in this creaking cage, this bone sculpture fragile as a house of cards, but it would be only to die.

"I've made arrangements for us to dine there," Beebe piped up, breaking my morbid reverie. He pointed to a well-lit building on the corner in front of us with several carriages outside. "It's in the European style," he added, a little uncertainly.

Despite my best efforts to remain generally unmoved, there are inevitably instances, not as infrequent as I might hope, when my fortifications crumble. Entering restaurants is one of those instances. Beebe did not help the matter by nervously straightening his cravat below me and removing his hat before we even neared the door. Go first, Beebe. Please go first. Beebe opened the door and gestured for me to enter. I fell immediately back into an old pattern of thought, one I'd hoped I had outgrown: I pretended I was going on-stage. I would now cross the threshold and enter a fabricated environment. The audience would be surprised, of course, but they also knew exactly what they'd paid to see.

The restaurant had dark wood floors spread over with richly patterned rugs of variegated, though muted, colors. I was surprised, at first, to see that the tables were all of different shapes, some round, some square, and two long, rectangular tables with several different parties seated along them. Even the chairs were mismatched. Lit by cut-glass sconces along each wall, the restaurant was lively and somehow intimate, with everything cast in a medieval glow. A young man with a frosty-pink rose in his lapel led us to a table away from the windows and other patrons. Thankfully, he placed me in a sturdy chair without arms, where my back rested comfortably against the wall.

"Well, this is all right, then?" Beebe, dwarfed in a high, cushioned chair decorated with a needlepoint hart and hound, again struck me as a schoolboy. I often received this impression of men, but Beebe in particular. He nodded. "I haven't been here before, actually, but one of my colleagues at the museum recommended it."

We were given menus. Consommé Grand Duke. Radish salad. Potatoes Gastronome. I wondered briefly if Beebe could read. You can, can't you?

"Ah," he said. "Bridgeport clams. To remind me of home."

"Tell me about where you grew up, then, Mr. Beebe."

Stuffed quail, demi glace. Would I dare order something in miniature? Loin of beef with mushroom sauce was more appropriate. The man returned, offering us claret in fluted glasses. Beebe ordered clams, I ordered consommé.

"Bethel Parish is a beautiful place."

"And what did you do there?"

"Tended hogs, mostly."

"Is that so." Beebe, no! A hog farmer? But then again, am I not a fisherman's daughter?

"It's not a fancy place. Farms of all different kinds, though. It's a fertile region. Abundant, I would say, in that regard."

Around us, ladies sat with men who had obviously never been hog tenders. A couple accompanied by a woman who looked as if she might be mother to one of them took a table near us. The mother, her white hair elegantly swept up and accentuated by a necklace of cut garnets, glanced at me and smiled as she looked quickly at her plate. It was a smile, though, that told me she was not shocked, but gently amused, perhaps, that the city continually tossed wonders in her lap, and I was simply the latest and nothing more than that.

"I also grew up on a farm," I offered, and then examined my menu as Beebe undertook the expected conversation: a comparison of crops, of fathers, of early frosts and late snow-fall. A platter of clams and a bowl of broth arrived. Beebe tucked his napkin into his collar.

"But there *was* something extraordinary about growing up when I did, in the place where I did." Beebe smiled. Small teeth, with rounded edges. He placed an empty clamshell on the tablecloth, despite the porcelain bowl he'd been given. He leaned forward dramatically.

"Because one of my friends was Phineas Taylor. We called him Tale, though, because his uncle was already Phin. We were neighbors."

"Barnum?" I lowered my spoon without taking the bite.

"There were two fields between us, and a thicket, but still our closest neighbor. I know!" he crowed, seeing my surprise. "It seems hardly possible now that he's . . . now that he's doing what he's doing. But back then, naturally, it seemed quite natural. He's just one year older than me."

"Mr. Barnum was your neighbor?" That Phineas T. Barnum was ever a boy seemed highly improbable.

"Yes!"

"He grew up on a farm?" Surely, not on a farm.

"Well, yes. It was his mother's farm, really. And his grandfather's." Beebe gestured with his fork, and I observed droplets of clam broth fly onto his coat.

"What kind of child was he?"

"Oh, well, not terribly unusual." Beebe relinquished his clams to make room for our dinner plates. He had ordered the quail, and I the beef loin. Beebe clutched his fork with one hand, his knife in the other. His table manners were awful. Could that be why people were staring at us? That would be something new.

"He had a knack for approximating. He could guess the number of logs in a woodpile, things like that. But I never saw him much after he went to work at the mercantile in town. Like I said, I stayed on the farm."

"With the hogs."

"Yes."

"And then he gave you the job of usher?" I could picture it: Beebe in muddy boots, fresh from the marketplace, all his hogs sold, appearing at the museum, having heard that his old friend was making a fortune. Barnum frowning at the disheveled man, but feeling some obligation to find a place for him.

"Eventually, yes. It's a whole other story."

"I'd like to hear."

"Well, I didn't mean to tell you my life history." He blushed, pinning his quail to the plate with his fork and taking a swipe at it with his knife. "But I moved here two years ago, to join the seminary."

"You!" I could not contain a laugh.

Beebe looked up sharply. "Yes. Why is that funny?"

"Oh, it's not," I lied gently. "Just unexpected." That he'd

succeeded in surprising me so thoroughly was highly endearing. Now that he saw my smile, he clearly relished it as well.

"Eventually I found that my own ideas about how to live in harmony with the Lord did not exactly . . . fit with the church. So I am no longer in the seminary. But I am continuing my path of faith. I am a Junior Warden at Saint Paul's Chapel. I live there and fulfill my duties as Warden, and also work in the museum three days a week."

"That's quite a pair of occupations."

Beebe nodded. "I know, but it makes sense, it truly does. What's funny is that I didn't even know the museum was Barnum's. I knew it changed owners, and I watched the outside of the building transform, you know, the red trim, all of that. But I didn't know it was him until one morning, I looked outside, and there was a huge banner strung across Broadway. I remember it advertised a Russian clairvoyant and a collection of serpents. Well, the contents of the banner weren't the problem. The problem was that on one side of Broadway the banner was anchored to the second-floor balcony of the museum, but the other side was most conspicuously harnessed to a tree on chapel property. You can imagine the difficulty. So I went across the street, of course, to speak with someone. And do you know, it was Barnum himself behind the ticket window! But I didn't recognize him at first. We hadn't seen each other in twenty years by that time. He pointed me toward the boss's office. As I walked down the back hallway I tried to figure where I'd seen him before, but it wasn't until I saw the name on his office door that I realized. I went straight back to the ticket window and there he was, smiling. 'Beebe,' he said. 'Have you come for a job?' And of course I hadn't, but . . . well, you know how it turned out."

"That's quite a tale."

He looked at his plate. *Ask, Beebe. Ask me how it feels . . . to be me, and I'll tell you. I'll try to tell you. The opening is now. Ask, and maybe I can bear your guileless eyes.*

"I thought you might enjoy it," he said, picking up the

quail's leg and slurping the meat off the bone. "It is strange where life delivers you."

We finished our meal in silence. I was quite comfortable, but as the silence grew, Beebe became anxious. Coffee arrived in mismatched cups. Beebe scalded his mouth and tried, quite gracefully, I thought, to hide his discomfort. But when it came time to pay for our meal, all traces of grace vanished as he poured a small number of coins directly onto the table and tediously counted them out. My skin crawled. Around the room, people looked at us. Because of me? Or him. Several crumpled bills appeared next to the coins and he leisurely smoothed and counted. He even paused to sip his coffee! I felt my face ablaze.

Seemingly oblivious to the spectacle he'd made of himself, Beebe talked all the way back to Ann Street, about the quality of the night, the gradual warming of the earth this time of year. Partaking in such talk is usually abhorrent to me; when you spend each day observing humanity in a setting like the museum, there is opportunity to ponder the superficial habits of man (and the even more numerous superficialities of woman). It is habit, is it not, that keeps us quietly busy in a world whose rules, dictated by others, we don't even question?

"Beebe, why did you invite me to dine with you?"

"Because I like you. Of course."

"But you are a man of faith, and even in the Bible giants are condemned as a corruption on earth. They are part of the reason God sent the flood."

"That's a harsh way to look at oneself, isn't it? The Bible inspires me to live righteously, it's true, but I think for myself, and obviously you do, too. You're a good person. Your perspective is unusual. I feel I can relate to that."

Outside the museum, Beebe took my hand, forcing his own arm to crook up at a comical angle. He bowed.

"Thank you for this evening, Miss Swift. I hope you were not too disappointed by my humble origins,"

"Why of course not, Mr. Beebe," I sputtered, startled that

he'd guessed that I had been. "Thank you for getting me out of the museum. You're right: It is a lovely evening."

I watched him cross over Broadway and, true to his word, unlock the iron gate at Saint Paul's. He paused to examine a patch of tilled ground near the church's front step before continuing along a path around the side of the building. As he disappeared I felt a sturdy tug of affection that I couldn't bear to dismiss.

Twenty-three

The whole morning was cast in a pall of foul humor. My legs ached from walking on cobbled roads with Beebe, and I struggled not to replay our dinner together too many times in my mind, which would quickly stale any remaining pleasure in it. I'd slept poorly and dreamed only of Pictou and the sea.

I'd always heeded you, Mother, hadn't I? You made everything sound so poetic, as if my life's scope were grander than anyone else's because of my greater mass. Whenever I came home overcome with girlish passions, you turned from your task at the woodpile or in the kitchen: *Love will not be easy.* You were the only one to ever speak to me of love. *Don't look for it, Ana. Never. Do not demand what can only be given freely.* You regarded me seriously despite my ugliness, my absurd shell. I never looked, Mother. I never did. *Be content in solitude. Only then are you prepared to receive love.*

But what of the trivial pleasures, the ones I observe over and over standing here? I appear as emotionless as a statue, but each couple who passes, each pair of clasped hands, each buoyant look is a dart pricking my skin, a rash spreading, itching to the point of distraction as I compulsively imagine all the rest, the hidden pleasures. *Concern yourself with practical matters. Then love will surprise you. That is the joy of it as much as all the rest.*

I felt for my bottle of Cocadiel's Remedy in one of the hidden pockets of my skirt. I took a drink. I wanted to improve my life, expand my scope, but how? I looked over the heads of the museum patrons and turned to this lofty matter, hoping to banish the rest from my mind. I would not leave the security of my profession. But a civic life, something outside the business of spectacle, would provide a necessary balance. Serve somewhere, something larger than myself, if such a thing existed. Where? A hospital? What do people do? Or was I just being a fool to think I could have a life outside of . . . this? The inky waters of Lake Ontario lapped at the edge of my thoughts. To slough off this weight, this world.

"Ana!" Thomas' fierce whisper saved me the stress of having no idea what a civic life meant, or how to achieve one. "She's here! Did you see her? She must have passed in front of you. Which way did she go?"

Thomas hopped and whirled in front of my booth, his ragged jacket flapping as if he were a crow half caught in a trap. He paused for a valiant attempt to tame the unruliness of his hair before resuming his hysteria. "Am I presentable?"

I looked down at his upturned face. "In the name of God, Thomas."

"It's Mrs. Corbett."

"Who?"

"She's here. She's much older! You must have seen her."

"I see approximately eight percent of what passes in front of my eyes. And that's when I'm feeling generous. Who is this person?"

"Mrs. Corbett. My teacher!"

"Fate knocking on the door?"

"Yes. *Yes!*" Thomas lunged toward the balcony, turned one hundred and eighty degrees, and made for the entrance to Gallery Seven. At the last moment he pivoted to the right and disappeared into the main hallway and stairwell.

Ten minutes later he bolted back into view, triumphant. "She's up from Boston!"

A woman, presumably the infamous Mrs. Corbett, appeared behind him. She regarded Thomas with flushed attention. She was an impressive sight, her generous proportions wrapped tightly in a flame-orange gown. Her dark, oiled hair was piled into sea-froth wavelets around her face, which showed the first embarrassed melt of age. As a finale, pinned to her head was a silk hat with a tiny red parakeet perched upon it. The bird, I observed, could have been stolen from one of the museum's own taxidermy collections. Mrs. Corbett stared at Thomas, who awkwardly introduced us before leading her to the balcony. Then he was back.

"She is here until one o'clock, when her husband will fetch her! I want to ask a favor. It is so crowded here."

"It's a muse —"

"Do you think I might presume to ask . . . it would be nice to have a quiet place to sit together. Even the rooftop will be crowded. And cold," Thomas complained, looking at the floorboards. "Could we sit in your room for an hour?"

I glanced toward the balcony, where a fiery orange shape stood at the railing.

"Isn't she marvelous?" Thomas breathed.

"Go." I handed him my chatelaine with its single key. I waved him away.

The gallery filled up and emptied out again. Bright beams of light divided the room and then diffused. Similarly, my mind flickered with thoughts, some vivid enough to blind me to the passing crowd before snuffing out. Memory replayed itself endlessly and would have driven me mad if I were not adept in skimming above my mind's meanderings with no fear of miring in the muck. At some point in the afternoon Thomas returned to his harpsichord and played an entire melancholic repertoire to the oblivious denizens of the street.

When the museum closed I went directly to the whist table, where Maud proceeded to interrogate me about the previous evening.

"What did you see?" she asked, with all the intensity of someone addressing a polar explorer.

"A whole room of bearded ladies," I said.

"You are so *sour,* Ana."

There had been no sign of Olrick the Austrian Giant at the whist table since the evening of Helen Barnum's death, and

Maud had managed, through sign language, to convince Mrs. Martinetti to bring her daughter as the fourth. The daughter, a long-limbed acrobat specializing in contortionism, sat straight-backed in her chair and stared at Maud and me. We dealt the cards.

I was partnered with Mrs. Martinetti the elder, and she spoke to her daughter in a conspiratorial tone throughout the first game.

"They could be cheating," whispered Maud. "Do you understand English?"

The women shook their heads.

"You don't?" Maud reiterated. They shook their heads again. "But you understood that. Perfect."

Mrs. Martinetti the elder spoke rapidly. Her daughter nodded and patted Maud's hand, giggling softly behind her cards.

"It would be so much *easier* if English were required," Maud huffed, studying her cards. "How are we supposed to have a decent game?"

I surveyed the Martinettis' faces. A single, ripe idea arrived. I could teach them English. Why not? It would give me something to do other than make a fool of myself for money. And it was helpful. Was it a step toward a civic life? It was at least a diversion. I began composing the handbill as Mrs. Martinetti and I lost the next three tricks.

When the game finally ended, I rushed back to my room. ENGLISH LESSONS. WEDNESDAY EVENING, IN THE APARTMENT OF MISS ANA SWIFT {GIANTESS}. I would write up the bills, hand them out . . . but those who needed my class would not be able to read them. I resolved to write them up anyway. I walked toward the drawer where I kept a sheaf of paper, but halfway there I turned. I sniffed the air. I scanned the room. Some unfamiliar muskiness hung in the air. Vague unease tugged the edge of my consciousness and I suddenly remembered my dream of the night before, of wading over the tide flats of Pictou. Warm seawater around my knees, my toes sinking in the rippled sand, I was a girl, just like every other, walking among the driftwood and the empty clamshells. I smelled the stench of drying seaweed and snails rotting in tide pools.

My bed had been disrupted, rumpled. Even the multicolored chaos of my quilt could not disguise the fact that more than sitting had occurred upon it. The stagnant air smelled of sweat and unknown brine. I ran my hand across the quilt. Was that a touch of dampness? And then I saw the evidence, right in the middle of the bed: a bright red feather. I held it up between two fingers. It curled incriminatingly. I twirled the feather and brushed it along my cheek, seeing flame-orange skirts spread wide across my bed, ample flesh spilling from silken constraints, and the particular ecstasy of long-imagined coupling.

I saw my own reflection in the mirror on the opposite wall, the red feather against my cheek, and also a scarlet blush rising there. My expression was unforgivable: slack-lipped and misty-eyed.

"You!" I growled at the image. "Always watching, aren't you? Is this what you want to see?" I lunged across the room and ripped the mirror from its hooks. I threw it as hard as I could and it exploded against the wall.

In the silence that followed, I knew Maud and everyone else was listening closely; they wondered if the mirror was the beginning of my rampage, or whether a single act of self-annihilation would suffice this time.

In front of me, cupped gently on the air, the red feather drifted sideways. I lunged for it, but the draft from my body whisked it away.

Twenty-four

The fifth floor was at its busiest at half past nine in the evening, with doors opening and closing, conversations audible from rooms away, and the heavy footfalls of the Wonderful going up and down the hall. I started with the Indians.

There had been some excitement when the Indians arrived because they refused to divide themselves into groups of two and move into the three apartments the museum had prepared for them. After mysterious negotiations, the Indians — they were Sioux we discovered — made themselves a sort of camp along one wall of the beluga's gallery. The whale, whose tank was still not complete, and who received meals consisting of buckets of fish, did not seem to mind. The Indians had constructed some small shelters from blankets draped over clothesline, and as I approached, I saw that they'd made their camp into a rather cozy affair. Seven cots in two tidy rows, each made up with a woolen blanket and sheets. Men lay on two of the cots, apparently asleep. Two others sat on the floor just inside the blanket structure, and a white-haired man wearing a violet waistcoat and a top hat stood at the top of the ladder. He leaned over the side of the beluga tank, his sleeves rolled to the elbow and a fancy hardwood pipe jutting from the corner of his mouth. He held the handle of a horsehair push broom over the water. When I reached him, I peered over the lip of the creature's tank; the whale was lolling on its side while the old Indian scrubbed its back vigorously. The whale emitted a long, continuous whistle and raised one fin lazily.

"Good evening," I said.

The elderly man glanced at me. One of the younger men came out of the tent and walked to where we were. He wore black trousers and an indigo shirt. He watched the older man and said nothing. One of the others sat up on his cot.

"My name is Ana Swift," I continued. The smell of wood smoke emanated from the Indians' blankets in a spicy tang, confusing me with a memory of my mother's house, my home, that place I'd never see again, a place of questionable existence.

"I'm hosting an English class. Wednesday evening. The night after tomorrow." I held out one of the yellow flyers. "To learn English."

The beluga croaked with pleasure, which made the old Indian smile. I gave the flyer to the younger man, who did not look at it. Another Indian appeared from somewhere on the far side of the whale's tank. She was a woman whose age I could not immediately tell; perhaps it was close to my own. Her hair was shorn close around her ears, and the planes of her cheeks were softened by two creases running horizontally, not denoting exhaustion but giving her face an unusual, wizened quality. Her look was a challenge, and curious. As she came close, I saw that the creases across her cheekbones were scars, made by what must have been an extremely sharp blade. The younger man started to shoo her away, but the elder one gestured to her, and she smirked at the young man as she drew closer.

"She will be the only one," the elder said. His English, muffled by the pipe, contained a faint British accent.

The other man gave her my flyer. She snatched it and scurried away.

I bypassed the apartment of the conjoined twins. The Martinettis took two flyers, nodding and clucking and waking their youngest son to translate. The Chinese giant, Tai Shan, answered his door wearing a brown silk tunic embroidered with turquoise peonies.

"I am teaching an English class, here in the museum," I said. "I presume you are not in need of such a thing."

"No," the giant said softly. "My English is excellent, as is my German. My French, however, could stand improvement."

"Well." How irritating.

I had seen this Chinese giant only once before. He obviously found better things to do with his time than spend it with the rest of us, so I did not go out of my way to befriend him.

I passed Olrick's closed door, and the albino twins and their parents, who came from New Orleans. At the end of the hall was a door I'd never noticed before. It was probably empty, but I knocked anyway. No sound from within. I slipped a flyer under the door and as I turned away I heard something move inside. I tapped the door again. "Hello?" I thought I heard a voice, and then I definitely heard the thump of something hitting the floor. As I turned the doorknob it occurred to me that whoever it was might not want to be disturbed.

A tribal man, an old African, probably, lay curled on his side on the floor of the empty room. He clutched a satchel of some kind to his shirtless chest. His face was ashen, his eyes closed. The window was wide open and dead leaves had blown in; a few of their tatters were caught in his hair and on his trousers. He was whispering something I could not understand. He seemed to be ill.

"Are you all right?" I went to him, ambushed by the pungent odor of his sweat and unwashed clothes. His eyes snapped open, revealing yellow whites and black irises. He continued to whisper and raised one of his hands in a gesture that appeared to beckon me. He must want food. He looked as if he hadn't eaten in days.

"Where is your manager?" The man didn't answer. He looked terrible, so I hurried to the restaurant and returned with two plates and a pitcher of water. He had moved to an upright position, sitting cross-legged. His satchel had disappeared. He did not move but accepted the first plate when I pushed it to him. He ate slowly, carefully, the pieces of boiled carrot. He dipped his finger into the mashed potatoes and ate those. He did not touch the sliced beef, but drank all the water.

"Where is your manager?" I asked him. "Who is your guardian?"

Most of the savages with whom I'd shared the stage were not authentic, or if they actually were from Borneo, or South America, or wherever they claimed, they were long accustomed to the entertainment business. There had been a "Batu Pigmy" in Jones' show who had worked as a barkeep on the nights he wasn't performing. He was just a dwarf born to slaves in Georgia. Most performers of this type traveled with managers, but from the look of this one, he did not have the benefit of such a relationship. Someone would have to be notified.

By Wednesday evening I had brought four chairs from the restaurant, a small stack of paper, and four pens and inkpots. I set the chairs in a tidy row. I waited in my room, but no one came. I opened the door and looked up and down the hall. I waited ten minutes and then I went to collect them.

When the Indians saw me coming, one called out, and the woman with the scars appeared. She followed me to the Martinetti apartment, which was unusually quiet. Mrs. Martinetti the elder was the only one there, and she bustled around, collecting her shawl and her sewing bag, appearing quite excited by the prospect of the class. I delivered them to my apartment and went for the tribesman. He was sitting in the same cross-legged way in the middle of the floor, but there were now cot, desk, chair, and even curtains on the windows of his room. The tribesman wore a new pair of trousers and a shirt and woolen vest and appeared more alert, thankfully, than when I had initially found him.

It was only when I had them sitting in a row in front of me, as I stared down at their three very different heads, that I realized I did not know how I would actually teach them anything.

I would begin with the broadest perspective possible, I decided.

"This," I began, gesturing to the walls, the floor, "is the museum. We are in the museum." But they will think *wall*, and *floor*, is *museum*.

I took up pen and paper and drew the building as best I could. I wrote the word underneath the picture and held it up for them.

"Museum," I repeated. The Indian laughed. Mrs. Martinetti looked over the tops of her spectacles, scrutinizing my face. She reached for her sewing. The tribesman did not move or look at the drawing.

"Museum?" This was ridiculous. I was ridiculous. The Indian was transfixed by the pieces of bright orange fabric that Mrs. Martinetti sewed.

"Sewing," I declared, pointing at Mrs. Martinetti's work. I pantomimed the rise and fall of a needle and thread. The Indian woman smiled. This wasn't working.

The class unraveled. I drew pictures of chairs, of beds. I announced, pointed, and proclaimed everything from shoes and stockings to the sun, moon, and stars. Mrs. Martinetti good-naturedly repeated my phrases and words but seemed entirely more interested in her needlework than the lesson. At first the Indian just laughed at the things I said, whether out of shyness or arrogance I could not say. But soon she just stared at the tribesman.

Even though he sat like the others in his restaurant chair, holding the small stack of paper, the pen, and the inkpot on his lap, and even though he looked in my general direction with his eyes open, the tribesman appeared to have disassociated himself from the present reality. He did not appear to be deranged; he seemed quite lucid in his movements, when he made them. His impassivity was not apathetic, somehow, and I believe that's what made him interesting to look at. It was as if he was so entirely occupied with other things, my laughable attempt at teaching was simply a collection of noises and images that had nothing to do with him. It was true, I realized. He was right. And he was humming.

After half an hour I had run out of things to say. I stood there, with the two women staring at me. I was sure the half smiles on their faces expressed contempt in addition to the effect of the comedy I had just performed.

"That's all, then. That's the end." They did not move. They did not understand English. "I've done the best I can, and it is obviously not good enough."

Mrs. Martinetti reached over and tapped the Indian on the arm. "Violetta," she said, pointing to herself. "Violetta."

"Kokipapi," replied the Indian.

Mrs. Martinetti made a hilarious attempt to pronounce the Indian's name. We all laughed, except the tribesman.

The Indian pointed at me. "Ana."

"Ana, sí," Mrs. Martinetti agreed.

The Indian rose from her chair and motioned for us to wait. She left the room, and we heard her running down the corridor. I remained at the front of the room while Mrs. Martinetti murmured the Indian's name until the syllables blended to nonsense.

When she came back, the Indian dragged a boy into the room with her. I had seen him among the others; he was the youngest among them and the only one, besides this woman, with his hair cut above his shoulders. The woman tugged him by the arm, speaking to him rapidly and pointing to us. Looking steadily at her, the boy jerked his arm out of her grasp.

"She is Mary," he finally said. "She would like you to know this." The woman looked sharply at the boy and grabbed his arm. She spoke to him in a harsh whisper. The boy extricated himself and turned to go, but the woman's voice stopped him. He did not turn. She spoke to him in a crooning whisper until he gave up and nodded.

"She says she will tell you her real name. In your language she is called They Are Afraid of Her."

She smiled at Mrs. Martinetti, pointed to herself, and repeated her name. The scars across her cheekbones folded to creases, transforming her for a moment into an old woman. Even though Mrs. Martinetti could not understand, she clapped her hands gleefully and repeated, *"Theyarfraiover."*

The boy moved toward the door, shaking his head.

"Wait!" I couldn't bear to see him, our only bridge, leave us to our fumbling silence again. "Could you tell us something more?" I blurted. "Her scars. What about those? Where did she get them?"

His expression did not change, but when he spoke to They Are Afraid of Her, he was obviously angry. He moved again for the door and made it halfway into the corridor before she caught him again. When he turned back, the boy's face had transformed from anger to sorrow. He spoke softly to her. She coaxed him back into the room, her voice almost a whisper.

"She would like me to tell you that her face was cut a very long way away from this place. As punishment for leaving her tribe."

"Isn't she part of your tribe?" I asked.

"We took her in. We are all Sioux, but she is from another place."

Looking shyly at us, They Are Afraid of Her whispered more to the boy.

"She says now this place is her home."

"Why did you come to this city?"

"She says the past doesn't matter."

The boy turned on her then, hissing in her ear and leaving the room without so much as a nod to the rest of us. When he left the room she did not pursue him, and something dark flickered in her eyes as she smoothed her skirt and waited for what would happen next.

The tribesman retrieves a small bundle from where he has hidden it. He hums the song, beginning with the note after where he'd left off. The sound wrings out the sea's stinging residue. It brings back what had been drowned. He holds the bundle close to his chest, still frightened that it has come to him. He should not be holding it. He is not even a carrier, does not possess even that much knowledge, and now, against his will and too far away from the home place, he is a keeper, a guardian. He pulls back the stained canvas to touch the hollow mulga root, running his fingers along the grooves and beveled ridges of the designs burned into the wooden surface.

Whenever the men would gather, the keeper came to them with the mulga root and its contents, placing it in the center of the circle. The keeper advised the men when to move camp to the stone country and how to prepare for the coming floods. When the old women gathered, they drew these same shapes in the dirt and spoke with the keeper. He advised them in the safekeeping of water, where to gather goose eggs, and where to light the cleansing fires when the season called for it. The keeper's knowledge guided the group, always, and now the keeper, who had been the tribesman's only brother, was gone.

The tribesman continued the song and eventually found the floodplain dry and cracked near the home place. Crocodiles swam tight circles, water caking to mud around them, water holes evaporating away. Gurrung it was, then, at the home place now: the season when the land lies dormant. He tried to stay there, using the song, and his heart nearly burst when he encountered the scent of paperbark blossoms, which melted into twilight and the shapes of feeding bats gliding like spirits above his head. His face grew damp from the heat or tears, but he did not move to wipe the moisture away. In the distance the people carried their things into the darkness at the base of the escarpment, making their way up into the stones, to the high place, to hunt goanna and wait out the floods. He tried to stay there, feeling the cool rock caves over his head and hearing the gentle sounds of the people making camp. But the keeper appeared, turning to him suddenly from a particular tone in the song. The keeper beckoned to him and pointed north.

He opens his eyes to the empty room at the top of the museum. He hears the multitude of museum visitors below him and feels the vibrations of their footsteps above. It is terribly cold. He has not been warm since they thrust him into the hull. He observes his surroundings as if from the innermost chamber of a woodworm's mindless tunnel. As the vision of the home place evaporates from his mind, he is left alone, no longer connected to a relevant world. There is no way forward for him, and since the keeper is dead, and the mulga root is here with him in this terrible place, there is no way forward for the people.

Twenty-five

Only a full moon gave this much glow. Blue shadows striped the floor and the whole room appeared to be dipped in silver. I did not even need a candle to write by, that's how bright it was.

I had been awake for hours with my mother-made quilt high at my chin, the squares of all my girlhood dresses turning me into a patchwork behemoth. Had I even slept at all? The night was all-encompassing and inside its long tunnel I was both comforted and disturbed, because it reminded me of the long months I was trapped in bed while my body grew. My published True Life History pamphlet lay on the counter of my booth, but I sat up and found my pencil and the stack of papers anyway. How could I characterize eleven months of chaos ravaging an exquisitely still body?

In the beginning I was a nocturnal creature. When night fell, my mind became more lucid. Not that I was churning out magnificent poetry or insight, not at all. Most nights I read, but in the darkness I could always feel some ethereal charge that alerted me to the silken threads that bound reality together. It was comforting because I was simply part of this graceful web, just one filament of many. Sometimes I'd lie in my bed, staring at the wooden ceiling, and listen to the breath of my parents above. The sound was so beautiful to me, and yet it seemed offensive that they slept through the limpid medium of night. The discovery of my new nocturnal nature was the first revelation of my convalescence. The second was that Evangeline, my beloved cat, knew something strange was happening; for the first time in her life she would not come near me, no matter how I called to her.

Even as greater and greater swaths of time were lost to pain, night was still my favorite time. It is the memories of day that are blurred and smeared together, almost entirely lost except for glimpses.

Once a week, before the morning's chores began, my mother brewed the laudanum. Through the doorway of my room I watched her pass, first with the pot of well water, then with the wood for the fire. After a while she ground the cinnamon and then the clove, and added sherry wine and opium. As the weeks wore on, the fragrance of that brewing tea became dearer to me than anything else. She hated how I reached for it, but there was no other way, was there? The bones of my wrists grated against each other as they grew, stretching the skin so I thought I would burst. Sometimes I itched so badly I scratched myself bloody. She began brewing laudanum every three days, and watched as I drank it and drowsed, unburdened but drooling, all afternoon. Eventually I took such large quantities that old Garvey, Pictou's only doctor, didn't know what to do. I would scream myself awake, certain that my bones had torn through the skin, sweating, unable to focus my eyes, and she would rush in with another cupful, a blurred, warm figure with spidery hands working my clenched jaws open.

Garvey brought a doctor from Halifax, who brought his colleague from Boston. They spoke with my mother upstairs as I clutched my bed frame, where my hands had worn through the varnish. I had already grown two inches by then; I was horrified, and I wanted to die. Finally they gathered around my bed, three men in black suits, the one from Boston looking rather excited.

"They've brought a stronger medicine, Ana. It's a new procedure. Would you like to try it now?"

"For God's sake," I whispered.

The Boston doctor opened a small wooden box and produced a lancet.

"We must pierce your skin, Ana. It may sting."

I laughed. "Don't mock me."

The lancet's brass handle was engraved with roses on a graceful vine and two doves, symmetrically stretching their wings toward each other. I stared at it as they administered the morphine. I could not look at the men, not to mention my mother, because the medicine was spreading in a ripening glow that sent tingling splinters directly to my most delicate parts. It aroused my senses so that I blushed and barely suppressed a groan as the morphine spread outward from my center in a great alleviating wave. Even now, thinking of those twining roses, those two birds arched in their languorous stretch, I blush. When I finally looked at her, my mother recoiled. I must have been smiling.

I can recall nothing but morphine for many weeks of my illness. These are not unpleasant memories, but hopeless to transcribe. Since the growth came in waves I did not always need the medicine, and during the lulls my mother tried her best to keep it from me. I wanted it, though. I still do. But I was ill for so long that the morphine, like the night and the novels I read, like my mother and each of the seasons that passed in front of my eyes, was just one of many companions. It wasn't until several years later that morphine saved my life, for good or ill.

My father was the one who was absent. At first he tended to me constantly, thinking this was an ordinary illness, but gradually, as we realized what was happening, he withdrew his care. She said the mackerel season had come earlier, was bigger than any other year; that he'd had to hire two more boys from town to help. The cost of medicine, too, she said. It's not cheap. He's upset, she said. I did not blame him.

Sometimes I listened to him make his way in from the barn late in the evening. I knew he kept a bottle of whiskey out there and I could tell by his footsteps that he'd been into it. I pretended to be asleep, and when he stopped in my doorway my heart pounded so loudly I thought he must surely hear it.

The bright cold day I finally sat up and swung my huge legs off the edge of the bed, I knew I had to move or die. I was groggy from laudanum — I hadn't needed morphine in a month — but determined. When I lurched to my feet I thought I would faint from the pain but I wobbled ahead, reaching the kitchen door in just a few steps. I staggered outside in just my too-short nightgown, the cold turning my bare bruised legs pink. Cold air hit the weeping sores on my back as I came down the few steps to the snow.

He was in the barn and I started toward it. I was so curious what he'd been doing in there every day, since the nets were long stowed and the boats out of the water. The snow numbed my feet deliciously, and gooseflesh prickled my skin. I heaved in cold air and walked through the clouds of my breath. I smelled wood fires and frost as I squinted dizzily in the sun. I ducked through the once huge doorway of the barn.

He was building a large wooden box with one side cut out. I did not recognize it as an exhibition booth until later, when she told me they'd read about a giant who made seventy dollars a week in London. We could pay off the boat, she said. Can you imagine that?

When my shadow filled the barn entrance he looked up. His eyes widened and he stumbled backward, tripping over his tools. He fell. My father.

He shouted for my mother, but she was gone to a neighbor's house. He was trapped.

"Da," I said. "I can walk again." The barn spun in front of me and I clutched the wall. Explosions of light blocked my sight. "I think I might —"

"Ana!" His voice reached me from very far away as I toppled from a new, great height.

Twenty-six

A sound pulled me away from Pictou and those people now lost to me. I stared at the door to my apartment, listening, but all was silent on the fifth floor of Barnum's museum. I wondered if I'd actually heard anything at all, but it came again, and this time I thought it must be Beebe, and my blood rose dreadfully. I put down the True Life History.

Poor, awkward Beebe, burning his tongue and laboring over his coins. I hadn't seen him since our evening together, even though I'd strolled by the theater entrance on more than one occasion. The idea that Beebe might have sneaked away from his chapel bed and across Broadway and made his way into the museum somehow and was now poised outside my door was oddly thrilling. I rose. Be that man, Beebe. One who would act rashly out of desire or, even better, simply to say, *Look how blue the night has become, how strangely silver.* If it's you, I will not even speak. I will just pull you in.

It was only Maud, though, standing there, holding a mostly melted candle in a tarnished silver holder. It was Maud, and she was the image of a nightmare: her head a nest of black tangles, her recently woken face bearing a crease from her bedding, her beard and eyebrows in complete, awful, disarray.

"I have incontrovertible evidence," she whispered fiercely, pushing her way into my room.

"Are you awake or asleep?" I asked.

"Don't be stupid. I *hear* them."

"Who?"

"The gaff."

"Not the gaff again!" Maud's persistent interest in the authenticity of the conjoined twins had become an irritating obsession.

"Yes. And this time I'm ending it once and for all. Come with me."

"I'm not coming with you anywhere." I stepped back but she grabbed my wrist with force.

"I need a witness, Ana. So it's not just my word against theirs."

"Well, if they're a fake, there should be plenty of evidence."

"Just come on." She pulled me into the hallway.

Regrettably, she was right. What sounded like two distinct sets of footsteps came from the closed door of the room. The few times I'd seen them, the twins had appeared real enough to me. I'd scorned Maud's suspicion. The identical dandies, with their slicked black hair, had claimed to be British. They were of the most common variety, connected across the torso, each half with his own arm and the tri-legged mode of transport on the bottom. They wore elevated shoes of different heights, and their trousers fit loosely enough to imply that their middle appendage was not monstrously deformed.

"What are you going to do?" I whispered to Maud.

She flung open the door.

We were transformed, then, over the course of one long moment, into villains. We had surprised them in an act of intimacy, although to use that word in the context of conjoined twins is to imply a far deeper meaning: intimacy endured to the point of derangement. They were no gaff.

They were kissing, and they seemed to have been dancing before that. One half of the twins wore a rather fine organdy gown in violet and a wig of yellow hair piled high with tiny jewels. His face was powdered, and at the moment of our discovery I observed several enamel bracelets on his raised, gloved arm, which was entwined with his brother's in the gesture of the dance. It was a picturesque scene, elegant as ballet and as tender as the most fervent couple. However un-usual, the caress thrilled me.

"Get out." The unbedecked twin's voice was not loud. He spoke with aplomb, though with no discernible British ac-cent. He made no move toward us. His mouth was smeared with lip rouge.

"Get out. Monsters," the twin repeated.

"Oh, Jacob." The one in the gown also spoke softly. "We might as well invite them in." He offered a strange smile, but we had already backed away. Maud shut the door and ran back to my room. We laughed, but there was wretchedness in it.

"The one question is answered," gasped Maud. "But I have so many more!"

"Do you? I find I have no question at all."

"How will we ever face them again?"

"We have no choice but to face them again. Probably to-morrow at breakfast."

When she was gone, and I had once again crawled into my bed and tucked the quilt tightly around my body, I re-alized that what I felt was envy. For their closeness. Com-pany. Companionship, however forced. I should have envied a normal couple, but naturally that was more difficult for me to imagine.

On New York Island

Twenty-seven

Above Murray Hill, mansions were replaced by factories set back from the road, emitting steam and occasionally foul odors. The view opened up on either side to pasture and thicket, with a few old oaks spreading their great umbrellas in the distance. These trees would be coveted in the city, but up here they were grand sentinels guarding nothing.

Guillaudeu passed an empty, reeking cattle market, a tidy brick building with a sign for Simeon's Match Company and a factory busy producing whatever it was the city needed. If he'd ever passed these buildings before, he'd been deep inside a carriage and never noticed them. He was getting tired, but he went on, unable to stop even when he came to a gray wooden tavern at a crossroad. A dozen horses in the tavern's small pasture looked up as he skittered past the open door and the men's voices erupting from within. Half an hour later he sat down on the wooden steps of a church. He got out the smoked sausage and realized he hadn't packed a knife. He made sure no one was watching before gnawing off a chunk. He checked his watch: four o'clock. He broke off some cheese and ate that, too.

A distant but growing rumble disturbed Guillaudeu's meal; he walked around the side of the church, looking east until the steam engine appeared. So he was still on Fifth Avenue. The sleek coaches of the new Harlem Railroad clattered by on what must be Fourth. The windows were crowded with the figures of sightseers. A blaze of orange caught his eye and for a fleeting moment he saw Celia, leaning against the glass in her ugly wool coat, waving to him. After it had gone he walked to the tracks and touched the still-warm rails. *I can't escape the city's tendrils. They reach up, always up.* He looked south. *I could be in my office within an hour if I catch the next train.* His heart leapt toward the idea of his freshly oiled worktable, the pots of resin and beeswax, and all his tools waiting in alignment, waiting for the next specimen and the application of his will over it.

But as the specter of Mr. Archer appeared, tapping his pencil on a stack of paper in the corner of Guillaudeu's office, poised to write unknown nonsense about Barnum's latest spectacle, one simple fact became utterly clear: The museum was no longer his home and there was nothing he could do about it.

For a moment he felt as if he'd been slapped in the face. He even raised a hand to his cheek as he stood there by the rails. Then from the gut he heaved, unsure if he was going to cry, scream, or vomit, and he found himself laughing.

Orphaned again, you fool! This time by a damned building! The hilarity crashed through him and his breath twisted free of his body in convulsions overlaid by squeaking mirth.

"I am *Lusus naturae*," he wheezed, doubled over and clutching his belly against a cramp.

As suddenly as it was upon him, the episode ended. He righted himself and mopped his face with his handkerchief, feeling a welcome calm. He had been observed by a little boy in overalls standing against a fence across the rails, who now ran off.

I will continue north, Guillaudeu declared to himself. He knew it wasn't a noble decision, or, more significantly, a logical one. Like all voyages of discovery, his was fueled as much by a determination *not* to stay in one place as a conviction to explore. He imagined Cervantes' approval.

Guillaudeu set off again. When he could see the river and the southern edge of Blackwell's Island he turned north, and a brackish breeze caught him full in the face.

The landscape now shifted to asylums, which seemed to

be everywhere and only grew bigger as he walked. They were formidable buildings, even with children playing outside some of them. Deaf and Dumb Asylum. Colored Children's Asylum. Lunatic Asylum. All catchments for the city's inevitable by-product. What if he'd been taken to an orphans' home up here? He'd have ended up an apprentice making matches.

Guillaudeu walked up a hill and past the gated estate that topped it. An orchard with newly unfurled leaves rustled like an audience whispering in the theater. He saw a cluster of buildings ahead, nestled at the water's edge in a shallow valley beyond the foot of the hill. Turtle Bay. He'd stop for a meal and a good night's rest in one of the village inns. Perhaps he'd have time to read a bit more of what Linnaeus had to say about voyaging in one's own country. Guillaudeu had already adopted the essay as his guide and companion, as if the words of the famous taxonomist were enough to create order around him as he walked, and to keep him safe.

Twenty-eight

"O grim look'd night, o night with hue so black. O night, which ever art when day is not. O night, o night, alack, alack, alack!"

Now that Guillaudeu stood in the shadows at the edge of the tavern's crowded garden, he saw that a rough theater had been erected at one end, lit by gas lamps now that the sun was setting. Two costumed men stood on the stage, holding open books in front of them. Women emerged from the tavern with plates and pitchers for the patrons, all of whom were busy heckling the players on the makeshift stage.

It had taken far longer than Guillaudeu expected to reach the outskirts of the village, and he was feeling light-headed.

"I fear my Thisbe's promise is forgot! And thou wall, thou sweet and lovely wall, that stands between her father's ground and mine . . . show me thy chink!" And the men roared as one player, acting the part of the wall, turned his back to the audience, bent over, and lifted his costume to reveal a pale and distinctly hairy backside.

If there had been some courage required for Guillaudeu to venture into this tavern, after pausing at the threshold the amount needed was doubled. He stood outside the gate, invisible (he hoped) to those within. Any remaining daring, which had sustained him as he started this adventure, leaked away. Clutching his satchel, tired and very hungry, he had now lost himself somewhere along the mutable border of things, trying to discern exactly where the world ended and he began.

"O wall, full often hast thou heard my moans, for parting my fair Pyramus and me."

An uproarious cheer accompanied Thisbe's arrival onstage. She was a massive woman with rouged cheeks, a piercing voice, and an expansive bosom barely contained by a half-laced corset. Aghast, Guillaudeu watched as she pranced to the wall, who had righted himself and now stood with his arms folded in front of him.

"My cherry lips have often kissed thy stones!" Thisbe shrieked as the wall reached out with both hands and grabbed her ample breasts. The men in the tavern roared, and Guillaudeu nearly turned and ran, but then he saw one of the cooks emerge from the tavern with a huge pot of steaming food. Salivating, he took a step forward. Then another. He kept his eye on an empty place at one of the tables. He unlatched the gate and entered.

"Oh, kiss me through the hole of this vile wall!" Pyramus cajoled.

"I kiss the wall's hole!" Thisbe crowed, and the wall broke his neutral stance to press his mouth to hers. She promptly pushed his head down into her décolletage, where he snuffled happily and perhaps began to suffocate. "And not your lips at all!"

Guillaudeu crept among the howling men until he was safely seated among them.

Onstage, the threesome shouted their lines and grappled one another from one obscenity to the next. Thisbe lifted her skirts to her knee and both Pyramus and the wall knelt before her with their heads invisible beneath the folds, braying like donkeys.

Sharing the table with Guillaudeu were three large men. These dark-complexioned specimens of *Ursus americanus* were surely brothers, or at least cousins. Their attention was firmly glued to the stage and their paws wrapped around hefty beer mugs. When they laughed, the closer one's elbow brushed Guillaudeu's side.

"Excuse me, sir, does this tavern have rooms?" Guillaudeu ventured.

"Rooms?" The closest brother swung his gaze momentarily in his direction.

"Beds. For the night."

"This tavern?"

"Yes," Guillaudeu said. "I'm exhausted."

The man really looked at him this time. "Not the Pick and Hammer. Never heard of anyone staying here, unless they end up under one of the tables out here. Don't see many city dandies on these roads, not on foot. They all take the train. Looks like you've been walking, though."

One of the tavern's cooks came into view and Guillaudeu waved her down. "Ah, a plate, please. What is it you're serving tonight?"

The red-cheeked woman seemed to be a matriarch of the tavern. "Meat. Potatoes. Cabbage. It'll be forty cents."

"And I'd like one of these mugs. Of ale, I suppose it is."

"Ten cents." The woman extended her palm. "Fifty, total."

Guillaudeu reached into the inside pocket of his overcoat for the leather purse that had been Scudder's so long ago. His fingers dipped deep enough that he should have felt it, but he did not. He pressed his flat waistcoat pockets. The woman watched him unbuckle his satchel and rummage through it; it was an act of denial, though, because he already knew the purse was gone. He had put it in his overcoat pocket.

The woman narrowed her eyes and now had both hands on her hips. "Well?"

"It's gone. My money." Color rose to his cheeks and again he felt the boundaries of the world dissolving around him. Beside him the cousins roared in approval of Thisbe and her lover Pyramus.

"If that's so, *sir,* you can leave my establishment now." The cook's voice was firm and loud. All three *Ursus americanus* swung their attention onto him.

"We got a downtown confidence man with us tonight,

Bernard." The cook addressed the closest man. "Do you think we ought to call Leo out here?"

"I must have been robbed!" Guillaudeu blurted, trying to extricate himself from the bench without disrupting anyone else. His panic was intense.

"At least we caught him before one of you boys bought him something," the cook went on. "Now you better leave nicely or I'll have to call my husband out here."

"You don't want that, old man," one of the cousins said softly.

"I'm going, of course! I didn't mean anything —"

"Sure, you didn't. We ain't fools; you can be sure of that."

Guillaudeu tumbled over the bench and trotted across the garden and through the gate. As he latched it behind him, another roar erupted, as if he were the joke, not the stage players. He reached the far edge of the tavern yard, now illuminated mostly by the rising moon. On the East River blinked the lights of several boats, and closer to him were the lights of Turtle Bay village, which now seemed forbidding and forbidden because he was penniless. Of course he'd been robbed. He remembered the sharp elbows bumping him as he rushed from the Points and the skinny children following him closely with sharp and hungry eyes. Of course they would snake their little hands into the pockets of a fearful, stupid man.

All along he'd thought if worse came to worst, or when he'd had enough of walking north, he'd just catch the Harlem Railroad home. Suddenly Fourth Avenue seemed as distant as the Sierra Nevada.

But now? A chaos of thoughts tangled in his mind until one pulled free and floated above the others: His time in the field, his exploration of his own country, had only just begun. He was not cold, his stomach was not yet completely empty — he still had a little sausage and bread in his satchel. And, he finally realized, he wasn't scared. This was New York Island, after all, not the North Pole. He pitched his satchel over one shoulder and like a ghost passed silently through Turtle Bay. Once the village lights were behind him he walked more easily into the night. It never had been places that scared him, even unknown places. It always had been people.

The full vault of heaven presented itself above the orchards, its topography of stars obscured only by an occasional cloud in the foreground. As Guillaudeu walked below it, a great calm unfolded. He stopped frequently to stare upward into the cosmos, and he was comforted by the dispassion he sensed emanating from between the distant stars, from the great humming ether that presided over the city at his back, all people, oceans and continents, and perhaps even harbored the vessel USS *Happenstance*, Scipio's ominous figment, somewhere among the planets.

A barn disentangled itself from a dark thicket on the far side of a field, and it seemed to be unattached to any visible farmhouse. It might be a safe place to sleep. He left the road, angling toward the structure with the tall grasses whispering against his legs.

The barn was a huge, octagonal husk. Patches of siding were missing and a faint smoky odor made him think it had burned, though probably long ago. He walked inside the massive structure and among the stalls arranged like facets around the center. A tear in the roof broke the symmetry of the barn's design. Listening to birds mumbling in the rafters, he walked to the center of the hay-strewn earthen floor. The cobalt patch of sky contrasted with the blackened jagged roof, and Guillaudeu peered up through the hole as if it were a telescope. On some unknown cue, the birds took to the air. Crows, he saw, as they silently rose through the jagged portal. They dispersed into the unbounded world, each black dot tearing its own tiny hole in the heavens.

Guillaudeu pushed as much hay as he could into one of the stalls until he had a decent pallet. He curled there under his overcoat, using his satchel for a pillow. He tucked his clasped hands between his thighs, and when he closed his eyes he was standing at his beloved worktable. Pots of resin, pots of beeswax. Arsenic. Cochineal, calipers, excelsior, camphor. He relaxed. His world collapsed immediately into sleep.

Undulating light danced across his office wall even though the room's one window was blocked, as usual, by a curtain. He examined his tools, arms folded across his canvas butcher's apron. Scudder's voice was in his head, saying words he remembered from long ago: *The flawless preparation of a large mammal is a taxidermist's greatest feat and proof that he is a master of his craft.* He smiled because, in the present example, every initial measurement had been accurate. The first incision had been a perfect longitudinal line leading him into the work on a straight and righteous path. The skin had graciously parted from the muscle to receive its salt and arsenic. The bones agreed to their excavation, and the ligaments seemed to release their grip with gratitude. Harmony was what he felt as the herringbone stitch entered his mind and he remembered what he'd been looking for: waxed catgut thread and a curved needle. The skin of a human is decidedly thinner than all other animals, with obviously less hair. It would be impossible to hide the seams, and so his tidiest stitch, the herringbone, would do nicely.

Celia's manikin was masterfully prepared out of pine, iron, annealed wire, wax, Formula 9 papier-mâché, and her own bones. The manikin now stood apart from the worktable where Celia, as he'd known her, had ceased to be. Her new skeleton awaited the cloak of skin, and Guillaudeu obliged; he could smell the acrid scent of carpenter's glue and knew he must be quick about it.

Beginning at the head and working down, he used high-grade Dutch beeswax to perfect her brow ridge and eye sockets and fitted two blue glass eyes before laying the veil of skin over her skull. Arranging a specimen's eyelids always took longer than he expected, but he did not panic. He would finish before the glue became too sticky to work with. The neck needed a few minutes of attention — a few more layers of papier-mâché created the shape of the esophagus just so. He had sculpted her arms exactly right, as well as her chest and rib cage. He began sewing at her armpit, his stitches catching the shoulders, and then the arms, in place. He then sewed down her sides to the waist to secure her torso. He politely sewed her well-intentioned but now uncloven femininity and continued on his way down her legs. He finished at the ankles, where the cured skin tucked nicely into the tops of the plaster feet. He tied a neat knot and cut the thread. With growing excitement, he made the final arrangement of her features — applying wax, using tiny spatulas and dentist's tools to get the shape of her lips, and then resin to get the color.

Guillaudeu unbound her hair and combed it. He dressed her carefully in soft old underthings, her thick woolen stockings, and a muslin shift. He unhooked all the buttons down the back of her dark gray velvet dress and lifted it over her head. As he pulled the sleeves up over her newly arranged arms, the fabric slid gently into place. He buttoned her up and fitted her favorite lace collar about her neck. He coiled her hair into a bun and tied it with a gray silk ribbon. Into her crooked arms he placed *The Seraphim and Other Poems,* her favorite.

He took off his bloodied apron and stepped back. A work of art, he recalled from his years as Scudder's apprentice, is not complete until beheld by its audience. From the sheath of her newly donned skin, the specimen regarded him slyly. He circled her. The height, her posture, the expression, and the way she held the volume of poetry. He'd gotten her just right.

His triumph sent him directly to the waking world, where for a few moments he could not move. His heart raced. Where was he? Gradually he made out some form in the darkness. He smelled the faint charcoal of a fire long past and the hulking shape of the barn surrounding him. His heart rate calmed as he recognized his surroundings, but accelerated again as the shadow of his triumph returned and he recalled the dream to which it belonged.

Twenty-nine

Guillaudeu moved through the morning's unbroken silence slowly and deliberately. He'd decided to forgo the road for the orchards that lay on the other side of the barn and he moved beneath the gray and lichened branches with humility, inhaling the scent of the grass he trampled and accepting the dew as it soaked his trouser legs.

The night had been infinitely long and the taxidermist was incredulous that it had given way at all, especially to such a delicate dawn. Enveloped in this misty shield Guillaudeu did not feel apprehensive as he continued north; if he was trespassing, which he surely was, he could explain. He groped his satchel until he felt the smooth ridge of Linnaeus' spine within. He was not sure of the words he would use when faced with the angry landowner, but they certainly pertained to the importance of traveling in one's own country. What is the difference, really, between an orchard on New York Island and sublime Dalecarlia, when both are approached with the same sense of wonder and exacting eye of the naturalist?

He walked on, among browsing cattle, past farmhouses fragrant with wood smoke, and across the dreamlike landscape of blossoming apple trees. With his mind finally quiet, he took simple joy in his own meandering path. He walked on a small path through a wild meadow, and as he came over a mellow rise, he saw a brown shape in the grass. A person? He stopped. But his eye, accustomed to certain forms, soon recognized a bedded-down animal. As he came closer, it took shape as an ungulate. A few more steps and he was certain: It was a deer. He moved toward it in an exaggerated creep that would have made an observer laugh, but creeping was entirely unnecessary since this creature was entirely dead, and had been so for some time.

The carcass was in that peculiar stage of decomposition during which the opposing forces of desiccation and rot waged war and it was not at all clear which side would win or how the two coexisted at all. The skull, already bleached in places, had broken through layers of dried hide, yet from the bowel liquid still seeped, teeming with what manner of animalcules Guillaudeu could not guess. The buck had died with its forelegs outstretched and its hind legs tucked as if he had just leapt, indeed, over the great divide. A small set of antlers now tangled with the meadow grasses.

He counted three holes in the animal's side. Guillaudeu knew nothing of guns or hunting, but by the placement of the wounds he deduced that no single shot had killed the deer. In all likelihood the creature had made its way some distance before it succumbed. Had the hunters not pursued their prey? Had they been turned away by the owner of this meadow? Guillaudeu looked around as if that personage were lurking nearby. Why hadn't the property owner dressed the meat for himself? The spectacle of the deer's body disturbed him. The disarray, the holes, the way the fur drifted away from the carcass on the cool air, it was ominous and wrong. *Creatures should die for a reason*, he asserted suddenly, *and this one clearly has not. It's as good as murder!* Outraged, he squatted near the carcass, noting the delicate hooves and the sockets where the eyes had been. The grass was dead where the creature lay and soon he saw small worms making their way out of the rotting meat into the ground. Disgusting, he fumed, but he could not turn away.

He saw more movement within and around the carcass. It was not just a few worms; myriad tiny creatures scavenged upon the buck. Flies preyed on its eyes, bees swarmed its wounds, and now he noticed that what he had interpreted as bullet holes may actually have been pecked by crows or some other bird. The buck may have just died here of natural causes. It may have been lame or diseased. All manner of woodland creature have supped on this feast, he realized.

He moved a few feet away and sat on the grass. He watched the buck. He thought about his dream. *This* is what happened to Celia, not the other. Her body rotted away. She was absorbed into the earth and gave sustenance to insects. Guillaudeu considered these facts for a long while, and when he did not become angry or afraid, he moved on.

Thirty

He must have walked more easterly than he thought, because by midafternoon Guillaudeu came to the river and now he walked along the edge of a great salt marsh. He observed the spiral shells of snails moored to blades of cordgrass. The brown mud was pocked with bubbles, and along its sulfurous surface scuttled small armored creatures. Whether they were crabs, sea beetles, lobsters, or scorpions, Guillaudeu had no clue, but he welcomed his ignorance on the matter and enjoyed the sight of two sailboats scudding northward in the distance. He spotted a great egret, *Casmerodius albus*, not twenty feet from him. With one leg poised out of water, the white bird arched its long neck forward and from it the great yellow knife of the bill was aimed and ready. The bird's head inched minutely closer to the surface of the creek, and Guillaudeu sensed its prey approaching. The air tightened. Guillaudeu held his breath and the world hung in suspension for two long moments. Suddenly the bird had a slim fish in its bill and Guillaudeu shouted, "Hurrah!" With a languid movement, the egret then flapped itself into the sky and away.

When Guillaudeu turned to go, he faced a well-used sandy track angling to the northwest. He'd been in the wilderness most of the day and hesitated to join up with civilization just yet, but the other option would require him to wade through the salt marsh, so he climbed onto the road.

As soon as he saw the hamlet with its small wooden houses clustered around the intersection of two tracks and the sign welcoming him to Pension's Creek, Guillaudeu's hunger became very intense. He had gnawed the last of the sausage early that morning and all that remained of the bread were scattered crumbs at the bottom of his satchel. He had drunk from a creek and not thought much more about food until he saw the well-fed villagers going about their day.

Shall I pass as quickly through town as I can, or shall I knock on a door, any door, and beg for food? He was incredulous even to be contemplating it, but this was real hunger, something he hadn't endured since he was a boy. He passed one house after another, feeling a bit dizzy and unsure how, exactly, to go about asking for help. This was, after all, a voluntary circumstance. He passed a mercantile bustling with activity and a building with boarded-up windows. From the façade of the next building hung a whitewashed sign: ZETETIC SOCIETY AND MUSEUM. Museum? He'd landed at a museum.

He walked into the dim interior, brushing crumbs of drying mud and flakes of leaves off his jacket. A pale boy in a coat whose sleeves were much too short stood behind a wooden counter.

"Is the museum open?" Guillaudeu asked uncertainly.

"Well." The boy cleared his throat. He couldn't have been older than sixteen. He examined Guillaudeu suspiciously. "Yes, it's open." He straightened up to his full height. "We are the largest Zetetic Society in New York."

Guillaudeu peered beyond the boy into the shadowy room. "I'm not familiar with that particular society."

"What! Surely you've read the Symmes' Compendium?"

"I have not," Guillaudeu admitted, looking around the room, which held several glass vitrines, paintings and maps on the walls, and an abominable specimen of *Ursus americanus*. "But whoever stuffed that black bear should be ashamed of himself. I hope it wasn't you."

"I am not concerned with those flea-infested specimens," the boy explained, his hands folded in front of him. "We now

197

focus exclusively on the more relevant and exciting field of Inverse Cosmogony."

"Oh?"

The boy extended his hand toward the museum's small collection. "This exhibit honors the work of the magnificent John Symmes." He leaned forward in his enthusiasm; his red-rimmed eyes beseeched Guillaudeu with the barely re-strained fervor of a zealot. Guillaudeu stepped away.

"Symmes' theory of a hollow earth inhabited by a more heavenly race of man guides our exhibitions and our fund-raising efforts." The boy gestured to a tall glass jar with a few coins in it. "We are raising funds for a journey to the North Pole, so we may discover what John Symmes already knew to be true: Great portals await us, leading to new realms of lush geography and civilizations of man!"

Guillaudeu regarded the glass jar. "It appears you have enough to get your expedition partway to New York City."

The boy bristled. "We're well on our way, I can assure you."

The skin of the black bear's head had not been sufficiently attached to the manikin; it drooped obscenely, revealing the edge of the glass eye at one socket, and a blackened portion of the lower jawbone beneath the peeling gums. The beast had been intended to maintain a threatening posture, but now it seemed to recoil in horror, as if it had just seen itself in the mirror.

"Even though your museum clearly has . . . higher pur-suits, it is these more common examples of fauna that will lure newcomers into your establishment." Guillaudeu ges-tured to the bear and spoke as gently as he could. He'd formed a strategy. "It takes something familiar to bring them in. But once they are inside, they will encounter Symmes' theory and undoubtedly lend their support to your worthy expedition. Still, this bear will not attract anyone in its cur-rent state. Just look at it."

The boy obliged, tilting his head and frowning. "It is rather tattered."

"How will anyone take you seriously with this atrocity on your premises?" He paused for dramatic effect. "I can fix the bear's major failings in one hour." Guillaudeu finished with a flourish worthy of Barnum: "For I am a taxidermist."

The boy considered this for a moment, and then contemplated the glass jar on the counter.

"I couldn't pay you."

"A meal would be quite satisfactory."

The boy took him out to a barn behind the museum to look for tools. It was his uncle's museum, he finally revealed. Until that soul had died, just three months earlier, the collection illustrated the diversity and color of the New York Island flora and fauna. But the boy had moved most of that small collection into the barn to make way for Symmes.

The former proprietor had been an amateur taxidermist, at best. His tools were meager and of poor quality. But Guillaudeu still managed to find some decent glue that hadn't solidified, and a few sharp tools. He even found thread and a pot of black resin to repair the loose skin and darken the gums.

The work took nearly two hours and by the time he finished, the sun was setting. The bear was repaired and the boy was ready with a plate.

Guillaudeu had never had such a feast: brined beef and pickled cabbage, a small fillet of smoked trout, a hunk of fresh bread, peeled carrots, and a mug of beer. He sank onto the front steps of the museum, dizzy with hunger and delighted with himself. He was a barterer, a man of action, a sly negotiator! He could not see the boy standing behind him in the doorway, but the boy stared at Guillaudeu as if the taxidermist were a dangerous or deranged man. Guillaudeu relished the meal like no other and, later, also felt some relief that *Ursus americanus* was restored.

Once every month for the past eighteen years Guillaudeu stayed all night at his museum to fumigate. Armed with canisters of sulfur powder and camphor, he walked slowly among the galleries, puffing and squirting, thoroughly checking each specimen for signs of decay. The restoration of the bear, and the meal that was his reward, had temporarily banished the thought that this task was now overdue, and in his absence his own life's work was falling to ruin.

Thirty-one

He opened his eyes into predawn twilight. A bright orange fox, *Vulpes vulpes*, was near, stepping meticulously between blades of grass, its body taut, eyes targeting something in front of it. Even the bushy tail with its black-and-white tip was angled in an attentive curve. The small lean creature moved silently, its pointed muzzle leading it toward its breakfast. In a practiced assault, the fox arched back on its hind legs, leapt straight up in the air, and pounced into the grass. Guillaudeu sucked in his breath. The fox lifted its head, the spread wings of a sparrow caught in its jaw. The fox trotted off. Guillaudeu closed his eyes and went back to sleep.

He returned to consciousness thinking of an aviary. A hundred birds lived in what used to be Gallery Nine, on the east side of the fourth floor of the museum. Some of the cages were too crowded. There were complaints from museum visitors that it was dirty, smelly, crowded. What happens when birds don't have the materials to make nests? He envisioned the floors of the cages lined with soiled and broken eggs, birds crashing against the glass windows, starving and panicked. Any hatchlings would be pecked to death. Eaten. Had someone fed them since he'd been gone? How long had he been gone? How many birds had died? What about the snakes? The octopus? The whale?

Exactly in the position in which he'd slept, Guillaudeu stared up through the branches at the layers of wavering green shadow. A hive. A Chinese puzzle. A steam engine.

The rogue echo of Barnum's words returned. The place shifted and transformed under the myriad gaze of the public. A steam engine. A puzzle. The deeper you go, the less you know. The words formed an incantation that Guillaudeu also applied to his journey on foot across New York Island. Barnum's was an endeavor that invited chaos into its design. Guillaudeu watched the fluttering leaves for a moment and then closed his eyes. Just like nature herself, he thought. No system exists that does not contain the element of the unknown, the egret's razor beak hovering above the water, or that moment you realize your purse has been stolen and you are far from home.

The crack of a gun made him jump to his feet. Leaves fell from him. He was cold but not unrested. There had been no nightmares. He looked around, unsure from which direction the shot had been fired. He had made a nest for the night in a copse of sassafras trees. Beyond them to the west was someone's orchard. Ahead of him northward was woods. Beyond that, he did not know.

From behind came the sounds of several men walking through tall grass, their low voices alternating in conversation. Guillaudeu stood unmoving as the flannel-jacketed trio saw him. From a rope slung over one man's shoulder hung two foxes, still dripping blood from their mouths, their tails adorning the man's neck like a woman's stole. Guillaudeu raised his hand in greeting, or surrender; the men acknowledged him, he thought, and kept on walking.

After his meal with the Symmes fanatic he had stayed on the thoroughfare for a few miles until he came to a walking track veering off westward. He'd followed that between properties and through wild thickets until he found the sassafras copse. Now, as he gathered his things and started off again, his hip ached in its socket and he favored his right foot. The sole of his left shoe had thinned and the ball of his foot was bruised. He picked up a stout branch to use as a staff. He had passed beyond the margins of his known world, and in his aching muscles and stiff back he felt his age: A younger man would have traveled more quickly, observed more, never would have had his purse stolen in the Points, he thought. But he had done it — slipped into the lifestream beyond the walls of his office. Slipped into a world of chaos, the only real world. And it had not devoured him, at least not yet.

The woods were dim and the branches around him were mostly dead, choked out of the light by the upper reaches of trees. Here was a mixture of pines and maples, sassafras and alder. A group of tiny gray birds flitted above him.

An aviary, he recalled. A real aviary was what the museum needed. All the birds out of cages living together in one big gallery. Trees could be planted. A water feature — a spring and pool of some kind — would be constructed in which they could bathe and preen. Maybe the sloth could live there, too. He wondered if anyone was feeding the beluga whale. Had the orang-outang starved to death? He looked down, watched one foot go ahead of the other. His trouser hem had frayed. The sleeves of his jacket were splattered with mud. He ran a hand across his cheek and felt bristles. An aviary where different birds lived and nested all together and could be observed by the people of New York.

When the woods thinned and then dropped entirely away he found himself standing on the skyward edge of a great escarpment hundreds of feet above a plain of waving grasses. Far below, four horses galloped, riderless, across the savanna. Almost level with him, riding the upward air currents near the rock face, soared several large birds. Hawks, probably. Too small to be vultures.

Granite outcroppings dotted the flats below and the high cliff continued northward. He walked its edge, marveling at the landscape. In the distance he saw the East River curving westward. From the other direction came the Hudson. He was looking across the Harlem plains.

He walked across the tops of granite outcroppings the size of his apartment building, heavily lichened and bearing the petroglyphic markings of water and time. He passed a boulder that had been split by a maple tree growing up through it and now lay in leaf-covered halves. He felt as if he were walking through the ancient epochs, medieval times or even earlier. He walked until he saw a path winding down to lower ground. Following it with his eyes, it stretched all the way to a village at the edge of the Hudson. "The Spuyten Duyvil ferry," he breathed, amazed to see something familiar in this wilderness. This ferry docked at the Christopher Street port, near the terminus of Franklin Street. He saw the moored ferry almost every day and had never given it an ounce of thought. He looked southward down the river, where several boats steamed or sailed toward the city. His heart lifted. He started down the path.

A lone woman stood at the end of the dock with a swarm of gulls banking above her.

She focused exclusively on her task, standing sturdily against the wind. She held part of a dinner roll aloft in her outstretched hand. Her olive-green shawl had come half unwrapped and one end of it fluttered behind her. She seemed not to notice. Guillaudeu walked onto the dock. River water lapped the pilings and Guillaudeu felt light, like he barely inhabited this world. Banners of sunlight on the silty water waved like the flags of Barnum's Aerial Garden. A sailboat tacked across the Hudson and Guillaudeu watched its pilot duck when the boom came across.

The woman took in his ragged clothes and tousled hair.

"Good morning," he offered.

"Yes," said the woman, brushing a brown-and-silver strand of hair away from her pursed mouth. She wagged the roll toward the gulls. He watched her.

"I don't know why they won't take the bread. They insist on fluttering around and endlessly bickering." She was irritated, her voice surprisingly gruff. And British.

"Maybe they're not hungry," he offered.

The gulls dipped and hovered. The woman tossed the bread into the air and recoiled from the screaming tangle of gray wings that dived upon it. Guillaudeu leapt back too, shielding his head with his arms. She pulled another roll out of her handbag and started again. Without turning from the gulls, she tore the roll in half and offered a piece to Guillaudeu. He ate it.

The ferry appeared, chugging northward toward them. The woman tossed the rest of the bread over the water and the gulls attacked it as it floated. She was older than he'd thought at first. Maybe even fifty. Her hazel eyes were attentive and her movements decisive. She looked him over again.

"I'm hoping to catch this ferry," Guillaudeu said. He felt oddly calm, unafraid of speaking frankly. "But someone stole my money several days ago."

"I'm sorry, I don't have anything to spare." She brushed the crumbs from her hands and started to walk away.

"Please wait." Guillaudeu hoped he didn't sound too desperate. He fumbled with his satchel. He had only one thing to offer.

"Here," he said. "This is all I have to offer."

"A book?" She stopped, curious.

"Linnaeus."

She came over and took the book from him. "The 1812 edition. The best one." She opened it up and scanned a page or two. "How much?"

"Two dollars."

"Enough for the ferry."

"Yes."

"It's a deal."

He handed over the book and took her money. For him the transaction was strangely intimate: She now held the pages that had spurred his journey in the first place, and her money would get him home.

"It's true what he says, you know." Guillaudeu pointed at the book. "You must have experience, real experience, to complement reason and book learning. That combination makes one a wise observer of life."

"The combination of experience and reason *is* life," the woman said. "Experience, reason, and perhaps a little stubbornness. Yes, that ought to do it." She laughed then, her face creasing to wrinkles around her eyes. "An observer of life is trapped in the margins, probably taking excessive notes."

Struck mute, Guillaudeu helplessly returned her not-unfriendly gaze.

"What a lovely coincidence to be presented with Linnaeus by a wandering philosopher," she said, shaking her head. Given a few more moments Guillaudeu probably would have thought of something to say, but the blast from the approaching ferry rattled his brain, and within seconds a small crowd of people poured out of the ferry landing's tavern and streamed onto the dock. The woman hurried toward the gangway.

The whole way back, Guillaudeu stood outside, his jacket wrapped tightly around him and his cap pulled down. He watched the passing landscape and gradually the thickets, orchards, fields, and villages of New York Island lost their intricacies and shrank smaller and smaller, until they fit into a foot-long diorama and could be seen only through the lenses of a brass Cosmorama viewer.

She Stands Up Again

Thirty-two

My wooden booth stood twelve feet high by six feet wide and five feet deep, with a door built into the side for me to duck through and a front counter the height of an average person's waist. The two carpenters had regularly disappeared from the job, probably called to some remote region to build animal cages, so the booth had remained unfinished until now, and I had occupied it without the benefit of paint or a sign. I had requested red and gold, and it had (finally) been admirably done in pinstripes all the way around, with a kind of faux gilt around the front. At my request the sign simply read MISS ANA SWIFT, THE WORLD'S ONLY GIANTESS.

The counter held stacks of new lithographs and a basket of Giant's Rings, given to visitors in exchange for a nickel. I had requested shelves underneath the front counter so I could stow a few things for my convenience: a shawl, several bottles of Cocadiel's Remedy. On a specially built ledge at my eye level, out of sight of the visitors, I put a volume of poetry. This was a luxury I had never yet known while working, and it was a great relief to think of reading a few lines as the hours passed.

The True Life History was already fifteen pages long and swerved hopelessly back and forth in its chronology. Eventually I would revise it but for now the simple act of writing mesmerized me: the symmetry of a stately *H*, the *r*'s small plateau, the continuing scrawl that could include any fancy, true or otherwise, that my mind could spawn. I had not written anything since my letters to you, Mother, and it was a strange relief, pouring memory into the imprecise mold of words. Writing is an imperfect alchemy. Why manufacture phrases to describe thoughts and imaginations that have nothing to do with an alphabet, with these scratched signs? Words have histories that span centuries, and what does that have to do with me? On the other hand, writing is a manifestation of our pathetic, inborn determination to leave a trace of ourselves, no matter how flimsy, to persevere beyond death. The journal is the simplest of legacies, the most intimate reflection of the supreme foolishness and arrogance of man and evidence of his most valuable illusion: *I matter.*

I recalled the recent story of Captain McCaffrey's failed attempt to reach the North Pole. After enduring countless dreadful hardships and exposing his men to his own acute case of polar mania, McCaffrey led his crew, one after another, to icy death. Near the end, after everything else had been abandoned, the captain sacrificed the lives of his last two men in an attempt to drag a trunk full of his journals onward, over the endless ice. One year later a team of Norwegians on skis found Captain McCaffrey's body draped dramatically over the trunk in a permanent, frozen embrace. So the journals were recovered, but the problem remains: All the valiant determination described in those pages was made ridiculous and void by the absurdity of McCaffrey's fate.

Despite this example, I squeezed pleasure from the act of transcribing my thoughts and also the simple momentum of the pen filling page after page. I wrote as if the True Life History were my last will and testament. I hunched over the front counter of my booth, staining my fingers with ink, until the visitors came in great numbers and began to whisper, wondering what a giantess could possibly have to write about, and I hid it away.

Out on the balcony Thomas played Lanner's Separation Waltz, one of my favorites. I affixed my gaze to the shaggy musk ox head mounted on the opposite wall and prepared to succumb to the hours. Randomly, a young couple danced across the gallery, disregarding everyone else on earth. I followed their progress without moving my head. They bumped Pa-Ib's glass casket and sprang away in a whirl and laughter. Envy misted my sight, but the lovers were not its object. It was Thomas who had conjured my reaction, sitting out of sight in his threadbare coat, the vagabond prodigy with ragged stubble across his chin and his eyes perhaps closed. His particular magic, his contribution to humanity floated, bodiless, on the air. It emanated from him, but it did not depend on the spectacle of his person. He had no idea of the waltzing lovers, but here they were, the consequence. He provoked the classical feelings of love and rapture, a range of emotions captured in the music of the masters. I, on the other hand, was responsible for (indeed, made my living by) the basest emotions: voyeurism, astonishment, and weird taboo. And I accomplished this by doing nothing, just providing my body.

Two hours later, this rumination led to my humiliation. It was a small leap from the effects of music to those of poetry, and from there it was a very small distance indeed to reach my beloved volume, *Collected Poems for a New Age,* on the shelf below me. I had arrived at the awful idea of sharing a few lines with the world.

Into the river of brightly colored bodies and the cacophony of voices in the gallery, I added my own. I put on my shawl, stepped out of my booth, opened the book to page seventy-three, and funneled my voice into a booming, yet, I hoped, inviting, timbre:

"In ev'ry age, and each profession,
Men err the most by prepossession;
But when the thing is clearly shown,
And fairly stated, fully known,
We soon applaud what we deride,
And penitence succeeds to pride."

Christopher Smart had long been my favorite poet, partly because he produced what the world considered his finest work only after he had been caged in a debtor's insane asylum for years.

"A certain Baron on a day
Having a mind to Show away,
Invited all the wits and wags,
Foot, Massey, Shuter, Yates, and Skeggs,
And built a large commodious stage,
For the choice Spirits of the age."

Under Mr. Ramsay's tutelage I had learned oratorical techniques and had recited countless passages, mostly from Shakespeare. Though I never detected much of a response from the audience, they always gave me a polite applause, and reciting a few verses never failed to excite me. Even now I felt heat rising into my face and a nervous constriction of breath. I didn't look up from the page, but I heard the silence spreading.

"But above all, among the rest,
There came a Genius who profess'd
To have a curious trick in store,
Which never was performed before."

"Look at 'er!" It was the hoarse voice of an old man. "She's red as a apple!"

"And tall as an apple tree!" a second voice responded to the call. The crowd then released an alarming amount of laughter. The sheer volume of it was more than I thought possible for a group of twenty people, and as I stood there, momentarily stunned by the wave of voices, I could hear each one individually: a woman's cackle hovering above a child's thoughtless squawk. And men's voices, so many of them, all twisting together into a thick, ropy sound. Their vulgarity was a shame: The poem was actually very good, and funny, but they didn't hear it.

Then I saw Beebe among them. He was looking straight at me, gently jostled by the crowd. He wouldn't approach me, would he? Don't make it worse, Beebe. As the din quieted, I realized he was clapping. My oppressors dispersed quickly, but Beebe remained, giving applause that I appreciated until it went on too long and I gestured for him to stop.

"Was that something you wrote?"

"Oh, no, and I hadn't even gotten to the interesting part yet."

"I've been wondering when I'd see you."

"I'm not terribly hard to find," I snapped, suddenly aware that I was standing in a glorified box. I could just nail up the front and save people the trouble of making a coffin!

"You know, tomorrow evening the choir is performing hymns. At Saint Paul's."

"Oh? What's the occasion?"

"It's the eve of Easter Sunday." He appeared to be examining the Giant's Rings.

"Is it Easter again already?"

Another familiar figure entered the gallery, leading what appeared to be a miniature army. Elizabeth Crawford, patron saint of orphans. She gestured her charges toward the balcony and, catching my eye, gave a little wave and swerved toward my booth.

"Oh, Miss Swift! How do you do?" She tipped her head, which had a tiny velvet hat upon it. Beebe responded with a barely audible *Ma'am.*

"Miss Crawford. Who have you got today?"

"They're from the Bowery Boys' Home. Most of them" — she lowered her voice — "are *criminals.*"

"Exciting," I said.

"But I notice that even they, hardened as they are, have become quite pale in the presence of Pa-Ib."

Miss Crawford had made it a habit to seek me out whenever she visited the museum, which was at least twice a week. She was always gracious and seemed genuinely interested in the trifles I came up with when she asked me how I fared. She curtsied gracefully and let two little boys jerk her deeper into the museum.

Beebe stood blinking at me, one of his hands jingling a handful of Giant's Rings. "Would you like to come?"

"Where?"

"To Saint Paul's. Our choir is quite good. And Easter is one of my favorite holy days."

"Do you sing in it, Mr. Beebe?" Certainly, attending a church would be an abhorrent act, but the prospect of poor Beebe singing in a choir somehow melted me.

"Well, I'm not the star performer, but yes, I do my best."

"Then I'd be honored to attend. Are you sure it's all right with your superiors?"

"Everyone is welcome at Saint Paul's, I can assure you."

"I may not be able to sit in a pew," I warned.

"Why not? There's no rule that only Believers can sit down," Beebe ventured.

"How do you know that I'm not a Believer?"

"I just assumed, but forgive me if —"

"I meant simply that I will not fit comfortably on a pew."

"Ah. Oh. I see."

"Don't worry, Mr. Beebe. The pew will be fine, as long as the concert is not terribly long."

That evening, I was horrified to find the conjoined twins sitting at Maud's whist table. Maud gave me a small shrug as I entered the room, and she gestured me to the chair opposite them. I should have expected that Maud would make them my partner, although the truth was, I preferred anyone to Olrick, who now sat across from Maud.

"I'm Jacob," one of the twins offered, giving no indication, in gaze or gesture, of the debacle that had occurred not twenty-four hours earlier.

"And I'm the Angel," said the other, nodding his head.

"Oh, come on," his brother said. "He's Matthew."

"We didn't realize the fifth floor had a high society of its own," said Matthew. "But now that we're on the inside," he whispered, "we won't tell anyone else." Jacob reached across their chest and dipped his hand into the far waistcoat pocket. Matthew slapped his brother's wrist. "Get out!"

"Oh, they won't mind if we have a little tipple, surely?" Jacob looked around the table.

"As a matter of fact" — of course Olrick would object — "I believe the museum is *dry*."

"That's what you think," snipped Jacob.

"It may be best to refrain for now, gentlemen," said Maud, shuffling the cards expertly. "But the night is very young." She winked.

The twins and I took the first two hands, but they were unskilled and drunk. Olrick and Maud took the next three, and they eventually won the first game. Maud made tea. I wanted to get back to my room, to leave the dull company of my brethren for the dullness of my own thoughts.

"I have an announcement," said Olrick, once he had a cup and saucer in his hand. "I've found a new manager in the form of Mr. Lawrence Bloom, who approached me several weeks ago."

"Mr. Bloom. Where do I know that name?" Jacob said, leaning toward his brother.

"He manages Miss Luella at Vauxhall Gardens," Matthew reported from behind his cards. "He's got people in Philadelphia, too. At the Melodeon. We know him."

"Ah," said Olrick.

"Scoundrel," muttered Jacob.

"Aren't they all?" finished Matthew, looking into his tea.

"They are," I confirmed.

"Well, I found him quite agreeable, with a contract for sixty dollars a week, which is ten more than Barnum offered. He guaranteed engagements not only in New York but also in Philadelphia."

I tried to hide my surprise at the discrepancy between our salaries. I made thirty dollars a week. Olrick's duties were significantly less than mine. He did not wander as I did. He did not even have a booth. He performed three times a week and twice on Saturdays, in the theater, in the company of General Tom Thumb and one of the professors.

"I am telling you this because Mr. Bloom has advised me

215

to leave Barnum's employ, and that is what I intend to do. He does not expect the museum to last another year."

"But it's only just begun," said Maud.

"Barnum is on Mayor Harper's blacklist. Mr. Bloom said —"

"That's only because Barnum is making more money than the mayor," said Jacob. "It's only because Harper isn't getting a cut."

"That may be true, but there are lots of safer venues in the city. In terms of stability," Olrick went on, a bit defensively.

"He has us *living* here, Olrick." Maud was getting annoyed. I hadn't realized her allegiance. "How much more stability do you want?"

"There are simply too many strange variables here. What about the beluga whale? It's been three months since the museum opened and the tank still isn't finished. It leaks, in fact. When is he going to finish it? Where is Barnum, anyway?"

"If he finished the beluga tank," said Jacob, reaching successfully for the flask, "where would the Indians live? And what would happen to our privacy? We would have gawkers right outside our door. I much prefer it this way."

"I'm not here to argue," huffed Olrick, setting down his tea and rising to his full height. "I simply wanted to alert you to the possible danger of staying here. Mr. Bloom said he wouldn't be surprised if Harper makes some kind of action against Barnum. There. That's all. I'm finished." He stormed out the door, ending our whist game.

"Some people," said Jacob, pouring a trickle of whiskey into his tea, "simply do not have the correct attitude for this business." He raised his glass. "Here's to the rest of us."

Thirty-three

I sat squarely on the pew with my tightened thighs supporting my lower half. Even so, terrible splinters of pain emanated from each of my spine's compressed vertebra. *You will
not take me so soon, will You?* The last time I'd been in a church
it was in Pictou-by-the-sea, and I was a child of average
height. *I am meant to live longer than the rest of my kind. That is
Your plan, isn't it?* An elderly woman in an unbecoming green
hat gaped at me, and I narrowed my eyes at her. My belief in
God had vanished as abruptly as my normalcy, and so wasn't
it nonsense to address him?

The service was an impenetrable tangle spewed forth by a
man made virtually invisible by a voluminous white robe.
He perched inside the pulpit like a dove in a cage, emitting
bits of an elaborate song: the disciples' sacred ignorance and
the so-called key to the Kingdom of God. These words did
not move me, except by spurring in me a desire to move
away from this church and everyone in it. But I had accepted
Beebe's invitation to listen to his choir, and I intended to
hear it. I shifted my weight as best I could and ignored the
hag in the hat.

Outside, evening had darkened the sky to oxblood. The
church was lit rather magnificently by hundreds of thick
yellow candles. *You know this is not my place. This is not my
story. You must be mad to think I could believe in this pomp and
posturing.*

Did the gathered flock truly believe that a Jesus of Nazareth, citizen of a distant desert country so many centuries ago, would return, would not only walk among the living but also offer supreme salvation to all Believers? Must I always take the sour perspective, as Maud points out again and again? But really. If Jesus appeared in this city, I'd wager he would be selling something. I snorted. But it would have to be something useful to people during their lifetimes. The promise of salvation after death would be too simple of a hoax. The whole thing sounded amateurish. No one would believe him.

The rector's twittering finally came to an end. The choir rose. I spotted Beebe in the first row in a scarlet robe, the hymnal held out in front of him. The organ blasted a frightening chord into the universe, as if the church were a machine grinding into life, perhaps rising on mechanical legs to lurch up Broadway toward heaven, or somewhere.

Arise, Sons of the Kingdom, indeed! The choir began their hymn as if their voices kept the sun on its accustomed track, each man's mouth becoming a small black O, and then a line, each man's body responding to the music as if all human life depended on it. I noticed Beebe's blissful expression in particular as he leaned into the verses.

Without self-consciousness, Beebe sang with his brethren about the apparent imminent return of God's only son. It was obvious he was actually singing *to* God. Eyes closed, even his hair popping upward, suppliant. This was his true face, and I found I did not want to see Beebe exposed in this way but I could not look away. The very thing that would sanctify him in another woman's heart made me recoil. Would everything that brought him joy either irritate or amuse me?

When the service ended, Beebe walked directly to me with his robe fluttering out behind.

"Miss Swift! I was delighted to see you in the audience."

"The church is beautiful. What a sunset."

"We are blessed that our windows face west."

"Blessed? It seems a purely architectural design."

"It's the same thing."

"I don't see how. One is divinely sent, the other created by the will of man."

Beebe smiled. Patronizingly, it seemed. "God's hand is evident in all our pursuits."

"Even the murder that happened last night in Corlear's Hook? That girl who had her neck slashed ear-to-ear?" I had not meant to slip, to spit this venom.

His expression intensified my regret. "I'm sorry." But of course I could not control myself. "I just mean to say, it is the architecture of the church that we refer to. Exact measurements and angles. Foresight. And the sunset itself is a product of nature, the natural turning of our planet and the effects of shifting light, which operates without interference by any supernatural being. Our emotions are a reaction to this natural beauty."

"It is God's unbounded mercy that gave us this wondrous life," Beebe said simply. "And it is our task while we're here to live gratefully in the face of His many wonders." He looked at me pointedly. "Wonders that arrive in all shapes and sizes."

"Well," I muttered, smiling. "That's one way to look at it."

Beebe stepped closer. "I would like to show you where I live, upstairs," he whispered. "But we must wait until the congregation leaves, and the senior warden, too. Stay here until the congregation is gone, and then leave by the front entrance. Around the back of the church is another door. Wait there for me."

"Is the secrecy really necessary?"

"Guests are not allowed upstairs," Beebe confided. "Also no one knows that I work at the museum."

"You're keeping it a secret?"

"They wouldn't approve. They don't exactly understand my faith."

I had to laugh. "Nor do I, Mr. Beebe. But so far the intrigue is quite entertaining."

"Coming from you, I will take that as a great compliment." He bowed playfully and stepped away.

I strolled the length of the church, avoiding the stares of both congregation and icon. Instead, I enjoyed being in a space whose proportions fit me comfortably, if not its contents.

When all but a few stragglers had left the church, I made my way out, deftly avoiding the eager gaze of the rector, whose desire to convert the unbelieving apparently was not strong enough to overcome his fear of speaking to a giantess.

The rector did not see me angle around behind the trees in front of the church, perhaps the same trees to which Barnum had tied the banners that had lured Beebe to the darker side of Broadway. I walked along the mossy wall of the building and into a quiet graveyard that I had not even known was there. The names carved on the knee-high slabs were too far below to read as I moved among them. The grass was lush and swished against my skirts. Without the distraction of daylight it was easier to feel the bitter rise of spring, the acidic smell of soil parting for the blind thrust of life. In Pictou they'd be tilling, I thought, but who *they* might be I didn't know; you are gone, and he left Pictou years ago. Even though some other family must surely inhabit it, I always imagined the farm decrepit, its doors banging in the wind during winter and bleaching when it's hot.

I walked to the other side of the churchyard and saw the museum. It came into view slowly, like the SS *Great Western* powering across the Atlantic. In the dark, from this different perspective, the museum was a great living thing: Black shapes streamed into its gaping maw in a constant flow upward, its food and fuel. Like a hundred blinking eyes, the building glowed from every window, and from the rooftop, the ascendant beam of Barnum's Drummond light presided over it all like a great, beckoning antenna. What was the museum signaling? What did it want from us?

"Miss Swift!"

I jumped at the sound, though it was only Beebe.

"They're all gone," Beebe whispered fiercely. "Usually the senior warden stays here at the chapel, but the rector called him to serve another congregation for Easter, so he's off to Manhattanville tonight by carriage. Come in, come in."

He stood in a disturbingly small doorway with his hair askew, still in his choir robe. "Follow me, Miss Swift."

I squeezed into a stone passageway. I had to stoop and within ten paces knots of muscle along my spine vibrated in protest. Steps led upward, and I twisted my body around the tight spiral, my feet hanging off the edge of each step. I grasped the stone banister with both hands, in case the steps, which had supported decades of clergymen, gave way under the weight of the infidel.

In Beebe's stone room, several lamps illuminated an unexpected jungle. Potted plants lined the sill of one large window and covered his small bookcase and bedside table, even spilling over much of the floor. His small desk, too, was covered mostly with clay pots, with only a small clearing for his brown leather Bible, whose cover was sprinkled with crumbs of dry soil.

"My primary duty here as junior warden is to care for the grounds," Beebe told me.

I brushed my hand across the fine green blades in one pot. "This one appears to be grass," I observed.

"Yes. The senior warden tells me it's silly to keep it, but I'll plant it outside when it gets a bit warmer. It was dug up for a burial last October and I hated to see it all die. I kept just a small amount."

"Naturally. And this?" I looked into a pot with one ghostly white shoot coming up.

"A crocus. I mean to plant those by the chapel door. I have an apple sapling, too, that the rector approved for near the front gate. The rector wants the grounds to remain simple, but you'd be surprised how many different things come up out there, blown here or dropped by birds, even here, in the heart of the city. All summer I must pull them up, flowers, vegetables, even. I plant as many as I can in here and give them away."

"Or keep them."

"Yes." Beebe turned this way and that, looking into pots

and inadvertently dragging his robe sleeves across them. *You are tangled with life, Beebe. You have one foot in the church, one foot in the museum, and both hands occupied by the fecund earth. And your heart? Could it be wide enough to hold a giantess?*

I sat on the edge of his bed; the chair he'd offered would have snapped like kindling. "Tell me, Mr. Beebe, why you are working for Mr. Barnum."

"Oh, oh I see. Yes." He straightened up and brushed his hands on his robe, leaving dark smudges. "You're probably curious." He stood directly in front of me. "I would be, I suppose."

I smiled. *We could go far away from here, Beebe. West, to the Territories, and make a home somewhere on the prairie, where the skies are wide enough to dwarf me. We'll watch the weather come across miles of open ground. If you like, we could even keep hogs.*

Beebe clasped his hands in front of him, appearing for a moment like a failed saint in his disheveled robe.

"I was in the seminary, as you know. Here, in New York. But right away I knew it was no good for me. It might have been different, if I was anywhere else but this city. But maybe not. Maybe I would have thought the same thing if I was out in the country somewhere. You see, the life of faith cannot be separate from the commonplace. It won't work for monks and clergy to be all the way over here" — he extended his left arm — "and the rest of humanity over here." He extended his right arm. "That's just not going to work."

"What do you mean, *work*? Is there a specific goal for that kind of life?"

"If holy men are separated by the clothes they wear, the way they talk, where they live, then they are not going to relate to the common man, and therefore they will not touch them with the Holy Spirit. And if they don't do that, then more people will be destroyed, who could be lifted to meet Jesus in the air. The Rapture will be swift as lightning."

Please, Beebe. Go no further. But of course I had to know more: "So why did you choose the museum? You could have worked at any trade in the world. Was it simply because you knew Barnum from Bethel Parish?"

"The way I see it is this: To immerse oneself in the world of vice is to give oneself the best opportunity to walk in true faith and touch many with the Holy Spirit. It was God's will that hung that banner across Broadway, Miss Swift, and brought me into the museum."

I rose to my feet. The top of my head brushed Beebe's ceiling. We will not go to the Territories, will we, Beebe? Thunderheads rushed away over a great, distant prairie.

"To declare that I am part of your world of vice is insulting in the extreme, Mr. Beebe."

Beebe's face crumpled in confusion. "What?"

"Vice, Mr. Beebe. Evil, degrading, immoral, wicked, and corrupt." I spat the words down on him as he peered up, a chick in the nest discovered by a fox. "I see that I am simply your dare with the devil, and I have no interest in indulging your conceit any further."

"That's not what I meant. Miss Swift! Ana." His voice hushed as he spoke my Christian name.

"Whether it is what you meant or not, you are still exposed."

"You are not at all sinful in my eyes!"

"I will not be judged by you, of all people, with that ridiculous fairy tale you cling to so fervently."

"Wait!"

I ducked out of the room and in a few strides was into the twisting stairwell. Even clutching the railing, my momentum was too great in the narrow passageway and I lost control, skidding down several steps before lurching backward to hit first my shoulder, then my head, against the wall. One leg flew forward, the other buckled, and I finally hit the stairs squarely on my bottom. I thought I heard the chapel's foundation creak. Wedged in place, I held my breath as my twisted right knee exploded in pain.

"God damn it all to bloody hell," I seethed. I opened my eyes and saw Beebe standing above me at the top of the stairs. He was shocked, frozen in place. "Don't play the innocent with me, Beebe. Working at the museum your delicate ears have heard much worse than that!"

"Are you all right? My goodness, are you hurt?" He took a step and reached vaguely in my direction.

"Just get out of my way and I'll be rightways up and out of this cursed tunnel." Using the banister as a crutch I crawled endlessly upward, balancing my weight on my left leg. I braced one arm on each side of the passageway and hopped down a step. I squeezed my eyes shut against the ricocheting ball of pain shooting up my spine.

"Please, allow me to accompany you, to see that you —"

"Certainly not." I hopped down another step, then another, and then I was around the corner and out of Beebe's sight. "Don't you follow me," I growled.

"Miss Swift, please! You have misunderstood my —"

I let out an ugly laugh. "I assure you that I have misunderstood neither you nor your intentions. Just to be perfectly clear, I will never be converted to your faith. And how could we be . . . friends, if you think I am sinful?"

"I never said that!" His voice was fading. At least he had heeded me not to follow.

"You didn't need to," I finished, and emerged into moonlight.

I hobbled away from Saint Paul's with my eyes upon the museum door, where the flow of visitors marched on. William the ticket-man saw me coming and hurried out of his booth.

"What in heaven's name happened to you?" He passed his arm partly around my waist; by placing my hand on his shoulder I was able to alleviate some pressure from my right leg. "Gideon! Wake up, you scalliwag!" The bleary-eyed boy popped into view from behind the counter.

William escorted me across the waxworks and into the back stairwell, which, thankfully, appeared to be deserted.

"What happened, Miss Swift?" William was quite breathless beside me.

"I went to church."

"Church? Whatever did you do that for?"

I sighed. "I don't know, William. I made a mistake."

Up and up we went, each step wrenching more of my spirit away. William, on his old man's legs, tried his best to help support me, but it made little difference.

"Could you just go up to the restaurant and get the biggest pot of scalding water from Gustav, William? That would be such a help."

"Of course." He continued up as I made my way onto the fifth floor.

In my room, I drank half a bottle of Cocadiel's Remedy. By the time the bitter syrup turned to blessed numbness in my veins, William had delivered the hot water and I'd shooed him away. I opened a jar of salts and dumped the gray crystals into the water. I shed my shoes, shirtwaist, skirt, and corset, pulled the steaming pot close to my bed, sat, and lowered my feet into it. I dampened a washcloth and pressed the hot compress against my shoulder, then my forehead. I pulled the quilt around myself. I won't be able to walk my rounds tomorrow. I'll need a suitable chair to bring to my booth. Perhaps there's a large one in the theater, backstage? I'll get Gideon to find one in the morning. Blast those steps! Both my legs throbbed gently in the water and I passed the damp cloth along them.

Maybe to remove the specter of Beebe as he stood at the top of the stairwell staring down at me, or to reassure myself after our disconcerting altercation, I pulled the True Life History from the bedside table to my lap and took up my pen.

If only I were not burdened with the memory of a life before I grew monstrous, I would not be touched by the affliction of hope.

Hope? Visible on paper, the word lay exposed as evidence of what had been lurking in the back of my mind. I had spent years of my surely abbreviated life as an entertainment, observing the disappointing ignorance of men (and myself) that keeps us chained to the charade of our habits, the affectation and infinite pettiness of daily life. There is no pleasure in viewing a disembodied arm in a jar of alcohol, a savage from a distant country, or a deformity such as myself, except the most fleeting vulgarity. Was it hope for a different life, then, that had urged me out of this museum and into a life with someone like Beebe? Or was my hope merely a perversion, since I cannot actually leave the spectacle of my body no matter where I go, except by suicide?

I am certain my hand would not falter in discharging my final exit, if that is the way I chose, except that a problem arises in the thought of my body left behind, helplessly vulnerable to unknown humiliations. The idea of someone pacing my length, scratching his head and wondering how he'll transport the body, and someone else lifting my cold arm to press his tiny hand to my lifeless paw, even these mild images unleash the most sublime terror in me; I could never let that happen.

If only I were not burdened with the memory of my life before I grew. The sunlight of Pictou suddenly bathed my face. I sat behind my parents, safely dwarfed in childhood, facing the way we'd come, my little legs dangling off the end of the wagon. We bounced behind the mule's uneven trot, through ribbons of sunlight, between boughs studded with blossoms. They laughed together as we drove away from the harbor, away from our farmhouse, across wild meadows that were the most beautiful, seething colonies of life.

Clutched in my hands, a glass jar with cheesecloth for a lid. Tufts of drying grass lay at the bottom of it with a few leaves and the tiny branch that bore a gently swinging cocoon. Every few minutes I examined this pea-green jewel, to make sure I had not missed the butterfly coming out.

"You hang on tight, Ana. The hill's coming up." My father's voice. Lost to me for all these years, yet there it was. But I would not put down the jar to hold on. Instead, I lay back among the damp nets, my family laughing again as we went up, up, into the bright sun.

I stayed in the wagon while my father unhitched the mule and let her loose to graze in the pasture. He came for me, then, even let me bring the jar with us. He lifted me up; I was a pretty feather in his arms, and I can smell his sweat and the sea in the memory.

"Here's a butterfly," he said, swinging me lightly in the air before setting me on the ground. He took my hand and we walked together to where all our friends had gathered near the church door.

If only he'd known what a bizarre metamorphosis we would undergo, maybe he could have prepared himself better. Within six years neither he nor I went to church anymore. She was the only one who did, hitching up the mule and riding up the hill alone as if nothing had changed. As if a line halfway to our neighbor's house did not form every Saturday at our farm, as if she did not walk the length of that line selling muffins and homemade peanut brittle to the strangers as they waited for their chance to see me in a homemade booth in back of our barn, out of sight of the road. It was his idea: one day a week for a couple of years, until we could pay off the boat. But he couldn't bear to see it with his own eyes. He always went fishing on Saturdays, leaving it to us and Fletcher's brother, who came up from Halifax each weekend to manage it.

They are fascinated by God's many wonders, she told me as I stood frightened in my first booth, smoothing my dress and crying. *They long for the extraordinary. Don't we all?* Not me, Mother. I would have known true happiness if only you had sewn me that dove-gray velvet dress for no other reason than to just make me feel proud (I would never say beautiful) with all those folds of dense, expensive fabric and matching ribbon flowing around me. But that dress was my first costume. I wanted to love it; I hadn't ever worn or imagined such finery, but how could I? I hated it as much as I hated facing him when he came home evenings, quietly asking how much money was in the box.

In a year, we decided on two days a week, then three. By the time I was nineteen, we'd paid everything off and bought two new boats. Father had two skippers working for him and six crewmen. The path to my booth had been worn to a gulley and we hired men to fill and cobble it. Each month I received a package of morphine from Boston, and because I was usually filled with it, that whole period of time was wrapped in warm layers of gold, rose, and purple, with only a tinge of darkness encroaching from the edges. If I had not had the medicine, I'm certain I would have found a way to die after the first hundred people viewed me.

Back in the museum, my pencil still hovered above the mostly blank page. I'd managed only the one stilted sentence. My leg throbbed and I had nothing for it. I slammed the book shut and threw my pencil across the room.

Thirty-four

By the time I arrived at Miss Crawford's address, I was an hour late for her soiree and crescents of sweat had dampened my dress under the arms. I had finally settled on the green velvet gown after sewing on a new lace collar and lightening the whole affair with my peach-colored wrap. It was still a wintry and somewhat dowdy ensemble, but it was the best I could do. I did not expect to enjoy the walk, and I didn't. I set off from the museum with a thoughtless confidence in my ability to find the address. It was north, of course, and west. I had asked William the ticket-man where it was, but north of City Hall Park the streets became tangled and crooked, and I lost myself almost immediately. It didn't help that my right leg still throbbed from my fall in Saint Paul's Chapel.

Miss Crawford had invited me to a party and I hadn't mentioned it to Maud or anyone else on the fifth floor, partially to hoard my pleasure at the invitation, partially to avoid Maud inviting herself along. But once I stepped through the wrought-iron gate and faced the ornate brass knocker on Miss Crawford's apartment door, helplessly experiencing trickles of sweat slide into the crease of my corset and down my back, I wished for Maud's presence by my side. My feet and knee joints ached, and I'd forgotten to bring a handkerchief to wipe my face. I was certain I looked even more ghastly than usual, but after a minute of standing there, imagining myself in the midst of the scene I was about to enter, I lifted my hand, almost as a punishment for my own self-pity. Thankfully, the elderly Negro who answered my knock waved me in quickly without so much as a blink of the eye.

Crystal dripped from the high-ceilinged foyer, reflecting the flames of hundreds of candles nestled in octopus-like candelabra, which themselves echoed the shapes of the sea serpents and mermaids writhing up from the mosaic floor. A painting of an English garden was suffocated by the thick floral of its gilt frame. Delicate lacquer tables held groups of porcelain vases and small sculptures. To call the space luxurious would be an understatement, but I would not call it elegant.

"The ladies are in the ballroom," the servant told me, gesturing up the stairs with one gloved hand. "Would you like an escort?"

"I'll find my way, thank you."

But the ballroom was empty. It had a small domed ceiling and scenes of the country life painted above the moldings. Several settees and armchairs were strewn about the periphery, and I found evidence, in the form of sets of gloves and crystal punch glasses, that the party had, at one point, occupied the room. I sat briefly on the edge of one of the couches, prepared to wait for the party to return from wherever it had gone to. Was there a terrace? A garden of some kind? I went to the French doors on the far side of the room only to find that they were not real, just an adornment. Perhaps I should go home. I could not even attend a party correctly. I arrive, and the party vanishes. I walked back to the hallway, and it was from there that I finally heard the sound of voices farther down the hall.

A thickly curtained study was stuffed with the tightly corseted taffeta and silk-clad bodies of thirty women, all chanting a hymn in muted but impassioned voices: *"Come, Holy Ghost, who ever One, art with the Father and the Son; Come, Holy Ghost, our souls possess, with Thy full flood of holiness."* The words were not sung; some women spoke them out, others whispered. *"In will and deed, by heart and tongue. With all our powers,*

Thy praise be sung; And love light up our mortal frame, Till others catch the living flame. Till others catch the living flame." Their eyes were closed, all except Miss Crawford's, whom I spotted on the other side of the room, and who gave me an encouraging smile. She pointed to a stack of hymnals near the door. It wasn't until I saw the mesmerist herself, tied to a chair in the middle of the room, that I realized what was in progress. *"Almighty Father, hear our cry, Through Jesus Christ our Lord most high. Who with the Holy Ghost and Thee, Doth live and reign eternally. Doth live and reign eter-na-lee."* I opened the hymnal to the page marked by its silk ribbon as the women began another round.

Of course I have encountered all manner of augurers: brain-cartographers, clairvoyants, biblical prophets, mind readers, ecstatics, ornithomancers, card and tea-leaf interpreters, even one optimistic boy who claimed to see the outline of a life in the shape of your biggest toe. The show business was no stranger to the public's desire to glimpse its own fate. But the business of communing with the dead had landed strangely in the realm of the church. In Cooper's Medicine Show there had been a short-lived experiment with a trance-lecturer, but her repeated omens in which famine destroyed the American republic were so unpopular (with audiences as well as her fellow performers) that she was asked to leave after only three shows.

"In will and deed, by heart and tongue, With all our powers, Thy praise be sung." The mesmerist was a very young girl. She had a silk band tied over her eyes and a heavy cross around her neck.

The women intensified their efforts. They repeated the hymn. I did not join them, but when I closed my eyes the words closed over me like deep, black water. *"Almighty Father, hear our cry. Come, Holy Ghost, our souls possess."* The voices went around and around. On the fourth or fifth repetition one voice began singing in a high soprano, managing a strange harmony with the more guttural sounds of the rest. Little by little, other voices began to sing, until after two or three more repetitions we had erupted into a triumphant, though somewhat cacophonous, anthem. I heard wails, especially from one deep voice somewhere to my right. The knot in my chest that had formed upon entering the room had loosened, and amid the roar I finally managed to whisper a few lines. We went on and on, I cannot even guess how long, before the sound of a bell called us back.

They were surprised to see me when they opened their eyes, but Miss Crawford called our attention to the matter at hand.

"We will now focus our attention on Miss Thibodaux and give her the benefit of our clearest thoughts and prayers. If she is ready, we will now proceed."

Miss Thibodaux bowed her head slightly, and Miss Crawford brought a small table to her side. A large sheet of paper covered the tabletop, and Miss Thibodaux's hand sought out a pencil resting in the middle. She nodded again.

"Now, please send Miss Thibodaux the name of your loved one, the one with whom you would like to speak from beyond the great divide."

There was a collective intake of breath. The faces of the women, all immaculately painted and coifed, focused with pretty intensity on the blindfolded girl. Almost immediately the mesmerist began to scrawl. The women fluttered and let out tiny gasps. The girl's hand shook, and a bead of sweat dripped from her forehead into the kerchief. She was good. I wondered if Miss Crawford was paying her. The girl's hand jerked across the paper.

"It looks like an *N.* Yes, *N,*" Miss Crawford whispered. "Then *O, R,* and *A.* Nora. She has written Nora." The women looked around with their hands over their hearts. Some shook their heads. "Who sent prayers and a request to speak with Nora?"

No one responded. After thirty seconds, Miss Thibodaux's fist banged on the tabletop.

"Nora," Miss Crawford repeated, but no one claimed Nora.

The next name, John, elicited a response from the deep-voiced woman on my right, who turned out to be wild-haired and elderly. "My brother," she whispered.

"He is here with us. What would you like to ask him?" Miss Crawford said.

"John, my dear, where did you leave the deed to Mother's house? We haven't been able to find it anywhere!" *The deed to a house?* But Miss Thibodaux's hand responded quickly to the question.

"Ask my neighbors," Miss Crawford read from the paper.

We waited for further messages from beyond the divide, but after several minutes of silence, Miss Thibodaux indicated that the spirits had left us. We all joined hands, then, and sang another few rounds of the hymn. At the end, a rosy-cheeked Miss Crawford untied Miss Thibodaux from the chair and removed the bandanna.

The mesmerist couldn't have been more than fourteen, and she looked straight at me. "I need water," she said.

"Let us all now retire to the ballroom, ladies, please." Miss Crawford put her arm protectively around Miss Thibodaux. I filed out with the rest, vowing to give no indication, now or ever, that the young mesmerist had written the name of my mother.

"Welcome to the fourth meeting of the Second Chapter of the Women's Empowerment League!" Miss Crawford stood in the center of the ballroom. We gathered around, dutifully raising our tiny glasses of punch. "We are dedicated to raising female civic, social, and spiritual consciousness!" The group gave out a tidy *huzzah!* "Through these meetings, our collective feminine powers are strengthened, for the betterment of our lives and our society!" The rest of the league responded with a decidedly feminine round of applause.

"I would like to introduce two very special women with us tonight for the first time. You've already met Miss Thibodaux. She visits us from the town of Savannah, Georgia. The other is Miss Ana Swift." Miss Crawford gestured to me. I smiled, politely, I hoped. "Who is currently employed in Barnum's American Museum. I ask everyone to please make these two ladies very welcome tonight, as you enjoy your drinks and the dessert that will soon be served. I believe our own Miss Evelyn Wilcox will now pleasure us on the pianola."

It really was a lovely room, filled with candlelight and the many-hued forms of the ladies, who now broke into small groups. Miss Crawford came to me, confirming that I had some punch, that I was comfortable.

"You didn't tell me this would be a political soiree, Miss Crawford. You should have given me fair warning," I chided her, glad for her attention.

"Oh, nonsense. It's just my closest friends. We formed the league six months ago, when we began the children's improvement plans and our efforts with the impoverished mothers of the ports."

"Mothers of the ports?"

"Prostitutes. With children." Miss Crawford's eyes flitted among her guests. "Oh, you really must meet Gloria. Gloria!" She waved her friend over, a sharp-featured woman with an unfortunate overbite, who eagerly reached out her hand to me.

"What a pleasure. How did you ever get her to come, Miss Crawford?"

"Oh, just the usual," she said with a wink. "I'll leave you two to get to know each other."

I looked down upon the impeccably straight middle part running the length of Gloria's skull, and the very minor cleavage she had tried to create at the top of her dress.

"You know," she said, "I've been interested in the American Museum for some time."

"Really. Have you attended any of the theater performances?"

"Oh, no." Another woman approached us. "Hello, Miss White. Have you met Miss Swift?"

"It's a pleasure to have you in the league." Miss White was a tiny blond woman in a bronze gown.

"Oh, I'm not a member."

"You are now!" laughed Gloria.

I felt more like its pet.

"We were just discussing the museum," Gloria continued. "My interest is more of a critical one, I'm afraid. You see, as chairwoman of the Association for the Improvement of the Condition of the Poor, I'm a sponsor at the Bethany Hospital for Orphans. It came to my attention recently that two orphans, a brother and a sister, had been *purchased* from Bethany Hospital. When I investigated further, I discovered that Mr. Barnum's American Museum was responsible. An agent from that institution had visited the orphanage and purchased them."

"It is quite illegal to *buy* children!" Miss White gaped.

"It is in*deed*," Gloria confirmed.

We each took an outraged sip of punch on behalf of purchased children. "Well, when I found out, I went straight to the museum and demanded to speak with someone."

I almost smiled. "Let me guess. Barnum was not available."

"Yes. I was quite insulted. I spoke with a naturalist of some kind."

"A taxidermist, I would imagine."

"He knew nothing. He suggested I speak with the theater manager, Mr. Forsythe. I waited two hours, and then Forsythe wouldn't say anything! He wouldn't even let me into the area of the museum where apparently many of these so-called *performers* live! Can you imagine? The children were probably somewhere in that building, but they wouldn't let me in, even to confirm their safety."

The women did not appear to realize that I, too, lived in the museum, or that I might have some knowledge of the children they sought. I was trying to think of who they might be.

"It's an abomination," said Miss White, "that children have no protection from those who would abuse them."

"I have written a letter to Mr. Barnum," Gloria continued, "requesting full access to the children. But unfortunately he is abroad and will not be back for several weeks."

"Where is he?" I inquired. After Barnum's latest disappearance, I had been only mildly interested in his whereabouts. The museum seemed to function just fine without him. But after hearing of Olrick's higher salary, I wanted a meeting.

"Haven't you been following the paper? He's in London, at the Royal Exhibition there."

"Miss Swift, perhaps you could investigate the matter of these siblings for us!" Gloria clapped her hands.

"Well, I don't have anything to do with other contracts or —"

"Oh, Bitsy! Bitsy, come here for a moment." Gloria called our hostess over, who seemed mildly annoyed to be pulled from her conversation across the room. "We've just had a wonderful idea. Miss Swift can look into this matter of the children from Bethany Hospital!"

"Oh?" Miss Crawford colored slightly.

"I won't be able to do anything more than you could," I protested.

"Well, I don't believe that at all," Gloria scolded.

"Just try," Miss White added dolefully.

"But if you can't, Miss Swift, then don't feel obligated," Miss Crawford said.

"Well, I certainly don't know that anything will come of it."

"Oh!" Miss Crawford blurted. "Good! Here comes dessert. Priscilla has made us a beautiful almond cream cake."

I managed to stay at the party for almost an hour, and toward the end I realized I was enjoying it. Miss Crawford drifted back and forth with ladies whom "you really must meet, Miss Swift." My favorite was Miss Pregler, who dispensed with small talk after politely introducing herself.

"You must have a terrible time with hats, Miss Swift. How do you ever find them in your size?"

As she escorted me to the door, Miss Crawford insisted I come to the next meeting.

"The ladies *adored* you."

Thirty-five

As soon as I went looking for the children I found Beebe pacing in front of the theater doors. I had avoided him quite successfully since my hellish visit to Saint Paul's Chapel, despite the fact that he'd left several reconciliatory gifts at my booth. The first was a small cake in a pink paper cup. When I saw it I thought an absentminded museum patron had left it on my counter and threw it away, but the next day, as I returned to my gallery, I saw Beebe scurrying away with his head down. Tucked behind the Giant's Rings was a tiny yellow-green elephant carved from soapstone. I kept it because it reminded me of a creature I'd loved in Methuselah Jones' menagerie. Since the elephant, he'd left a tin of peppermints and a tiny cut-glass bauble, but I hadn't sought him out. When I saw him I felt a curious lurch in the gut; my rage over our botched liaison had cooled to a simmering annoyance over the fact that he apparently did not have the courage to face me again.

He froze mid-stride when he saw me, and then, astonishingly, he smiled shyly. "Miss Swift, do you hate me quite thoroughly?"

"I —"

"Wait! Do not answer! I've been so confused as to whether to leave you entirely alone or pursue a further explanation of my ill-received but, you must know, benignly spoken words that night. You made it clear you wanted nothing to do with me." His voice became rather mournful.

"You lodged me firmly in a world of vice, Mr. Beebe. How was I supposed to interpret it?" I found my rebuke less sharp, less firmly believed, than expected. I suddenly saw quite clearly a fact that dried up my ill feeling: He cared for me. This knowledge hung in the air between us so palpably that I was left quite speechless.

"You misunderstood me," he insisted.

"Perhaps," I conceded. "We must all release our iron grip on our beliefs once in a while, mustn't we?"

"Perhaps?" His face broadened. "Perhaps? Then you do not hate me?"

"How did you know elephants are my favorite animal?"

"I didn't! I didn't, Miss Swift." He opened his palms as if this coincidence were God's will. Certainly he believed it was.

"Well." I could not help but return his smile. "Let's not speak of it again, shall we?"

"Speak of what?" he cried. He lunged forward and took my hand with both of his. "I'm so glad you came to find me!"

"Actually, I didn't."

"Oh?"

"But I'm glad I did."

"Yes."

I told him about Miss Crawford's party, and that I was curious about the number of children employed by the museum.

"Well, there are the albino twins, the General Tom Thumb, the four Martinettis. And these." He pointed to the sign behind him. THE AZTEC CHILDREN. "So, eight."

"Are the Aztec Children new? I haven't heard of them before."

"Yes, they've been here only a couple of weeks. They're onstage right now. *Straight from the heart of the South American jungle, ladies and gentlemen.*" Beebe aped the master of ceremonies. "*After all trace of the great Aztec civilization vanished into perpetuity, only these royal children remain, captured by a group of*

Brazilian Pigmies and subsequently rescued by our own Professor Chatterton! I've heard it so many times, I could scream."

"And do they live on the fifth floor?"

"I don't know. If they did, I'm sure you would have seen them."

I remembered pushing open the tribesman's door; that musty room, his starving gray face. "Not necessarily. You wouldn't mind if I peeked in the theater, would you?"

"I'm not supposed to open the doors if the show has been in progress for ten minutes. And they've been going for twenty." Beebe stiffened a bit reciting his duty.

"Mr. Beebe, really. I just want to get a look at them."

"I'm really not supposed to."

"Well, then, I'll just have to go around to the —"

"Oh, all right, Miss Swift. You see how my resolve crumbles! Let me get the door for you." He pulled it open soundlessly, motioned me in, and then slipped in himself before easing the door closed.

The Aztec Children stood in the center of the brightly lit stage surrounded by painted set pieces depicting pyramids and various jungle animals. A professor stood to one side, addressing the audience: "They were malnourished and frightened, but over time I was able to gain their trust. Through a system of sign language, I began to learn the story of their Royal Heritage in the grand city of Iximaya."

The Children themselves regarded the audience with dazed expressions. They were brown-skinned, quite young, and dressed in furs of some kind. Gold jewelry adorned their necks and wrists. One, a girl, I thought, was much smaller than the other, and she wore a circlet set with stones around her forehead. Their heads had been partially shaved, exposing high, strangely sloped foreheads, with matted black hair cascading down their backs.

"Eventually, they led me back into the jungle to the site of their former glory. In those caves, I found urns full of gold! So much of it that Cortés himself would have been jealous. Unfortunately, the area was patrolled by bloodthirsty

Brazilian tribesmen who would have killed us instantly if we had tried to reclaim the treasure."

Could these be the siblings Miss Crawford and her friends had mentioned? I told Beebe I had seen enough.

"Why are you interested in them?" he asked once we'd returned to the empty foyer.

"It's nothing, really. I was just wondering how they are taken care of. Who arranges their meals, things like that."

"I believe there's a nurse with them, although I'm not certain."

Applause erupted from inside the theater and Beebe jumped to attention. "I must go, Miss Swift." He straightened his usher's cap and took a step toward me. "I have just a few seconds until the masses descend upon us." He reached for my hand.

"All right." I was blushing like a girl, and so was he. "So good-bye?" A bizarre giggle erupted from my mouth. I should have been turning away but I moved toward him, extending my arm. It is a delicate matter to make love to a giantess, Beebe. I will not give you more than half a minute to act.

He used both hands to clasp one of mine. He raised my hand to his mouth in the ancient manner, but at the last moment he flipped it over and kissed the center of my palm. His lips were unexpectedly soft even as they pressed against this hardened pad. Quickly he kissed again, and again, working his way past my wrist. I cupped his face, felt the contour of his skull with my fingertips. He pressed his cheek against my hand with his eyes closed. He rested there for a moment before springing back, walking slowly backward toward the theater door, keeping hold of my hand as long as he could.

At the end of the day I set off to find the Aztec Children. It wouldn't be difficult, since I knew who occupied all the rooms on the fifth floor except two, and I was fairly certain that one of those was empty. I approached the one at the end of the hall on the right. My knock was answered by the smaller of the children, still wearing the furs and tiara.

From where I had stood against the back wall of the theater, I did not perceive what was now immediately clear: The children were weak in the mind, perhaps to the point of idiocy. One child stared up at me while her brother sat on the floor, rocking slightly, a thread of saliva hanging from his lip. Their foreheads, which the professor had described as *ritually shaped,* were actually the bloated cones of encephalitis. They were alone in the room, and a cursory look yielded enough disarray to indicate neglect. Dishes, some broken, were stacked in the corner near the door. Their chamber pot was pungently full and looked as if someone had knocked some of its contents onto the floor. The boy seemed to be crying, although his assonant yelp could have meant anything.

If these children were the siblings Miss Crawford and her friends were looking for, their anxiety was more than justified. I could already see the women's horrified faces, each vermilion set of lips pursed into a perfect O as I explained the situation, and their relief and gratitude when I described the children's' rescue. It wouldn't be difficult to verify that these were the right children.

Outside the museum entrance I found Beebe, transformed by our earlier encounter into a dashing stranger, non-uniformed and standing with two other men. The sun had just set, and the whole avenue was cast in lavender. Visible between two buildings, a line of flat-bottomed clouds reflected angled planes of fuchsia.

"Isn't it extraordinary?" Beebe came to me, gesturing aloft.

"Do you know where Bethany Hospital is?"

"Don't tell me that's where you're going."

I turned away from him, looking for a carriage for hire.

"I know where it is," he said.

"Could you point the way? I have a quick errand there."

"Ah, I'm afraid I won't help you. Unless you agree to have me as an escort." Beebe appeared as startled as I was by this bold assertion.

I laughed. "Such drama, Mr. Beebe."

"No. I'm quite serious. Saint Paul's has several aid programs in the Points. Lives have been lost delivering food along those streets. Please. Allow me."

He caught the attention of a hack driver and we both ignored the obvious list in the four-person carriage as I stepped aboard. We lurched northward in the twilight, veering right onto Chatham Street alongside City Hall Park. Against a backdrop of buildings tinted mauve and reflecting panes of orange sunset in their windows, I explained to Beebe what I was after with the siblings and the children's aid society. He was unconvinced that the museum would have obtained children from the Bethany Hospital.

"That would be terrible. And I'd be surprised if Barnum's scouts even know Bethany Hospital exists."

It was only a minute before the marble buildings gave way to red brick, and the people moving up and down the street faded from the well-heeled Broadway shop owners and businessmen to the drab tones of foundry men, laundry girls, and finally rag pickers. We turned up Mulberry Street; the hooves of our mare clacked dully as the cobble turned to clay brick. Beebe leaned up and spoke a few words to the driver, who nodded.

We were in a realm of clapboard shadows. On first glance, the street was strangely deserted. As we drove on, I picked out various gray forms of humanity, most lingering in doorways or disappearing into subterranean stairwells. The glass of each gas street lamp had been broken. Our driver tried to light the lamp dangling from the carriage, but our jostling prevented it, and it was clear he would not stop. One door, attached to a plank building tilting even farther to one side than our carriage, burst open as we passed, expelling two old men, a wave of raucous voices, and the sight of one candle burning on a table.

The orphanage, a two-story brown brick building, was just above Cross Street.

"I'll wait ten minutes," said the driver. "No more."

"How much time do you need?" Beebe asked, fumbling for a coin while flailing to help me down from the carriage.

242

"That will be enough."

"I'll ring the bell before I leave and give you one minute, no more, to get back," reiterated the driver.

I felt as if we were jumping from a ship. "Fine."

After emitting a painfully shrill shriek when she saw me, the young girl who opened the door for us was struck speechless. I won't deny that I would have been, too, if I was a thirteen-year-old orphan opening the door at dusk to the silhouette of a seven-and-a-half-foot-tall person. But her shock did not help us get the information we needed. I questioned her briefly, but she just shook her head, nearly toppling the candle she held out in front of her like a ward against evil.

"I . . . I don't know, miss. I don't know."

"It's a matter of some urgency." Beebe spoke gently. The girl let us into a dark foyer.

Another woman appeared, this one much older and in the black cloak of the church. "What is it, Gretchen?" She crossed herself when she saw me.

"I need information about two children taken from here," I said.

"Who are you?"

"Miss Swift. This is Mr. Beebe."

"We're not open for visitors." The nun's round, eyebrowless face lacked all definition, but her words were sharp.

"I just need to know —"

"Show them out, Gretchen." The nun turned away.

"Wait!" Beebe dug into his pocket. "We just need to know one thing." He handed the woman two coins. She dropped it into the small pouch hanging from her belt. "But we don't have much time."

"Come with me." The nun led us through one door into a narrow hallway. She extracted a key from her apron pocket and unlocked the next door. We followed her into a hall filled with children. The palpable odors of hair, dirt, excrement, and old sweat made the air a poignant swamp. Some children slept on straw pallets but most sat huddled together, wearing long dirty shirts. A girl held a big-headed baby with mucus dried on its chin who screamed upon seeing me. One boy lay on a pallet with his wrists tied down and his eyes following us closely. Beebe looked neither left nor right, his fists clenched. I was fleetingly glad the room was not well lit.

The nun led us to an office on the far end of the hall. She sat on one side of a small desk.

"What is it you want to know?"

"Did the American Museum take two children from here?"

"Which organization are you with?"

"None."

"None? Why are you here?"

"We simply want to confirm that it was two children —" Beebe began. The woman shamelessly held out her hand, and Beebe laid another coin in it.

"Yes, they took the two. Brother and sister, if I recall. Some weeks ago. Encephalitics."

"Where did the children come from?"

The nun laughed. "Come from? Those two arrived on our front step nine years ago, drooling babies, both of them. Probably half nigger, half Indian. That always comes out idiots." She laughed again.

"That's all. That's all, Miss Swift, isn't it?" Beebe was already pulling my arm.

"Who bought them?"

Still smiling, the nun placed both hands on the desk. "Oh, we don't sell children, ma'am." She rose to go.

"I find that difficult to —"

"Let's go now, Miss Swift." Beebe looked over his shoulder toward the distant street.

"Funny, though," the nun continued, leading the way back out, "I've never seen a rich person come for children like that. Real rich lady, and young, too. Came late at night."

I could not look at the children again, so I looked at the stained and crooked floor passing beneath my feet as we made our way out. The carriage had waited for us. I could see it surprised Beebe that it was still there.

"That was horrible," I whispered. "I didn't know it would be like that. Miss Crawford said the women sponsored the place. I thought it would —"

"At the chapel we try to be involved, but we still don't always know where the money and food go."

"They're better off at the museum," I realized out loud.

Beebe said nothing, but he seemed to me more dignified in the evening light. He looked upon the city with grave concern, and solemnly placed his hand over mine.

All I could think about was getting back to my room and pouring hot water and sea salts into my basin and dipping in my feet, scrubbing my hands. But there was a commotion on Broadway. We stopped behind a cart carrying a load of barrels. Carriages and horses blocked the way forward.

"Must be a collision ahead," said Beebe, "we're almost there. Let's walk back." He paid the driver and we disembarked.

"They still don't have rights," said Beebe, "in the museum."

"But anything's better than that orphanage, you must agree!"

He buttoned his jacket, his light brow furrowed.

Something had happened at the museum. A river of people poured out of the main entrance and a crowd leaned over the balcony. As we approached, a knot of blue-coated policemen emerged dragging a man. More officers followed.

"It's the Martinettis," breathed Beebe. "Look. They've arrested them." Mrs. Martinetti and her daughter, both walking stiffly and wrapped in someone else's coats, were escorted into the police wagon. Beebe pulled out his watch. "They would have been in the middle of a performance!"

We pushed our way toward the entrance and found Mr. Archer near the doorway. The ad man leaned casually against the wall.

"What happened?"

"Oh, this? This is the just the beginning." Mr. Archer shook his head, smiling. "Lewd and obscene behavior. And with children, too."

"Was it their new costumes?" Beebe gasped. "They have these new costumes. A few of us thought they might be slightly revealing, but they assured us —"

"Costumes, suggestive performances, certain anatomical exposures during acrobatic routines, not to mention they're immigrants." Mr. Archer raised an eyebrow.

"You must be so pleased," I hissed at Archer.

The ad man turned his palms upward. "Pleased? My emotions hardly seem relevant here."

"Last I heard, you were Barnum's employee, not his destroyer."

"Ah, you underestimate us both, Miss Swift. Don't you remember Zechariah?"

"Zechariah the prophet?" Beebe asked.

"He's smarter than he looks, your usher," Archer said coolly. "There must always be an accuser, you see. It's an ancient, perfect game, it is. Just being played out here now, in the newspapers. Barnum knows the rules. He set it all up."

"I can't stand to look at you," I huffed as I pushed past the ad man. Sensing Beebe's hesitation about what to do next, I pulled him into the museum with me.

"They don't deserve this," I sighed. From the balcony, we watched the police wagon full of acrobats disappear down Broadway. Even without a spectacle to watch, the crowd on the street did not disperse right away. "Lord only knows how much money they brought Barnum."

"I'm sure when he finds out he'll rescue them," said Beebe. He wandered over to Thomas' harpsichord and played a few inappropriately cheerful notes.

"I'm not so sure."

"Of course he will."

"He could have arranged this whole thing, Mr. Beebe."

"Samuel."

"What?"

"Please call me Samuel."

Beebe was standing by the harpsichord looking up at me. In his own clothes, canvas pants and a woolen vest over a thick flannel shirt, he seemed less familiar and I enjoyed seeing him anew. His ledge of curls still hovered above his ears, but out from under his usher's cap even they struck me as pleasingly tousled, or at least less comical than before.

"Well, Samuel, shall we see if Gustav will give us some supper?"

From where they hung on flagpoles and in the trees, gas-lights illuminated the rooftop garden against the gathering night. In the distance a second city shimmered in a reflection on the surface of New York Harbor. Candlelight emanated from the windows of Saint Paul's, and Beebe stared at the chapel as we strolled along the promenade.

The people who gathered around the glowing stoves were all employees. I saw the Human Calculator staring into space, clutching spoons in one hand and a bowl in the other. William the ticket-man and his nephew, Gideon, ate next to Clarissa, whose massive heft extended into the darkness beyond the stove's light. Everyone was talking about the Martinettis, but Beebe and I moved past the conversations of our companions to the outer edges of lamplight. We found a stove with empty chairs around it. Beebe fed it a fragrant piece of wood and I fetched a stone bench to sit on, lifting it easily in a feat some would pay to see.

"We could be around a campfire somewhere," I mused. "Far away from cities."

"In Bethel Parish," Beebe said, "some nights you can see every star in the heavens."

"I was thinking of the land farther west. Somewhere in the prairie where there's no one for a hundred miles in every direction." Bright clouds gathered on that unbroken horizon, dappling the grassland in great, whalelike shadows that would quickly envelop me. "Sometimes I think about going there," I admitted.

Beebe was looking at me, but I was staring at the coals. "To the Territories?" His voice was gentle.

"People say there are trees five hundred years old out there. Big around as a house. I'd like to see those."

"We could start a church," said Beebe.

I frowned in the dark. "Or a farm."

"Or a farm," he agreed. "I know it's difficult for you to imagine yourself a preacher's wife." Disconcerted, I looked at him. His gaze did not waver. I very rarely considered myself any kind of wife at all and I found the notion quite disturbing. Beebe, however, looked calmly into my eyes as though it was the most natural idea in the world.

"I don't know what to think about that," I mumbled, securing my eyes on the coals. Suddenly Beebe was at my side! He'd hopped up on the bench where I sat. Standing, he was almost level with me.

"I know what I think about it," he whispered, leaning so close to my ear that his breath warmed it. I hardly had time to remember the various difficulties posed by two such disparately proportioned people kissing before we had overcome them. His lips were soft yet bold, and they sent a ringing chord through me as they worked their way across my own.

Thirty-six

I didn't see Miss Crawford until the following Saturday, but I had spent many hours, in my booth and also outside of my working hours, coming up with a plan. I was certain I could convince the museum's performers to create an alliance, especially since the Martinetti debacle. We could meet formally, with the intention to draft certain regulations about pay and length of contract, as well as guidelines regarding the care and guardianship of child performers. If we did this with the support of Miss Crawford's Women's Empowerment League, we would have the endorsement of a well-known social group. The plan would succeed. I had even begun mentally composing the agenda for our first meeting.

I saw Miss Crawford strolling into the gallery early Saturday afternoon, thankfully without her usual train of disheveled children. She walked arm in arm with a woman in a highly adorned feathered cap. I left my post to meet her.

"Miss Swift! How is the museum life?"

"Very well."

"This is Margaret Goodwin. Her husband is one of Mayor Harper's deputies."

I bowed slightly. Mrs. Goodwin visibly recoiled, her eyes ricocheting between Miss Crawford and my sternum.

"Miss Swift is the museum's most striking employee," Miss Crawford told her friend. "Almost eight feet tall. Just look at her hands."

She had never mentioned my physical appearance before. Instinctively I looked at my hands.

"Miss Crawford, I wanted to tell you. I visited the Bethany Hospital."

"Oh?" She looked quickly at Mrs. Goodwin. "You *went* there?" She stared at me.

"Some of the children were tied to their beds. It was abominable. I couldn't believe the conditions."

"Our improvement program is new. Change takes time, you see. Perhaps we should speak about this later, Miss Swift." She took her friend's arm. Her face had become uncharacteristically pinched.

"I just wanted to tell you, though. It was horrendous. But the children did come from there. The Aztec Children. They were brought here from there by —"

"This *really* is not the best time to discuss this." She yanked Mrs. Goodwin away as I abruptly realized why Miss Crawford had abandoned her perpetual grace and courtesy.

She backed away with Mrs. Goodwin hooked to her arm. The pieces now lay in front of me, obvious. She visited the worst orphanages in the city for her "charitable" work. She frequented the same circles as Barnum, who had undoubtedly offered her a respectable sum to abandon her morals. He must be paying her to bring troupes of orphans to the museum as well as to buy them, to spread the good word among those circles and cover up the ugly deeds.

"You should be ashamed of yourself," I hissed as she retreated.

"Wasn't there an arrest made here a few days ago?" Mrs. Goodwin inquired mildly.

Miss Crawford again pursed her lips and blatantly glared at me. "Yes, there was."

"I read about it in the *Herald*," Mrs. Goodwin continued. "A group of jugglers, wasn't it? Italians, wasn't it?"

"Yes," Miss Crawford snarled. "They were arrested for exposing themselves in a most lewd and obscene manner. The police department took very appropriate action, I must say. It's a comfort to know how *easy* it is to take care of situations like that," she said. "I read that the costumes did not even reach to the knee. We really must be on our way, Miss Swift."

"Miss Swift would probably be interested in knowing about the program we discussed on the carriage ride over," Mrs. Goodwin cluelessly said.

"What program is that?" I inquired, my eyes still fastened on Miss Crawford.

"We are considering training a number of Christian charity workers who would be sent to work at various business establishments, mostly in the Bowery, with the intent to improve and rectify certain issues of morality. We've targeted this museum as a possible recipient of this service."

Miss Crawford was now examining her own hands. "Let's move on, Mrs. Goodwin."

"That's an interesting proposition," I said. "But I think you'd have a hard time convincing Mr. Barnum to let someone else infuse his establishment with moral pretension. Especially when the people supposedly infusing it are blatant hypocrites."

"Phineas T. Barnum," Mrs. Goodwin announced, "is the scourge of the city."

Miss Crawford moved away, towing the fuming Mrs. Goodwin.

"It hardly makes sense for you to say so," I called after them. "Since you paid your quarter just like the rest of humanity."

I swung away from them and was immediately faced by a dozen museum visitors gaping at me like a row of carved pumpkins.

"Yes, even giants lose their tempers," I snapped, feeling the scope of my anger flash outward beyond the bounds of the museum and any wrongdoing among its patrons, inhabitants, or creator. The people around me scattered. "As difficult as that may be for you idiots to fathom."

Spira Mirabilis

Thirty-seven

Guillaudeu looked up. He reached up. He tried to catch the sloth's attention, but it would not look and did not move from where it hung on the branch by its long, curved claws. It was only when he gently shook the trunk and the sloth dropped from the limb in a swirl of hair, landing with a thump next to his foot, that he realized the animal was dead.

He carried it to his office. He laid it on the worktable and brought a pencil and his set of measuring rods and wooden rulers. Arm span: sixty-three inches. Top of the head to the tailbone: thirty-one. Lower legs: twenty-three. Dusty flakes dropped from the animal's stiff limbs. Guillaudeu smoothed the fibers of the sloth's gray-brown coat. He rolled plugs out of raw cotton and filled the nostrils, the mouth. The words of the banished Cuvier came to him from the cellar: *Courage means the courage to look steadily.*

He put on his apron and surveyed the tools hanging on hooks at eye level. He chose the curved scalpel. He made the first incision from the top of the pubis upward to the collarbone. He worked slowly, relieved to feel the tools in his hands. He allowed himself to enter the microcosm of the body and forget everything else. Without disrupting the abdominal muscles, he pulled the skin of the lower torso back as far as he could, dabbing away beads of blood and grease. Using his knife, he separated the femurs from the pelvis, and after a single cut across the intestinal canal he was able to remove the lower entrails to the sawdust-filled waste box. He removed the pelvis and set it aside. He skinned the animal, slipping the handle of his knife between the musculature of its lower back and the skin, and sliding it upward.

He detached the long forelimbs from the shoulders and continued skinning up under the creature's narrow shoulder blades, around the neck, all the way over the head to the point of the nose, being especially careful with the eyelids, since they were the most important feature in establishing an exact expression on the specimen's face. The head came easily off the neck; Guillaudeu carved off its musculature and set the skull aside.

He worked for hours, barely noting the changing light from his office window, or the occasional knock on his door. Mr. Archer returned from wherever he had been. If Guillaudeu had looked over his shoulder, he would have seen the ad man, newspapers under his arm, staring openmouthed at the taxidermist, returned from exile, at his cluttered and bloodied worktable. It was the only moment when the contents of the museum completely surprised him.

With the animal skinned and its skull emptied of its contents, Guillaudeu gathered the ingredients for the next steps: arsenical soap in an earthen pot, preserving powder, brushes, annealed iron wire, and Formula 9 papier-mâché.

Even though he'd always hoped for something greater, Guillaudeu's most lasting contribution to his art was the invention of Formula 9 papier-mâché. Adding a simple tincture of clove oil and salt to the ancient flour-and-water mixture eliminated all chance of mold, even if the gluey layers were still a touch damp when the skin went over them. He now mixed up a batch in his baker's bowl and cut open a new package of hospital linens already torn into strips.

He added water to the arsenical soap and coated the skull and the hide, careful to keep the fur side dry and clean. He mixed preserving powder with the chopped tow and flax fibers that would fill the body's cavities, and he wondered if any of the museum's other animals had died.

Guillaudeu used pliers to twist a length of wire around the

central rod that would support the head and torso of the specimen. He added a second axis for the lower limbs. Using a file, he sharpened the ends, then slowly hooked one of the wire arms into a forelimb as if hanging a coat. He continued with the other limbs. He would need to keep records of the live animals from now on. He would observe them daily to make sure they were fed. He needed information. As he put on his leather gloves and mixed more preserving powder into the cotton, he surveyed his library, noting the irrelevance of many volumes, the dustiness of their spines: Aristotle, Aldrovandi. *It is only really in one's study,* Cuvier insisted, *that one roams freely throughout the universe.* Guillaudeu slid the sloth's upper arm bones into the skin and attached them to the iron wire with brass piano forte strings. Had he ascribed to that idea? It seemed suddenly preposterous. It was Pliny, perhaps, who had spoken the truth when he described man's ultimate presumption . . . *as if owing to our craving for some End, the problem of immeasurability would not always encounter us. It is madness to investigate what lies outside, as if the measure of anything could be taken by him that knows not the measure of himself.*

He stuffed the first handfuls of chopped cotton and preserving powder into the arms of the sloth. Hours had passed. He lit a lamp, his mind now racing ahead to the various people he wanted to contact, the scientific circles he must infiltrate, the new knowledge he must seek out and gather in order to ascend to his new position as true keeper of animals. It did not matter that when he'd returned to the museum after his walk across New York Island, full of explanations and justifications for his absence, he found that no one had even noticed he'd left, not even William the ticket-man. It did not matter that the museum flowed swiftly around him, shape-shifting all the time to accommodate the public's fickle and shortsighted fancies. He recognized why he was here and he went ahead with his plans.

He did not finish mounting the sloth until well after the museum's last performance had ended and the trickle of footsteps outside his door had ebbed to nothing. He closed the incisions with catgut and secured two black glass eyes in place. He painted over the paw pads and nose with gum arabic and arsenical powder. He had arranged the specimen to appear as he had first seen the creature, sitting like a child with its arms around its knees. During this final hour of preparation, Guillaudeu wondered where in the collection the sloth belonged. Certainly not among the rodents or the monkeys. He lifted the specimen into his arms.

Guillaudeu's footsteps echoed as he walked up the marble stairway. He paused at the top to observe moonlight saturating the air. It had been a long time since he'd walked the empty halls, absorbing the pale friction that seemed to fill the place to bursting. He walked slowly through the portrait gallery. Any confusion about where to put the sloth dissolved as he realized the creature had already established its true place in the collection.

Guillaudeu's hands were sore and stained, and the bloodied tools in his office attested to the creature's transformation from corpse to sculpted impersonation of life. Essentially, though, the animal's role in the museum remained the same. Aware that he was participating in his first act of deception, Guillaudeu returned the specimen to its pergola, under the sign marked SLOWEST CREATURE ON EARTH.

Thirty-eight

Guillaudeu finished clearing off the shelves in his office, and now he was terrified. He had removed a dozen dusty specimens that had lived in the shelves for as long as he could remember. As he did it he felt relief, catharsis, even. He had packed away the books he hadn't touched in years. He was overcome by the need to get rid of more, more than he'd planned. But now it was done; his volumes lay in crates and boxes, and the old moth-gnawed robin, his very first experiment in taxidermy, lay hidden inside a cotton handkerchief to be taken home. Instead of satisfaction, Guillaudeu felt very old and very scared. It had taken a lifetime to accumulate what he had discarded in an hour. What time did he have left? Suddenly the thought of dying with empty shelves in his office was the most terrible thing he could imagine. He fought the urge to put everything back where it had been. Instead, he turned to the thick-leaved logbook he'd requested. It was filled with entries made by the two boys whose job, up until today, was to feed the animals. Guillaudeu had taken matters into his own hands, reappointing the boys to cleaning cages and giving himself the primary duties of caring for the animals. The specter of the sloth's light body drifting to the floor in a cascade of brittle hair haunted him and strengthened his resolve that no other animal would come to such an end.

The logbook reeked of fish. Each page held a list of animals, divided by floor, with a description of the type and

quantity of food given, space for a checkmark beside MORN-
ING and AFTERNOON to indicate the food had been delivered,
and a margin for any general observations.

Guillaudeu looked over the entries. The longspurs were
building a nest in a potted myrtle. Most of the fish, too, continued to thrive. There was some concern over the seahorses
disappearing. Guillaudeu had assumed cannibalism was the
cause, and he had increased their daily dried shrimp allotment. No one understood why they kept disappearing until
one of the night custodians, sweeping the aquarium galleries, swore he saw the octopus creeping across the floor, leaving a wet trail from the seahorse vitrine. It returned to its
tank, squeezing through the inch-wide opening at the top.

But it was the orang-outang that continued to be the most
worrisome problem in Barnum's menagerie. The animal had
been given two servings of fruit and vegetables per day, taken
straight from the restaurant kitchen. Despite this special
treatment, however, the orang-outang remained the only
animal in the logbook with a regular commentary scribbled
in the margins: *Food untouched. No fruit eaten. Would not eat.
Only water gone. Would not eat. Did not move.* It surprised Guillaudeu that the creature was still alive. He had found illustrations in his natural history volumes, but no useful information about the small ape, and it was not without a certain
dread that he finally decided to go up to the third floor to see
the animal.

He passed Mr. Archer on his way out and made his best effort to avoid eye contact as the ad man raised his head from
his newspaper.

"I can't believe what I'm reading here. It's —"

Guillaudeu simply raised a hand as he passed, and Mr. Archer offered no further comment.

The mermaid had vanished from the museum when her
monthlong reign in the spotlight ended. In her place sat a
heavy, gently swaying woman with closed eyes and draped
in bejeweled scarves. Dropping a coin in Valkyria's jar would
dramatically awaken her to the task of shuffling a stack of
thick cards, from which she would draw out destinies.

A troupe of Swiss bell ringers had taken the place of the Italian acrobats, and the daily matinee had changed to *A Ceremonial Display of a Vanishing Indian Culture*. Guillaudeu took comfort in the immutable marble stairway under his feet, and the familiar stretches of oak floor and plaster walls that he'd always known. These different entertainments were simply changing wind patterns on the surface of the ocean. He continued up to the third floor.

The orang-outang lived in a small gallery where the only other attraction was a full-sized black lacquer carriage that had supposedly belonged to Queen Victoria. Museum visitors could climb a small set of stairs and spend a minute or two sitting inside the carriage, passing their hand along the very same railing and their bottoms along the very same bench as royalty.

Guillaudeu navigated the mass of early-afternoon visitors. Halfway to the gallery, he almost turned back. The museum was at its most crowded, after all. It would surely be more comfortable, and probably more enlightening, to observe the orang-outang this evening. But he was already approaching the gallery. It would be even sillier to return to the office. Guillaudeu suddenly had the sense that someone, maybe God, was watching him, taking note of his actions, certainly, and quite possibly his thoughts. He had the sense of a moral obligation. I am in charge here, he thought; I *will* proceed.

The ape's cage was a square of delicate metal latticework over a straw-strewn floor eight feet in diameter. Visitors swarmed the cage but were held away from it by a length of velvet rope. The people were quieter here than Guillaudeu expected, except for the inevitable collective squeal emitted by the children who formed the layer innermost to the cage. From the doorway, Guillaudeu couldn't spot the orang-outang at all. Strange, because the cage contained only straw and what looked like a few strips of fabric. As he reached the far edge of the crowd, though, a reddish lump became visible in one corner. The ape *had* died. Its leathery black feet were positioned sole-to-sole and everything above the creature's knees was covered by a piece of burlap. Guillaudeu looked at the faces of the people around him. A mother to his left watched her boy with a bemused smile. A gentleman holding the arm of his daughter or niece stared at the lump with a decidedly expectant expression. He considered emptying the gallery of people. He could say the orang-outang was scheduled to have a medical examination. Then he could find someone to dispose of the creature's body. The children squealed, though, and the lump made a small move. A hand emerged from under the burlap and very slowly an ovoid face peeked out. The orang-outang looked at the children before withdrawing again behind its makeshift curtain.

That evening Guillaudeu returned to the orang-outang's cage with a bucket of fruit. Empty of visitors, and lit by six wall sconces, the gallery contained an almost firelit glow. The animal sat in the middle of the cage. It did not have the wide cheek flaps shown in the illustrations. Barnum's monkey was female, Guillaudeu decided.

He unlocked the small door on the side of the cage and set the bucket down. The orang-outang sat with her hands in her lap and did not acknowledge his presence. Perhaps she ate only when she was alone. He strolled casually back to the entryway and watched her from a mostly hidden vantage point. He held still for five minutes, listening to the sounds of the custodial staff somewhere behind him and the sounds of the street somewhere in front. She finally pushed up to her feet and went to the bucket. She looked into it, picked up a triangular piece of melon, and dropped it. She stalked to the other side of the cage and resumed her cross-legged seat.

Guillaudeu decided to try an experiment.

"Now, what is this all about?" He spoke softly as he retraced his steps to the cage. "You can't be so picky about your food that you would starve yourself to death, would you?"

He opened the door and retrieved the bucket, pulling it out of the cage and setting it on the gallery floor. He picked up the melon. "This looks delicious to me, you know." He made appreciative sniffing noises. The orang-outang pretended not to notice. He picked through the fruit. It was ripe and clean. When he looked up, the orang-outang was standing at the edge of the open cage door, only two feet from him. She had long, tufted red hair, with brown-black skin showing through on her chest and lower legs. She swung down from the cage and walked, with quiet propriety, past him toward the window.

If she escaped, Guillaudeu would appear a fool. He imagined her in a cloud of feathers as she tore apart the tundra swan specimens. She hurled vases from the glassblowing display. He did not know how fast the orang-outang could run, but he imagined it was very fast indeed. Because the gallery had no door to seal it from the rest of the museum, Guillaudeu blocked the entry with his body. The orang-outang watched traffic on the street below. She moved her head slowly from side to side. Twice, she observed pigeons flying. She walked to the second window and looked out from there. She moved, Guillaudeu noted, with surprising grace. I should write that down somewhere, he thought. *Movements like that of a particularly agile child. Exceedingly long forelimbs and the hands of an old woman.*

The orang-outang turned from the window and Guillaudeu immediately spread out his arms to make himself look bigger so she might think he could stop her if she tried to escape. The ape did not look at him but walked directly to Queen Victoria's carriage and climbed aboard. She was still for a few minutes. Guillaudeu could just see the top of her head through the carriage window. She slid out the other side and proceeded directly to the food bucket. Guillaudeu imagined her hurling it against the window. Instead, she picked it up, carried it to the carriage, and, using her two hind legs and one free forelimb, climbed expertly to the carriage roof and ate her dinner, beginning with half an apple.

Guillaudeu returned to his office smiling despite himself. He opened up the logbook. The ape had eaten every scrap of food, groomed for ten minutes, and returned to her cage for a nap. He opened the heavy logbook and pulled out a pencil. *This young lady prefers her meals on the carriage roof.*

Thirty-nine

"He's in London, you know. Then he's going to Paris."

For once Guillaudeu welcomed the interruption. He was staring at the empty bookshelves again. He could not think of where to begin, or how to find the books that would help him proceed: animal behavior, accounts of the wilderness, whales, and orang-outangs in particular. On a slip of paper he had written *Lamarck?*

"Who told you?"

"Who told me? *Who* told me?" Mr. Archer had burst into the office with startling vigor. The ad man waved a newspaper. Guillaudeu recoiled.

"The *Atlas* told me, that's who. Barnum has set up a regular column with them. A *Public Correspondence,* as they call it." He looked away, as if the newspaper were an unfaithful lover. "He didn't even tell me. And I'm supposed to *know* these things."

Guillaudeu took the paper. Archer walked stiffly to his side of the office and sat down.

"It's brilliant, of course," Archer muttered. "Even when he's gone, he's here."

"*London. May the eighteenth. A missive from the Royal Exhibition.*" Guillaudeu looked up. "Or would you prefer I didn't read aloud?"

"Go ahead. I didn't get through the whole thing anyway."

264

"Dear Editors and People of New York: Nearly all the exhibitions in London employ a dozen or two men to go about the streets carrying their billboards far above their heads, being attached to a pole, which they carry on their shoulders. Thus you will meet these itinerant advertisers with their lofty placards, announcing the place and time of exhibiting the Chinese Collection, Ojibeway Indians, Wilson's Scottish Entertainments, and others.

"While taking my morning ride the other day, I discovered a new moving sign of this kind, many rods ahead of me. It had large brass letters of the highest polish, and they glistened in the sun like burnished gold, and therefore could be seen at a great distance. There! Thinks I, here is another show arrived in town, and a formidable opposition it may prove, for really they are cutting a splendid dash.

"As we approached the moving sign board, I began wondering what exhibit could it be — whether it was a cannibal, a trained tiger, a learned pig; but my question was soon solved, for we came so near that I could read the show bill, and what do you think it was! This was the whole inscription: PREPARE TO MEET THY GOD. *On the reverse side also the same. This brass bill contained not another word, and of course gave no clue to the names of its projectors; but I felt quite anxious to learn what gentleman had opened this new branch of show business, and where they exhibited themselves. So I asked the boardman what show shop he belonged to, and what was the object of this brass mandate. He replied that 'Church meetings were held three times per day at present, at Exeter Hall,' and that he was sent out from that church!*

"What blasphemy it is thus to make a show and merchandize of the Word of God! But there are some fanatics in the world who would reduce the character of the Almighty to that of a Connecticut itinerant peddler. Such wretches are wolves in sheep's clothing, and they deserve to be sheared twice a year. They inflict more injury on the pure principles of the gospel and the glorious and sublime doctrine of Christianity, than all the infidels in the universe combined.

"I have obtained many new curiosities, including numerous Cosmoramas and the smallest pair of ponies in the world — only 23 inches high. The same ship which takes this letter will convey them, and all interested parties can (for 25 cents — don't forget that part of

*the story!) see them in detail, and ten thousand other wonderful ob-
jects of curiosity at the American Museum in New York, a place uni-
versally acknowledged as the most respectable, best conducted and
worthy establishment, blending instruction with amusement, in the
WORLD. In fact, its proprietor is looked on very justly as a public
benefactor; and if he is not presented with the freedom of the city of
New York by this great city's recently new mayor, I shall look upon
that new mayorship corporation as a set of ignorant dolts, who ought
to be sentenced to a six months' diet of bread and water without the
benefit of clergy! As ever thine, P. T .B."*

Guillaudeu folded the newspaper. "Interesting to think of
Barnum as a religious man."

"Oh, he's religious all right," Archer said and snorted.
"He's just about as religious as a man can get under the
broad, vague wing of Universalism. No" — Archer began to
pace — "Connecticut itinerant peddler, indeed! I'm *sure* no
one would *ever* accuse Barnum of selling trinkets at the temple. I cannot believe that he would set up this column without even telling me. I am, after all, his advertising *agent*. Did
you know that an hour ago I was having a steak pie at Sweeney's, when Mr. Bauer, managing editor of the entertainment pages in the *Atlas*, no less, slapped me on the back and
gave me his congratulations. 'Congratulations?' says I, looking around to see if it was some kind of practical joke. 'Well,
yes,' says he, and shows me this published letter from London. Unfortunately I could not hide my surprise, and so Mr.
Bauer immediately perceived the whole scheme was executed without my knowledge or, more important, my guidance. The whole thing was exceedingly embarrassing, and in
Sweeney's, of all places! Half the city's newspapermen were
in there with us. I fear it has shattered my credibility."

"That sounds like an overstatement, Mr. Archer. I'm
sure —"

"One can *never* be sure of anything in this business, Mr.
Guillaudeu. That would undoubtedly be the end of you."

"So you can be sure of uncertainty. That means there's one
thing —"

"I do *not* appreciate your attempt at wit," Mr. Archer snapped.

"Well, I do not appreciate you invading my office."

"Good Lord, not that again, please!" Archer looked at the ceiling. "Your precious office. Just because you have no life to speak of, outside of this building."

"Get out."

"You get out."

"Get out!" Guillaudeu found that he was shrieking. "You superficial, conceited, slave . . . to the coin!"

"I am leaving of my own accord," Mr. Archer announced with a queer, fixed smile on his face. He paraded to the hat stand for his coat and his cane.

"No, you aren't! I am throwing you out."

"You're wrong." Archer turned. "I simply humor you, old man." And he vanished.

Guillaudeu sat unmoving in his seat for a full minute, waiting for his heart to quiet and his breath to return to normal. He could not remember the last time he'd been in a yelling match and it disturbed him. Then it delighted him. He huffed out a chirpy hiccup that could have been a laugh, and shook his head, rising from his chair. He straightened his waistcoat. It was two o'clock: time to feed the whale.

Two buckets of herring were waiting for him as usual outside the museum's side door on Ann Street. He hauled them back into the hallway and past Barnum's office toward the waxworks, but he could not carry them both and had to make two trips up the back stairwell.

When he arrived with the second bucket he was panting and wishing he were a younger man. Across the fifth-floor gallery the tribesman stood at the top of the ladder at the beluga tank, with the first bucket of fish in one hand.

Despite all the changes while he'd been walking through field and valley, Guillaudeu had seen no evidence that this tribesman had been on display. No pamphlets, no transparencies, none of Mr. Archer's hyperbolic effusions in the newspaper. The tribesman had barely crossed his mind since the day he'd banished Cuvier to the cellar. But here he was, wearing decent trousers, leaning over the edge of the tank. He must be sixty years old, Guillaudeu observed. The man dipped his hand into the bucket and held out a fish. In a moment the delicate white maw of the whale appeared under his hands and delicately plucked the herring from his hand. The tribesman held out another fish with the same result.

Guillaudeu watched the tribesman daintily feed the whale, the expression on the older man's face not changing in the slightest, even when the beluga cooed appreciatively and clucked in apparent satisfaction. When the first bucket was empty, the tribesman handed it down to Guillaudeu and beckoned for the other.

Guillaudeu handed it up. "Thank you," he said uncertainly.

When the second had been doled out, the tribesman climbed down from the ladder and looked at Guillaudeu.

"I could use your help with these buckets in the morning," Guillaudeu ventured. It seemed odd to ask an older man for help. The two men blinked at each other.

"Museum," replied the tribesman and walked away.

On the roof, the Happy Family was looking decidedly bedraggled; now that the weather was warming up they needed some shade. Guillaudeu unlocked the wooden door to the cage and ducked inside. The prairie squirrels immediately ran up and all three sat up on their hind legs, tapping their short tails.

"All right!" Guillaudeu laughed, filling their bowl with chopped vegetables. The coyote retreated to the farthest corner and stood with its back to Guillaudeu. He filled each food bowl one by one. The snake lay sleeping, still half inside the remnants of its old skin, which hung in crinkled tatters.

On the way back down, Guillaudeu visited the aquaria on the fourth floor: the octopus tank, seahorses, huge vats of tropical fish. He had been astonished to discover that museum visitors were in the habit of tossing things, usually food detritus or ticket stubs, into the animal cages. He would need to conduct several daily patrols to make sure none of the animals were harmed.

He skipped down the stairs of the back stairwell two at a time, his head full of the animals. He would conduct patrols, keep a detailed journal of the animals' behavior, perhaps even initiate a correspondence with one of the zoologists in Philadelphia. He wondered if Barnum might consider placing him in charge of obtaining new members of the menagerie, so that Guillaudeu could realign the methods of acquisition with taxonomic propriety.

Guillaudeu stopped abruptly as he approached the second-floor landing. A strange shape flitted across his mind. He closed his eyes to see it better: a soft, delicate creature housed in a curved horn was hovering in the black sea of his mind's eye. Wavy brown lines against a milky white shell. He saw it clearly now: *Nautilus pompilius*. Guillaudeu gasped, delighted. Not a puzzle, though there were many interlocking parts. Not a hive, but a nautilus.

On the surface, of course, the museum would appear not to be a spiral. But the longer he kept the nautilus in mind, slowly spinning in the black abyss of deepest water, the more certain Guillaudeu became: The museum resembled this strange creature. The main stairway, drawing people up and around, was the siphon. The dense crowds streaming through acted as water, gaining pressure and generating propulsion. The museum itself did not move, of course, except with the current of public fancy and at the bidding of Barnum's hidden will. But like the mollusk, the museum contained chamber after chamber, instinctively constructing its graceful architecture to facilitate its own growth, as well as to house the movements of the public's imagination. But wasn't there also a distinction, Guillaudeu mused, between the expansive, outward spiral and the destructive inward one? This museum, it seemed, accommodated both the galaxy and the maelstrom. Wasn't the nautilus, after all, one of the most famous examples of the divine proportion, so fundamental to the universe? And if the museum could accurately, if poetically, be described as a nautilus, how big would the spiral grow, and where was it propelling itself? Toward some new age, whose rules and form were still malleable ideas in the minds of the populace? Or was it spiraling toward its own violent implosion?

Exhilarated by his revelations, and buoyed by the sense that he had gotten the better of Barnum by discovering such a profound symbol for the building he loved so well, Guillaudeu hurried down the last flight of stairs toward his office to write it all down.

"Emile!" It was William, leaning out from behind the ticket counter with something in his hand. "A letter came for you."

Guillaudeu grabbed the envelope without looking at it and continued through his office door. On the other side he found Archer, whistling ostentatiously.

"Don't worry, my dear Guillaudeu," said the ad man, tipping his hat. "Our problem is solved, and I hold no ill feelings. You will once again have dominion over all of your lands." He gestured at the room. "I've found a new abode."

"You're moving out?"

"Yes. To a somewhat more . . . discreet location."

"But I thought —"

"Yes, well, let's just say sometimes it behooves a person to fade to the background for a time. You shall soon see what I mean. I'll leave it at that. Someone will be here for my things in an hour or so. I'm taking the remainder of this day off. I have . . . well . . . I will not regret the time we've spent together, despite our . . . differences. My office will be along the inner hallway." Archer continued, pointing away from the street. "Beyond the waxworks. Not too far from Barnum's."

"A good place to work. Quiet." Guillaudeu did not know what else to say.

"Quiet. Good. Well."

When he left, Mr. Archer closed the door silently behind him. After the noise of the crowds and the animals, Guillaudeu found the office gloomily silent. Wasn't there something he was going to do? His momentum gone, he tapped the fingers of one hand on his desk and looked anywhere but the empty shelves. He slumped into his chair. Still staring blankly ahead, he fingered the envelope William had delivered. Slowly, he registered the embossed lettering, the stamped insignia, as those of the Lyceum of Natural History. Gawking, he smoothed the letters lightly with his fingertips and held the envelope for some time before he opened it.

Impressed with the importance of the study of Natural History as connected with the wants, comforts, and the happiness of mankind, and particularly as it relates to the illustration of the physical character of the country we inhabit, We the members of the Lyceum of Natural History do hereby invite you, Mr. Emile Guillaudeu, to associate yourself with us as a Resident Member, for the better cultivation and more extensive promotion of the above.

The meeting was tomorrow. Tomorrow! He knew there was an intricate and often lengthy procedure for inducting new members. How had he even come to their attention, after all this time? Could it have been Barnum himself who nominated him?

Years ago he'd petitioned the society and practically begged for admission, but after receiving no reply, and no acknowledgment from Lyceum members who had visited Scudder's collection over the years, he'd given it up. He'd always hoped they would one day see him as one of their brethren, and they finally had. Excitedly, he looked around his empty office.

Forty

When he saw the Lyceum of Natural History building for the first time, Guillaudeu was forced to correct his expectation that the establishment would at least attempt to imitate Aristotle's original school in Athens, in which scholars paced under ornate covered walkways, hypothesizing the parameters of Nature's great scheme amid gardens that reflected those patterns in miniature. He thought, at the very least, that its interior would be an enlargement of an Italian virtuoso's study, with geodes and astronomical instruments crowded among half-unfurled maps of Patagonia.

He was disappointed to see that the Lyceum was housed in a narrow brick building identical to the residences on either side. As he stepped through the nondescript foyer, his remaining illusions dissolved. He was startled to find a medium-sized room, bare except for several tables on one side and a grouping of chairs in front of a small podium on the other. The only thing filling the room at the moment was conversation, emanating from the twenty or so men standing among tables not covered with instruments or specimens but with sandwiches.

Guillaudeu recovered quickly and approached these men not with his accustomed dread, but eagerly. He recognized some of their faces, even knew one or two by name. Before he lost his nerve he introduced himself to the first man he encountered, a friendly ornithologist called Dr. Putnam.

Soon he'd met five other members of the Lyceum, all recently graduated from Columbia College's new School of Natural Science.

"Mr. Guillaudeu is guardian to the creatures in Barnum's American Museum," Dr. Putnam explained to the younger men. "You'd be surprised how many zoological displays Barnum has installed."

"I'm not sure I'm capable of being surprised inside that building," said one of the men, a rotund young fellow by the name of Standish who appeared even younger than he was by the thick blond curls hanging about his face. "When I go to Barnum's museum, I *want* to be surprised. And yet there is such a plethora of anomalies that it's impossible to retain one's sense of wonder. After an hour I expect surprise, which is most unsatisfactory. I can only imagine the effect of being there on a daily basis."

"It is a strange place," Guillaudeu agreed. "My attention is primarily devoted to the natural history collection and the new living menagerie," he went on calmly. "I let most of the museum's other contents pass by me without much consideration."

"That's all well and good," replied Standish. "Until those other contents begin to affect your livelihood. I've been following the story of the family of acrobats in the *Atlas*. They're still being held at the Tombs. I think it's a shame that the museum hasn't gotten them out by now. There are three women, one of them a grandmother!"

"Yes, that was an unpleasant business," Guillaudeu replied. He did not say that he hadn't kept up with the story beyond the headlines, or that ticket sales at the museum had jumped thanks to the press after the Martinettis' arrest.

"So you are the keeper of Barnum's menagerie!" Another man, also very young, joined in the group. He was a specialist in tropical fish, he was quick to assert.

"How in the world did he get those magnificent seahorses? I believe they are the only ones to be found on the eastern seaboard, if not the entire country."

"Barnum has scouts all over the world," Guillaudeu replied, feeling distinctly knowledgeable. "They bring the fish by boat to —"

"He must have a special arrangement," Standish interrupted. "Because as far as I know, all imported fish must pass through the customhouse. I know for a fact that none of Barnum's acquisitions has ever —"

"Let's not get into the minutiae of it," Dr. Putnam interjected. "I am so glad, Mr. Guillaudeu, that you have joined us. I believe our speaker for tonight is ready to begin. Are you acquainted with the work of Quincy Kipp?"

"No." Guillaudeu hoped his ignorance would not be too noticeable.

"Well, Kipp didn't have much to say about birds, which is a shame, but his work was interesting nonetheless."

Dr. Putnam led Guillaudeu to a chair, and Guillaudeu now saw one of the Lyceum men guiding a woman toward the podium.

"Sadly, Kipp passed on several years ago, but his daughter has become something of a champion for his work here as well as in Britain."

The woman waited for the voices of her audience to subside. She appeared to be examining the men in the audience very closely. Her face brought to Guillaudeu's mind the sound of gulls and the taste of a sour dinner roll.

"My name is Lilian Kipp," she said crisply. "As some of you know, I have been in America for several months, presenting the work of my father, Professor Quincy Kipp. I am grateful for the opportunity to address members of your Lyceum, especially on an evening as lovely as this."

His eyes going wide, he remembered the landing at Spuyten Duyvil. This was the woman who'd bought his volume of Linnaeus. He shrank in his chair.

"My father traveled the globe in the service of the British government. It may surprise some of you that as a youth his interest was chiefly in the fine arts, sculpture in particular. Before anything else, he was an artist. It is not my intention to give his entire biography to you tonight, nor to chron-

icle his personal journey from art to science, but let me just
say that in nature my father saw an artistic genius more
perfect than Michelangelo. He saw geometry more impressive than that of the Greeks. In nature's mysteries he
found lessons comparable in number and meaning to those
contained in any holy book. It was his belief that catalog-
ing and organizing nature was not enough for a thoughtful mind to accomplish. Serious contemplation of these
subjects is evident in his work. Philosophical thought. But
more than anything else there is compassion. A human soul
reaching for a personal relationship with the spectrum of nature."

Miss Kipp had clenched one of her small fists. She spoke
with fervent conviction. Her bearing evoked a feeling of so-
lidity, of squareness and exact alignment. Guillaudeu was
rapt, simultaneously wanting her to recognize him and also
wanting to run away.

"His work is intimately connected with poetry, it's true.
Some have argued that there is no place for this kind of work
in the annals of science. But I believe the boundary between
these disciplines is malleable. That a healthy line of inquiry
can contain threads of poetry braided to the filaments of natural philosophy. We need only to look to examples like Eras-
mus Darwin and Leonardo da Vinci to see the precedent for
this mode.

"I have brought several of my father's notebooks with me
tonight, which will be displayed on these tables following my
presentation. It is my hope that you will find much of interest and enjoyment in these pages. I have also published a
volume of his writings and drawings, which will be for sale.
At this time, I would now like to read to you from one of
these volumes, entitled *Quincy Kipp's Epistemonicon: Toward a
New Understanding of Beasts and Men*."

Lilian Kipp obscured her face by raising an open book in
front of it. Her voice was clear and strong.

"Bradypus tridactylus, *the three-toed sloth, rarely comes down from
its tree. With its disproportionately long limbs, a sloth on the ground*

cannot even support its own body weight, and this predicament reduces the creature to an embarrassing, spread-eagled grope.

"Safely aloft, however, the sloth maintains its lifestyle of nineteen hours asleep followed by five hours of mild wakefulness, the highlights of which include twig-eating and prolonged gazing. The sloth lives its ten-year life span in this way, high in the crooks of trumpet trees. It does not hunt or utter a single sound. It is nonterritorial and cannot fight. Eventually, we must ask: What is the sloth for?

"It's no surprise if you can't picture the face of a sloth. Its closest relative is the armadillo, but what help is that? The sloth has no first cousin and is solitary by nature. It may appear to be an evolutionary orphan, but before we find ourselves weeping in sympathy, notice the greenish hue of the sloth's unusually long, coarse coat. Its fur was made with a certain aptitude for attracting algae, and there it grows, especially during rainy seasons. Along with this primeval colony, the sloth's coat harbors moths and beetles that live off the algae. The sloth is even known to lick its own fur to get a taste of it, perhaps at those times when pulling a leaf is too much bother. And so, if we take the time, we see the sloth is not alone at all.

"Bradypus tridactylus is endowed with three hollow claws on the ends of each of its limbs. By hooking securely around slim branches, the curved claws allow the sloth to hang comfortably in its natural position: upside down. If you happen to see a sloth hanging this way, you might notice an unusual fact. While the coats of other longhaired animals fall down their sides from a sort of middle part along the spine, the sloth enjoys a part on its belly, with its long hair hanging with gravity toward its back. The sloth is so well adapted to this position in the world that it even gives birth and sleeps while firmly attached by its claws, a living hammock.

"If you're trying to make sense of the sloth, simply look beyond the bias of its name. Could it be this animal is simply more aligned with its dream world? That it climbs high into the canopy because, to its sensibility, the earth is distracting, if not irrelevant? Perhaps the sloth is a deft navigator of its own soul and, if it ever decided to speak, would answer all of our questions in a soft somniloquy."

Lilian Kipp spoke for three-quarters of an hour, and when she had finished, the members of the Lyceum followed her to the display tables where she had laid out her father's notebooks. Guillaudeu waited until she had extricated herself from the first group of men who accosted her before he approached.

"I believe we almost met," Guillaudeu offered. He felt strangely elated. "At Spuyten Duyvil."

Lilian Kipp cocked her head, her forehead creasing. Then she gasped. "Linnaeus?"

Guillaudeu made an exaggerated bow. "I hope you enjoyed it."

"I have. Although I wondered over the inscription. This Edie person really wanted you to have the book. I felt awful after I bought it from you. In fact, I looked for you on the ferry. To give it back. I'm sure Edie would want you to keep it."

"Edie and I . . . are no longer close. You probably didn't see me on the Hudson because I was outside on deck for the whole voyage."

She laughed, showing her small white teeth, straight on the top row and crooked on the bottom.

"Well, here we are, in an entirely new place and time. I see that you've another set of clothes after all."

"I'd been traveling on foot for some time when we met." Guillaudeu made a formal introduction of himself.

"Barnum's museum!" Lilian Kipp laughed. "My favorite place on the whole island of New York. I've written to all my friends in London, telling them it is worth the voyage just to see it. I've been at least six times. More!"

Guillaudeu was taken aback. "More?"

"My favorite is the sewing dog!"

"Cornelia? Really?"

"Among the popular displays. The diorama showing Vesuvius' eruption is also impressive. What's your favorite?"

Guillaudeu had never considered such a thing. "My work is taxidermy."

"But among Barnum's hoaxes? His exhibits, his so-called Representatives of the Wonderful?"

"I don't usually pay them any attention."

"How is that possible? Don't you walk among them every day?"

Guillaudeu was afraid Lilian Kipp was about to dismiss him as a terrible bore. Several men were circling their way closer to her, clearly hoping to catch her attention for a question or two.

"There is one exhibit I've grown very fond of, although you haven't seen it."

"Oh, I'm sure I have. I've explored every salon and gallery in that building. I'm quite sure."

"No, I'm certain there's one you haven't seen. It's quite intriguing. In fact" — Guillaudeu leaned closer to Lilian Kipp and felt something of Barnum in his words — "it's a bit of a secret; I cannot speak of it publicly."

"Oh?" Lilian Kipp leaned closer, and Guillaudeu smelled licorice. "There is a region of Barnum's labyrinth I haven't discovered?"

"Yes. I don't know how long it will remain a secret, though. Perhaps you'd like to see it?" As he spoke he was aware only that it was a simple invitation that she accepted just as the circling Lyceum members closed in and swept her away from him. After he had found Dr. Putnam and made arrangements for him to visit the new aviary the following morning, Guillaudeu emerged into the full dark of the street. He noticed the particularly deep blueness of the sky. He felt his spirit scooped up into that blue, and for a moment he imagined himself aloft, his ankle tethered by a rope to the lamppost to keep him from drifting into the atmosphere.

Forty-one

"But what is a bird without a tree?" posed Dr. Putnam, standing a few paces from Guillaudeu at the center of the gallery. "My single suggestion for this aviary is foliation, my good man. *Foliation!*"

Dr. Putnam rotated on his heel, his eyes searching out the shadowy forms of birds along the aviary's moldings. His round, blunt face and bony elbows resembled the mantis *Tenodera sinensis*.

"Improve this habitat by bringing in more potted trees. Install a section of tall grasses, some flowering shrubbery! And certainly more pedestal drinking pools. It would be a dire injustice for these animals to be deprived of the leaves and grass to which they are accustomed. Dire." The ornithologist's fervency was a bit disconcerting.

"As I'm sure you know, these birds have been living in a state of anxiety since the moment of their capture. Just behold that pair of evening grosbeaks. When does one ever see evening grosbeaks so still? To endow them with trees is a necessary service. If I were you, I would even paint the walls. In the form of trees, perhaps, or even simply the color green. The birds won't be bothered by the paint and afterward they will feel much more comfortable."

Guillaudeu scrawled Dr. Putnam's recommendations in a small notebook. The room was not entirely devoid of foliage: a few saplings leaned in heavy urns, and someone had provided bundles of branches, some quite large, and attached

279

them by rope to the ceiling. Each of these makeshift perches, as well as the window moldings and ornamental woodwork, swarmed with birds.

"And as to the species, Dr. Putnam, what do you recognize? I was left no notations, no indication of what type of birds are here."

Dr. Putnam shook his head sadly. "Most distressing. I would like to speak with Barnum about this. He seems to have very little compassion for his avian comrades."

"I suspect he hasn't given these comrades much thought at all."

Dr. Putnam removed a pair of tiny brass binoculars from his jacket pocket and raised them to his eyes. "It is admirable that you are improving this situation," he remarked as he scanned the room. "You will strengthen the impact of the birds on museum visitors. Ah! Someone has brought you a horned lark! And it even looks like the western variety. And its mate, good. Aviaries are wonderful places. Just think: Is there anyone who would not get a thrill to have one of these cardinals fly close overhead, from one branch to another? Just imagine a mother pointing out a monk parakeet in the process of nest-building to her child. The true question in my mind is this: What is the world without birds?"

"I am grateful for your help!" blurted Guillaudeu. "I am grateful. I am new to this whole business."

"Birds are a wonderful business!" Dr. Putnam chuckled. "And we aviphiles are not a cutthroat bunch. Call on me whenever you wish. What in the world is a purple gallinule doing here? It appears to be without a mate, unfortunately. You will need to build a small pond or pseudo-marsh for it. And a wood thrush! Oh, how lucky you are! What a voice on that little fellow. And it looks like . . . wait, I can't see" — Dr. Putnam swung wildly, following the darting glides of a small bird high above them — "yes, cliff swallows! Gorgeous! Unbelievable that they are here! And already building nests! Up there where the wall meets the ceiling. Where are they getting mud for that? Wonderful, just wonderful."

Dr. Putnam watched the birds for several more minutes,

swinging his binoculars to and fro. As Guillaudeu escorted him toward the burlap curtain that hung in front of the door, the ornithologist paused.

"I am so glad Miss Scudder recommended you to join us at the Lyceum. Sometimes we members can become somewhat insular. It is refreshing to draw in new perspectives."

"Edie?"

Dr. Putnam was puzzled by the expression on Guillaudeu's face. "Why, haven't you spoken with her? She sent such a beautiful nomination letter, co-written by her father. Usually, you know, the process for inaugurating new members is more scientific. But since the Scudders are so dear to us, and she was so fervent, there was a unanimous vote. And if you must know, the Lyceum's coffers are quite empty at the moment, so all new memberships do help."

Something caught Dr. Putnam's eye. "Oh heavens, oh no!" He gasped and dropped the binoculars from his eyes. "A shrike!"

"A shrike?" Guillaudeu repeated stupidly. His head pulsed with shame. Edie?

"It seemed as though all was well with your birds, but here's a shrike, a notorious cannibal of the smaller songbirds. You must capture it at once and remove it to its own cage. At once! Where did they get a shrike, of all the birds out there in the world!"

Guillaudeu was not sure how he would go about capturing a shrike, but he certainly wouldn't attempt it in the company of Dr. Putnam. He assured the other man he would isolate the bird, thanked him for his recommendations, and escorted him from the aviary. When the ornithologist had gone, Guillaudeu grabbed his coat and pushed his way against the crowd at the museum's entrance. He launched himself onto Broadway, where a light rain misted his skin. Too impatient to wait for an omnibus, he crossed Broadway and started south, signaling the first cabriolet he saw. Its two black mares carried him swiftly to the Front Street port. He bounded up the stairs to Edie's office and found it empty, the door ajar.

With the curtains drawn back, the huge windows of her

office framed the harbor as a portrait of commerce. Gulls circled the ships moored in the distance, and in the foreground was a forest of a hundred swaying masts. On the docks below the windows, men speaking many different languages unloaded the myriad cargo that fed the city, while others loaded provisions for the next voyage. It happened here just as it had for centuries all across the world's oceans, Guillaudeu ruminated, temporarily distracted. The cargo changed over time, but some of these ships had been sailing unchanged for decades, recognized by generations of captains as they passed one another at some distant ocean crossroads.

By the time he saw Edie she was staring up at him from the rain-slick dock where she'd been directing the sailors, her hands on her hips. His heart jumped. She motioned to him, raising both arms and pulling them down near her temples. He cocked his head, confused. She pointed to him accusingly and then motioned to her own head. Was she telling him to get out of there? That she didn't want to speak with him? That he was crazy? He had ruined everything.

Frowning, she jabbed her fingers toward him again, and then she started shouting. Guillaudeu wanted to flee, but no, he would face this. He deserved her anger, every ounce of it. Had he not turned his back on her, his closest friend? He opened one of the windows.

"Bring me my hat, you silly man! I'm getting soaked!"

Cautiously, he brought it, a floppy old felt thing that would hold more water than it repelled. Her hair was a dripping net of tangles and her skirt streaked with creosote. She embraced him immediately. "I was wondering when you'd come."

He delivered mumbled apologies to her damp shoulder. He'd been foolish, he told her. Brainless! How could he blame her for Barnum's changes at the museum?

"You are so stubborn, Emile. I knew there was nothing I could say that would reach you." By her tone he knew he was forgiven. "But when Father saw you outside the house, you appeared to be quite mad! That's what got us worrying. He misses you! How many times must I say that to you? You pretend to be so alone in the world, when your family is right here! Why you didn't come to live with us after Celia died is really beyond me, but what can I do? You won't listen. You don't have to say anything, just don't be silly anymore. Now, come with me to lunch. I'm starving."

"I'm starving, too," Guillaudeu murmured. He followed her up the dock, abashed and suddenly very glad.

Forty-two

The next morning Guillaudeu set to work. The aviary door bore a sign reading TEMPORARILY CLOSED. He obtained various supplies at Dr. Putnam's recommendation and could already envision the finished aviary: Netting would hang like a high-topped tent. Below, a path winding through the trees would give the visitors an entire journey with the birds, with several benches and a small fountain along the way. Perhaps there would be a small plaque, engraved with the words of Audubon and including a small dedication to Celia, the beloved wife of museum naturalist Emile Guillaudeu.

Within ten minutes of setting to work, he became uncomfortably tangled in the netting he had purchased. It was not particularly fine netting, but in an attempt to lay it out flat, Guillaudeu had caught the buckle of his shoe and then two waistcoat buttons. The more Guillaudeu fumbled with it, the more entrenched, and panicked, he became. After five minutes of struggle, he lay at rest on the floor with both of his feet thoroughly enmeshed. He had not thought to bring a knife, and he had already bruised his hand trying to snap the hemp cord. If he attempted to return to his office, he would drag fifty feet of net behind him.

The purple gallinule crept toward him, clenching and unclenching each three-pronged foot before setting it delicately down again. The gallinule turned one eye upon him and then the other. It stepped closer.

"I am an imbecile," he told it.

"*To too two terp t too,*" the gallinule replied.

Other birds came close, flitting to the sill above him and swooping overhead. Guillaudeu became uneasy. The gallinule's eyes were beady, the gestures of its head and legs eerily human. He couldn't keep track of the smaller birds that flitted around him. Two pearlish brown doves pattered across the floor toward him with speed. He recoiled. They cocked their heads and ruffled. Guillaudeu renewed his efforts to untangle himself. He felt he was being watched. His eyes caught too many flickers of movement all around. The swallows dipped closer, seeming to close in on him. Distracted and trapped, he cursed the birds of the world. He pictured Dr. Putnam's horror at such a gesture. High above him, two ravens, *Corvus corax,* emerged from inside the bowl of the chandelier. They perched on the rim. They watched him.

Finally, after removing his shoes, his socks, the buttons from his waistcoat, and his dignity, Guillaudeu wriggled free of the netting. He scrambled back into his clothes before addressing the birds.

"There now, then. Much better." He brushed his knees and backed away from the doves, who queried him with a round of head-bobbing. "No need for alarm. Just your keeper making a mess of things." He continued backing away until he reached the aviary door and slipped outside. He breathed deeply.

William's nephew, Gideon, was nowhere to be found and Mr. Forsythe, the theater manager, had recently forbidden his workers to leave their posts to help with other museum tasks. Guillaudeu didn't want to spend all day searching for someone to help him with the aviary, so he climbed the back stairs all the way to the fifth floor.

The tribesman had been hauling the buckets of fish up each morning and administering the whale's morning feeding. After his initial concern, Guillaudeu was delighted by the man's diligent and solemn execution of the task, and grateful for the help. Most mornings he would meet the tribesman at the beluga tank for a few minutes before proceeding up to the roof to feed the Happy Family. He picked up the neatly stacked buckets on his way back down.

Guillaudeu crept past the Indian camp, where someone was snoring on one of the cots. He passed through the door to the hall of apartments and made his way to the final door on the left.

"It seems I need another pair of hands," Guillaudeu offered when the tribesman opened his door. He must be closer to seventy, Guillaudeu noted. He pointed to himself, then the other man, and back to himself. "Will you help me?"

Guillaudeu made a poor imitation of a bird with his thumbs hooked together and both hands flapping. He pointed up the hall. "In the aviary."

The tribesman nodded as if he'd been expecting the request. He carefully removed a wool shirt from a hook on the wall and buttoned himself into it.

"You will help me?" Guillaudeu hadn't expected it to be so easy. The tribesman tacitly agreed. On the way out, Guillaudeu picked up the beluga's ladder.

"The things you've seen, coming all the way from Botany Bay." As they returned to the fourth-floor aviary, Guillaudeu had the unexpected urge to converse. "You could be quite a lecturer on the subject of your travels. There are many in this city who would be interested in you. You would have no trouble finding sponsorship. To lecture. If you wished. Which I don't think you do, but I can't be sure.

"You know," Guillaudeu continued. "I'm a bit of a traveler myself. I know, it may be difficult to imagine, but it's true. I walked almost the entire length of New York Island." The tribesman was the first person he had told.

Once inside the aviary the tribesman seemed to understand the purpose of the room, and after a few seconds watching the birds he disregarded them completely. They set up the ladders and began to nail up the netting.

"Well this seems to be working much better," Guillaudeu remarked. "And strange as it may be, I am enjoying your company very much. Is it unusual to prefer the company of one with whom I do not share the benefit of language?" He glanced at the tribesman, who worked without pause. "I believe that says something about my interest in my fellow man, doesn't it? The truth is, I am relieved to find a person to whom I must give no explanations of any kind."

The men ascended and descended parallel ladders, raising netting and retrieving dropped nails.

"If you are not obliged to perform," Guillaudeu said, starting up the conversation again after twenty minutes, "I wonder what you are doing here."

The tribesman paused for a look in Guillaudeu's direction.

"In other words, what is keeping you here? You could walk outside and never return, if you pleased. Not that I want you to do that, of course. I should like to know your name, but that seems entirely impossible."

Presently, the tribesman began to sing. It was an unusual piece of music, with barely enunciated vowel sounds rising and falling between intervals of throaty tones. The song continued for a period of minutes and Guillaudeu recognized a kind of refrain, but the verses between seemed to grow consecutively longer and bore no discernible resemblance to one another. After ten minutes, Guillaudeu gave up trying to characterize the song, and after twenty minutes the song seemed to have always been there. As with the tribesman's general presence, the song put Guillaudeu at ease. He hung the netting and drifted into an enjoyment of the work and the warm sunlight on his face.

When the tribesman stopped singing, it wasn't at the end of the song. By that time Guillaudeu had correctly supposed that the song couldn't possibly have an ending. For a minute or two Guillaudeu didn't notice that the other man had stopped, but when he did, the silence hit him abruptly, and he felt an unexpected sadness. When he looked down from the perch of his ladder, the tribesman was at the base of it.

"What is it, sir? I do wish you'd keep up the song." Guillaudeu hummed a few notes as he came back to the ground.

For the first time in their brief acquaintance, the stranger responded to Guillaudeu's voice. He put his hand on the taxidermist's arm and gestured for him to follow.

The gallery adjoining the aviary on the fourth floor held the glassblowers and their furnace. The glassblowers drew large crowds, and the heat of their fire added to the day's spring warmth, making the gallery uncomfortably hot and a vivid contrast to the cool aviary. In the far corner, Cornelia the sewing dog panted and pumped the pedals of her machine.

The tribesman led him straight to a small cabinet in the corner of the next gallery, which had drawn no crowd. The *Ornithorhynchus anatinus* sat on its pedestal, its brassy fur gathering dust and its broad, fleshy bill absurd as ever.

Amid the clamor of the forge and the intermittent call of the cold-drink vendor, the tribesman spoke in a low voice, drawing invisible figures on the palm of his hand using his right index finger as a pencil. The *Ornithorhynchus* had some special meaning to the man. Guillaudeu listened to the tribesman, whose voice was just barely audible.

"I suppose there is no translator, maybe in all of New York, who could enlighten me as to what you say," Guillaudeu said softly. "And you are probably giving me the information about this creature I looked for in all the books."

The tribesman continued marking lines on the palm of his hand.

"I have a pencil in the aviary. Let's see if that helps," Guillaudeu said. They returned, and he found a sheet of thick brown wrapping paper and handed it and the pencil to his companion. "Show me," he encouraged.

With his eyes, the tribesman asked Guillaudeu what paper and pencil had to do with anything. Guillaudeu again made writing gestures, and finally resorted to humming a few notes of the tribesman's original song. After a few seconds of rumination, the tribesman began to draw.

The tribesman worked slowly, beginning on one edge of the wrapping paper, making seven small circles arranged in a rough crescent. He then marked out a path through them. His lines branched out from the seven circles, and he followed one branch, creating what seemed to be geography around it as he went. The tribesman worked so slowly that Guillaudeu went back to work, periodically checking on his progress as he moved his ladder and continued with the netting.

When the tribesman finally brought it to Guillaudeu, the map covered nearly the whole surface of the paper. Extending out from the seven circles, which Guillaudeu sensed were hills or mountains of some kind, were what appeared to be streams, ravines, and broad expanses of flat terrain. Approaching the right-hand side of the map, the desert transitioned to rolling hills, which the tribesman had crosshatched with the pencil.

"Forests?" Guillaudeu pointed to the crosshatched marks. "Trees?" He raised his arms above his head in a gross approximation. The tribesman did not respond to Guillaudeu's effort, but he traced a route across the map, from left to right, ending at what appeared to be a coastline. He then backtracked a finger to a stream, or river, running through the crosshatched section. He tapped this region several times and pointed through the aviary wall toward the *Ornithorhynchus*.

"A-ha! Is this where the creature lives?" Guillaudeu tapped the paper. The tribesman tipped his head in a gesture Guillaudeu interpreted as affirmative.

That evening, when Guillaudeu returned to his office, he brought out a map published by the United States Exploring Expedition of sections of Australia, primarily the eastern coastal areas of that vast continent. He spread it out on his desk with the tribesman's drawing alongside it. After several minutes of looking between them, he recognized the same river outlined on both. Setting the tribesman's map against the other, he saw that the tribesman's map extended deep into the unmapped interior of the land, hundreds of miles beyond the last lines of the American cartographers. The scales of the maps were different, of course, and one was based on geometry and precisely measured distances. It wasn't until he sat staring at the strange continuum between the high-quality paper and inks of the one and the penciled lines of the other that he wondered how the tribesman could have drawn the terrain in the first place, as if he'd flown over the land on the back of a giant bird.

The tribesman could navigate by landforms, winds, and by the night sky. That's why he left the home place with the keeper. He always went with the keeper to visit the oldest places, walking a full twenty paces behind him so he would not hear the song, but he had heard it despite this precaution, and he had learned it by the time he was thirty, though he dared not sing it aloud. He went with the keeper many times a year, to Nanguluwur, Ubirr, and Burrunggui. Sometimes they did not go to the old places; they went walking across the savanna, or by raft during the wet seasons, so the keeper could listen for information that came from the water, from the dry ground, and from the cliffs. They returned to the people after days, sometimes weeks, with guidance and news. Incorporating the new knowledge, the people would move to the next camp, or they would stay until the eucalypts flowered or the magpie geese took flight.

But the last time had been different; the tribesman knew it right away, even if the rest of the people did not. The keeper beckoned to him in his usual way, and pointed east. The tribesman prepared for a journey but he could not feel the reason for it. The old women talked among themselves: He was going now? With the thunderheads building? They did not understand it but they trusted the keeper, as they should.

The keeper led him to the east. The tribesman thought they would go to Nourlangie, but after a day's walk away from the camp the keeper turned north. The tribesman's unease grew. This was not the way toward any ancestor, unless the song had given the keeper knowledge much deeper than anyone knew.

On the evening of the second day of walking the keeper had come to him. Brother. The keeper's white hair glowed in the nighttime. Brother, we are going to the sea. The tribesman knew he was smiling. It is the sea we need to ask. The keeper's voice was strange, different. He squatted next to the tribesman, rocking gently back and forth on his heels, twisting a length of his hair between his fingers.

The tribesman noticed his eyes were red-rimmed and watery. The keeper was very old. He held centuries of knowledge, but could he walk that far? The people knew the sea only by what they heard in stories. Those stories had nothing to do with life at the home place. Why? whispered the tribesman. We have never gone there. What is the need? We have never gone there for anything. Something is changing, the keeper told him. That is what I know. We must find out what it is and bring the news back. Now is the time to go and get this information.

For four days they walked across dry floodplain, through forests where the rustling of leaves blocked every other sound. They watched thunderheads pass above their heads and drop their rain far to the west. The keeper walked steadily in his uneven gait, limping from his old wound. As they went farther and farther the tribesman's fear grew, and he mourned. He hated to leave the home country more than anything else in his life. The aunts and grandmothers had always teased him, ever since he was a boy, saying the only reason he learned how to read landscapes, how to mark paths and navigate by the night sky, was so that wherever he was, he could return very quickly to his bed.

As they walked, he tried to keep the home place with him. He saw the men poised ankle-deep in the shallow wetlands, spears raised. Faster than you could see, they speared turtles through the neck. The hunters walked back to the stone cliffs before dusk, watching the wood swallows roosting in the high crevices. The women plucked the last geese of the season, storing the down and stringing flight feathers and hanging them among the rocks. The tribesman wanted more than anything to return, to feel the first drops of the rain on his back. He wanted to walk into the shelter and breathe the scent of roasting bird, of coming storm. But without the tribesman the keeper would be lost. And the people needed a keeper, so the tribesman could not turn back.

The song on his lips tastes metallic, brings a vision of rain and the smell of wet eucalypts. He moans when he feels the wooden floor of the museum under his feet and hears the sound of horse's hooves and clanging metal harnesses on Broadway. He covers his ears, but nothing helps. He is nowhere, dying, waiting.

Forty-three

"But where did they come from?"

"Chicago, probably. Most of the Indian shows originate there."

"I mean before that. Where are they from?"

Guillaudeu was incredulous. Lilian Kipp's interest had swerved almost immediately from the enigmatic white whale, the secret he'd used to bring her to the museum, to the Indians who lived beside it. The presence of the beluga had startled her, of course. She had scaled the ladder, even extended a hand to the creature, which had given it a hesitant nibble. But she was entirely more intrigued by the Indian camp, even though no one was there.

"These baskets," she had exclaimed. "I saw some like them at the British Museum before I left home. The motifs remind me of Greek mosaic, do you see the similarity? I haven't had a chance to see any of your Indians yet. I would love to travel west, but I don't have the time right now. I'd better go soon, though. Tribes like this won't last long."

"They've been living here for several months." Guillaudeu struggled to recall another detail about the Indians. "They perform two shows a day. Dancing, I believe."

"We should see them! Could we? Ever since I was a girl I was always envious of you Americans with your Indians. I imagined if I'd been born here I would have run away from home and been adopted by some."

"Oh?"

"Isn't that silly?"

"Not at all, Miss Kipp."

"Oh yes, it is. If we're to be friends you must tell the truth, Mr. Guillaudeu!"

Guillaudeu blushed. Once again, Miss Kipp had slipped into a directness that he found exciting, terrifying, and somehow a relief. Linked to her, he felt himself anchored to the ground instead of stumbling over uneven, undulating terrain.

"To be quite frank, then, I am at a loss. I showed you the museum's greatest treasure and greatest secret. It is the only beluga whale in the country, and yet you are entirely more interested in the Indians."

"A-ha! That's better, Mr. Guillaudeu. The answer is simple: I have seen the whale before."

"That's not possible! The public isn't allowed into the fifth floor at all."

"No. Not *this* whale. I've seen belugas in the seas of Greenland. I accompanied my father on one of his last voyages, and we watched the whales, hundreds of them, as they foraged in Baffin Bay. This is a fine whale, though. I will pay it more attention if that makes you feel any better."

"But that would not be truthful, Miss Kipp! No need for you to cater to an old man's delusion. I simply assumed that, like me, no one had ever glimpsed one before."

"Most people haven't."

"But I managed to find the one woman who had."

"I was glad to be found."

Guillaudeu offered Lilian Kipp his arm. "As I understand it, there is an Indian show at eight o'clock this evening. If we want to see it, we should ascend now to the Aerial Garden and Perpetual Fair for supper."

The evening was windy and warm. Clouds in the shape of all manner of pastries scudded low against a purplish backdrop. He seated her at a table near the railing. It was the first time Guillaudeu had eaten supper on the roof. The prospect of navigating the crowds had always been distasteful enough to send him into the streets instead, or home. Now that he was here, the people did not bother him. The view to the harbor was spectacular, and off to his right he could see the Happy Family in its cage. The coyote seemed to be watching him specifically. Hoping for food, he suspected.

Lilian Kipp regarded patrons, restaurant waiters, even the tableware aligned in front of her with the same exacting scrutiny she had given to the Indian baskets. Now she gazed over the railing at the city below. Guillaudeu felt he would lose her completely to the many-layered vista if he didn't engage her in conversation right away.

"You inherited the naturalist's capacity for information."

"Something of it. Compared with the others I am a dilettante. In some it borders on mania. Useful mania. An accepted one, but mania nonetheless."

"Was your father afflicted with it?"

"Mania? Perhaps. He *was* considered something of an oddity. He was always abroad, and when he was home in Bradworthy he walked through the fields and woods, taking down notes and observations of things the farmers could not even see. He wandered and wandered, in circles and loops, backtracking and cutting his way through thickets. Yes, some people considered him a bit off. And then after a few months out would come an article, published in London or Edinburgh, making some new sense of the grub or the blackbird. I adored him, of course. I would stumble along behind, making notes of my own, which he insisted I read to him. He would pretend to augment his findings with mine."

"You moved to London when he died?"

"Yes. The contours of my life have been wholly determined by his."

"I'm sure that's not true," said Guillaudeu. Lilian Kipp had issued her comment casually, without blinking. If it was intended for humor he could not say, and he experienced an unpleasant memory of his wife's cholera-stricken face.

"Oh, it certainly is! The farm was Mother's. But we stayed there for him. He could not bear to live in the city. But as soon as he died we were off. Once again, he prompted our move. And the Royal Society offered me work only because I am his daughter."

"It seems a sad way to look at things, doesn't it? An over-simplification."

"But it's true," she said and laughed.

"But no one is forcing you to publish his writings, are they? It is obvious to anyone who hears you speak that there is passion behind your efforts."

She examined the black tulip in the vase on the table. The wind lifted the corner of her shawl and delivered a pleasant whiff of fennel to Guillaudeu's nostrils.

"What is *your* work, then?" he asked gently.

Lilian Kipp replied quickly. "I classify botanical and ento-mological specimens for the Royal Society. I sit at a table with Miss Bedard, who sketches each beetle while I look it up in Albin's natural history. Miss Martin fills in the sketches with watercolor."

"That sounds like the work of the Royal Society, not your own."

"You're making fun of me!"

"Not in the least," said Guillaudeu. "I truly want to know."

"I have no work of my own."

"I don't believe it," snapped Guillaudeu.

"Whyever not?" Lilian Kipp snapped back.

"Because I am convinced that everyone spins a web of their own design inside their own head. Everyone creates some personal taxonomy with its own meandering logic, some small prism of ideas and passion, no matter how deli-cate or unusual or unspoken. No one can implant such a thing in another. It springs from one's own vision."

"What a pretty thing to say," said Lilian Kipp.

He saw she had not expected it. Neither had he.

"What is yours, then, Mr. Guillaudeu?"

"I won't let you turn the conversation that way, Miss Kipp," he said. "The question was first put to you."

"Well," she began, "I *have* been investigating something over the years. It started with frogs at the pond in Bradworthy. The development from polliwog to frog is remarkable; I have countless sketches and observations of it. But several years ago my mother and I were walking in Kew Garden. We looked at the leaves of a flowering cherry tree, and I found a chrysalis. Have you ever seen a chrysalis, Mr. Guillaudeu?" Lilian Kipp appeared a bit breathless.

"I have not."

"Not many people have, which is surprising, considering there are over fifty thousand species of caterpillar in the world, and those are just the ones we've classified! There are untold thousands more, I have no doubt. A chrysalis is a thing of real beauty. Extraordinary beauty. Rare beauty. For example, if you look at one through a magnifying glass, you will see imprinted textures and patterns on its surface. These patterns, I've discovered, reflect the markings of *both* the caterpillar *and* the inchoate butterfly. But inside the shell, the actual creature has dissolved into a pulpy liquid. Liquid!" Lilian Kipp paused for a drink of water. She shook her head. "In fact, I met a man in London who kept a colony of *Smerinthus geminatus*. He was the only other person I found who was conducting his own inquiry into the process of metamorphosis. I realized his aim was much different from mine when I entered his laboratory and found that he was draining the liquid contents of the cocoons into cocoon-shaped glass vials and selling the substance to ladies of rank as an elixir. *Skin like the wing of a butterfly.*

"A frog's metamorphosis is not quite so otherworldly as that of the moth or the butterfly. The frog sprouts its limbs in plain sight. True, it changes from breathing water to air. That is no small feat." She laughed. "But consider the caterpillar! It emerges into the world and the first thing it does is consume its own leathery egg. From that moment on, all it does is eat. Its body is a simple vessel blessed with the flame of life! It doubles and triples its size within three hours of its birth. It splits out of its first skin into a bigger one, with different coloring and contours. It repeats this process two more times, evolving into several different caterpillars on its way. Then, according to some indicator still unknown to man, it hangs itself under a leaf. It is perfectly still for almost exactly twenty-four hours. Then, its skin splits apart one more time to reveal the chrysalis. From the wormy, earthbound crawler emerges this liminal phase, a hanging cocoon, more of a place than a being. Inside, slime somehow organizes itself into a powder-winged creature, an iridescent aeronaut, one of our universal symbols of beauty. Does the butterfly remember eating the leaves upon which it now alights? All of its mechanisms for survival are different. Its whole architecture has transformed. Are they two creatures, five, or one? Only when I examine the chrysalis itself, as I told you, with the magnifying glass, do I see how the caterpillar is linked to the butterfly."

Guillaudeu sat back in his chair. He observed Lilian Kipp beginning to blush. He could not speak. He felt as if she had split open her own skin and shown him a damp and unfurling wing. He looked down at his clasped hands.

"I know," she mumbled, rearranging her silverware on the napkin. "It is a relatively small concern. In the face of the great studies, of Buffon and the rest, my scrawlings and rambling thoughts are hardly . . . Isn't it a bit of a folly that I spend most afternoons studying worms, when surely there are better ways to address the troubles of the world, or at least to make one's mark upon it?"

"My dear, you have forgotten to whom you are speaking. Consider my own line of work," Guillaudeu said and smiled. "Somehow, through the convolutions of my mind, I am convinced that it does matter, though, that mine is in some way an admirable pursuit. We are both concerned with transformation. Who isn't?"

"Metempsychosis," blurted Lilian Kipp, "manifests not only in art and poetry, but in science, I am convinced. The passing of the soul at death into another body. Because the caterpillar *dies*. That much is certain. And yet it is reborn, with wings! It is a miniature phoenix. And we are too busy to ever see this phoenix rise. It baffles me. Wouldn't it make sense for us to keep caterpillars in cut-glass terrariums, to preserve them in reliquaries, worship them, even? How can we pass through the world without even considering them?"

"You clearly have not made that mistake, and you have my utmost respect in that regard."

Lilian Kipp laughed. "Why thank you."

"I am very serious. You must publish your findings."

Lilian Kipp again dropped her gaze to the tulip. Her hands, Guillaudeu noticed, were twined together tightly.

"What is it?"

"I have published," she said softly.

"How wonderful! And where might I find this work of yours?"

Lilian Kipp dipped her hand into her velveteen purse and produced a slim gray volume.

"*Kipp's Epistemonicon*?"

"I am the Kipp who wrote it," she whispered, as if someone who might report the forgery might be listening. "Not my father."

Guillaudeu blinked.

"I am a terrible fraud, I know." Lilian Kipp looked over the railing at New York Harbor, her brow creased. Guillaudeu had the fleeting desire to place a finger on that crease, to smooth it away. "I would never be published otherwise."

"But your father —"

"He was an explorer, a naturalist, all the things I said. But his works were simple treatises. Scientific only. The philosophical musings are all mine."

"The sloth?"

She turned back to him, the line of her jaw set. "Yes. I shouldn't have told you."

"I'm glad you did."

"Do you not hate me?"

Guillaudeu laughed. "Hardly. After your lecture at the Lyceum I was most disappointed that I could not speak with the author of those wonderful words." Guillaudeu smiled. "I do think you could have published it under your real name."

"Not in London. Maybe here. But it's quite too late for that."

"And it will be too late for us" — Guillaudeu sensed he should not pursue the matter further — "if we do not descend to the theater for the performance."

Forty-four

Because the Human Calculator retained top billing in the theater, the Indians performed their evening show in the portrait gallery. By the time Guillaudeu and Lilian Kipp arrived, most of the wooden folding chairs were filled and the gas lamps were blazing. The audience emitted a disorienting buzz, and as they navigated the crowd Guillaudeu offered Lilian Kipp his arm as much for his own comfort as hers. He would have preferred to retire to his office and continue their conversation, but Lilian Kipp was obviously interested in the show. She led him very close to the stage, to the middle of the second row. The first row was entirely empty.

"Isn't this a bit close?" Guillaudeu ventured.

"I want to be able to see their clothing and any art objects they might have," said Lilian Kipp. "Isn't this exciting?"

A figure in a dark suit appeared at the end of the row and bent to speak to someone. Guillaudeu had not seen Mr. Archer for some time and his visage gave him something of a shock. Archer whispered into the ear of a seated man whose face Guillaudeu could not see. Archer rose quickly, and as he turned, he saw Guillaudeu. The ad man's eyebrows shot up and the two of them exchanged mutually surprised expressions before Archer walked briskly away.

"It's beginning," whispered Lilian Kipp.

Because there was no backstage, the Indians filed down the aisle from in back of their audience.

"Oh, look. How beautiful," breathed Lilian Kipp. The man at the head of the procession carried a cut sapling in front of him as if it were a flag on a pole. The sapling was festooned with strips of red and blue cloth, and lone feathers fluttered from strings. Other shapes dangled from the sapling's dead branches, small bundles of fur that Guillaudeu finally recognized as animals: a small dead ground squirrel of some kind, or at least a part of one; a whole bird, a finch perhaps, wrapped in string; other creatures too small to identify.

Once onstage, the elderly man set the sapling down. Boards had been nailed to its base for stability. The man sat down underneath the tree. The rest of the Indians had gathered on one side of the stage. They wore thin white cotton robes painted with red and blue shapes. Some of their faces were painted bright red, with black half-moons or chevrons on their foreheads. A young man holding a drum joined the man under the tree.

Without acknowledging the presence of the audience, the old man began to chant.

Beside Guillaudeu, Lilian Kipp leaned forward. The younger man beat the drum. The remaining Indians formed a tight circle and swayed toward the center of the stage, picking up their pace as the drumbeat quickened. Guillaudeu felt his mouth pinch into a frown: Shouldn't someone explain what the Indians were doing? What kind of dance was this? He fingered his collar. The crowded hall was becoming uncomfortably hot.

The drummer accelerated his rhythm into a pounding crescendo and the old man suddenly leapt to his feet, stomping and emitting a high-pitched yodel. Just as abruptly, the drum ceased. The circle of Indians silently parted, revealing one shrouded figure in the center. The old man assumed a predatory stance and crept to the cloaked figure in an exaggerated tiptoe. The figure took one step backward and the chorus of people around it let out a synchronized yell. The drum started up again. As the chorus shuffled backward, the old man lunged forward. He swept away the shroud to reveal a woman, clad only in a thin cotton tunic that barely covered her knees. She stared at the ground. Her hair was shorn to her skull and she wore no paint except a black line running across her cheekbones and over the bridge of her nose. As she began to move, the chorus followed. She stumbled toward the tree, but the old man leapt toward her again in his stylized attack. The woman seemed disoriented; members of the chorus surged up when she appeared to lose her balance. Like the others, she did not regard the audience but lunged and teetered and seemed to be held up by the rhythm of the drum.

"What are they doing to her?" Lilian Kipp whispered. Guillaudeu felt the warmth as she leaned into his shoulder. "Has she been drugged?"

"Certainly not! I certainly hope not."

Onstage, the chorus accelerated its song. These six people moved in unnerving synchronicity while the woman continued her delirious movements. The old man settled beneath the tree as the chorus fanned out to fill the periphery of the stage. They stomped and shuffled sideways, bent halfway over in one moment, and the next reaching toward the ceiling.

The temperature in the gallery was decidedly uncomfortable; women in the audience fanned themselves using pamphlets and Guillaudeu was tempted to take off his jacket. Beside him, Lilian Kipp sat very still. The woman onstage wriggled and spun with the chorus' chant. Guillaudeu could see that underneath the cotton tunic her skin was bare; in certain moments when the woman bent forward or changed the direction of her dance, he could discern the curve of her hip and the shadows of her breasts. His hands were sweating and he dared not look at Lilian. He noticed that every man on the stage had closed his eyes. The woman's eyes were open but she seemed not to perceive her surroundings. She stumbled again; women from the audience gasped.

Guillaudeu looked furtively at Lilian Kipp, who remained transfixed by the performance. Beyond her profile, the man at the end of the row stood up. He looked toward Guillaudeu, who averted his gaze. At the other end of the same row another man rose. It was clear these two knew each other; they were coordinating their movements. Guillaudeu watched as the men walked toward the stage. He was able to cover his ears before the first man blew a piercing note from a metal whistle.

"In the name of Mayor James Harper, we command an end to this abomination!" cried the second man.

They approached the stage. The Indians took no notice of the intrusion. The drummer continued, as did the woman's unnerving dance. The audience, however, emitted a powerful chorus of exclamations.

In a sudden move Lilian Kipp gripped Guillaudeu's forearm. "Is this part of the show?" she whispered.

"Stop!" yelped the man with the whistle. He blew the instrument a second time. The mayor's deputies regarded each other for a moment and then ascended the stage.

Beneath the sapling, the old man opened his eyes. Guillaudeu noticed his expression was not one of surprise; if anything, he revealed a bemused half smile. Guillaudeu felt a knot tighten in his gut.

The deputies approached the performers with outstretched arms, as if they were pursuing errant hens. Continuing their dance, the chorus watched the deputies. The young drummer was the only one who broke from the performance. He did not stop his music but rose and took a few steps toward the woman. The old man grasped him by the ankle and shook his head. The drummer jerked his foot away but made no further movement. The deputy with the whistle removed his jacket in a swinging motion. Quickly he wrapped the coat around the twirling woman's shoulders. The moment he touched her, the drums and the dancers stopped.

The man blew the whistle again, unnecessarily. "On behalf of Mayor James Harper and the upstanding citizens of this great city, I now make the following *official* announcement: As of this moment, Phineas T. Barnum's American Museum is closed! The closure, which should come as a surprise to no one, is due to repeated offenses to the morals and sensibilities of our citizens. These offenses, typified by the obscenities perpetrated in this Indian show, target the more delicate audience members: women and children."

"What is he talking about?" whispered Lilian Kipp. "All women have seen the skin of women. And children? If anyone, it is men who should be banned."

"Since its opening day, Barnum's American Museum has been a den for illicit and morally corrupt spectacles, such as the one behind me. This, in addition to numerous illegalities of the museum's operation, has led the mayor's office to gather all its deputies together and close the museum. It will remain closed until further notice. As we speak, dozens of the mayor's faithful servants are at work in this building, escorting people to the nearest exits and explaining the situation. If you will all please now rise, we have stationed deputies at each door."

A few people in the audience applauded and Guillaudeu wondered briefly if the whole thing was one of Barnum's schemes. But the policemen stationed in each of the museum's doorways convinced him otherwise. He shielded Lilian Kipp as best he could from the pressing crowd and led her down the marble stairway.

"Does this happen often?"

"This is the first time."

"It's terribly exciting, though."

Guillaudeu wondered if the mayor meant to evacuate the museum employees as well as its patrons. Who would care for the animals? If Barnum's museum was being shut down for moral reasons, did that mean the mayor was shutting down half of the Bowery? What about Niblo's Garden?

As they approached the main entrance, Guillaudeu saw a cluster of people just outside the door on Broadway arguing with one of the deputies. He had not seen the giantess for several weeks and now she bent over the man, her face red and one arm pointing toward the entrance. At her side, two men with slicked hair stood very close together, also gesticulating wildly.

"Amazing!" said Lilian Kipp. "What a sight!"

"Come with me," he whispered.

Guillaudeu grabbed her hand and led her through the crowd. With a swift turn of the key and whirl of a skirt, he pulled her inside his office.

Forty-five

They stood with their ears pressed to the door. Deputies escorted dozens of museum patrons out into the street.

"Let me phrase it differently for you, *sir.*" The giantess' irate but controlled voice reached them easily. "You and your minions have just barred us from returning to our *homes.* Is this so difficult for you to understand? Look up there. Can you see that row of lit rooms on the top floor? That is where we live. Now if you and your mayor want to pay the costs of a hotel for twenty people, this story might have a different ending. But I doubt very much —"

"She will get her way," Lilian Kipp whispered. "Listen to her!" And she was right. Soon they heard the giantess and several others return to the building, passing on the other side of the door, cursing under their collective breath as the exodus of museum patrons went on and on.

Lilian Kipp turned from the door. "Your office?"

"It is." He lit the wall lamps.

Lilian Kipp ran her finger along the length of his bookshelf, which was still empty except for a worn copy of *Birds of America* that Dr. Putnam had thrust into Guillaudeu's hands at the end of his visit.

Outside, someone slammed the museum's main entrance doors, and they heard the slide of the outer gate.

Lilian Kipp raised her eyebrows. "We're trapped!"

Guillaudeu opened the door slowly and peeked out. The entry hall was dark as they stepped into the corridor, and the ticket window was closed up tight. They heard the sound of people talking, milling in groups on Broadway. Someone kicked the door and demanded a refund.

Lilian Kipp covered her mouth with her hand to laugh. She turned and pointed. "Let's go up," she mouthed, moving toward the marble stairway, her form striped by shadows. The street sounds ebbed to nothing and as they climbed the broad marble steps, Lilian Kipp's footsteps clicked satisfyingly across the faintly luminous, veined surface.

None of the usual crowd noise cluttered the air, and so the portrait gallery echoed their whispers. Guillaudeu and Lilian Kipp walked among a chaos of chairs, some toppled, some leaning against one another like drunkards, detritus from the Indian show. Onstage, the Indian's wrapped tree still stood, and Lilian Kipp climbed onstage to examine it. Far away, on the other side of the gallery, the draperies swung gently on slow breaths of air. No windows were open that Guillaudeu could see; it must be the museum's own breath.

They passed through the galleries on the second floor, looking mostly upward beyond the displays, both of them tending toward the vacuous reaches of the upper air.

He suddenly wanted to see his sandhill cranes, so they climbed to the third floor and stood among them. He refrained from his usual explanation of the behaviors their poses displayed. The cranes' deep, spread-winged curtsy and mirrored arching salute had come straight from the lithographs in Geller's anatomy book, but here, in the blue night, the postures spoke for themselves in gestures as graceful as calligraphy.

"Your work is stunning," she whispered, and he did not brush away this compliment.

They walked arm in arm, as if they were admiring the blossoms in City Hall Park. They stayed well away from the balcony in case the mayor's men were standing guard below, but Lilian Kipp climbed into the giantess' booth and stood upon the stool there.

"Greetings!" she cried from her perch. "How is life in the lower atmosphere?"

In the aquarium gallery they watched sleeping fish drift from one end of their glass worlds to the other. The octopus pulled itself up the side of its tank, tracking them as they moved around the room. The seahorses swayed, only anchored by the curling tips of their tails wrapped around sea grass.

They walked among automatons, mummies, totems, and optical illusions. He showed her the Cosmoramas, the sloth, the Bengal tiger he had mounted what felt like centuries ago.

"Everything looks different in the dark," he whispered. "I never thought I'd see the museum like this. That it would be like this . . . again."

"Amazing," she said. "How unexpectedly the familiar regains its mystery."

Guillaudeu felt such relief, then, that his vision blurred and he clenched his fists tightly. He wanted to trap this moment in a specimen jar.

He led her to the roof, where briefly they shivered in the open air. The door to the kitchen swung open on its hinges, so they went inside and used a big kettle to make two cups of strong black tea.

On their way down they heard distant laughter coming from the fifth-floor apartments.

"Let's go see what they're doing!" Lilian Kipp whispered.

"Oh, I don't think that would be a very good idea."

"Why not? We're all stranded under extraordinary circumstances. The rules of our everyday life are void here, of all places." In her excitement Lilian Kipp was already opening the door to the fifth-floor gallery.

Someone had opened all the gallery windows, and several torches smoked near the Indian camp and the whale. Lilian Kipp took a few steps into the gallery and looked around.

"Well? Are you coming or shall I meet you back here?"

A group of people stood along the edge of the beluga tank, their feet propped against the scaffolding for what would someday be a viewing platform. One person, an Indian boy, sat on the edge of the tank with his legs dangling. A murmur arose from the group, and they saw the boy's legs lifted up by the curved white back of the whale as it passed. The boy laughed and hung on to the edge. The whale passed, the boy remained sitting on the edge, now just splashing the water with his feet.

"The apartments must be just there, through that door," Lilian whispered.

"Yes."

They crossed the threshold into the corridor and almost ran into another Indian, a woman with close-cropped hair and a scarred face who leaned against the wall. She was knitting, of all things, holding her ball of wool under one arm, and when she saw Guillaudeu and Lilian Kipp, she bolted past them back out to the beluga gallery.

"She was the one from the show today," murmured Lilian Kipp, already looking ahead with eyes full of wonder.

"Was she?"

The apartment corridor was cozily lit and much warmer than the rest of the building. It emanated the sounds of people at home: conversation, teacups clinking into their saucers, footsteps across rugs.

The next door on their right was open but the room was empty. Barely furnished, what was visible looked slightly off: The bed was half propped on wooden crates and stretched half the length of the room, and the mirror was hung at a level high above their heads.

They passed two closed doors, and then came upon an open one leading to a lavish apartment hung with rugs and silks, with several carpets covering the floor in an ornate, mismatched collage.

As Lilian Kipp stepped up to the doorway, Guillaudeu automatically stepped back as invisible but impermeable barriers rose between him and the carpeted room. He fought sudden panic.

A card game was in progress among the hirsute woman, the giantess, two young men with slicked hair sharing a seat, and a woman of tremendous girth who sat with her back to the door talking animatedly. Amazingly, the Australian tribesman sat a little apart from the game, straight-backed in an overstuffed chair and looking neither right nor left.

"I'll wager Barnum set it up himself," the obese woman said. "Profits are down. They say he's spending all his money abroad doing — what? What is it?" With great effort she wrenched herself half around. For a moment the room fell completely silent. "What in the hell is this? I thought the museum was closed!"

The card players glanced briefly at one another.

"Who are they?" one of the slick-haired men said.

"Didn't the deputies get all of them?" said the other.

"Hello!" Lilian Kipp offered valiantly.

"It's the taxidermist," said the giantess, who had gone back to studying her cards.

"Makes no difference to me," retorted the hirsute woman as she rose. She lumbered to the door with the same expression, as if the bread were burning in the oven.

"Good night," she said curtly and shut the door in their faces.

When she turned to Guillaudeu, Lilian Kipp had lost her going-to-a-picnic demeanor.

"We *are* in their private living quarters," Guillaudeu remarked.

"I suppose so."

Down the hall another door opened and two ghost-children scampered into view, chattering in French. Their hair and skin were identical shades of pale, milky yellow. The boy ran past and pulled the edge of Lilian Kipp's shawl. He let it snap back, then ran to the end of the hallway and out into the beluga gallery. The little girl stopped short, her crimson eyes darting between Guillaudeu and Lilian. She turned daintily on her heel and skipped back from where she came.

"Yes, we should go," Lilian conceded.

They retraced their steps and were almost back to the beluga when a bird called sharply behind them. When Guillaudeu turned, the tribesman was standing there. He addressed them by hooking his thumbs together and flying his hands upward.

Guillaudeu laughed. "I *know* him!"

The tribesman, who was only as tall as Lilian Kipp's shoulder, led them back to the apartments and to the end of the corridor. He gestured for them to enter his room and sit on his narrow bed while he settled upon a rough stool across the room by the window.

"He's a fine fellow. No English, as you might imagine. This is Lilian Kipp," he told the tribesman by way of introduction. "He sings a most intriguing bit of music."

The tribesman folded his hands on his lap and looked from one of them to the other.

"He is breaking my heart somehow," Lilian murmured.

"To my knowledge he has never performed. I have a theory that Barnum has forgotten all about this one."

"Why doesn't he leave?"

The tribesman continued to regard them with the bemused patience of a grandmother, occasionally contemplating the rising darkness outside the window or gazing across the room to a small bundle of burlap in the corner.

"He was carrying that when he arrived here." Guillaudeu pointed to the bundle. "Your belongings? From home?"

They all observed the bundle.

"Isn't it strange," Lilian Kipp mused. "We are so accustomed to our social graces. We are so dutiful. We carry out our meaningless, expected parlor conversations, never saying what we truly mean, or what is important to us. How easy it is to exist in the company of others and yet remain completely alone. Without all the talk, as it is with this man, I see how conversation is all too often just a clutter. It makes me sad, all the time we waste. He is looking at you so strangely."

It appeared that the tribesman had made a decision. He went to the corner and brought the burlap sack. He pulled his stool so close that their three pairs of knees almost touched.

From the wrapping he pulled a hardwood root, thick and serpentine. Along it were etched designs burned into the wood: circles within circles, chevrons, and parallel lines. He cradled the root in his arms with an expression that wavered between mild alarm and resignation.

A lone ant, larger than any Guillaudeu had ever seen, emerged from one end of the root. As soon as he saw it the tribesman began to hum. The ant moved directly to the highest point on the root without any of the mindless zigzagging typical of its kind. The tribesman pulled a tiny piece of food from his pocket and set it on the root next to the ant. The creature lifted it high, retraced its steps, and disappeared.

A whole procession of ants now emerged, some like the first one, others with taut, distended midsections bloated to the size of amber marbles.

"*Yerrampe,*" said the tribesman. The ants marched to the highest point and the tribesman put crumbs out for each one. He began to speak, slowly at first, navigating the buoyant, rolling words and rapid repetitions of his native tongue. He spoke softly, but soon his recitation took on some urgency. Occasionally he looked over his shoulder, gesturing toward the window.

When the last ant disappeared into the branch, he rewrapped the bundle very carefully and placed it back in the corner, still talking. He returned to the stool and continued his story.

There was no one in New York who could translate these words. It was a chasm of centuries, of millennia, that separated their worlds. It was the least he could do to listen carefully despite this obstacle.

After a while the speech turned to the humming song with its unfolding layers. The shadows shifted on the walls, the night poured in. The man hummed and sang. Lilian Kipp nodded to sleep with her cheek on Guillaudeu's shoulder, and Guillaudeu kept very still so as to enjoy every moment and every square inch of her side snugged warmly against his.

In the song he heard subtle harmonies and strange tilting narratives. No system of categories contains this, he observed. He felt Lilian's breathing deepen and he wondered if she dreamed of cocoons swaying under canopies of sunlit leaves. What purpose is there in looking for order when new species are discovered all the time and when all premises shift and bend and crumble with time? Why look for order when the deeper you go and the more closely you look, the greater the mystery?

The song continued for a length of time that Guillaudeu could not measure.

And then at a certain point it was time to leave.

"What is your name?" Guillaudeu asked the tribesman before he roused Lilian Kipp.

The tribesman frowned and nodded and did not say.

All the apartment doors were shut and the corridor was silent. The only sounds on their way out were the snores coming from the Indian camp and the swish and ripple of the whale swimming in slow circles. Sadly, Guillaudeu realized this night would end. The steady march of daybreak had started somewhere beyond the distant horizon; the clockwork of the universe proceeded.

"Come with me," Guillaudeu whispered. "I want to show you one more place."

"Yes." Lilian Kipp was still waking up. "What do you think he was telling us?"

"He was telling us about a place we'll never see. A place where we would know nothing and recognize nothing."

"My father once traveled to India. A man there blessed him. Spoke a prayer over him before his sea journey home. He asked the man to translate the words but the man wouldn't. He said the prayer had already entered his soul and would do its work despite my father's ignorance. Who knows." Lilian Kipp yawned. "Maybe the man was really cursing my father and simply made up a pretty explanation for it."

Guillaudeu led her into a green and leafy world. Hemp netting billowed down the pea-green walls and formed a canopy above them. He lifted the netting's hem and they ducked inside. Potted myrtles and shrubs of varying heights had become the major thoroughfares for a bustling ornithopolis. A small fleet of juncos beelined among the dark trees, their white tail feathers flashing. A bluebird glided between low-hanging branches, streaking cobalt. The purple gallinule stalked delicately behind them on the sawdust path. Higher up, shapes silhouetted by the dim upper air glided by. Higher still hung the chandelier, where two ravens presided from a half-built nest made from bird bones and strands of netting, and decorated with buttons lost from Guillaudeu's waist-coat.

They sat, leaning against one of the great ceramic tree pots. Lilian Kipp dozed again, and Guillaudeu listened to the movement of birds. Gradually, light gathered strength, rising across the windows in slender bars. A wren flitted across the path at knee level to light on the topknot of a bush. It bowed and cocked its tail and emitted a much grander song than its appearance implied. The morning must have achieved some critical brightness, because following this diminutive herald, the birds let loose and sound drenched them from above. Lilian Kipp raised her head, smiling.

From invisible perches they sang single long notes and wavering trills. The juncos twittered past again and added *chuups* and *chips* to their recital. Thrushes dropped reedy whistled spirals, which floated down in loose coils and lay among the leaves. Birds sang as they flew, trailing banners behind them. Small choruses came from the shadows, while a puffed-up robin, which Guillaudeu did not remember seeing before, hopped just ahead of them, posing dramatically for his familiar aria. The air brightened quickly and the chorus intensified. Every molecule of air seemed to be used for song. Each exhaled breath was swept up by feathers, transformed into music. Lilian Kipp's upturned face met the cacophony straight-on, eyes closed. In an action Guillaudeu never dreamed he was capable of, he placed his hands lightly on each of her shoulders and delivered a kiss to her cheek.

She smiled and did not open her eyes. "Your mustache!" she murmured. "Listen."

And they did, until the day was simply day again and the birds' work was done.

"I do wish I could stay here. From what people are saying,

Barnum's got some tricks up his sleeve," Lilian Kipp remarked as they walked away from the aviary. "It would be such fun to find out what happens, but I've got to get home."

"Home?" This word left him at a loss. "To your hotel?"

"No. Home." Lilian Kipp smiled. "To London."

The idea that she would leave had not occurred to him.

"I leave in three days," she added.

"What! Why?" Guillaudeu sputtered. "So soon?"

"According to the schedule of the HMS *Providence*."

"Why didn't you tell me before? We haven't — We were just —"

Lilian Kipp straightened her skirt and tightened her shawl around her shoulders. "Why would I want to ruin a perfectly lovely evening? If I had told you, we never would have had such a wonderful time."

He stared into her eyes until he understood she was right. She stepped closer and faced him squarely.

"I know you are a New World species," she said. "But perhaps migratory? Passage on the HMS *Providence* wouldn't be the most difficult thing to come by."

She regarded him unabashedly and for a moment he saw the voyage with perfect clarity, standing with her on the upper deck, watching a seabird glide against a thickly overcast sky and the open sea spread beneath them, dividing the world cleanly without the obstacle of land.

"I couldn't possibly." He was out of breath. His voice was tight. He gestured helplessly at the museum. "My life's work."

"It was a ridiculous idea," she finished briskly. "I knew it was. I just thought I'd articulate it. I don't know why, other than I enjoy your company. Now walk me to the hotel, Emile, please?"

He delivered her there and they promised to meet again after her day's engagements. She disappeared into the hotel foyer and by the time Guillaudeu had reached his dark apartment building, the day was bright and he had thought of a dozen things he wanted to tell her.

The tribesman and his brother walked for twenty days, the tribesman marking their path and the keeper guarding the bundle and singing, always singing. They walked across wet savanna, eating goose eggs until the land dried to dusty earth. They walked between termite mounds as tall as trees and made their way into woodland of unfamiliar trees where silent birds followed them from high in the canopy. The tribesman's mind grew darker, but the keeper's shone more brightly. The keeper watched the birds above their heads. *Good companions,* he said, nodding. *Good.*

They waded through open fields of wild grasses growing higher than their heads. The tribesman worried that snakes of this unknown country hid at their feet. His brother stopped, half enveloped by the grass. He turned to the tribesman. *Brother. The sea shifts under the wind just like these grasses, creating patterns and signs for us to read. Like the clouds,* the keeper continued, *except that we can immerse ourselves in the water's moving.* He would not stop talking about the sea, but instead of comforting the tribesman with his confidence, the keeper's words frightened him. *What of the people?* he asked the keeper. *They will be expecting us back. From the direction we went, they think we are at Nourlangie, a two-day journey from home.* The keeper dismissed this idea with a wave of his hand. *The people do not understand what I understand,* he hissed, and went on through the grass.

It was the only time in his life that the tribesman heard his brother disparage the people, and even recalling it now, from the distance of continents and ocean, the tribesman shudders. As the brothers continued their journey, the keeper spoke incessantly of the sea's mysteries. It contained, he insisted, the answers to all their concerns. *Brother, I dreamed of our people living near the sea. We did not have to move every season; we lived in one place. I have seen it already.* When he heard the keeper's words, the tribesman's heart screamed in pain, and it screams now, as he lies on his pallet covered with two blankets and the wool coat given to him by the skin-and-bones man. He shivers, clutching the bundled mulga root to his chest.

He slips into the song and pouring rain immediately drenches him. Of course, Gudjewg: the flooding time. He tilts back his head and lets the sweet water fill his mouth. Water cascades down the many faces of the stone, flooding the savanna, sending goanna, snakes, and possums into the trees, where they are hunted by eagles or the people. Thunder reverberates across the yellow-gray sky, echoes off the cliffs and back across the wetlands. This abundance fills the tribesman with joy as he sings. He sees tender shoots rising out of the water, sees the tightly curled fronds that will become great lily pads and the plump, rosy buds of lotus flowers. In the distance, he sees the aunts and grandmothers, bare to the waist, and barely covered above except for great bark hats that stream water behind them. They wade slowly across the flooded plain to the sedgeland where the geese are nesting. They squat, gathering the big eggs and setting them carefully in baskets. The tribesman strains to hear their laughter until he is trying so hard to hear beyond the monsoon that he is no longer singing, and he is back in his room at the museum, terrified of the cold, of the walls all around him. He waits for a sign until he cannot bear the emptiness, and then he waits for his breath to return so he can start the song again.

She Stands Up Again

Forty-six

Finally, after scouring the *Herald,* the *Evening Post,* and most of the *Subterranean,* I found the listing. I saw it only because its small headline was posted underneath the death announcement of one Nicholas Willard. Nicholas, aged ten years, had recently met his end by leaping (for what purpose?) into a large bin of grain on his family's farm in Newholm, Kentucky. Before he could leap out again, he was smothered to death by a fresh load from the harvester, operated by his father. Was he America's youngest suicide? Or simply the victim of his own exuberance, killed by love of leaping? Was his father a murderer? Even if the law did not call him so, what did his own heart say as he lay in his bed at night? And how did the report of young Willard come to be listed in the *Subterranean,* a workingman's newspaper whose aim was the glorification of the agricultural life, not its many perils?

After perusing the papers hour after hour, I had given up any hope of understanding the logic that governed their layout. Notices for the latest inventions in India Rubber ran next to announcements for a newly revised *Atlas for the Geography of the Heavens,* published by London's Royal Academy of Sciences. The article describing street repair schedules in the fifth ward bumped margins with an editorial written by the mayor of the city in which he took on a peculiarly intimate tone to announce plans for a great municipal park that would not be finished for two decades.

The museum had been closed for three days. The first I spent celebrating with Maud and the rest of the residents of the fifth floor. Then, when we learned that despite the wording of our contracts, our "vacation" had no guarantee of recompense, the celebration turned sour. Jacob and Matthew had drunk themselves into a stupor in Maud's parlor and no one but I could move them. In the morning they arrived for breakfast with bruises on both of their faces and they would not speak to each other.

I spent the second morning cleaning my apartment and airing bedding on the roof. I soaked my feet in the last of my salts and read the latest installment of *Barnaby Rudge* in the *Herald,* reprinted in honor of Dickens' recent visit to America. While strolling in the museum after lunch I saw Beebe across the street, kneeling in the chapel yard. I watched him dig in the soil next to the chapel steps; no doubt he was transplanting some seedling or other now that the weather had warmed fully to spring. After a few minutes he saw me and came across Broadway. He joined me in the empty museum, and we walked together for a while. Our time together was slightly awkward; without the crowds wreaking havoc around us, with the museum so quiet it was almost invisible to us, what, really, did we have to talk about? But it was pleasant enough, this man beside me, although I wished he were taller.

That evening I joined a group in Maud's parlor for our usual pastime. Thankfully, Matthew and Jacob had recovered themselves to the best of their ability and even indulged us after the game by singing a rather astonishing operatic duet from *The Barber of Seville.*

During this third morning, my time had been entirely consumed by newspapers. The listing that I now underlined with my pencil announced a meeting to be held tonight at Niblo's Garden: *The New York Alliance of Actors and Costume-Makers meets at its usual location for its biweekly gathering at nine o'clock, immediately following the half past six performances.* I had never expected to find a giants' guild, but I had even given up on finding an organization of acrobats, albinos, clairvoyants, or human anomalies of any kind at all. Until now, the closest match I had found was the button-makers' alliance.

Since my confrontation with Miss Crawford, I had been thinking incessantly of how to remedy the issue of the Aztec Children. Maud and I alternated caring for them to the best of our limited ability. We had no way to fathom how deeply their minds were contaminated by illness; all we could do was gauge the patterns of emotion that flitted across their faces like cloud formations. They were unaccustomed to human kindness. They seemed most comfortable spending their waking hours sitting together, usually with their arms entwined around each other, rocking gently, sleeping, and occasionally communicating with each other using an invented language of clucked syllables and intricate gestures. We called the boy Henry and the girl Susan. They were a doleful pair. The only time I saw them smile was once when we brought them chocolate cake.

Thus far, I hadn't found the solution to their dilemma. The only idea that had come to me was to have a talk with Barnum myself. I wanted to prepare, however, for such an encounter, and this Alliance of Actors seemed to be my best prospect.

It was hours until the meeting, and I was becoming impatient with the other residents of the fifth floor. I gathered up my True Life History and went downstairs to the aviary, for a change of view.

Even the birds seemed to sense that the routines of the museum were disrupted. The aviary was somewhat stuffy so I opened a window before slipping into the mesh tent. Most of the creatures were invisible among the potted trees, but occasional flurries of chirping gave them away, and a few sparrows hopped among the bark chips on the ground. I sat carefully on one of the wrought-iron benches and looked upward into the trees. Several nests were visible among the branches; life goes on and on, doesn't it? No matter where you are.

Without their usual work, Maud and the others had fallen into a disappointing pattern. All they did was lounge around in their dressing gowns and sip spirits, smoke their pipes, and talk endlessly about the same subjects: aches and pains, people they once knew, one another, themselves. The fact that I was no different made it even more irritating to be near them. We had all chosen this profession in one way or another, even if our deformities made it seem like the only life available to us. Didn't they all remember, as I did, the exact moment they chose it for ourselves?

How could I have resisted them? By the time Methuselah and Beatrice Jones stepped out of their filigreed carriage and came through our gate in Pictou, our sideshow had been shut down for eight months and Mother and I inhabited the farm like the ghosts of an earlier generation. It wasn't even a farm anymore. Now we had enough to buy everything from the mercantile in town and we'd sold all the animals except three laying hens and let the kitchen garden go to seed. It was summer when they came for me; Father hadn't been home in four days. At the height of the season he spent nights on one of the boats, which was just as well for us since he hated to see me, and Mother hated him for that. The changes, first mine, then his, had corroded her spirit and now she lurked around the empty farm pretending she could still care for me when it was obvious she had nothing left to give.

I remember I had shut myself away from the light. Even the oblique northern sun gave me horrible headaches, especially if I hadn't had enough medicine, so I stayed behind drawn curtains, watching motes drift up and down in the narrow shafts that managed to angle in.

I watched the two strangers come across the yard and felt Mother watching, too. When we heard the gate we thought it must be Father; he would be coming home anytime now. Methuselah Jones' beard was still dark then, and it tumbled down his chest in unusual curls. He was elegantly dressed in a violet vest and lavender cravat, all the rest black, as I recall. And it's a good thing he was dressed well, because his finery just barely offset the fact that his black hair was blatantly unkempt, some of it even tangled into felted clumps. His mustache obscured his mouth completely, and his wide-set eyes held more than a glimmer of chaos. Bright blue and constantly flitting from one thing to another, Methuselah Jones' eyes were proba-

bly the primary attractions of Jones' Medicine Show. They were painted, in the manner of the Turkish evil eye, on all the carriages and even over the entrance gate.

Madame Jones tempered the effect of her husband exquisitely. Slim, just old enough to be trustworthy, and dressed in tawny shades of gold and amber that accentuated the blond hair swept back in a simple bun, she was his conduit into the realms of society. She walked slightly ahead of him toward the house, her arm already reaching for the bell and a charming smile spreading on her lips. I heard my mother's hesitant steps toward the door and returned to my chair. I preferred to meet them sitting down.

"Hello, Miss Swift," Mrs. Jones said as they came into the room. My mother parted the curtains, and both strangers bowed courteously. Mrs. Jones stepped forward. "You are surely aware, by now, that you are the only giantess currently working in the world?"

"Actually, no." This took me by surprise. "But I am not actually working. I'm sure you saw the booth in our yard. It has been overtaken by brambles."

"We are hoping to change that," Madame Jones said bluntly. Methuselah Jones had faded into the shadows behind his wife. It was one of his many strategies. "I hope you will hear our terms."

It was the subject that Mother would not dare to raise with me. It was totally beyond her scope to urge her only child (even if she was already twenty years old) away from home, especially a female child into a world of commerce. My mother left the room.

"Our medicine show tours six months of the year," Madame Jones continued. "We employ all kinds of people, maintain a menagerie of animals from all six habitable continents, and additionally produce special exhibits and performances during winters from our permanent theater in Halifax. We are known worldwide, and have been in operation eighty years, since Methuselah's father started his traveling menagerie. As our employee, you will see the world; every other year we take our best people and animals (of which you will be one, that we guarantee) overseas, to London, Paris, Amsterdam, Prague, and Saint Petersburg. All our accommodations are exquisite. You will have your own custom-built living coach while we travel on this continent, and private rooms in Halifax."

I listened to her, already sensing Pictou slipping away. I had destroyed our lives here, the farm was gone and my mother worn almost entirely away. If I left, she would return to real life, wouldn't she?

"The truth is, we are surprised you haven't been approached already," Madame Jones confided. "If there are special things you want, you must really let us know."

I said nothing. Years ago now I had stepped out of one life, leaving the husk of a little girl behind like an abandoned cocoon to blow away in the wind. I would do it again.

She came closer to me, glancing quickly over her shoulder to make sure my mother wasn't there.

"To really live, Miss Swift, you must expand yourself into many identities. You are constricted here, I can see." She gestured to the shabby room. "This world is just one of many. Very many. You can belong to different worlds, Miss Swift. The Greeks! Folklore and fantasy are open to you. And there are so many others who could be a new family. You must try being with them. You will be independent. You will have money. For them." She gestured toward the kitchen. "And for you."

I nodded. "How soon can I go?"

Madame Jones clapped her hands. "Soon! We must talk terms, and then we'll arrange your passage."

Methuselah Jones then stepped into the light, leading with his eyes. "You come with us, miss, you quit the morphine. That's part of the deal."

I nodded. Outside, the gate creaked. He'd returned from the boats. I heard no welcoming footsteps from my mother toward the door. Methuselah Jones looked at his wife. She nodded. He stepped into the kitchen to meet my father.

"We have other remedies," Mrs. Jones assured me. "Many others. You'll see. We employ doctors of our own who are accustomed to the specific conditions of our employees. You won't need the morphine, Miss Swift. I promise. A new world awaits."

Forty-seven

As Maud and I left the museum that evening, my chest constricted in the usual manner. Although I had celebrated the
museum's closure with the rest, these unstructured days
were wearing on my nerves. Each morning I slept as late as I
wanted to, without the usual pain in my feet and legs from
walking through the galleries. But when I rose out of bed
and stood at my window, panic descended like a dark fog
upon me, lodging in my chest, a tight bridle. What would I
do with the day? I had a new routine, but it occupied me for
only an hour or two: a thorough foot and leg massage; a trip
down the hall to check on the Aztec Children, who were
usually still sleeping in their new cots. Then breakfast on the
roof. After that, however, I was on my own until dinner. I
did not visit the galleries. Why would I? And I had not ventured into the city. I needed new shoes and a new dress, but
I had been trapped by inertia. It was the actors guild that finally pulled me from my disgusting ennui.

Maud led the way. The address was on Broadway at Prince
Street, well north of the museum. Maud had worked at
Niblo's Garden for six months prior to joining Barnum's museum and when she had discovered I was going to the meeting, she would not be left behind.

"They employed me before their *conversion*," she said as we
approached the building. It had a façade similar to Barnum's,
but instead of marble Niblo's building had been created with
bricks of a rather fiery orange. "Yes, Mr. Niblo the younger

married into the Van Hoek family, and after that a hirsute women would never do."

The lobby was wide and accented with three frescoes painted in brilliant tones that depicted tigers in a jungle scene. Rugs of incredible dimension lay across the promenade, and an elegant hanging sign pointed the way to the fountain. Other signs advertised the evening's entertainments: PERFORMANCES TODAY COMMENCE AT HALF-PAST SIX WITH THE OVERTURES TO ACTÆON, AFTER WHICH WILL BE PRODUCED THE HIGHLY LAUGHABLE BURLETTA, OF ANIMAL MAGNETISM! (WITH A NEW SCENE WRITTEN FOR THE OCCASION). IMMEDIATELY AFTER THE FIRST PIECE, AND PREVIOUS TO THE INTERMISSION, MR. BUTTON WILL SING A NEW SONG, CALLED "RHYMES AND CHIMES ON THE SIGNS OF THE TIMES!" BETWEEN THE PIECES, AN INTERMISSION OF HALF AN HOUR WILL BE ALLOWED FOR PROMENADE AND REFRESHMENTS IN THE GRAND SALOON, WHERE ICE CREAMS, FRUIT ICES, AND REFRESHMENTS OF THE CHOICEST KINDS AND IN GREAT VARIETY WILL ABOUND.

Compared with Barnum's enterprise, Niblo's Garden was a rather breathtaking manifestation of elegance.

There was no one about, but we found a sign propped against a high mahogany counter on one side of the lobby, ACTOR'S GUILD, GREEN ROOM, with an arrow pointing the way. I passed by the doors to the main theater. Through them, I witnessed the elaborate gallery, layered with so many varieties of velvet, so many tiers of balcony, so many baubles and gilt-framed alcoves that I was nauseated and squinted to dim the glare. It was spectacularly silly.

The green room was a spacious and well-lit den with about twenty people gathered near the front. I sensed immediately that the actors, who are always recognizable by the slight arrogance of their stance, had taken one side of the room and the costume-makers the other.

"I recognize the tall one," Maud said. "And the two women sitting down. They're German."

By the way their gazes lingered on Maud, I deduced these people recognized her as well.

"It's remarkable. The manager here encourages the actors to meet like this. Can you imagine if Barnum did the same thing? Oh, my Lord! Look who it is, the Emperor himself!"

How could I have not immediately seen one of my own kind? Tai Shan, the Chinese giant, the most elusive of Barnum's Representatives of the Wonderful, was standing against the room's far wall. He was reading a pamphlet, which he held between two fingers of each hand. His head was level with a crystal wall sconce, and it illuminated his face quite dramatically.

Each of the few times I'd seen the Chinese giant he'd worn a different, richly patterned silk tunic, with similarly colorful loose trousers underneath. Tonight he was swathed in a robe of red silk alternating with bands of purple and panels of a textile embroidered with poppies. I had to admit the clothes looked exceedingly comfortable. I watched him put on a pair of spectacles and lift the pamphlet to eye level. His face was impassive, strikingly angular and made more so because of his bald pate. I guessed he was younger than I, but it was impossible to know for sure. He was the recluse of the fifth floor and never made an effort to talk with any of us, so we never bothered to speak to him. Neither Maud nor I went over to him.

We found two seats and in due time a man rose to address us. Based on his humble manner and long, elegant fingers I assumed he was a costume-maker. He welcomed the group, and then welcomed the *newcomers,* looking pointedly in our direction. He paid no attention to Tai Shan.

The costume-maker continued by summarizing the previous meeting, which included various items almost unfathomable to me, including guaranteed annual contracts and schedules that included ten Saturdays off work each year. He sent a petition around the room, the subject of which he did not reiterate for those who had missed the previous meeting.

"But before we continue these discussions, we have an item of new business. We are a small group here," he continued.

"When newcomers arrive, we like to give them a chance to tell us something about themselves. Please, ladies. Indulge us."

Everyone in the green room turned to scrutinize us; in a maddening gesture, Maud looked at me as if she'd never seen me before, her lips pursed. It was a clear sign that I was to be our spokesperson. I did not stand.

"We're from Barnum's American Museum. There are certain issues among the employees there, including unfair pay, inadequate care for children, and a prevalent general disorganization that precludes the resolution of these issues. You may have heard of the recent arrest of the Martinetti family of acrobats. They are entirely without representation, legal or otherwise. I saw your advertisement in the *Evening Post* this morning. We are not actors in the conventional sense of the word, but I believe we fit into the same arena. I'm hoping to listen to your discussion and ask for your advice and guidance to help remedy the situation at the American Museum."

None of the actors regarded me, or the details of my little speech, with particularly friendly expressions, but I was still unprepared for what followed. From one corner of the room, a voice that was registered somewhere in the lowest regions of the bass clef and shockingly loud emitted a mind-splitting barrage of language. Everyone jumped, including the mild costume-maker who stood in front of us. The instrument of this noise was a robust male, of above-average height and stormy complexion, who had risen from his seat and now glowered at Maud and me while spewing chains of words in German.

It also soon became clear that everyone else in the room knew the German language. I was incredulous. On the fifth floor of Barnum's museum, one could not find a group of more than five or six who spoke the same language, English included.

"They're *all* German?" As I whispered to Maud, the terrible shouter began waving his fist at us, and at the costume-maker, who visibly recoiled.

"Most are. That's one of the reasons I left; they revert to German to discuss real business."

"I thought you were fired."

"It was practically mutual."

"Sir?" I raised my hand and addressed the costume-maker. "Would you mind enlightening my friend and me as to what is going on?" At the sound of my voice the shouter paused.

"There is some discussion —" he began.

"That is clear," Maud snapped.

"Why should we help you?" The shouter switched languages seemingly mid-sentence, his voice retaining the volume and force of a pipe organ. "Since your museum closed, attendance here at Niblo's has doubled. Why should we help you?"

"Not everyone is agreeing with Mr. Messner, madame," the costume-maker offered. Mr. Messner had reverted to his native tongue and now addressed the seated actors. The costume-maker cleared his throat and switched to German, calling out to the group. Mr. Messner did not immediately back off, and several of the assembled people shouted their opinions in German over his voice.

"Your meetings are advertised as open to the public," Maud shouted over the din. "I'm surprised that you would put in the effort and money to place these ads if you did not really mean what they say."

"Mr. Niblo places the ads" — Mr. Messner growled from his seat — "so people will think his establishment *progressive,* as they say. Nothing more."

I could see this detail ruffled Maud, but it was clear by the set of her jaw and the tilt of her shoulders that we would stay to the end.

"Entschuldigen Sie bitte." The racket ebbed suddenly with this new voice. Tai Shan had stepped away from the wall and now addressed the group. "I hope you will allow me to translate my colleagues' concerns. They are asking for your help. Surely you will give it to them?"

He was graceful. He gestured for me to continue. I hardly knew what to say.

"In Barnum's museum there is no recognized method for us to enact change. All of our contracts are privately signed."

Tai Shan's voice was gentle and steady even as it navigated the rugged topography of the German tongue. People's heads turned from one to the other of us as we alternated.

"Barnum is constantly expanding the museum according to his whim. I'd like to negotiate with him and try to centralize the contracts, and to include certain benefits for us, like what you're doing with your schedule of Saturdays off work."

After Tai Shan concluded his translation, an actor was the first to speak. He addressed me directly. "You must show him that you and your group have power in the museum. Without you, he would have nothing to exhibit!"

A costume-maker nodded. She could have been my mother's age, wearing a faded kerchief around her gray hair. Tai Shan translated her words. "There can be only one representative of your group. You and you only must negotiate with him. Everyone must agree to the terms of your guild. She says the guild will work only with this unity."

By the end of the discussion, people talked excitedly about the museum, the change that was possible. I nodded and tried to remember everything that was said. When the meeting ended, several actors nodded good night and wished me luck with the endeavor.

Maud stayed at Niblo's to talk with several of her former colleagues, so Tai Shan and I left the theater together.

On the street, the evening air promised summer. Families walked in groups beside lone men hurrying home. We walked in silence, two pillars above the swarm. An old man and his stooped wife approached us from the opposite direction, barely holding steady in the throng. They hobbled between faster-moving pedestrians, the man navigating not just his two feet but a cane as well. The woman seemed to be the eyes for the pair; while he focused on the ground in front of him, she peered up Broadway, perhaps scouting for obstacles. When she saw us she nudged her husband and they straightened up a bit to look. They beheld us as if we were a miracle, their expressions simple wonder. Perhaps I was just exhilarated by our success at Niblo's Garden, but their faces filled me with an abrupt joy; they had received our gift. I wanted to turn to Tai Shan. Had he seen them? But in the end I didn't, because I didn't want to break our silence and lose the delicious sensation of struggling to keep up with someone else.

The two policemen stationed at the entrance opened the doors for us before we had even reached the museum side of Broadway. They were in the process of tipping their hats as we brushed past them when a voice stopped me.

"Miss Swift! Wait!"

I swung around in the entryway. As Tai Shan continued on, disappearing into the museum, both policemen lunged forward to apprehend a smallish figure.

"Not you again," one of the policemen growled. "It ain't gonna work."

From between their arms I perceived the pianist Thomas Willoughby struggling to free himself. The police held him in such a way that his legs windmilled uselessly.

"I know this man," I told the officials.

"He's been trying to tell us he lives inside. But our orders are no one but performers and cooks go in. He ain't a cook; that much is certain. And he doesn't look like a performer to me."

I had never seen Thomas looking anything but rumpled, but he had exceeded all previous levels of disarray, appearing now with ripped trousers, a dark stain down the front of his frayed overcoat, and at least three leaves stuck in the chaos of his hair, one of them a particularly bright shade of green. He cast furtive looks at the policemen.

"I've been trying to tell them, but they won't believe me."

"Oh?"

"That I'm a clairvoyant," he said flatly.

I wouldn't have believed it, either. Oh, Thomas. Why didn't you just say you were one of the animal keepers? I suppressed a smile.

"We asked him to prove it by telling O'Connor's future, but he won't do it."

I took a deep breath. "He performs in the theater on Tuesdays and Fridays at two o'clock," I offered. "He has a booth as well. On the third floor. But I suppose my word isn't enough, is it?"

"He just doesn't *seem* like a clairvoyant, is all." The one called O'Connor scrutinized Thomas. "We don't trust him. And isn't it only the real freaks that live in there, anyway?"

"Barnum includes Mr. Willoughby among his Representatives of the Wonderful because of the unwavering accuracy of his predictions and the delicacy of his constitution. Just look how the harsh city has affected him! He really must return to his apartment. The crowded streets overwhelm him."

"I can sense people's destinies," Thomas offered softly.

"Then what is mine?" O'Connor leaned ominously over the pianist. "I'm sure if you tell me a little something about my future, we can allow you in."

I couldn't help. Thomas gulped some air.

"The reason I am so hesitant, sir, is simple enough." Thomas still had a wild look in his eye, and I wondered if he had been out somewhere smoking opium. "Generally, people are eager to hear their fortunes when there is love on the horizon, or exotic travels." His voice settled into a surprising, authoritative tone. "But it's altogether different when the news is bleak. For example, when the unforeseen event is an accident" — Thomas raised his eyebrows suggestively — "people are far less interested to know the details."

O'Connor took a step back.

"Yours is a profession fraught with danger, Mr. O'Connor. Given this warning, do you truly want me to continue?"

"I don't believe I do. No, please don't." Mr. O'Connor stepped away from the door, and I pulled Thomas inside by the collar.

"Good Lord, Thomas. That was a bit extreme." I let him go and we ascended the marble stairway.

"I could think of nothing else!"

"You look as if you've slept on the street."

"I have."

"You have?"

"But I am inside now, thank God. I shall eat and play the piano and look at the whale."

He trotted to keep up with me, his head bobbing up and down with its crown of leaves. He caught me looking at him and smiled.

I stopped on the landing to laugh. "I've seen worse clairvoyants, Thomas. But, '*I sense people's destinies'*?"

"It's true, in a way."

Thomas revealed that for a full month leading up to the museum's closure, he had slept each night in the glassblowers' studio on the fourth floor. Quite comfortably, he insisted. It was easy to keep a bit of a fire going in the forge, he said, and now it was warm enough that he didn't need one.

"Don't you have an apartment? You must be making enough money here to sustain yourself."

"I have a room on Hester Street, yes. But it's a difficult neighborhood. I had an unfortunate incident involving my neighbor and one of her . . . clients. She's a pleasant woman, really. But I'm afraid I made an enemy out of her. Since then I've been hesitant to go home. And the truth is, there's no piano on Hester Street. It suits me fine to stay here. I like it."

It was true, now that I thought about it, that Thomas was always at his post on the balcony in the mornings when I made my first rotation of the galleries, long before the fiddler and the horn player arrived. And he was always there at the day's end, when I retired upstairs. The museum opened at sunrise, it was true. And closed at ten o'clock.

"Why didn't you tell me?"

"No need to pull anyone else into it."

We made our way across the galleries to the corner stairwell. We took one flight up. Thomas stopped at the landing.

"You're coming with me," I told him. "I'm not leaving you down here to nest like a squirrel when there is a perfectly civilized apartment building upstairs."

"Squirrels are resourceful creatures," Thomas muttered. But he followed me.

A handful of oil lamps lit the Indians' camp but the rest of the fifth-floor gallery gaped like a great cavern, with only slivers of moonlight casting white shadows into its farthest reaches.

"This might be my favorite room in the museum," I told Thomas. "It seems to me that every museum should have an empty gallery. For balancing the senses. I am truly fond of the effect of walking through an emptiness like this. It makes me feel . . . the right size. The Giant's Lament, Thomas. You finally heard it."

"But this gallery isn't empty. It houses the museum's greatest marvel, remember? I'm going to have a quick look." Thomas swerved toward the beluga tank.

Only three Indians sat together in the makeshift living room of the camp. As I approached I realized that one of them was not an Indian at all, but the Australian tribesman, sitting on a stool next to the eldest Sioux. The third figure was the young man who had translated for They Are Afraid of Her during my English class. The old man, in his black wool frock coat and satin top hat, was speaking to the tribesman so softly I could not recognize the language, or even hazard a guess as to which it could possibly be, for them both to understand. The younger man rose to apprehend me before I could interfere.

"He can't understand you," I said.

The man did not look at me, but the corner of his mouth curved into a sneer. "If you say so," he said.

"Who is he?"

"Who do you think he is?" The Indian took a step toward me. Mocking me somehow, though I didn't understand his parameters. "Who could he possibly be, in this place?"

"Someone whose home is a long way from here. As it is with all of us."

"And so the Grandfather welcomes him." With that, the man abandoned me abruptly to return to his grandfather's side.

Out in the middle of the gallery Thomas had climbed the
scaffolding up the side of the tank, facing away from me. I
could see his head moving side-to-side as he followed the
animal's movements. He did not see or hear me approach,
even when I stood near him and peered over the edge of the
tank.

The beluga was not alone. It slipped through the black
clear water, luminescent as usual and silent for once. A
woman glided with the whale, equally luminous and equally
silent, her arm flung over the animal's barely discernible
neck, her body, barely concealed beneath the soaked fabric
of her blue shift, lying flush against the beast. The whale propelled them both with slow vertical sweeps of its tail. They
went around and around, the woman with her eyes closed,
her short hair lying flat and smooth against her skull.

Thomas stared at the two creatures until he saw me. Then
he turned crimson and tripped over himself to descend the
ladder.

"Who is she?" he whispered.

"An Indian. They Are Afraid of Her."

"Why?"

"No, that's her name."

"She must be cold. I've never seen her before."

"And now you've seen more of her than most."

They Are Afraid of Her, who must have heard Thomas'
commotion, hoisted herself out of the tank. She wrapped
herself in a blanket that she'd hung on the scaffolding.

"Wait," she said softly. She came halfway down the ladder
so that she was level with my head.

"Hello!"

"Your English is improving," I observed.

"Practice. My cousin knows."

She regarded Thomas, who simply stared at her. She extended a hand and fluttered her fingers. "You," she offered.
She reached her other hand out and fluttered both hands
until her blanket slid precariously and she clutched it around
her.

"Yes! I play the piano!" He pointed at himself. "Thomas."

They Are Afraid of Her nodded.

She looked between us, and then over her shoulder toward the encampment where a couple of Sioux sat on the floor, leaning against the wall.

She pointed to the door to the apartments. "I want to live."

"Me too!" Thomas responded excitedly.

"That's not what she means, Thomas. She wants an apartment."

"Don't you want to stay with your people, your relatives?" Thomas asked.

She shook her head.

"I'll see if an apartment is available," he gushed.

"Thomas, don't make promises you can't keep." I tugged his arm. "Let's go."

Thomas tipped his hat as he backed away from her. "It is an exquisite pleasure to meet you."

They Are Afraid of Her watched us go.

"That was a bit rude, Ana."

"We can't get ourselves involved in something we don't understand."

"Speak for yourself. If I avoided things I didn't understand, I'd never do anything! I'd have to avoid music, for goodness' sake. Where would I be then? She is very beautiful, you have to admit."

I led Thomas to the Martinettis' abandoned apartment, the largest on the fifth floor. Since the arrest of the acrobats, the other residents had been arguing over who would move in. Of course they could not decide, so the two adjoining rooms remained empty. I ushered Thomas into them and got him settled, reassuring him that no one would mind if he joined us. The pianist was delighted, and he began to fret over what he would do first: go back to the whale or downstairs to his piano.

I continued down the hall and knocked on Tai Shan's door. He appeared in the doorway, already changed into a soft white robe and trousers. "I don't mean to disturb you, but I just wanted to thank you again for what you did at Niblo's."

"It was your idea to get their help. Thank *you.*"

How had I convinced myself he was pompous? Tai Shan was elegant, certainly more educated than anyone else on the fifth floor, but the arrogance I had seen was actually a reserve that now seemed closer to shyness. How could I have misread him? My eye for seeing through layers of pretense clearly was not trained for my own kind. Nor had I noticed that his head was not entirely shaved; a thin, tightly braided plait hung over his shoulder all the way past his waist, at least four feet in a shiny silken cord. It was quite stunning.

"I also wanted to apologize for being unfriendly toward you," I stammered.

"I didn't think you were unfriendly."

I laughed. "No? I can't imagine how else you could have interpreted my coolness. Good Lord! Your room is half the size of mine! Less!"

He smiled and pushed the door open wider.

"Is this a joke? Do you really live in here?" The room was ten feet square with a minuscule window facing Broadway.

"Of course."

"But there's no furniture! I'm sure Barnum would switch you into a larger room."

"Yes, there is furniture. Don't you see it? I have a table there, and a rug made for me by my uncle." He pointed, and then I saw it: a very low narrow table along one side of the room, too low even for an average-sized person. The rug was woven from coarse fiber. He gestured me in. The room smelled pleasantly of beeswax.

"Where on earth do you sleep?"

"There." He pointed to a cylindrical bundle of rolled blankets. "I put it away during the day."

"But where do you sit?"

"Here." He pointed to the floor. I looked dumbly down. He sat, as if to demonstrate it could be done. From his position, the table was a good height for eating or work.

The table was covered with small tools, pieces of bone, and stones of various colors. On one side of the tabletop stood several rows of tiny carved animals: two rabbits, several monkeys, a bone owl, and a horse with a gracefully fluted tail. They were the same figurines I had seen for sale at a concessionaire's booth on the third floor, the same as the yellow-green soapstone elephant Beebe had given me.

"*You* make these?"

Tai Shan surveyed his work carefully. "Yes."

"You could double your profits if you advertised that these miniatures were made by a giant."

"I know. But this is my hobby. It is my own private joke. Besides, my cousin sells the animals; he operates the booth downstairs and makes a good income from the statues."

Tai Shan fiddled with a small pair of pliers. I hated towering over him so I sank to the floor, my skirt billowing and my corset pinching. I felt decidedly silly with my legs sticking out in front of me. Tai Shan appeared not to notice.

"Were you born in China, or here?"

"China." He pointed to a scroll on the wall. It was covered in spidery crosshatched characters. "I lived in the Imperial Palace."

"So it's true. Your story, the one out there" — I gestured in reference to our booths — "it's true?"

"Of course. I arrived in this country only last October. I was briefly employed in Paris, but I wanted to live in New York because my remaining family lives here. My uncle and aunt, their son and his wife."

"Is that where you go when you're not working? I've noticed you're rarely here in the evenings."

Tai Shan smiled. "I go to them quite often. I stay with them for the night and return here in the morning. My cousin's wife is expecting a baby. I've been helping with the preparations."

The more I watched Tai Shan, the more baffling his delicate angularity became. He exuded lightness despite his physical bulk. He sat comfortably cross-legged, creating a nest of his lap big enough to hold several children. Above his peaked cheekbones his eyes remained fixed on me as he spoke softly about his family. I took in the details of his room: more animal figurines on his tiny sill, a painting of a gibbous moon over pyramidal mountains. He had very few possessions, even for a performer. In comparison with his sleek and simple dwelling, my room was a chaos of ill-fitting furniture, my booth a self-administered prison cell, and my life, in its floundering and self-importance, a terrible mistake.

Astonished, I began to shed tears. My eyes stung fiercely and my breath grew ragged.

"Here." Tai Shan's voice was soft and neutral. He held out a blue silk handkerchief.

"No, it's all right."

"Take it."

"But it's too fine. I would —"

"Please." Tai Shan laid the handkerchief on my knee. I started to rebuke him but he held up his hand and shook his head. I patted my eyes with the cool fabric as deeper shudders racked my rib cage. Tai Shan gazed at his folded hands as I continued crying.

"I lived in the emperor's palace for ten years," he began. "In my quarters hung portraits of the giants who had come before me. Seven generations. When a court giant died, families with children like us appeared from across the country to seek an audience with the emperor, to apply for the post. Usually there were a dozen giants to choose from. My father prepared me for this interview from a very young age. He taught me languages, swordsmanship. There would be no greater honor for him than to be associated with the court.

"When we arrived for our interview, we found that it was not the emperor himself who chose the giant, as in earlier times, but a deputy. A man no one recognized. Instead of the elaborate performance that my father had taught me, I simply stood in a line with four other men. The emperor's deputy chose me, I believe, because I was the tallest.

"Soon after I moved into the palace, I realized that giants had fallen out of fashion. Most days I had no appointments. During festivals I dressed in red and joined in the parades with the rest of the court. When dignitaries from abroad visited the emperor, which wasn't often, I would sometimes be called upon to serve tea or perform some small entertainment. I was treated with respect, but my duties gradually shifted, until my main occupation was tutoring the children. One day the emperor called me into his chamber. He said I was to be the last court giant. There would be no successor. It was then that I decided to leave."

"It was that simple?"

"Yes. My father was dead. My mother was dead. The court was indifferent, occupied with bigger troubles. My only remaining family, as I've told you, was here. There was nothing for me in China except a dead tradition."

"And you don't mind working in a place like this?"

"There is no other place like this museum! Not in Philadelphia, London, or anywhere. That's what makes it interesting. This kind of work is easy; in America I meet people from all over the world. Yesterday, I spoke with a Portuguese duke and duchess visiting the museum! Very nice people."

Very nice people. When had I ever thought so well of museum visitors, or anyone? I sniffled.

"In China everyone has seen a giant. It's unusual, of course, but nothing extraordinary. Not like here. And you! You are the most extraordinary of all Barnum's wonders."

I coughed. "How on earth do you mean?"

"The world's only giantess. Who else can claim to be the world's *only* anything?"

"A lot of people, in this business. Whether the claims are valid seems to be beside the point. But in all my years traveling and working, I haven't seen another giantess, it's true."

"Amazing." Tai Shan shook his head.

"They must be out there somewhere."

The gale blowing through my rib cage subsided. Tai Shan sat with his legs neatly folded. Behind him the small rectangle of sky deepened to indigo. A flock of pigeons spilled across it, the undersides of their wings flashing in unexpected unison.

"Doesn't it bother you that we die so young?" My voice was childlike, full of breath.

"Fear of death is common to all of us."

"That's a diplomatic approach."

"If I lived as if I'd been cheated, that wouldn't be living at all. It does no good to covet a type of life that is not in our nature."

"Yes, but . . . it's horrible. It's not fair!"

Tai Shan laughed, his angularity breaking into pleasant ripples. "It sounds like your particular justice has a narrow parameter —"

"What were the odds that I would be born this way?" I sputtered, leaning toward him. "A million to one."

"Some would call that a miracle."

"I call it Nature's terrible sense of humor."

"No one sees the world like you. People could benefit from the way you see it."

"I see death in every shadow and behind every door."

"So did the sages, Miss Swift," said Tai Shan, still chuckling. "That's what gave them a sense of humor."

Forty-eight

The audience assembled as planned on the front lawn of City Hall Park just off Broadway and Park Row and by ten past one o'clock, it collectively began to wonder when Mr. Barnum would appear. Men flapped their hats in front of their faces even though it was the brightness of the May sun, not its heat, that was distracting. Shouting children ran among the crowd; several boys had climbed the scaffolding that hid the new Croton Fountain from view. Since its grand unveiling the previous October, the fountain had been overflowing its basin and inexplicably drying up. I hoped it wasn't an omen for the whole Croton waterworks. Leaves and bits of trash had collected in the basin; soon children chased one another around and around it. Weaving through the crowd were several concessionaires I recognized from the museum, selling cold drinks and trinkets. At Barnum's instruction, Representatives of the Wonderful were spaced evenly throughout the crowd. I saw Tai Shan on the other side of the park and his visage, suddenly familiar after our visit in his room, calmed me in an unusual way. He waved from above the sea of heads. We were two ships above the storm.

I saw Clarissa, the museum's Fat Lady, sweating profusely, cooling herself with an outsized peacock fan. Thomas Willoughby stood beside me, fidgeting incessantly and peering over his shoulder as if he suspected he was being followed. I looked for Beebe but could not see him.

Besides the staff, who milled and squabbled over patches

of shade, and the two dozen journalists with notebooks in their hands occupying the area directly in front of the empty podium, at least two hundred citizens populated the lawn; they appeared to be average citizens from all over town who seemed to require nothing but Barnum's name to appear. They were probably expecting acrobats, or a crocodile. My neck emitted electric pulses of pain and my jaw ached, but it was good to be off the fifth floor, where the stagnant air was infused with the restlessness of eighteen professional performers on hiatus.

When a sleek carriage stopped outside the stone piers at the park's entrance we were sure Barnum would emerge with some flourish, larger than we remembered, smiling grandly. The crowd leaned and voices rose. But a dozen constables on the backs of horses came around the corner instead. They lined themselves up along the perimeter fence, their horses jostling and sidestepping daintily. The audience recoiled, our collective head pivoting. The shouts of children faded to murmur.

The carriage door slammed open and two men stepped out onto the sidewalk. A third man emerged and remained balanced on the running board with one arm hooked around the carriage window for support. "It's Mayor Harper," a voice whispered somewhere below and to my left.

I glanced behind me to where Maud stood with a black lace veil obscuring her face. She was talking with Oswald La Rue, the Living Skeleton.

"This meeting is now canceled!" The new mayor's youth surprised me. He was a slip of a thing with a thick mop of dark hair, and his voice rang out as if he were a schoolteacher losing control of a rowdy brood of children.

"We now ask you to vacate the park. Barnum's museum remains closed." He looked around. "There's *no* place for Barnum at our great City Hall. Please, make your way out immediately.

The crowd stirred near the gates. Was it that easy to dispel them? Would they come out for Barnum and immediately turn tail for the mayor? But a familiar figure emerged from the crowd and walked between the stone piers to face the mayor.

"Good afternoon, Mayor." Barnum's voice was friendly. Harper's shape grew rigid. "I admit I do not see what the problem is. This park has been the site of countless public gatherings, including speeches by statesmen, celebrities, even visiting dignitaries from abroad. Would you deny those who live in this city access to their own parkland?

"But now that I think of it" — Barnum paused dramatically — "that is exactly what you propose for this grand central park of yours. Access to only those who can pay!"

"Barnum, I insist you leave the premises now."

"Indeed." The crowd was now condensing in a push toward Broadway. Children were no longer laughing. Some people hurried toward the side entrance, but most remained to see the show.

"Yes," Barnum continued. "You indeed hold this particular power, Mr. Mayor. *Dominion* is the old term. But do you know Mr. Suskin?"

From his running board Mayor Harper made no response.

"Mr. Suskin is one of your secretaries, and it was he who issued the permit for this gathering." Barnum removed a folded paper from his trouser pocket and walked directly to Mayor Harper to hand it over. "It is a gathering for members of the *press*," Barnum went on, waving toward the journalists who were furiously scribbling. "To begin now and extend until two thirty. There are children and mothers here as well, Mayor Harper. If you'd like to keep your constabulary on guard at the fence to ensure their safety for the length of this meeting, we would be much obliged."

Barnum turned to the crowd, who responded with applause. He made his way toward the podium as the mayor of New York slipped back into his carriage.

"This is how it begins," Barnum intoned when he reached the podium. "Exactly like this. Those in power begin to make judgments on behalf of those they govern, instead of listening to the judgments and opinions of the people. Where we can gather together peaceably. Where we can go on our well-earned day away from the workplace. We must keep an eagle's eye on those above us. Remember the rights of the citizen as written in our great Constitution, that sacred text that *they*" — here Barnum gestured behind him to the granite columns of City Hall — "claim to hold above all others.

"Friends, I was a penniless man when I arrived in this city. The list of my occupations during the first months I lived here would surprise you, and embarrass me. I struggled not only to survive and to provide for my wife and infant. I wrestled with my soul.

"Come closer, please. There is plenty of room up here on the lawn." Barnum gestured toward the steel fence at our backs. "Come, friends."

It was a good approach, I had to admit. Barnum knew exactly what he was doing, and his audience stepped closer with childlike expressions.

"From my earliest memory I knew I was not made for the farming life, the life given to me by my family. My interest and my calling lay in a different realm. But where? It was not in the landscape of meadow and forest. As a child I worked in the Bethel Parish mercantile, and in the world of commerce I found myself a step closer, yet my destiny remained mysterious.

"I rode into Manhattan on a donkey. It was my own Jerusalem, if you will allow me the comparison. I still did not know where my search would ultimately lead, but I had found the city of my dreams. I was soon impoverished, invisible in this great tide of humanity, adrift amid thousands upon thousands of people and opportunities, bumped and knocked down, even trampled. I admit that my good wife returned to Connecticut in shame, to await my rise from the gutter.

"A man is given a certain allotment of fuel in this life for the engine of his career. Would I run this machine on an established path, would I enter banking, shipping, or some post in municipal government? Or would I follow the compass of my deepest yearning, even toward an unknown destination?

"Most of you know the story of my first venture as an itin-erant entrepreneur of the show business." Again Barnum re-garded the newspapermen. "With those first explorations, I had hit upon it: To make men and women think and talk and wonder was the end at which I aimed. In their wonder-ing lay our humanity, my destiny, and my fortune. I knew it with certainty. Any doubt that had polluted my faith dis-solved." He pointed south. "My museum is a manifestation of that faith.

"The human mind wanders far afield. It wanders as far as the ships of the United States Expedition Company, and far-ther even than Europe's most powerful telescope. There are no officers of morality patrolling those peripheries, for better or for worse. And would we want someone to decide for us whether we are allowed to learn of the distant cultures of man? Would we avert our gaze from the image of a celestial body brought close to us by the inventions of man, simply because one opinion is that the star blasphemes? Of course not! We have a right to marvel at these existences!

"I have brought nothing into my museum with the inten-tion of offending the citizens of this city. I have brought strange, wonderful things to the light. That is my livelihood, my passion, my constant study and occupation. Is there any-one here who would challenge the people's right to view and form their own judgment of the contents of a museum that declares itself to be as diverse and infinitely surprising as the variety of human souls? Would anyone challenge me?"

The newspapermen scribbled. Barnum trolled the audi-ence, passing his gaze over the rear sections and then scan-ning forward.

"I would speak." The voice came from within a group of theater employees.

"Samuel Beebe, it that you?"

The scribbling stopped. Barnum's voice had betrayed sur-prise. Shocked, I did not turn to look. Good Lord, Beebe! Not you.

"Why don't you join me up here, Samuel." Barnum

quickly recovered his composure. "I would like to hear your view."

"I see no need to ascend the podium, Mr. Barnum. I'm perfectly comfortable addressing you from here." Beebe's voice was unusually level. "I am repulsed by the arrogance of your analogy, Mr. Barnum. By the time Jesus rode into Jerusalem he had healed a hundred lepers and announced a New Kingdom for the community of man. The kingdom he professed is based on the substance of Jesus' life and teachings: love, compassion, faith. *Humility.* He rode into Jerusalem for one purpose only: to suffer and die at the hands of the adversary, on behalf of all of humanity. On *our* behalf. Do you not recall Jesus' first action once he had reached the holy city? *Jesus entered the temple and drove out all who were selling and buying, and he overturned the tables of money changers and the seats of those who sold doves.*"

"But Samuel," Barnum countered, "I have never announced this enterprise as anything but popular entertainment. Furthermore, it is you who have forgotten an integral part of Jesus' earthly ministry. How did word of his miraculous powers reach the multitude? He did not have newspapers at his disposal! His disciples were not journalists! No, he performed. In public spaces, he healed demoniacs, lepers, paralytics. He magically produced massive quantities of bread, of fish. He calmed the Sea of Galilee. Crowds gathered. Crowds spread the word of these spectacles, these miracles, these performances. But whenever someone approached him, he did not confirm even his own identity. And what was the effect? Word spread even faster because people wondered, Who is this man? And within the questions that swirled continuously around him, using the strength of people's curiosity and their willingness to believe, Jesus birthed his new kingdom!"

"Mr. Barnum, I am once again shocked at your presumption. Making a spectacle out of the primitive cultures has nothing to do with Jesus' ministry, nor does serving brainsick children to a ravenous public appetite for grotesquerie.

Indeed, capitalizing on the plight of an immigrant family who is even now imprisoned and suffering in the Tombs, of all places, is quite the opposite . . . Surely the audience gathered here has no trouble understanding my point."

I had never heard Beebe speak with such authority. He appealed to the audience with the confidence of a seasoned orator, his words unhurried, lucid. He was, indeed, buoyed by his faith. But instead of lifting my heart toward him, his performance (what else could it be?) immediately wilted my inchoate love in the bud. I suddenly saw him behind the rough-hewn podium of his own church, somewhere on the prairie. Near the front pew, I sat in a custom-built chair, my hands folded in my lap, my eyes faithfully locked on his as he expounded earnestly to his flock. But even then he looked a little ridiculous in his white rector's robe, and people wore bemused smiles as they listened, wondering, "But how can he say such things, when his own heart holds such perversion. Just look at the size of her — " No, there was not room for that faith *and* me. It would be a lie anywhere, even far from this city. Enough. Lightning flashed over the prairie and a sudden gust swept the church away, and then the wild grasslands themselves dissolved in torrential rain.

"Your hypocrisy and loose words are shameful," Beebe continued. "What would your own family, your own uncle Phin say if he were alive and could hear you now?"

Barnum stared at Beebe through a veil of silence that pricked the hairs on my nape, before he rent it with a guttural laugh. He threw his head back and clutched his middle. The journalists could not write fast enough.

"Yes, yes, my dear Samuel! Of course! It was only when Jesus returned to Nazareth that the people ran him out of town! *Isn't this just the carpenter's son?* they said. Do we not have his mother and his sister here in the village with us? Isn't this the man we knew as a boy, throwing rocks and playing in the dirt just like the rest?

"But I'm afraid you've picked the wrong relative to illustrate your point, Samuel. You should have invoked the name of my father, about whom I am more sensitive. Or my mother, God rest her soul. But you picked my uncle. With this choice, all you have done is provide the context for the greatest pleasure known to man, a pleasure that the author of every gospel well understood. Do you know what this pleasure is?"

Barnum paused, but only for dramatic effect. Beebe had no chance of recovering now. "It is the pleasure of a good story," he finished.

Barnum stepped out from behind his podium. "I have already stated that from my earliest memory I knew the farming life was not for me. In large part I owe this conviction to my uncle Phineas, the man for whom I was named, of whom Mr. Beebe has kindly reminded me. This uncle is the recipient of my utmost love, respect, and gratitude.

"Upon the event of my birth, my uncle presented me with a slip of paper. This paper eventually had the power to open my eyes to the infinite possibility in the world and it gave my vision a scope larger and grander than Bethel Parish. In my early years I read the writing on that piece of paper so many times that even now I know it by heart: *I, Phineas Taylor of Bethel Village in Fairfield County and State of Connecticut, for the consideration of that natural affection that I have to Phineas Taylor Barnum my nephew and son of Philo and Irena Barnum, release and for ever quit-claim unto the said P. T. Barnum to his heirs and assigns for ever, all Right and Title that I have a piece of land at the Ivy Island, a place so called containing ten acres and is bounded Westerly and Northerly on East Brook, Easterly by a ditch that conveys the water from the Ivy Island into the natural stream.*

"Ivy Island may have been only ten acres, but in my mind it grew to the size of Connecticut. The land itself was forty miles from Bethel, and my uncle made me wait until my tenth birthday before allowing me to visit my property. In the meantime, stories of this island permeated my childhood. Most evenings, when my family had finished its supper, Father would light his pipe and say, *What's that I hear about Ivy Island?* And Uncle Phin would reply, *It's the best, most fertile land in the country!* And he would describe it to me, undoubtedly delighting in my excitement. In my mind hazelnut trees dropped carpets of nuts and the soil sprouted fat-kerneled heads of corn the size of brook trout. The beets grown on Ivy Island were dense and heavy. He even said a vein of silver ran in the granite below Ivy Island.

"My dream was not to tend this land. No, I imagined all of this great bounty turned to heavy coins in my purse. By the time I was ten, my plan was fixed: I would work the land until I had enough money to hire others to do it for me. I would then open a store, sell my bounty, and make deals with suppliers in New York City to bring new goods to Bethel. When I had enough money I would open another store, and then another, and yet another.

"As you might imagine, I was beside myself on my tenth birthday. My father loaded me into the cart, and I was surprised that Uncle Phin was not coming with us. I shall never forget how he looked, standing in the doorway just as dawn lightened the eastern sky. *You must face your destiny alone,* he said. As I recall, I caught a glimpse of my young friend Beebe on the way out of town. I believe he ran alongside the cart on his little legs and tossed a stick into the air and caught it again just as we passed.

"We rode all morning toward Ivy Island, but my imagination flew above our rough cart. The fecundity of my island would take me beyond the world of dirt tracks, hog farmers, and a livelihood bound to the seasons. I dreamed. I plotted. I knew beyond all doubt that my destiny was entangled with something far greater than ten acres.

"When we arrived, I leapt from the cart. My father pointed to the far end of a field of uncut hay. *See that stand of sassafras? Beyond that boundary lies your land. Look for the stream. Follow it until you see the island.* Again I wondered that my father was not coming with me, but I was too excited to pause for long. I ran as fast as I could. In my mind I had already sown the best seeds and diverted the stream for water. I had already pulled up to the Bethel village mercantile in my own wagon with barrels of vegetables. Old Seeley the store clerk had already shaken his head, wiping his hands on his apron. *You've*

*done it again, Barnum. We're going to have people coming all the
way from Bridgeport for this corn.*

"I ran through the trees that divided me from my property
and followed the stream for several hundred feet before I
came upon the island. I had a good view of it from where I
stood on the sandy bank. I tried to look everywhere at once.

"First, I saw stunted alders leaning together like a group of
bent old women. Second, I saw the dusty, hard soil. A strange
feeling formed inside me. Third, I observed one sugar maple
with dried-up leaves, choked by a network of green vines
grown tightly around the tree's trunk. I recognized the red-
stemmed crawler. Ivy. Poison ivy. My eyes followed the network of tangles down one tree and up another, down again
and across the ground. The island was a wasteland.

"Suddenly all the years of stories made a new sense to me,
especially the ricocheting glances between Phin and my father. The neighbors smiling and calling out to me, saying,
Here's the Duke of Ivy Island. The deed. Now I could see my
uncle at the courthouse, drawing up the papers himself, and
my father with a small smile behind his pipe. I understood
what they had done."

Barnum blinked out at us as if from a great distance. The
silence in the park was profound until a clear voice came
from the journalists.

"But *why* did they do it?"

Barnum shook his head. "Answering that question took
many years. It was a diabolical practical joke, no question.
And I thought of it in exclusively that way until my wounds
had healed and time had diluted my memory. Inevitably, my
feelings changed. I realized that through the hoax of Ivy Island, my uncle had given me the two most important lessons
of my life: First, I would never let anyone fool me again. Second, through their trick, they gave me the opportunity to
feel the exuberance of pure belief that my destiny was larger
than the hay fields of Bethel Parish. Ivy Island allowed me to
dream of infinite possibility. Without that dream, I would not
be here today. In fact, and I mean this quite literally, if it

were not for Ivy Island, none of you would be here today. The American Museum would not exist.

"You see, when Mr. Scudder put the museum up for sale, I admit that I lacked funds. At the time I had many friends in this city who would attest to my entrepreneurial skill and the seriousness of my intentions. But my lack of financial resources eliminated me from the owner's consideration. I knew I could make the museum a success, if he would only give me the chance. So when I met with Mr. Scudder, I had in my hand a slip of paper that read: *As collateral, with the promise to reimburse you ten thousand dollars within two years, I present you with the deed to ten acres of Connecticut's finest farmland, near my ancestral home.*"

Barnum raised up his arms. "You can guess the rest of that story!"

When the applause subsided, Barnum returned to the podium. He peered over the heads of his employees and patrons. "I trust that you now understand that my relationship with this enterprise is one of unswerving belief. Mr. Beebe, have you gotten the idea?"

"The only idea that came to mind during your delirious rant is that this place will no longer be the means of my livelihood."

The other ushers had moved away from him, and he reddened visibly as he spoke. You are already fading from me, Beebe.

"I believe your exhibits are amoral, blind to human dignity, and in many cases mean-spirited. I will have nothing more to do with them, or you." Beebe turned stiffly and walked through the crowd. There. It is done. You yourself have closed the door between us.

"So be it," Barnum intoned. "The museum does not ask for approval."

Because of my height I could follow Beebe's route through the crowd as he left Barnum's meeting, and his employ. He weaved between citizens. Some recognized him as the speaker and moved aside, and some ignored him so he had to push against them to gain passage. When he reached the park's wrought-iron fence and the relative spaciousness of the street he broke into a run. Good-bye, Beebe. I kept his bobbing head in view as long as I could but soon he disappeared southward on Broadway. Godspeed.

"And now let us turn to the matter closest at hand." Barnum called his group to order. The journalists suddenly vied for his attention, raising their pen-tipped arms.

"Yes, Mr. Haley."

"Harper shut down your museum eight days ago. In that time you have not spoken to the press at all. The mayor's office cites numerous instances of lewd and obscene behavior, including the Martinetti family of acrobats, the Circassian Clairvoyant, and a group of Indians. What really happened?"

"Very good. What really happened is this: Several weeks ago, Mayor Harper attended an elite luncheon cruise around New York Harbor aboard Commodore Vanderbilt's schooner. Also attending the luncheon were the Duke and Duchess of York, as well as a pair of German aristocrats about to join a Lyceum-sponsored paleontological expedition to Dakota. Conversation during this event was dominated by accounts of my museum. All parties had made numerous visits to see as many of the exhibits as they could, and each guest sang the museum's praise. I believe the orang-outang was a special favorite among the royalty. The mayor was understandably annoyed that our friends from across the sea were more enamored by a popular entertainment than the city's ports, its public grounds, its civic buildings!"

"That's why he shut down the museum?"

"Believe me, morality and so-called lewd behavior are fabricated reasons, merely excuses. Another question? Yes, Mr. Emmett."

"When will you reopen the museum?"

"I have a team of legal assistants hard at work as we speak. Don't quote me on this" — here Barnum winked at the newspapermen — "but if the museum isn't open by this Wednesday I'll dance an Irish jig in the middle of Broadway, right in front of Saint Paul's Chapel! And I'm not even Irish!"

The men laughed.

"Another question? Yes."

"How will you counter Harper's attack on your museum?"

"A-ha! You're my kind of man, Mr. Whitman. As Mayor Harper should know by now, depriving the people of New York the entertainments they most enjoy will do nothing but fan their appetite for those very entertainments. In the time the museum has been closed, the attendance recorded at Vauxhall Gardens, the Park Theater, and Niblo's have increased threefold. Each day a line forms outside these museum walls, even though the sign reads SHUT! It was an ill-advised strategy. I don't mean to give you gentlemen any ideas, now, but he would have been much more successful plotting an assault on my personal character instead of that of my employees." Here the newspapermen erupted in laughter. "If the good people of this city truly thought me a scoundrel, I guarantee they wouldn't flock as they do to my enterprise.

"I was going to wait until the museum reopened its doors to make my plans public. However, because of your interest and your willingness to listen to all I have said today, I will let you in on some tremendous news. James Harper is under the backward notion that the citizens of New York City prefer to be kept apart from the diversity of human races that populate the globe. Exposure to exotic costumes and ways of life is not education in his mind. Instead, he views such exposure as *unchristian*. I do not understand it, and from the public outcry I have heard, I trust you do not understand it, either. It is the Sioux Indians who draw the largest crowds to the museum. It is our collection of African weaponry and ceremonial relics. We are a generation fascinated by the diversity of our world as we see it vicariously through the eyes of our national expeditions and glimpse it, however dimly, through the silver eyes of Daguerre.

"And so it is with the aim of augmenting this fascination and contributing to the education of my countrymen that I announce what will become known as the largest and most comprehensive gathering of disparate, uncivilized races ever seen on American soil; no diplomatic agency or scientific institution has ever done what I am about to do, either here or abroad. It is a veritable human menagerie and my greatest gift to the world thus far! It is the Grand Ethnological Congress of Nations! In just a few days time, my American Museum will become home to members of every primitive race of man now living on the globe. As we speak, representatives of the Zulu, Hindoo, Afghan, Nubian, even Esquimaux from the polar North are aboard vessels bound for New York Harbor. And that is just the tiniest hint of what will come. Prepare yourselves for this tide of humanity, for this cavalcade of Orientals. Get out your dictionaries, my good fellows, because you will need entirely new vocabularies to describe this event in your papers.

"Mayor Harper thinks the people of New York City do not want to open their eyes to the diversity of human cultures. He believes they would rather pay admission to stroll in a dull municipal park filled with man-made ponds, landscaped gardens, and footpaths designed to take them in circles. And he wants his citizens to pay for the park's construction! I know better. I have no doubt in my mind. But you can decide for yourself. Every one of you is perfectly equipped to decide for yourself. It is upon that simple fact that all my endeavors hinge."

As we speak, they are aboard vessels bound for New York Harbor. As we speak, Zulu, Hindoo, Nubian, Esquimaux. I watched Barnum gesticulating and waving his arms, but what I saw were lines of fur- and hide-clad exotics marching up Broadway from the port and pouring into the museum. What I heard was myriad languages spoken at once. Chaos and thousands of dollars in revenue. Barnum described torchlight parades to *Welcome Manhattanites to A New Age of Diversity*. The audience cheered. The Congress was a brilliant, devious plan. It would draw the biggest crowds the museum had yet seen. And we would use it for leverage.

Forty-nine

The evening after Barnum's performance, every door in the apartments of the Wonderful was open and an incredible cacophony of voices and music met me as I came in.

Maud's room was bright and jumbled. The white-haired albino twins were at the far end against a backdrop of purple and red rugs; the boy jerked in time with his fiddle's tune and his sister perched on a stool with her concertina on her knee and one small foot tapping. Around them in a loose half circle sat the rest, some clapping, most cheeks flushed with liquor. An abandoned game of whist and the detritus of supper littered the table, where Maud sat talking with Clarissa, whose massive girth spilled over both sides of the chair. I was surprised to see the Aztec Children, Susan with Maud and Henry almost lost in the great landscape of Clarissa's lap. Susan clung to Maud's skirt, her eyes fixed on her brother, who had fallen asleep despite the terrific hubbub.

In the eight days that the museum had been shut down, Maud's apartment had become the official parlor of the fifth floor. People brought the chairs and couches from their own rooms and some of them spent most of their time there, like the conjoined twins, who occupied their usual bench in the middle of everything.

"How did you get so many people in here so fast?" I asked Maud.

"Eight days without work is what did it. It was the fourth day when people lost the last of their inhibitions, and since then it's been like this. Haven't you noticed? Look who even came out to join us." Maud pointed across the room to where Tai Shan sat in a massive wooden chair a little separate from the others, but tapping his fingers in time to the children's music.

"Where did that chair come from?"

"We brought it up from a display on the third floor. Placard said it was Elizabeth the First's. Unlikely. Thomas! There you are, you rascal. Have some cake. We were just speculating about what our old friend Mr. Olrick might be saying, wherever he is at the moment."

"Gloating, I'm sure. He was certain Barnum's museum wouldn't last."

"The museum will be open again within the week. I have no doubt," Maud said. "Barnum is losing too much money to enjoy this kind of attention for long, although I'm sure he has enjoyed it. The newspaper stories have been spectacular."

"Maud, did you see in the papers that the Martinettis really are in the Tombs? That nephew of theirs was here again. Looking for Barnum. He said that without Barnum's written support they wouldn't be released anytime soon."

Maud shook her head, but I could see she wanted to be swept up in the festivities around her, so I let it go. I thought of Beebe, and he appeared again in the rough-hewn church, another world, this time extinguishing candle after yellow candle.

Oswald La Rue, Living Skeleton and supposed father of the albino twins, rose from a couch and joined his children where they played. Mr. La Rue and Clarissa had indulged the public, and greatly enhanced their professional careers, by "marrying" each other in a public ceremony in the museum's theater, becoming New York City's first thin-man-fat-lady couple. Their actual relationship was entirely professional and their guardianship of the twins was mysterious in origin, but the children were well groomed and relatively cheerful; no one questioned it.

Mr. La Rue clapped his bony hands as he passed like a

shadow between chairs and people. By the time he reached the twins he was dancing, kicking out his stick legs and cocking his arms with both elbows out. He leaned over and sidled side-to-side, looking like nothing other than a ghoulish marionette, with lips pulled back and the corrugations of his skull visible beneath the thinnest cover of skin. He danced his skeleton dance to the music played by two translucent, squinting children, and we all clapped, urging them faster and faster until he twirled in a tangle of loose limbs, his surrogate daughter shouting French phrases and all of us hooting and calling out for more. Amid this frenzy, in a dimming corner of my mind, Beebe snuffed out the last yellow candle and disappeared completely.

Across the room, Maud waved at me to look. Susan, the Aztec child, was clapping her hands. On her face was an expression I'd never seen: delighted eyes and a droopy smile. Maud grinned ridiculously and put her hand on the girl's head.

Despite the raised hairs on my nape and the sudden clutch of fear behind my sternum, when the music stopped I stood up. If I didn't speak now, I would have to endure the even more uncomfortable nagging of the idea on my conscience.

"I have a request," I began weakly. All heads turned. "We have in our midst two children, billed as 'Aztecs.'" I gestured across the room. Susan immediately lost all trace of her smile and instead stretched her mouth into an unhappy, exaggerated yawn. This was her gesture of protest, normally used when she didn't want to eat or leave her room. Thankfully, Henry remained asleep, or else he would have mimicked his sister.

"It will not surprise you to learn, if you did not know already, that these children were acquired illegally, in a maneuver that may or may not have been an improvement to their lives. It is not my intention to make a moral judgment about all that. I am here to ask that you sign your names to a petition, to be delivered to Mr. Barnum as soon as I can meet with him. The petition requests a full-time guardian for the children as well as regular medical appointments, as they suffer from illnesses, both of the body and mind."

Matthew, sitting below me to the left, held out his hand. "Well, come on then. Where is this petition? Do you have a pen?"

"While we're at it, we should appeal for guaranteed pay while the museum is closed," said Jacob.

"It's a bit too late for that," I replied. "But we can do better next time. It would benefit us all," I added, "to understand that we are more powerful together than as isolated individuals."

"If only I were an isolated individual," Matthew sighed, and received a sharp jab in the ribs from Jacob.

I retrieved the petition from my room and watched it pass through the hands of the Wonderful. Maud signed and gave it to Clarissa. Clarissa passed it to Oswald La Rue, who put on his spectacles and read every word before making his mark. He passed it over the table to Tai Shan.

Thomas Willoughby was the last to sign, and he returned the now-wrinkled papers to me. "I hope you take this to the Sioux, Ana. Everyone on the fifth floor stands to gain something from your petition's success." He bowed and extended the petition.

"Yes, the more signatures the better."

The sound of the festivities in Maud's parlor faded in the empty gallery. I looked for They Are Afraid of Her as I neared the encampment, but I did not see her. The elder Sioux, wearing his usual top hat and purple waistcoat, met me at the threshold. Figures stirred in their cots, and it was impossible for me to see if others sat in the recesses of their tent.

"Good evening, Miss Swift." The man's eyes blurred out of focus behind the smoke that rose from his pipe.

I explained the petition. The words that had struck the Wonderful as valiant, or at least promising, sounded hollow under the scrutinizing gaze of this man.

"Why should we sign such a thing?" he said. "We will be moving on soon enough. What is the benefit for us?"

"There will be others arriving for this Congress of Nations. The petition will help protect us, and them, from unfair treatment."

The old man laughed. "If a piece of paper could protect us from anything, we would know it by now." He sucked on his pipe. "That hasn't been my experience so far."

"No one will force you to sign," I said. The man chuckled again but reached for the petition and pen.

Across the gallery, a dim shape moved. A rounded figure that I recognized as They Are Afraid of Her, wrapped in the blanket, came toward us.

Her hair was wet and she was barefoot. She must have been swimming with the beluga again.

She looked at me eagerly. "I can go?"

She looked at the old man, then at the floor. In a quick, cruel movement he grabbed her by the wrist and shoved her toward the tent. He released a torrent of incomprehensible words in their language as she tripped over the blanket she wore and fell to her knees.

"She is a fool," he said by way of explanation.

"She is certainly not! She has learned quite a bit of English since she's been here."

He shook his head. "When we found her she was half dead. She was wandering in the heat on open ground. Those cuts were bleeding. She had dried blood all down her face. The buzzards were circling her. That's how we spotted her. She should have died."

"She said she was not from your tribe."

The man laughed. "No, she is not one of us. But she is Sioux. We took her with us. If we had known what she'd done, we would have left her for the buzzards."

"What did she do?"

"She left her family to marry a man from another tribe. He was an enemy of the Sioux. But her lover's people would not accept them, either. So he abandoned her. But her family wouldn't take her back."

"What about the scars?"

"We think she did it to herself. Or else her people gave them to her. She will not say. Foolish woman."

No wonder she wanted to leave the Indian camp.

When I returned to Maud's apartment, I did not meet Thomas' curious gaze, though I felt his eyes on me. The albino children were still playing their instruments, but now the sound was cacophonous, and those who had been drinking talked too loudly. Gradually, though, amid their congratulations and toasts to the success of my petition, my mood lightened. I talked with Tai Shan, and when he left I sat in the massive chair and soon I, too, was clapping along to the uneven rhythm of the music.

Fifty

"How is your father?"

"I beg your pardon?"

"Your ancestral home is Pictou, is it not? Nova Scotia? I presume he is still there?"

"No. He moved to Halifax after he sold his fleet. And how is your wife?" I countered his strategy. "We were all very sorry at the loss of your daughter."

"Mrs. Barnum is doing her best. Her grief has been difficult. We miss our girl."

"Of course." My gaze was level. "Wasn't Mrs. Barnum expecting a new baby?"

Barnum shifted in his seat. "No."

We eyed each other; his expression became satisfyingly clouded.

"Well. All of us on the fifth floor certainly miss them. They were such *fun*."

He moved a book to one side of his desk and revealed a copy of my True Life History. "This reads like the beginning of a novel."

"It's selling," I managed to reply. I had no idea he even knew I had written anything.

"Yes. Giants' histories are among the most profitable pamphlets. Yours is particularly well done. Brilliant, your decision to tell different versions of your story. Reading it made me ponder a question that has haunted me for quite some time." Barnum pressed the tips of his fingers together and studied his joined hands as if they were an architectural model. "The question of art in my enterprise. Is there a place for it? Does art, literary, painterly, or any kind at all, draw? Are people *really* as interested in art as they claim? My own interests are diverse, Miss Swift. The interests of the public, however, are of the utmost importance to me. And I have deduced that the public is largely indifferent to art, despite what they insistently claim."

"You can hardly expect me to believe that, Mr. Barnum."

He was shaking his head, trying to hide a small smile. "I'm afraid I can convince you quite easily, if you will allow me two minutes."

His confidence irked me.

"I was in London, as you know, with the General Tom Thumb. We booked the Egyptian Hall for our performances. During the few days it took to organize the show, I traveled back and forth from my hotel to the Egyptian to oversee the rehearsals and concessionaires. During this time, I noticed there was a small gallery next to the theater, and inside the gallery, one man worked, day after day. I observed him first washing the large windows facing the street. I even saw him sweeping the sidewalk in front. Then he set up two easels, one in each window, and set two large paintings upon them. He whitewashed the walls in the gallery and soon he was hanging paintings along the walls. Finally, I strolled to the gallery, hoping to invite this hardworking soul to the General's performance, which was scheduled to open the following evening.

"He eyed me warily, and when I invited him to the show he insisted he would not come. Since my gesture had been made out of nothing but friendliness, I was annoyed, yet remained courteous as I bid him good day.

"I asked the house manager at the Egyptian who the lad might be, and he told me a story that truly softened my heart. His name was Benjamin Robert Haydon, a painter fallen on hard times, who was putting on his exhibit as a last resort to retain his freedom. His debts were leading him to debtor's prison, you see. He hoped that with the proceeds of his sales, he could lift himself up and resume his business of portraiture. The manager told me that Haydon had rented the gallery for one week, with his exhibit opening the following evening, coincident to Thumb's first performance.

"You may already have guessed what follows, Miss Swift, so I will be brief: Thumb's opening was a gala event, the house crowded with London's elite classes, including royalty and Members of Parliament. The following evening was the same. I glimpsed Mr. Haydon walking toward his gallery as I approached the museum one morning, several days after I had extended him my invitation. As I passed him on the street, I asked him about his sales, simultaneously noticing his grim and haggard visage. He glared at me, saying not a word.

"Two days later I learned that the poor man had sold nothing. Not a single canvas. In fact, only a handful of people had attended his opening; among them, a London critic who disparaged the work the next day in the *Times*. The artist's hope had been dashed completely. I do not intend to shock you gratuitously, Miss Swift, but when Mr. Haydon did not appear for the fifth and final evening of his show, an acquaintance went to his small garret and found him sprawled on his bedroom floor, quite dead, having ingested some quantity of turpentine."

I let an appropriate silence punctuate the air.

"An interesting tale," I remarked. "You seem to have a fable for every circumstance."

"Apparently the young man left a note, condemning me personally, and the type of entertainment I represent. He believed that if his show hadn't coincided with Thumb's grand opening —"

"Suicide is a compelling finale to a miserable life, especially for an artist. I suppose all of Haydon's paintings sold after he died?"

"I don't know." Barnum's voice was thoughtful. "Do you think that could have been his hope?"

"Isn't it the wish of every artist who perceives that his end will come before his success? Your story reminds me of someone I once knew." I leveled him in my gaze. "If you can spare two minutes for a tale in which you do not feature, I will tell you.

"You probably haven't heard of Miss Juliet Besalu. I made her acquaintance a very long time ago, in Halifax, where we worked together in Jones' Medicine Show. She came from Mississippi, a slave, and was sold to the first traveling show to come through her town. They had to teach her everything. Up until then, all she could do was sweep and care for chickens. No small feat — if you forgive the pun — given the fact that she was born without arms. So they taught her the act, you know, pouring tea and lifting cup and saucer, painting, eating with silverware. She learned very quickly; by the time I met her she was playing piano and had a short equestrian routine. She almost never spoke, but occasionally we'd pass the time together, reading or playing cards.

"I believe the clay pigeon routine was her own idea, although I don't know for certain. But soon she was practicing with a small lady's pistol. She cocked it with her toe, and when her manager tossed the pigeon she shot it out of the sky. The shards tinkled like glass. I remember that. In a matter of weeks she had mastered it. Now, Mr. Barnum, I don't want to shock you gratuitously, but Miss Besalu had a plan entirely outside the parameters of her act. As you might surmise, her ultimate aim was not to obliterate a clay decoy. She succeeded in her true intention on a warm evening when the tent was packed. I must admit it was a graceful and perfectly executed maneuver; she shot the second of her three allotted pigeons and before the fragments had reached the ground she turned the pistol around with her feet, closed her eyes, turned her head to the side, and discharged one bullet precisely into her temple. It was not a powerful firearm; she knew she must hit her mark.

"At first the audience cheered, not perceiving what was obvious to the other performers. But the truth dawned on them as Methuselah Jones threw his coat over her form and carried her away. And while it is true that the suicide yielded publicity for Mr. Jones, it was of the variety that drove him

quite to the depths of despair, and ultimately to the utter destruction of his enterprise."

"I remember Methuselah Jones," Barnum said.

"He was a small-time showman compared with you." I
was practically cooing. "But don't doubt what happens when
the performers mutiny. They are perfectly capable of turning entertainment into horror. Just imagine the scale of your
ruin."

I didn't let too much time elapse. "I have a petition."

Barnum laughed suddenly. "I should have guessed! Brilliant, Miss Swift."

"My concerns are twofold: First are two individuals currently in your employ. They are known as the Aztec Children."

"Ah, yes. Wonderful specimens of the lost race of Iximaya." Barnum spoke as if he still addressed the journalists.
"Discovered by our own Professor Chatterton."

"My interest is not tearing the web of those particular de-
ceptions. I do not even care to cause a stir over how these
children came to be in your employ, although that would be
satisfying to me personally." I raised my eyebrow in what I
hoped was the equivalent of a checkmate. Barnum made
no move. His face was curious, unhurried. I realized that we
were on equal footing.

"These children must be cared for properly, however they
·came to be here, with special attention to their particular . . .
fragilities. These needs are not being met at the current time.
I have a petition here, signed by each one of your Representatives of the Wonderful."

"I see your English lessons haven't extended to handwrit-
ing," Barnum said, perusing the signatures. "I assume these
marks are for the Indians."

"No, the Indians write very well. The marks are Oswald
La Rue's and the tribesman's." How did he know about my
short-lived English class?

"The tribesman?" Barnum looked at me vacantly. "My
memory does not conjure that one. I'll take your word for it.

This looks reasonable enough." He tossed the paper lightly onto a stack of papers. "I'll see to it."

"Good." I hadn't thought it would be so simple. "And the Martinettis. They must be released from the Tombs."

Barnum swiveled in his chair and looked out the window. He appeared to be finished with our conversation.

"Agreed," he said.

I was just getting up, feeling the blood flow back into my legs, when he spoke again. His voice was altogether different: soft, ruminating.

"You know what I could never understand, Miss Swift? How it is that the word *museum* is unrelated to the verb *to muse*. It's a linguistic fluke! A coincidence, if you fancy that term. Palace of the muses. Place where we muse." He shook his head. "The world is strange."

Fifty-one

It was as if Barnum conjured the Congress with his words. Within two days of his speech in City Hall Park, eight more Indians appeared on the fifth floor and efficiently constructed a camp along the far wall of the gallery, on the opposite side of the room from the Sioux. Between the two camps swam the little whale, still unseen by the paying public.

Barnum also reopened his museum. As far as anyone on the fifth floor knew, none of the acts that had offended the mayor's office had been changed, except that Zobeide Luti, the Circassian Beauty, had altered her costume to more tightly restrain her abundant bosom.

Although there is no great pleasure associated with my vocation, and the particular miseries I have encountered in the course of my professional career have been many, on a good day I am convinced they are no more than is usual for a working person of my years, whether an alderman or a button-maker, and I try to never lose sight of the reason I continue my work: independence. For each day that I did not earn my salary in Barnum's museum, I felt a fraction of my independence slipping away. This was not an entirely financial anxiety; after my tenure with Mr. Ramsay I decided I would never work under the hand of a manager again. To operate under the direct instruction of another was to work with the mindless ease of a trained animal, with no eyes to see and no ears to hear, no matter how well you understand your instructions. However inverted it may sound, returning to my work as a public spectacle meant maintaining my dignity.

Blossoms from City Hall Park sweetened the air on the balcony. The breeze was strong but tunneled warmly toward the harbor. Thomas nodded to me from the depths of a sonata. The keys to his harpsichord were visibly worn; he and the two other musicians looked disheveled as ever, the ophecleide player seeming nearly asleep as he played. Several museum patrons stood at the railing with eyes closed and faces upturned, as if they rode the prow of a great ship, but instead of a glinting sea below there was a river of traffic on Broadway.

It was only nine o'clock in the morning and the building was almost full. A tremendous line of people snaked out from the museum entrance, and the buzz of their voices blended with the music. Strange, how calmly determined this line of customers appeared, as if they wanted nothing more in life than to wait all day on the street to hand their money to Phineas T. Barnum.

Parallel to the line was another clump of people, moving slowly up and down the street. A few of them carried signs, and many of them seemed to be calling out. As they came closer to the balcony I saw they were opponents of the museum. Their signs read DO NOT ENTER THE DEN OF SIN! and BARNUM IS STEALING FROM YOU! Several policemen escorted the opponents, and I could see more of them gathered in the garden of Saint Paul's Chapel. Among them, Miss Crawford waved her sign, flanked by two women I recognized from the soiree at her house. I watched her until her gaze rose to where I stood on the balcony. It passed unflinchingly over me and back down to street level.

"Ana, we are back to our old routine," Thomas called to me from the other side of the balcony.

"Indeed." I turned and walked into the shade of the galleries.

I was a rare visitor to the third floor, but I decided to go there before standing in my booth for the day. Apart from the orang-outang, the third-floor displays were mostly mechanical contraptions, including reproductions of Greek astrolabes and the Gutenberg Bible. These displays did not draw crowds, so among them Barnum had sprinkled some of his most unusual specimens to lure people upstairs. I was there because I wanted to have a look at the conjoined twins.

Jacob was becoming increasingly aggressive and I'd been fretting over the twins' erratic behavior. It was not uncommon for them to appear with violent marks on their arms, with Matthew bearing the brunt of them. He seemed to be retreating, a heartbreaking notion given the circumstance of his physical life. Evenings, if I heard a thump from somewhere among the fifth-floor apartments, I pictured Matthew receiving some abuse, and a hopeless feeling came over me.

I half expected to find their booth empty. A few times we'd had to rouse them from their bed halfway through the day. In these cases they were groggy and irritable, having apparently consumed large quantities of liquor the night before. But this morning they were in their proper place. They moved across a small stage, executing the steps of their Scottish folk dance perfectly for the spectators who stood before them.

Matthew still had a bright red scratch along his cheek that disappeared into his collar. He had applied powder to it, but that only accentuated his natural pallor and the wound itself. As they danced, Jacob's mouth moved in a constant stream of whisper to his brother, and both of their faces were held in neutral and unsettling masks.

I watched these two who were also one and suddenly in their struggle I saw my own: A war waged within me, between two opposing wills. For me the stronger side was a clear, quiet voice proving again and again that I am alone. I will never be part of society, it said, and so it's best for me to live, and especially die, by my own rules. Don't even try to belong, this voice advised. The other side was weaker, a kernel of hope that the world finally will stop staring and embrace me. It was a war without end, a division where unity should prevail. The twins made these internal adversaries visible. Seen this way, they surprised and frightened me, and I hurried away without making contact with Matthew, which had been my reason for coming up there. I let the crowd's current sweep me away.

A few galleries away from the twins, Maud sat on the edge of an upholstered chair, her feet firmly on the ground. A basket of delicate yarn sat on the floor by her chair, and she knit the filaments into lace on a pair of tiny needles. I had always admired Maud's choice in presenting an entirely domestic scene as her backdrop. Nothing more was required. No one who viewed her would recall the backdrop anyway. A velvet rope cordoned her from the public. There must have been a new advertisement; I had never seen so many people before her. This time they were mostly women and I recognized their reactions to Maud. I had experienced the same thing countless times, although Maud generated a much more poignant strain of aversion than I. I did not often hear the word *disgusting* in reference to my body. But Maud presented a different story. She was brilliant, sitting there, making lace and sipping what I knew to be very expensive Oriental tea. She earned more than any of us, because there was only one other hirsute woman in all of New York, and that woman had been touring in France for close to a year, with no sign of coming back.

I climbed upstairs and walked through the galleries on the north side of the fourth floor that were filled with artifacts, including numerous stone statues of horses and men, gold figurines of hundred-armed idols encrusted with glowing red stones, ceramic urns said to contain the ashes of queens, cases of swords in ebony sheaths, and, in the far corner of the northernmost gallery, Tai Shan on display.

His sign proclaimed that he spoke ten languages. A MASTER OF THE ANCIENT ARTS OF WAR AND ALSO SKILLED IN CALLIGRAPHY. There was a table with a diminutive Chinese attendant, probably Tai Shan's cousin, beside it, selling paintings of simple brushwork made by the giant.

He was the tallest human I'd ever seen. As usual, his body was draped in loose folds of silken fabric, this time in shades of green and gold, embroidered with cranes. He had no booth, no velvet rope, and yet the crowd stood well away from him. Tai Shan wore a faint smile and stood so still he seemed to be listening. His gaze fell somewhere beyond the spectators, which made it easier for them to stare directly at him. Even to me he was an impressive and puzzling figure; he was a massive specimen of man, and yet he bore an unmistakable feminine quality. His face did not have the usual clumsy exaggeration of most giants. It was delicately sculpted and, even more strangely, he emanated a soothing, gentle feeling. Peace, even. I watched from the doorway as Tai Shan slowly modified his position with a soft movement of his arm and shifting of weight, which provoked a ludicrous gasp from the crowd. As I watched, the muscles in my own shoulders loosened, which quickly prompted a series of shooting pains up my spine. When he saw me, Tai Shan smiled and that sense came over me again, the one I'd felt ever since I'd sat splay-legged yet comfortable on the floor of this other giant's apartment: I liked him. It was a relief to drop my usual hostility toward another giant, but if I did not hate other giants, that meant I did not hate the world. This was such a foreign idea, I quickly dismissed it. Yet later, when I once again approached my own booth, in comparison with Tai Shan's it appeared to me as a ridiculous self-made cage.

At lunchtime the taxidermist was feeding the beluga from the new platform that had been built around the periphery of the tank. Instead of the ladder, people could now climb eight or ten plank stairs to the platform, which allowed them to peer over the edge of the tank. How much longer before this gallery was opened to the masses? The Australian tribesman stood at the taxidermist's side. The most elderly Sioux Indian, wearing his black satin top hat, was shouting from his encampment. He was addressing one of the new Indians, all the way across the gallery. From a distance of two hundred feet, this newcomer was standing with his back to the Sioux, going about the business of packing or unpacking some kind of trunk. The Sioux seemed to become more agitated, although who knows what he was saying.

Light came from the Aztec Children's open doorway, but instead of the children I found Maud there alone. She sat on the edge of the children's bed with her shoulders slumped forward in a posture I'd never seen. Her face was partially obscured by her hands. Was she *crying*? Maud, is it possible for you to be crying? The thought was alarming. When she saw me she straightened herself up.

"Where are the children?"

"Gone."

"What do you mean? Where could they have possibly gone?"

"One of Barnum's scouts came, almost an hour ago. I came up by chance, fetching more yarn, or else we'd never have known what happened."

"Why didn't you find me?"

"He went into their room. I followed him and he was gathering up their things. They were just looking at him. The children, Ana. They didn't even react."

"Maybe they're still here. Didn't you try to stop him?" I lunged toward the door but stopped to hear what she said.

"He told me the Aztec Children weren't drawing enough of a crowd. Barnum had approved —"

"We'll go to Bethany Hospital. It's terrible there. We'll at least try to place them somewhere better."

Maud shook her head. "There was another man with the scout. He runs a theater somewhere in the Bowery. He had the papers; he's going to show them. It's all done. You know very well how it all works."

"But what should we do?" I looked around the meager room.

"We should forget them." Maud rose abruptly. "Even if we somehow got them back, what would we do? They can't live here if they're not performing."

She was right. Livid, I left her and went to my own room, where I stood at the window until the bright flame of my anger subsided. Barnum had accepted my petition. He had agreed, graciously even, to do his best to remedy the children's situation, and now he had flagrantly walked all over my intentions with his own. Yes, he was the ruler of those children's fate. Why would he take the interests of anyone else into account? The flame rekindled. But why couldn't he at least have been honest when we spoke and told me that he intended to pass the children off rather than care for them properly? He has made a fool out of me.

I strode the length of my room and back again. I stewed in my fury until I realized I had not given so much as a thought to Henry and Susan's actual welfare. At least it's coming into summer, I thought compulsively. At least they won't freeze to death at Bethany Hospital.

Fifty-two

"Yes. I heard something about that," said Mr. Archer, who was partially hidden by a massive pile of newspapers on his desk.

"You *knew* they would be taken away?"

I had come to Archer's office to inform the ad man that the Aztec Children had been sold for the second time. People on the fifth floor were talking about whether Mr. Archer had been involved in Mayor Harper's closure of the museum. Some even thought he'd been behind the Martinettis' arrest. If he was interested in seeing the museum falter, then I had something to bargain with.

"They weren't drawing, Miss Swift," Archer remarked as he resumed reading a newspaper.

"But they were bringing in hundreds every week! The advertisements were everywhere, in all your newspapers."

"They drew until last Thursday, when Vauxhall Gardens introduced their Amazon Pigmy Family. The Pigmies are a raving success, largely thanks to the advertisements *I* was commissioned to write." He smiled, raising a finger to his lips. "Shh."

"Do you know where the children have gone?"

"No." Archer turned the page in front of him. "One of the smaller theaters. Belmont's maybe."

"People would be outraged if they knew what was going on," I said.

"You think so?" For the first time, I had Archer's attention.

"There is a significant children's protection movement in this city, as I'm sure you know. The wives of many powerful men are involved. They would not *rest*" — I had him now — "until their voices were heard."

Now Archer was looking at me skeptically. "But why do you want to create controversy for the museum? You're paid well. What's in it for you?"

"I had a personal stake in the welfare of the Aztec Children. Do you require more information than that? Negative press makes no difference to me unless Barnum finds out that I played a part in it, if you get my meaning."

We faced each other. I saw Archer calculating factors about which I knew nothing.

"But what about you?" I ventured further. "We're all wondering why you are set on disparaging the museum."

"My livelihood is *there,* my dear." Archer gestured to his stacks of newspapers, visibly brightening. "Not in any one establishment. Not in the success or failure of any single man. No, my interest is a little more elusive. I have worked for nearly every newspaper in this town. I ride the tide of human error and triumph. Whim and popular taste. I am a kind of touchstone. My allegiance is to no one. The only item in my reliquary, to which I occasionally light a proverbial votive, is the holy steam printing machine. Other than that, I simply comment on what happens in this godforsaken city."

"But don't your comments contribute to shaping the future? What is printed is read. What is read is believed as truth. Belief spawns action, revolution, progress. Your business is augury, more than any clairvoyant working in these halls."

He smiled. "It's not only in tea leaves that one can read the language of cause and effect. But what you describe sounds more like politics than magic."

"Well, illegal commerce in children may not interest you personally, but there are many in this city whom it does."

Archer looked straight at me. "I will write the article, Miss

Swift, if you tell me one thing: Why do you really care about this? What is this personal stake?"

I had hoped he wouldn't press me, but I would not let him see me falter. "I presented Barnum with a petition signed by all the residents of the fifth floor, outlining our needs, including the care of the Aztec Children. He agreed to my terms, and then promptly sold the children. I am angry, naturally."

Mr. Archer nodded. "Naturally."

He pulled a leaf of paper from a drawer and uncapped his pen. "Tell me again the name of the hospital where the children were originally found?"

Later, as I returned to the fifth floor, a barrage of shouts met me at the threshold. A group of four Sioux, including the old man in the top hat and an equally elderly woman I did not recall ever having seen before, stood in a line outside the boundary of their camp, sending what I could only assume were obscenities or threats across the gallery. I did not see They Are Afraid of Her. The newcomers calmly went about their business, folding blankets, unpacking, and reclining with their backs against the wall. The only one among them who reacted at all was a little boy wearing an oversized cutaway coat. This boy faced the Sioux at the edge of his own camp in the attitude of a Bowery fighter, head lowered, fists raised. I wondered if this was a deliberate insult: Only the youngest among them would deign to respond. The strategy seemed to be working: The words I imagined as insults had grown to an alarming pitch and as I crossed the gallery I covered my ears. An object whizzed by amid shouts of surprise from the Sioux. A slender arrow embedded itself into the wall high above their camp. Everyone looked at the arrow. Across the room, the child had disappeared and the rest of the newcomers went slowly about their business. I shook my head. Who needed a group of bickering Indians as neighbors? All I wanted was to take off my cursed shoes, drink half a bottle of Cocadiel's Remedy, and sleep.

I lit the two sconces in my room. With the door closed, the noise from the Indian camps faded to a faint fluctuation. I undressed in flickering patterns of lamplight. Unbound, my body creaked and snapped like a dying oak. I sat on the edge of the bed and pulled off my stockings, hanging them over the arms of my chair for tomorrow. I rubbed my feet, kneading my fingers into the soles, gritting my teeth as bands of searing pain ribboned up my legs. I kneaded harder, suddenly determined to squeeze all of it out. Needles of heat alternated with cloudy numbness in the small of my back and my shoulders emitted their usual unfocused complaint, without beginning or end. By the time I loosened my hands, my head throbbed. I lowered myself down on the bed.

I lay mired in self-disgust. As I grew conscious of it, the feeling thickened to fill my whole room and even, I imagined, spilled out into the hallway. I was too tired to dismiss it. Images of Mr. Archer, the fighting Indians, Barnum's terrible grin, Matthew's stricken face, and the Aztec Children surfaced out of the murk and sank away. Mother, what would you tell me now? There you are in your nightdress, standing among the hens in the yard, wearing his boots. You face away from me and I know I'm young because I stand straight in the doorway and I look at your back without looking down. You take a few quick steps and catch a hen, tucking it under your arm and then swinging the creature out and extending the arm that holds it, wringing its neck in the first momentum of the arc. When you turn, your face holds a faint smile, you're thinking of something else. You are already pulling at a handful of feathers as you clomp toward the house; the image dissolves before you see me standing there.

I was angry about the Aztec Children only because Barnum had made a fool of my petition, of me. Predictably, I had steered by the compass of my own pride, and not out of any real compassion for the idiot children. The truth settled uncomfortably around me.

Fifty-three

They Are Afraid of Her appeared in the rooftop restaurant
the next morning near the end of our breakfast hour. The
museum was not yet open for the day; the dining area was
full of employees. It was the warmest morning of the year,
the sweetest smelling, and even those curmudgeons, like
Clarissa and the conjoined twins, who always insisted on
breakfast in their rooms, had come blinking out into the
sunshine. I sat with Maud and Thomas, admiring the way
the sun illuminated the orange juice in my glass. They Are
Afraid of Her appeared in the doorway and stood there without moving for close to a minute.

"Look who it is." Thomas put down his fork and made a
futile attempt to smooth down his hair. "The Indians *never*
come up here. She looks beautiful, doesn't she?"

"Look what she's wearing," whispered Maud. "That was
one of the Martinetti daughters' dresses, wasn't it?"

Thomas looked at his plate. I had only ever seen this
woman in the plain layers of beige muslin that all the Sioux
women wore, with the same, barely tailored blue overdress.
Now, as she stepped uncomfortably into public view, she
wore a skirt of raspberry taffeta buoyed up by a layer of tulle
just visible at her ankles. She had buttoned herself into a
dove-gray velvet jacket, hiding the top of the gown. She
must have been terribly hot.

"Maybe the dress doesn't fit her," Maud commented.

They Are Afraid of Her looked straight ahead as she stalked between the tables to the edge of the roof.

"She probably pillaged what the Martinettis left behind." Maud sniffed. "What is she doing up here?"

"From what I understand, she would prefer us to the company of her brethren," I said.

"That's awful," Maud muttered.

They Are Afraid of Her looked out over the city. When she finally turned back toward the restaurant, Thomas jerked to his feet as if he were attached to a string. In his crooked gait he fetched her.

Her new costume accentuated the fine scars slicing across both cheeks and made her shorn hair all the more striking. With scarlet cheeks she sat among us and carefully folded a napkin onto her lap. Thomas poured a glass of juice for her from our pitcher and stared at her until Maud prodded his knee.

"My goodness, dear," Maud began. "It seems as though you've ventured far from the nest."

"Maybe she couldn't stand the fighting last night," I commented. "Lord knows it kept me up."

They Are Afraid of Her looked between our two faces, smiling vaguely. "Hello," she said.

Thomas whistled and sent his finger in a long arc from right to left, impersonating an arrow flying across the gallery.

"What is happening out there?" he asked her. He shot the arrow again, this time impacting it against the flat of his other palm.

She stared at his raised hands. When she lifted her glass to her lips, she clenched the stem of the goblet so tightly I expected it to snap. She shook her head and hissed a few words in her language.

Thomas nodded sympathetically.

The Indian regarded him and then glanced over her shoulder toward the stairwell.

"Our enemy" — she paused, looking into her glass — "is

come." Her voice was much calmer speaking these words than in her own tongue. We all stared.

"You must be a better teacher than you thought," Maud observed. "She's speaking English much better."

"Someone in her own group is teaching her," I said. "It appears that she's the only one among them who isn't fluent already."

They Are Afraid of Her shook her head and pointed toward the floor. "Our enemy."

"Are you married?" Thomas asked.

Maud covered her face with her napkin. "Thomas!"

They Are Afraid of Her pointed at the stairwell and spoke words that sounded like they came from the middle throat, damp and hollow. Her brow furrowed and she made a fist of her right hand, shaking it furiously. She looked at Thomas the whole time.

"It won't end," she finished in English. "They are devils. Always. *This* is my home now."

Of course we were at a loss and our silence was awkward.

"I wonder if Mr. Barnum knows about this," Thomas said.

"I doubt that. If he did, he'd probably put the two tribes on a stage together and see what happens," Maud said bitterly.

"He wouldn't go that far," I said.

"Wouldn't he?" Maud was tiring of the conversation, I could tell. Soon Thomas and They Are Afraid of Her rose from the table, with Thomas saying something about finding someone to translate for them, so they could continue talking.

"Good luck," I said as they walked away. "I think I'll sidestep that conversation."

"No good will come of that," Maud commented when they were out of earshot.

"What, Thomas' obsession?"

"No. The girl leaving her tribe."

"This museum strikes me as one of the best places to leave your tribe. She could just take up with the Circassians, or learn an art that would keep her employed." Compared with what the Sioux elder had told me about the woman's history, a life in the museum would be easy.

"But she is fundamentally defiant. Couldn't you see that in her? She will fight what contains her, whether it's a tribe, a museum, whatever. I've seen women like that before. She brings trouble."

"You sound like an oracle, Maud. Do you have secret talents hidden away?"

"I just might. Shall we have a walk before retiring to our cages for the day?"

"That sounds lovely." We strolled along the promenade, pausing occasionally to peer over the edge of the building to see the swarm of humans below.

Fifty-four

In my booth I swayed like a sleeping elephant, half in a trance, vaguely noting the undulating current of spectators as they passed by me, my mind somewhere between Pictou and the sea, when Barnum materialized directly in front of me. It was a magician's trick, as if he'd stepped out of someone's shadow or unfolded himself from behind a child.

"Who is this *Advocatus Diaboli*?" Barnum demanded.

Was it a figment? I blinked down at him.

"I don't know."

Was it a riddle? Incredibly, none of the passing horde seemed to recognize Barnum. As he stood in front of me, two men even bumped his elbow in their jostle to view me.

"Who is it, Miss Swift?" His voice shifted to a strangely loving tone. From the crook of his arm he unfolded a newspaper and handed it to me. The headline: *Idiot Children Purchased Illegally from Five Points Orphanage for Barnum's Collection by Miss Elizabeth Crawford (Heiress to the Crawford's Boot Black Fortune) Only to Be Sold Again by Barnum*. The byline: *Your Advocatus Diaboli*.

"There is only one person in this establishment who 'cares' enough about the so-called Aztec Children to have an article written about them and we both know who it is. I will be honest: The particulars of your grievances do not interest me. I *must* discover the author of this diatribe! Who signed his name so blasphemously? I do not wish to stop him, necessarily. But I absolutely must know who he is."

"I'm sure you have your methods," I replied. I handed him back the newspaper.

"I do. But I would rather find out right now." Barnum scrutinized my face.

"You say you do not care about my grievances. And yet it is we human performers, your own so-called Representatives of the Wonderful, who are responsible for much of your revenue. Have you forgotten that it is us, the living tableaux, who most attracts the public? Isn't it to your advantage to give fair attention to our requests, as we are the vessels of your fortune? I am formally requesting that you give serious attention to the injustices among your employees, beginning with the release of the Martinetti family. If you agree to liberate them I will forget about the Aztec Children."

Barnum stared at me. "You are promoted. To forty dollars per week and the title of Manager. Of the fifth-floor residents. Including the Congress, which will arrive in due time."

"Mr. Olrick made fifty a week and performed far less than I," I countered. I hoped my voice did not waver or otherwise betray the shock I felt at his offer.

"Mr. Olrick had an astute manager." Barnum smiled slightly. "Fine. Fifty it is. Keep a registry. For all human performers and Representatives of the Wonderful. Collect names, rates, arrivals, and departures. Inform them they are to register complaints with you and you will deliver them to me. Agreed?"

"Only if those of us who have been in your employ since the beginning are guaranteed ten Saturdays off from work per year. And you must negotiate the Martinettis' release immediately."

We faced off, the flimsy boards of my booth seeming to melt away as the showman gazed at me. He extended his hand. "Agreed."

I pantomimed pulling an arrow into a bow. "Your *Advocatus Diaboli* has an office in this very building, Mr. Barnum." I let fly the arrow. "I'm surprised you did not suspect him."

Fifty-five

"That word is a curse. Why would we choose it for our name? We'd be better off inventing something new. Something people haven't heard before, so they won't make assumptions. We don't want them to think of that dog-faced boy they saw at the Bowery Theater in '38." Clarissa flushed with the exertion of her speech. Squeezed in beside her on the sofa, Oswald La Rue and Maud nodded in agreement. "How about something like Barnum's League of Anomalies?"

"His name shouldn't be part of it. We don't want to give him the added publicity," said Maud. "The New York League of Anomalies?"

Oswald La Rue shook his skeletal head. "Anomaly is too . . . medical. We should have something more grandiose. Prodigies."

I was stung. We'd gathered in Maud's parlor to celebrate the return of the Martinettis, who had arrived on the fifth floor the evening after I spoke with Barnum. They were fewer in number; several of the younger family members, including the lady contortionist and her two children, hadn't come back to the museum after their release. We didn't know why, and Mrs. Martinetti the elder would not speak of it, or say anything at all about their ordeal at the Tombs. After a celebratory feast prepared by Gustav, she sat in a corner of Maud's parlor over a great swathe of shimmering blue fabric. She was sewing new costumes for the family. They had taken a different name, as well: O'Malley. Apparently Barnum's negotiations had been with Irishmen.

The gathering was festive enough, with wine and cakes and music, but all too soon the conversation among my colleagues had barreled headlong into the impossible question of a name for our emerging guild.

"Guild of Unusual Diplomats!" Clarissa blurted.

"Why not call ourselves by our true name?" Jacob growled from the settee. "Citizen Horrors."

The room quieted. By now everyone was aware of the severity of the twins' condition. Matthew had succumbed to complete silence. Jacob had reacted by trying to provoke him, first verbally and then with his fists. One evening, Oswald La Rue had tried to stop Jacob from becoming drunk, but Jacob struck him a blow and then locked himself, and of course Matthew, into their room. An hour later, Tai Shan broke down the door because of the screaming. One of them had tried to cut the ligament that connected them. We didn't know which one inflicted the wound, and no one asked. They emerged from the room blood-spattered and wild-eyed and Oswald La Rue escorted them to the hospital to be stitched. They returned bandaged and sullen. Tai Shan and Oswald La Rue tried to talk with them the following morning, but nothing came of it.

If we had been traveling in an itinerant show, each of us would have moved our wagon away from theirs. Some professional problems could be addressed by the group, but this clash of wills was too deep for an outsider to approach. I continued to feel bad for Matthew, and on numerous occasions I paused outside their door, imagining a conversation in which I offered some aid or insight, even comfort, but any urge to intervene was tempered by a fact our kind knew all too well: If they needed to die, they would do it. Who was I to meddle?

"It seems to me the question of our name can wait," I remarked. "The Martinettis have returned to us, safe and sound."

"What about this Congress of Nations?" Oswald La Rue leaned forward, planting his bony elbows on the knobs of his knees. "I've been hearing strange things —"

"We should know what they're to be paid," Clarissa interrupted her partner. "Don't you think we have a right to know what he's paying them? I think we have a right to know, to make sure it's comparable to our rates."

"I've heard something about that." Tai Shan spoke softly. Everybody's head turned. "My uncle operates the concessions booth in Gallery Four. He heard from someone that these tribesmen are coming here because they think Barnum's Grand Ethnological Congress of Nations is an actual diplomatic meeting organized by the president."

The trio on the couch laughed. From his corner, Jacob snorted.

"I don't know if it's true, but if it is, there's a chance Barnum isn't paying them at all. Just their passage."

"Ludicrous," Maud breathed. The laughter diffused and all three of them appeared rather startled at the idea.

My head was beginning to ache. "What are we supposed to do about *that*?" I asked the room. No one responded.

"Perhaps we should start with a smaller problem," Maud ventured. "Something we might actually be able to solve. Something manageable that would improve our immediate situation."

"For example?" How irritating it was, that we could not even come up with a legitimate concern.

Oswald La Rue straightened up in his seat. "Well, those Indians are causing an awful ruckus out there. Kept me up the last two nights. They've shot more arrows than I can count. Between that and those two" — Oswald scowled at the twins — "it's a miracle anyone gets any sleep at all around here."

"I can hardly imagine that fighting going on for much longer without someone getting hurt," Maud chimed in. "What are they fighting over?"

"I don't know," I said. I looked around the room and

spotted Thomas cowering behind Clarissa. He shared a narrow chair with They Are Afraid of Her, who had somehow made herself very small. I hadn't even noticed that she was there.

"Would you enlighten us, Mr. Willoughby?" Maud piped up. "Did you succeed in your mission to discover their — or should I say *her* — secrets?"

Thomas' face turned scarlet. "I don't think I'm the best person to explain what's happening with them," he offered hesitantly. "I hardly know." He looked at They Are Afraid of Her. "You'd be better off asking the Sioux."

"We've tried to ask all of them! They won't tell us a thing," Maud snapped. "No offense to present company."

"I know the Sioux have been traveling among New York, Chicago, and Philadelphia for two years. That's as long as she's been with them. This new group is some kind of enemy."

"We've gathered *that* much," Oswald La Rue huffed.

"They are called Absarokee," Thomas continued. "She said they have been fighting them for a hundred years."

"Absarokee," They Are Afraid of Her repeated. She looked around the room. "I hate."

"Maybe you can tell us more, Thomas? About the Absarokee?" Oswald's voice was gentle. "They don't have costumes with them, as far as anyone can see. No one knows who brought them here — they don't appear to have a manager or a spokesperson."

The Indian woman stood up. She held her arms with unnaturally stiffness at her sides, with both fists clenched.

"Absarokee fight since they walked, since they could move on two feet. They fight in the other land, and they fight here. Anywhere. Time finds them, puts them together with us." She put her palms together as an illustration. Her face reddened. Her hands trembled. "They hate us. I hate." She paused. "They come here to get something back."

"She's mentioned this before," Thomas interjected. "She says they are here not to perform, but to get something back that was taken from them."

"Something that the Sioux have?" Oswald asked.

"The museum have," They Are Afraid of Her answered.

We considered this.

"She wants to leave the Sioux," Thomas said. "I've let her move most of her belongings into my apartment."

"Not very Christian of you," Maud chided.

I cleared my throat. "So what we've learned so far is that the fighting between these Indians isn't going to end until one or the other of them leaves. Unless we decide to throw one group out ourselves, we're back where we started."

"How about the Guild of Living Wonders?" Oswald offered suddenly.

"That's too close to the name Barnum gave us," Matthew countered. "What about the Guild of Human Curiosities?"

"Lacks imagination," Maud judged.

"Marvelous Monsters!" That came from one of the albino children, and it was then that my patience ran out. I left as unobtrusively as a giantess can.

Fifty-six

Below us a new transparency snapped against the building. Unlike most of the illustrated sails Barnum hoisted from the side of his building, this one was ocean blue. On it floated a familiar white shape.

"Can you see the date?"

"It's moving too much. They haven't secured one of the corners yet." Tai Shan leaned over the railing of the aerial garden.

"Ah! June fifteenth. I think. Or fifth."

"The fifth! That would be the day after tomorrow!"

"Fifteenth. Yes, I can see it now." Tai Shan righted himself, adjusting his sleeves and collar. "It's about time they finished the beluga exhibit."

"I suppose," I said. "But imagine what will happen when the fifth floor's open to the public."

"They won't be able to get into our half of the gallery."

"But they will be right outside our doors! They will drown us with their noise and their obnoxious chatter!" I was half joking, but the prospect was truly alarming. "We hear them. We feel them. We see them as soon as we open our doors. There is something necessary about walking across the empty gallery before we descend to the crowds each day. Do you agree?"

"I don't know that it matters to me," Tai Shan said.

"You don't notice the hundreds of people passing before your eyes each day, gawking at you incessantly."

"I notice lots of things about them."

"Well isn't that convenient for you. I only notice how horrid they are; and then I notice my own reactions to them."

"This *is* a museum, Miss Swift. And as far as I know, you are here of your own accord. "

"True." Whining to Tai Shan was embarrassing. "Here's a question I've been wondering about: Is a whale really a spectacle? Do you think it will draw?"

Tai Shan shrugged. "Why wouldn't it? Hasn't it been a draw for us all these months?"

"I suppose you're right."

Some children moved along the promenade in a straggling mass, following a figure I recognized as the taxidermist. Beside him, attached by a lead, toddled a large monkey with long red hair. The children screamed and ran behind them.

Thomas sidled up to the table. He had returned to his usual haggard self.

"How quickly love fades," I teased.

"I must speak with you," he whispered.

"Go ahead, Thomas," I told him. Tai Shan resumed eating his lunch, kindly showing no interest in Thomas' intrusion.

"Not here. Would you come with me, Ana? I'm sorry, but I'm afraid it's urgent and I don't know what else to do."

"All right. Forgive us, Tai Shan," I rose and followed Thomas as he scurried across the rooftop garden. Tai Shan waved us away and pulled a book from one of the many hidden pockets of his tunic.

Thomas would say nothing until we had returned to the fifth floor. He passed the Sioux Indians without speaking, without even looking in their direction. The Absarokee, if they were in their shaded camp, were silent. He led me to his room.

Thomas had inherited the largest apartment of all, and the only objects inside it were a heavy wooden bed, one footlocker that had a corner of flannel hanging out, a broad expanse of bare floor, and an array of strange musical instruments strewn around the room. I guessed that most of them were borrowed from the museum's collection.

He led me to a small pile of things in the far corner: one striped wool blanket, a basket, and a folded dress.

"Something's happened," Thomas repeated, still whispering. "Something is definitely going on. I can't figure out exactly what it is, but she's involved. She would be so angry if she knew I was telling you." Fearfully, he peered down at her folded clothes as if they were, or could become, animate.

"Maybe you shouldn't tell me what you're trying to tell me," I reasoned. "It's better not to meddle in certain kinds of conflicts."

"She's in danger. That's what I'm trying to tell you. Or she's dangerous." Thomas lifted the sleeve of They Are Afraid of Her's dress. "I don't know what to do! I woke up in the middle of the night last night. I opened my eyes just in time to see her slip out the door. She was barefoot. I followed her."

It sounded like the beginning of a fairy tale.

"When she reached the door to the stairwell, she turned back. She could have seen me, I don't know. I ducked behind the beluga's tank. I waited until I heard the door close behind her. I followed her down to the second floor."

"What could she want on the second floor?" I wondered out loud. Besides Pa-Ib, the Egyptian mummy, and my own gilded cage, I could think of nothing that might interest her.

"She moved so quickly among the cabinets. I am convinced she didn't know I was there. If she had wanted me to follow, she would have slowed down a little bit, just to be sure I could keep up with her.

"Eventually, she stopped in front of a large case. I'd never noticed it before, it's just one among a hundred identical cabinets. She used the hem of her dress to wrap her hand. So quickly, Ana! She wrapped her hand and then sent her fist through the glass. It splintered like an iceberg and then crashed with a terrible sound. I sprinted back to the stairwell. I was certain the commotion would call the night guards in from the street below. I climbed the stairs and ran back to my room. I hopped in my bed, calming myself as best as I could.

She returned a few minutes later. I watched her put some object among her things and change into a fresh nightgown. Blood had stained the first one, you see. From her hand.

"My breath had not yet returned to normal by the time she joined me in the bed. Maybe she knew I followed her. But maybe not. What do you think?"

Thomas stared somewhere in the vicinity of my neck.

"If she had wanted you to follow, why would she set up such an elaborately subtle ruse? You can speculate all you want, Thomas. But it will be an endless convolution, and a fruitless one." I pointed at the pile of her things. "Well?"

"Yes." Thomas knelt and put a hand inside the basket, keeping his face turned away as if something might bite him from inside. He pulled out an object and cupped it in both hands.

"It's made out of an . . . organ."

And it was. Inflated and dried, the membranous gourd had an unmistakable shape.

"It's a heart."

Inside the translucent pouch, something rattled. It was decorated with strips of buckskin and black glass beads.

"What is it?"

Thomas turned the thing over in his hands. "I don't know." His voice trembled.

"Look, Thomas, this clearly doesn't have a thing to do with you. Whatever this thing is, and whatever the reason is for her to steal it, it's beyond your control."

"But I love her." He was like a little boy and for a moment I felt weirdly maternal. I forced myself not to reach out and touch his cheek.

"I love her. So it does have something to do with me. That's how I see it, Ana. For better or worse. God's will must take me into account." He scrutinized the heart in his hands.

Fifty-seven

The next afternoon, on my way to my booth, I found They Are Afraid of Her's broken cabinet. One of the custodians had nailed boards over the hole and swept up the shards, but the artifacts still lay on exhibit. There were a pair of beaded buckskin slippers, some spears and arrows, an object that seemed to be a rattle, and a sheath decorated with geometric designs. Next to where the heart had been, a small label: PAGAN IDOL. Very informative.

Thomas did not appear on the balcony at all that afternoon, but his musicians stumbled along without him. The ophecleide player was very drunk and the fiddler, though sober, barely kept a tune. The music that resulted from their ineptitude served to elongate the hours, and I, trapped within earshot, did my best to become a statue.

When I returned home for supper, I saw that someone new had arrived and set up camp near the Absarokee. A stained canvas tarpaulin obscured the contents of a large cage. Beside it a lone figure lay wrapped in blankets. Some distance away Gideon, the ticket-man's nephew, sat on a wooden stool. Oswald La Rue, the Living Skeleton, was talking with the boy; when he saw me coming, he loped across the beluga gallery in his silent, wraith's gait.

"He's asleep. Can't even get a good look at his face. Snoring like a forest of falling timber."

"Who is it?"

"That's what I was trying to find out."

"What's the boy doing there?"

"Apparently Barnum sent him to stand watch. Told him to fetch him when the stranger wakes up. I don't like standing over that side of the gallery," Oswald continued. "Those Indians could freeze hell over with their evil eye."

"Have you seen Thomas?"

"Been in his room all day. One of those Sioux finally got shot by an arrow, did you hear? Savages." Oswald shook his head.

We stopped at the Sioux camp.

"Who got hurt?" I asked, searching their faces for They Are Afraid of Her. She was not there.

"Joseph," the old man said. It was one of the younger men. We knew "Joseph" was not his real name. Several of them used that name when speaking to white people, just as they called their women "Mary."

"Joseph" sat on the floor, his back against the wall and his upper arm bandaged and bleeding. We asked if they needed any medical supplies or help of any kind. They didn't. Oswald went whistling off toward Clarissa's room and I knocked on Thomas' door. When he finally answered, he looked worse than Joseph: pale, unable to look me in the eye. He did not invite me in.

"She won't speak to me," he whispered. "They've shot her cousin. They think he stole the . . . that thing."

Behind him They Are Afraid of Her sat on the floor facing the window.

"What are you going to do? Have you considered telling Barnum, or the police?"

"No. What would they do?"

"Well, that thing is Barnum's property, and it was stolen."

"Then she'd be punished."

"But it might scare off the Absarokee."

"No, no." Thomas dismissed my suggestion with a cringe.

"Thomas, you can't just hide up here. The band —"

"I won't leave her like this. She needs me here."

"Does she? She doesn't exactly look like she's crying on your shoulder."

"She needs me, Ana." Thomas lowered his voice. "I'm going to speak to them."

"Who?"

"The Absarokee."

"But they just shot someone."

"It's the only thing I can do. Her people won't listen to me."

"Do the Absarokee speak English?"

"I'll find out."

"I don't think that's a good idea —"

"Good night."

He closed the door softly.

Tai Shan was not in his room, and neither was Maud. I wanted their opinion on what to do about Thomas, but in the end I returned to my room alone.

In order to manage the members of Barnum's upcoming Congress, I must keep a registry. I had obtained a ledger, wherein each performer (or should I call them participants?) would give his name and a description of himself, including rate of pay. I could start with the newcomer, the one who slept by the side of that cage.

Later, as I lay in bed, the murmuring of the protesters outside the museum lulled me comfortably as if their cries were waves lapping the sides of some great ark. They stayed late each evening, sometimes sounding more like a celebration, singing hymns and shouting prayers, than the band of righteous hypocrites that they were. Didn't they have some better cause to promote? Didn't they know it was exactly Barnum's strategy to keep the museum in the papers?

I woke later than usual. I was afraid I'd missed breakfast so I hurried across the gallery. I was into the stairwell before I realized that something was different: The Absarokee camp had disappeared. I walked back. Their corner was empty. Only the newcomer remained, wrapped in blankets beside his draped cage, with Gideon curled up on the floor next to his stool, also asleep. The Sioux sat in a circle eating food and talking. I turned back toward the apartments.

This time Thomas didn't answer my knock so I opened the

door myself. They were both on the bed. The blankets had been thrown off and the sheets were in such disarray it looked as if they'd been fighting. Thomas squatted on the mattress wearing a ridiculous nightshirt with puffed sleeves. He hovered over They Are Afraid of Her, who was obscured from my view until Thomas shifted his position to regard me. He clutched one of her arms.

"How did they do it? How did they do it?" His was the compulsive voice of a parrot. "I told them nothing!"

I came to the bedside. The woman was dead. Thomas scrutinized her arm again. He pushed up the sleeve of her nightgown and examined three rows of parallel scars near her shoulder. He looked dumbly at the skin. He rolled her body slightly to one side to look at her leg. She had the same scars above her knee. Three rows, like dashes across the plain of her flesh.

"Thomas! Stop that."

"How did they do it? There is no wound, Ana."

"Thomas. Stop. Come here." I reached for his arm but he slapped me away. They Are Afraid of Her's eyes were still open, her ashen lips ajar.

"I talked to them last night because I thought it would help but they would not speak to me. They just stared, Ana. It didn't help . . ."

I did not try very hard to pry him away from the body, but I cradled his shoulders with one arm. He leaned into me, still clenching They Are Afraid of Her's arm. "We can't know what is between those two tribes, Thomas."

"They came in here. I locked the door and held her, but that didn't matter. I fell asleep and they got in. How? Why did they kill her? How did they do it without hurting her?" His voice had reached a level of hysteria. Someone walked by outside and Thomas leapt up, standing on the bed, almost to my height.

"They're gone, Thomas."

"*She's* gone."

Across the room, the pile where she'd hidden the heart looked exactly as it had when Thomas showed it to me.

"It's gone," he whispered.

"That's what they came for."

"Yes."

I straightened the sheet around They Are Afraid of Her and closed her eyes, grimacing at the cold putty of her skin.

Tears now streamed down Thomas' face.

"Will you come now? It's time to tell her people," I coaxed.

"Those aren't her *people*," Thomas hissed, wiping his face with a corner of bedspread. "I have nothing to say to them."

I lifted him from the bed and placed him gently on the floor in a gesture that felt natural in the moment but would have been bizarre in another circumstance.

"Then you stay here and pick out a dress for her to wear." I pointed him toward her pile of things. "When you are finished, come downstairs and find me. All right?"

Thomas wept and nodded. I left the room.

"She's dead." I spoke directly to the grandfather, who was eating his breakfast from a wooden bowl.

"We are aware," he replied. One of the men beside him burped.

"*You are aware?* Did the Absarokee give you a report on the murder before they left? Aren't you going to do something?"

"Why? You yourself said she is dead. There is nothing to do."

"Where did they go?" I jerked my head toward the empty gallery behind me.

The grandfather shrugged and lifted the bowl to his lips.

"Why did they kill her?"

The old man drank his gruel then wiped his mouth with his sleeve. He regarded me. "I don't think you have time for that story. I don't think you can understand it."

"You are a terrible old man," I managed to say. "I know they killed her because of that . . . thing. That heart."

"Like I said, it's not your story." The man turned from me and retreated into the tent.

I had been standing in my booth only a few minutes when

Thomas started playing on the balcony. At first, the sound resembled music, but the chords stumbled. Not out of clumsiness, I was certain of that. Thomas was too good for that, even in his current state. A recognizable melody hovered at the edges, but it was as if randomness, instead of measurement, structured the sound. A lilting phrase was knocked away by a pounding cacophony from the lower register. Bars of a familiar waltz tipped into an unrecognizable storm of half notes. It was precarious music, unsettling and hypnotic. I left my booth and stood in the balcony doorway.

These sounds sputtered out of him and he played in his shirtsleeves. The two other musicians stood in the opposite corner of the balcony, banished and looking as if a wind had swept them there. I leaned against the door frame to listen. Thomas watched the sky, as if he were totally removed from the movement of his arms.

The protestors circled below us with their useless signs, keeping up their vigil against the museum like a wake of vultures beside a mountain of carrion. Beebe and Miss Crawford were not among them today, but I had seen them often, flushed and triumphant, walking around and around, caught in the eddy of their own righteousness.

"You won't get rid of us with that racket," one of the sign-carriers shouted from the street. "We are not so easily dissuaded of our convictions!"

Thomas' song soared. Two disparate melodies converged. I walked to the railing and leaned over the edge. Several people below stopped walking and turned their faces upward.

"You should be ashamed," I called down. "Why don't you go home?"

"Barnum's Congress is an abomination! It must be stopped!"

Thomas finished the song and pushed himself away from the piano with a look of disgust. Whether the expression was directed at the protestors, his instrument, or the failure of love to prevent the death of They Are Afraid of Her was a mystery. He stood at the railing for a moment, clutching it with both hands as if we rode the swell of an oceanic storm.

He brushed past me, walking swiftly into the gallery, hands stuffed deep in his pockets. I called to him, but he didn't heed my voice. He disappeared, and I had no doubt that this image of his slumped and receding form would be my last glimpse of him.

Fifty-eight

Gideon, the ticket-taker's nephew, swept past as I ascended the stairs and I listened to his steps recede below. Each of my steps jolted my spine with an ungodly spasm and I envied and loathed the boy's speed and lightness. Who would tend to me when I could no longer move, when my limbs petrified into brittle boneposts? Who would massage my legs and tell me of the world once I was confined to bed? Would my decline be a swift avalanche into the abyss or a bumpy, horrified ride down a long and gentle slope?

In the beluga's gallery the stranger had awakened. He crouched with his back to me, rolling up his blanket. Gideon's tipped stool was still rocking nearby on the floor.

I hurried to my room for the registry; this newcomer would be the first official member of the Congress and as manager of Barnum's human menagerie I would duly catalog his details.

As I made my way back to the stranger, Barnum himself appeared in the opposite corner of the gallery and strode toward me; we converged upon the man.

As far as I knew, Barnum had never been sighted on the fifth floor, not even, Maud had told me conspiratorially, when his wife and daughters had resided here. Barnum grinned broadly as he approached. I thought he might break into a run.

"We were beginning to think you'd been struck by the

exotic sleeping sickness we've been reading about in the papers!"

"Phineas."

In one graceful motion the stranger rose and swiveled to reveal a sharply planed face half obscured by a dense gray beard. The overhanging contour of a misshapen fur hat shadowed his brow, but not enough to hide the man's strangely light blue eyes. "You know very well no such sickness has infected America."

The stranger pushed back his hat, which I now saw was made from the skin of a deer's head. The animal's face had been crudely molded above its wearer's, but its visage was half melted and grotesque. The man wore buckskin trousers and shirt. His hair was long and matted, and his voice bore just a trace of a New Englander's inflection.

Barnum embraced the man, slapping his shoulders and laughing. "Adams! At long last we meet again!"

"Indeed," said the man, chuckling.

"Miss Swift, may I present Mr. James Adams, whom I like to call James the Baptist for all his wandering. He's come to us straight from the wilds of the Sierra Nevada."

"No locusts where I've come from, but wild honey aplenty," murmured the stranger.

"Miss Swift is one of our biggest attractions," Barnum gestured to me ambiguously.

"I should think so," replied Adams.

"She is also one of my personal assistants. Miss Swift, I'm sure you've heard of Grizzly Adams," Barnum went on. "Tamer of a hundred bears, not to mention countless mountain lions, panthers, and eagles of the air."

"I have not," I replied. "But I'm glad to make your acquaintance."

"Indeed." Mr. Adams tied his bedroll with a length of frayed twine and pulled a soiled handkerchief from the pocket of his shirt.

"What do you think of my enterprise, Adams?" Barnum addressed the museum with an upturned hand. "A verifiable Pandora's box, wouldn't you say?"

"Lucrative, I'm sure." Adams squinted, looking around the gallery. "Perfect for the city right now. John Scudder's old place. A good location." Adams continued bundling his belongings.

"That's it?" Barnum laughed loudly. "That's all you have to say about my great ark?"

Adams laughed along with the showman, and their laughter went on a bit long. I could not see what was funny. When Barnum finally stopped laughing he looked a bit disconcerted.

"There's no doubt you've outdone yourself, Phineas. It's your most beautiful dream. I just wouldn't bother bringing it west, is all I'm getting at." Adams chuckled again to himself. "You'll need more than a tiny whale to impress the folks out there."

Barnum snorted. "The good people of the Territories have as much reason to gawk at a bearded lady and Tom Trouble's arm as the Vanderbilts!"

"I'm afraid you're mistaken, sir. But you shouldn't worry. You've got a bottomless treasure chest right here in New York. No need to expand it westward."

"Because of the missionizing? Is everyone already converted?" Barnum's voice had grown somewhat cool. "I cannot *bear* the thought."

Adams laughed and shook his head. "There *is* quite a currency of souls, but I'm referring to something else altogether. These are people who walk out of their cabins at night and see great curtains of green light moving across the sky. They see hundreds of whales sporting off the shores of their coast, singing in otherworldly tones. They see Indian canoes lashed high in the treetops and child-priests who lead whole clans of men, speaking the language of dreams and prophesying on the tidelands. No museum contains these things, Phineas. These wonders are out walking the earth, to be encountered unexpectedly. If they were in museums, no one would ever see them because no one has the time and no one has the money to spend on such a place. Your business feeds on leisure. Believe me, Phineas, I mean no offense by telling you. I am a peddler of entertainments myself, as you well know. And what I've learned is that the Territories are not the America you and I know. And if you don't believe me, just take a peek under that tarpaulin. For you, it's only a dime. Not you, Miss. You'll have to wait like the rest of them."

Barnum smiled awkwardly as he placed a coin in Adams' palm. "Still up to your old tricks." He took a few steps toward the tarpaulin. "I thought you left your beasts at the stables in Brooklyn. Didn't they have room for this one?"

"Most all of them are there, but this one stays with me."

Barnum daintily lifted the cloth and leaned under it for a look. Then he jumped back with force, tripping over himself and then Gideon's abandoned stool. Adams did not move to save him from falling.

"See? You're going to have to come up with something else, Phineas, if you want to exploit the Territories."

Barnum sprang to his feet. He stared at the tarpaulin with a dazed look. From within I heard claws scrabbling.

Grizzly Adams lifted the corner of his hat. He scratched above his ear and peeled the deerskin upward. It caught, as if it were stuck to the man's own skin, as if it were his own. He cringed as he tugged harder. Barnum and I watched him. Adams looked steadily at Barnum as he lifted his hat, which finally pulled loose to reveal a glistening wound on the side of his head. His skull was more than cracked; a small piece was missing, and the coagulated rim of the crater outlined a portal onto the great organ itself. He gave us just a glimpse of waxy gray slickness before he readjusted the hat, closing the curtain.

"Old Fremont's still giving me trouble," he said wistfully. "He gave me a good one up top, didn't he? I miss him, though. Left him in Saint Louis this time. That's about as far east as he'll tolerate."

"I'll send for a doctor, James," Barnum said grimly.

"No need, Phineas. I won't let him touch me."

"We'll get you set up with a more comfortable bed."

"I'm most comfortable sleeping on the ground."

Barnum shook his head. "You never change, do you? I'm

sending for the doctor, James. I'll call for you later. I'd like to take you out for supper after the museum closes."

Barnum walked briskly away. Adams brought Gideon's stool over to the tarpaulin. He set himself on it and picked up the rifle that had been leaning against the cage. He cradled the weapon in his lap and nodded to me.

"In case it gets out," he explained. "It was a pleasure to meet you, miss," he said.

I held out the registry. "We're recording the members of Barnum's Congress."

"What Congress?"

"The Grand Ethnological Congress of Nations? Didn't you see the transparencies outside? Isn't that why you're here?"

"Oh, I suppose it is," he said and chuckled. "Phineas didn't describe it to me that way, but if he had I wouldn't have come." He took the registry from me and set it on his knee. "Now that I'm here I might as well make a show of what I've got. Though it will cost Barnum a pretty penny." His looping signature was as graceful and precise as that of a governess.

Once they left the savanna, the keeper and the tribesman walked in a cracked-earth desert of red dust. The tribesman found water by digging up mulga roots and breaking them open with his knife and a rock. They killed strangely scaled lizards that barely moved when the men approached. They walked at night, the keeper now mumbling to himself continuously and the tribesman trying not to hear. The sea is the most beautiful thing, Brother. It is not! the tribesman finally shouted, the home place is the most beautiful! But the keeper just shook his head, his hair now matted with red dust, both of them looking like mimi spirits, but without a spirit's grace. We must go back, the tribesman said. We must reach the sea, his brother answered. That is where the new knowledge is. Nights, the keeper stared into the fire, rubbing his legs and singing the song but not listening to it. The tribesman realized his brother's obsession was the symptom of a sickness within him. Keepers were given training in self-diagnosis; their role in the group was so important that they must have methods and protocol for when they, themselves, became ill. But this keeper could not see it. Was it old-man sickness, the collapse of all memory? The tribesman watched the keeper closely. They were close to the sea; the tribesman smelled salt on the wind that blew directly from the north, so he kept following the keeper across the desert. He wondered if the keeper would return to his senses. Perhaps the foreign lands they now journeyed through confused his mind; perhaps these lands had their own songs that infiltrated those of the people. Perhaps when they returned to the home country the keeper would return to the man he had been. But for now, the keeper walked like a child, poring over each stone he found on their path, jumping and pointing at each buzzard that followed them. The sea, he said. Always the sea.

The tribesman leaves his room only to feed the whale. All the rest of his waking and dreaming life he is in the song, asking it to help him, to show him what to do now. He is frightened; he has none of the training that the keeper had, none of the initiations, none of the dreams. But he sings anyway, sensing it is wrong but unable to stop returning home, where the rains have ceased and the jacana now walks across the lily pads with three speckled eggs under his wings.

The lotus flowers have unfurled into globes of layered petals, the same color as sunrise. All the trees are fruiting and the people are happy. A wind is just starting to push the morning mists up and away, and the men gather to discuss which areas will dry out the fastest. The women hunt frill-necked lizards among the rocks and bathe in the pools beneath waterfalls. Geese, gorged on the abundance of flood time, are easy to kill. On high ground the bowerbird carefully builds its dome out of dry grasses. When it is built, the bird flies away. It returns with a coiled white snail shell and places it at the entrance of the bower. It brings back another. And another. And two white bones. Several white feathers, and small white pebbles. With the help of these trinkets, the bowerbird will have a mate by the time the wetlands recede at the end of this season, Banggereng, the time for fruit and blossoms.

Metamorphosis

Fifty-nine

Guillaudeu hid in his office for as long as he could, which did not turn out to be long at all since dozens of creatures relied on him for food. At least that's what he told himself, and it was true enough, but it was also true that the museum was shape-shifting; finally his curiosity got the better of him.

During the museum's closure, Barnum had appeared every few days, escorting groups of men among the galleries. Although Guillaudeu never knew exactly what they were doing, he learned from William the ticket-man that they were architects, exporters, financiers, theater managers, and showmen from across America. They carried rolled plans under their arms and, according to William, their meetings in Barnum's office lasted late into the night. These were the men Barnum had enlisted to help him create his Congress.

Next to arrive was a fleet of carpenters. Guillaudeu watched them file up the marble stairway carrying lumber and ladders. They swept through the museum, moving exhibits aside, clearing the space to begin their work. They hammered and shouted in the empty galleries, sometimes stopping to gawk at the mummy or to pet Cornelia, the sewing dog, who roamed the halls freely, taking handouts from the carpenters' dinner baskets.

When the museum reopened, Barnum allowed the construction to continue during the day. Stages appeared in every corner, some only five feet across, others framed by elaborately carved wooden scaffolds. One was positioned in the round so the audience could view performers from every angle. The museum's patrons strolled among the half-built structures, exclaiming over them as if they were the ruins of Pompeii or the rising temples of a new age.

Guillaudeu ignored the changes as best he could and also harbored a painful feeling that the museum, which he now imbued with a majestic, disdainful spirit, had rebuffed him once again. Hadn't he watched this building rise from the ground, conjured by John Scudder? Guillaudeu had inhabited the new halls eagerly and filled them with the work of his hands, but he had never commanded its shape. He could only watch helplessly during the museum's second transformation as Barnum's vision had capsized the ark of Guillaudeu's silent menagerie and replaced it with, among other things, the furred and feathered lives that now shaped his days. With injured pride he watched yet another transformation begin without him. He sulked in his office, and went about his rounds trying not to look or listen as the carpenters shouted to each other from ladders and scaffolds while they carved the museum's next face.

Returning from the beluga's morning feeding, an empty bucket swinging in his hand, Guillaudeu encountered a young man wearing a stained smock and holding a large open book in his hands. Despite himself, Guillaudeu looked to where the man's attention was focused. It was one of the new stages, embellished with two very tall carved wooden trees, one on either side of the stage, which had been painted shades of yellows and greens. There was an easel set up on the stage, and Guillaudeu immediately recognized the half-penciled and half-painted backdrop. He stopped.

"Lareux's African savanna! A wonderful depiction!" Guillaudeu gushed, his attitude of aloofness abruptly derailed. "The colors are very close to the original lithograph. That must be from his *Histoire Naturelle?*"

The young man's eyes widened. "You know it?"

"Of course!"

The painter shook his head. "I can't quite seem to get it right."

"But what have you done here?" Guillaudeu pointed to a mounted specimen that had been placed threateningly on one side of the stage. "Is this some kind of joke?"

"No," the painter said doubtfully. "We've been directed to set the stages as dioramas. You'll see there are plants, there, as well as the leopard. When the performers —"

Guillaudeu laughed. "The *leopard*?" Guillaudeu ascended the stage and stroked the spotted cat's head. "Allow me to clarify that this creature never lived on the African continent. It's a jaguar. *Panthera onca*. A New World species. You'll see the spots are in a distinctly different pattern from a leopard's."

"They look the same in the drawing," the painter muttered, climbing onstage and flipping through the pages of the book.

"You are mistaken, I assure you. For the sake of authenticity, I suggest you go up to the third floor and retrieve the lion for your display. Unless you are not concerned with taxonomic accuracy." Guillaudeu narrowed his eyes at the painter.

"There's a lion?"

"Of course. What kind of collection doesn't have a lion?"

"You work here, then?"

"I'm the taxidermist."

"What other African animals are here?"

"Aardvark, baboon, gazelle, hyena, impala, lion, oryx, well, an oryx head, warthog, zebra. Those are the mammals. There are also many birds, of course. And a cobra in Gallery Eight, unless someone moved it."

"A cobra! That would be wonderful in the diorama."

The painter trotted toward the stairs. Guillaudeu examined the glossy-leaved plants on the stage. Convincingly exotic, he decided. And the painted backdrop really was good.

He returned to his office, but within the hour another painter appeared at the door.

"Silas told me you're one of the curators?"

"Curator?" Guillaudeu had never considered this title, but he liked the sound of it. A curator was a guardian for all museum exhibits, his taxidermied creations *and* the creatures of Barnum's menagerie.

"I suppose I am."

"Are there penguins at the pole?"

"That depends upon which pole."

The painter looked puzzled. "They didn't say which one."

Guillaudeu accompanied him back up to the galleries, to a stage set with a curtain of white velvet and painted icebergs like house-sized crystals. Above this landscape hung a banner advertising THE POLAR WORLD OF THE ESQUIMAUX.

"No penguins," Guillaudeu confirmed. "And you're going to need at least three men to help you carry the polar bear down the stairs, assuming you *want* the polar bear."

By the end of the afternoon Guillaudeu had advised three more painters as well as the artist responsible for designing a new transparency that would hang on the side of the museum to advertise the Congress. Guillaudeu knew this young artist mistook him for someone legitimately in charge of the preparations, but he did not demur. Giddily, he suggested that instead of a scene from one particular region of the world, since the breadth of the Congress spanned the whole globe, why not depict a scene like Scipio's Dream? A scene of the entire world with a spectator peering at the whole thing?

Workers called to him as he went on his rounds. His specimens became elements in colorful, correct dioramas; on the third floor he worked with the builders to create a temporary cage for the orang-outang on the set for a Bornean wild man. Various birds were captured in the aviary and put in hanging cages to augment the scenery, with Guillaudeu keeping meticulous records of where they were and when they should be cared for. These stages were exhibits unto themselves, Guillaudeu thought, with their backdrops and dioramas of mounted creatures. He wished that no performers would come, that chairs and benches would be set up on the stages so that visitors could simply sit among the creatures and the painted landscapes and imagine for themselves these distant places.

Barnum had invented new methods for advertising his Congress of Nations, and in the end even Guillaudeu could not resist the growing excitement. Barnum had saturated the papers, of course, and hoisted a banner across Broadway, anchored on the other side to the Emory Building. Men holding signs walked up and down the thoroughfare shouting advertisements for Barnum's Grand Ethnological Congress, *Commencing this Friday with a Spectacular Torchlight Parade!* Bannered wagons driven by men in brightly colored coats traversed Broadway, with women riding in the open air tossing confetti and pamphlets. Barnum hosted fireworks displays above the museum, and when those ended, the Drummond light broadcast its white saber into the heavens just in case anyone orbiting the earth cared to descend for the show.

As he scurried happily from gallery to gallery, carrying buckets of food for the animals and random specimens for various stages, Guillaudeu kept track of the days, and then, when the numbers became manageable, the hours, until Barnum's torchlight parade. The only thought that dampened his spirits was that Lilian Kipp would not be there to see it with him.

Lilian Kipp's delight in Barnum's enterprise had loosened Guillaudeu's knotted and resistant heart. Twice a day, when he was beneath the aviary's netted canopy, he allowed memories of her to flood his mind. As he tossed seeds along the aviary paths and trimmed the now abundant hedges, he recalled her laugh and the warm weight of her against his side after she fell asleep in the tribesman's room. Once, he revisited the table where they had eaten supper in the rooftop restaurant and recalled, with perfect clarity, the edge of her shawl caught in the wind. The abrupt and total sadness that had then engulfed him prompted his decision to think of her only while he was in the aviary. This forcing of his mind did not work, of course, but he could not help trying to impose order where his emotions roiled in chaos. He had written to Lilian Kipp twice since she left on the ship to London but had not yet received a reply. He convinced himself that she'd forgotten him completely. That her life in London had swept her neatly back into its routines and society, and she would never think of him again, ever.

One afternoon, sitting in his office about to begin his third letter, he counted and recounted the days. Only twelve had passed since she left, which meant she had not yet reached London! And two letters already! He flushed, crumpling the piece of paper in front of him. *What an old fool I am.*

He sat in the silence of his office and looked around. The tidy shelves of bottles and the rows of tools did not arouse the old sense of balance, peace even, that he'd always cherished. His bookshelves were mostly empty, and dust had gathered on his worktable. A few stray leaves of paper still lay on the floor near where Archer's desk had been, and the whole room now seemed vacant, even though he inhabited it. He searched for something that would trigger the old feeling of home. Instead, for the first time, what fascinated him was the sound of the crowd as it moved into the building, as it dropped its coins into William's hands, as it started up the marble stairway.

Sixty

Carried along by the morning crowd, Guillaudeu made his way from one stage to the next. The African savanna glowed in shades of yellow, orange, and rose, with the arching black silhouettes of acacia trees painted in the foreground. The jungle scene was crowded with plants and a vertiginous backdrop that suggested the dense green landscape extended back through the museum wall. The polar stage had been built with jagged edges and the whole thing painted white and gray in the style of an ice sheet.

He looked for the carpenters but they were gone. Outside, the new transparency spanned the length of three floors and bore a luminous depiction of the earth, with several smaller scenes of the world's exotic civilizations ringing it like a corona. To one side, a fashionable couple beheld the scene. Guillaudeu had wanted to congratulate the young designer, but he, also, was nowhere to be found. The men had disappeared. Barnum's Congress was two days away and the whole museum, the whole city, it seemed, was poised to receive it.

He had fed all the animals and so he wandered, admiring the carpenters' handiwork and examining exhibits he had never seen before. He felt no urge to return to his office. For the first time, he bought a paper cone of popcorn from a concessionaire. Miss Ana Swift, the giantess, glided past him, her gaze somewhere above the crowd. When he followed the sound of applause he discovered a glassblowing demonstration in progress and he stood with the others watching the blowers spin molten, opalescent globules into bowls and slender chalices. When they finished, he turned to leave and couldn't remember which way led to the main stairway. He walked into the next gallery not knowing what to expect, astonished that he was lost in the museum. Within minutes he had regained his bearings but not the old intimacy he had shared for so long with the place. He felt the distinct sensation that in this brief disorientation, the museum had displaced him completely, and now he was no different from any other visitor.

The Cosmorama salon had not changed at all, and he walked into its depths with relief. The dim lights hushed the crowd, and the circle of metal viewers ringed the gallery just as they'd always done. He wandered across the plush carpet, not looking into any tiny worlds but seeing the salon itself as a timeless capsule that would exist forever.

Someone beckoned to him from across the room. It was an old man, sitting alone on one of the circular velvet couches. Guillaudeu started toward him with a strange feeling and then recognized the face of his old friend. Sudden tears blurred his vision and he fought the urge to flee, but then he saw the man's expression and he went to him.

John Scudder raised both his hands, as if presenting the salon to him.

"Emile."

"Yes." Guillaudeu sat down. Scudder, appearing very frail but wearing a neat maroon wool jacket and a black-and-white-striped cravat, reached over and touched Guillaudeu's wrist.

"Isn't it wonderful?"

"Yes, I suppose it is, John."

"I knew I made the right decision." Scudder tapped the top of Guillaudeu's hand. "They tell me you take care of all these animals. Is it true?"

"Yes."

"Marvelous!" Scudder shook his head, smiling.

Guillaudeu found that he could not look at Scudder's

broad, ursine face for more than a second or two. He looked at his knotted hands. He sensed Scudder regarding him.

"Do you understand now?"

"I think so, John. I'm sorry —"

Scudder raised his hand and swiped it in a short, abrupt wave. Guillaudeu had been on the receiving end of this gentle dismissal too many times to continue what he was going to say.

"I was *ready* to move on, Emile."

"I wasn't."

Scudder looked around the salon. "It was time for me to retreat to my library, to let Rebecca and Edie care for me. I wanted to watch what that Mr. Barnum was going to do, but from a safe distance. You know what he has accomplished, don't you?"

"Accomplished? He has just taken his first steps!"

"I wanted our work to be incorporated into this. To be carried forward."

"I didn't."

"You didn't know what you wanted, Emile."

"You're probably right."

The two men leaned against the velvet cushions. The crowd emitted a gentle rustling whisper, and the shadows of people paraded across the brocade walls. Guillaudeu settled in beside Scudder and together they watched the ebb and flow of visitors who bent to look through the lenses, who traveled the world.

The Congress and the Conflagration

Sixty-one

I sat in my room, scribbling away on my True Life History. Compelled to record the strands of my life, I did not care that most of them did not twine together into a braid; these strands were not meant for anyone's eyes but mine. I set down the look on Thomas Willoughby's face as he turned away from his harpsichord for the last time. Matthew's slumped posture when he and Jacob emerged from their bedroom each morning. Maud's expression sitting in her booth downstairs. They Are Afraid of Her's body, which was still bundled tightly in blankets, lying on one of the cots among the Indians. Tai Shan, eliciting awe.

"Miss Swift." One of the carpenters stood in the doorway. Breaking the flow of images, cutting the filament between a mind's scrawled record and reality, this man, holding a hammer, had a simple message: "They've come."

I approached a group of angular, stern-faced women with the leather-bound registry under my arm. The women carried baskets and wore narrow skirts of indigo and canary yellow, their hair wrapped in scarves of the same cloth. One woman spoke for them all. The Bella Luna Sisters, from Hispaniola. I copied their names into the register and explained the communal accommodations. They shrugged and nodded and arched their elegant necks this way and that like dark brown cranes until they spotted a serviceable corner with three narrow beds.

A white-haired patriarch appeared next, followed by two

women at each end of a heavy trunk, their black hair hanging in sheets down their backs. Three children scurried along behind them chattering in English. They were Esquimaux most recently from Philadelphia, with their native costumes in the trunk. Close at their heels were more Indians, these from the northern coast of the Oregon Territory. They wore bark shawls and carried wooden boxes painted with red-and-black ovoid designs. Their manager, a red-bearded voyageur, filled out the registry and then hurried over to speak with Grizzly Adams.

And so out of thin air, Barnum's Congress arrived. They filed to the fifth floor in a steady stream for two days, Wednesday to Friday. I set up a chair for myself, and a small table, and from there I cataloged them. Warriors from Central Africa: the thinnest, most aristocratic humans I'd ever seen. Roumanian gipsies with tiny mirrors sewn into their skirts, smoking pipes and arranging curtains around their beds. Laplanders in thick woolen pants, sweating and laughing at the beluga. I signed them in, page after page after page, satisfied by this attempt to organize such a cacophony of lives.

It was not as if I'd never seen performers of this sort — I had, of course, at almost every place I'd worked — it was the sheer number that amazed me, that struck me as wonderful, as well as the simple fact that most of them were exactly who they claimed to be. True, some had exhibited themselves in America for years, but many seemed to be new to the continent. A Saharan nomad spread his blankets on a cot beside a Japanese Yamabushi. A group of sunburned men wearing conical felt hats erected a cylindrical tent and disappeared inside. The Congress filled the beluga gallery until it was as crowded as anywhere else in the museum.

Barnum gave a short address on Thursday afternoon, shouting a welcome amid the babble of translation. He explained they would be debuting at the parade, which would begin at the museum entrance on Ann Street at precisely nine o'clock on Friday evening, and progress from there up Broadway.

I became the source of information for the Congress. They didn't have many questions, though. No one seemed to mind the strange accommodations, and they accepted the food that appeared, carried by a dozen waiters, from the restaurant above.

These people were a new kind of nomad. I hadn't seen it clearly until now, perhaps because I, too, am one. The city, the venue, the performances, those were all unimportant. By now there were established trade routes for the show business: Philadelphia, Boston, Albany, New York, Halifax. These people created their homes wherever they happened to be. The children of the Congress gave the clearest illustration: Two Chinese boys, the Esquimaux children, and a tiny African child had found one another among the multitude. They made a kind of playhouse underneath the beluga's platform, with a stool and an overturned washtub for a table. A parent or two would stop by, bending down to pat the littlest one on the head before continuing on. History holds whole cultures like this, which have had to carry it all with them: their homes, their religions, the memory of where they come from. How much more interesting and skillful is this than the average American life, especially a female life, anchored in place, satisfied with one mundane perspective when a kaleidoscope is actually possible?

A group of Chinese monks arrived. Someone from Natchez, Louisiana, wearing bones around his neck and bells braided into his beard. A Pigmy. A druid. A dozen Indian elders.

By Thursday evening I was exhausted; not by keeping track of the Congress but because I'd been talked into looking after several children while their mothers went about various errands in the city. I held two on each thigh and one in my arms. They were peaceable children, content to construct a tent under my shawl and occupy it, giggling, playing patty-pan and occasionally nodding off against my back.

By the time I returned to the apartments of the Wonderful it was midnight and Maud, flushed and fuming, was pounding on the conjoined twins' door.

"Damn them, Ana. They won't come out!" She intensified the percussion of her fists. "I know they're in there. I can hear them scraping around."

A sound, muffled as if someone was shouting from underneath a pile of blankets, reached us.

"They stole my brandy," said Maud. She stopped her banging and looked at the door thoughtfully. "*Stole* it. As if they couldn't buy their own. It's time for them to move on. What good are they doing anyone here?"

I lay my palm against the door. "Should I break it down?" But wars never end by invasions of kindness, do they?

"I suppose not," Maud said. "Wouldn't do any good. Come on, I have another bottle squirreled away. Let's have a drink."

An hour later, as I walked back to my room, I noticed the twins' door was wide open. The creaking of the boards under my feet seemed to echo off the walls as I moved closer. The room was wrecked, with bedding on the floor and books and clothing scattered everywhere. I looked up and down the corridor. Where had they gone?

For weeks Matthew's face had been an ashen mask and I had done nothing to help. I had looked away, and now my casual dismissal seemed as brutal as a physical act of violence. I set off after them.

When I reached the top of the stairwell I heard them. Clutching the banister with both hands, I descended as fast as I could. They must have heard me because the sounds below intensified, as if someone were carrying too much firewood and the pieces were falling, one after another. Around we went, spiraling down.

I caught up with them on the second floor. They stopped in the middle of the shadowy portrait gallery and Matthew was slumped at an odd angle. He was on Jacob's right as always, away from me. Jacob turned as I approached.

"Well, if it isn't the inimitable Ana Swift, high above the clouds and all human concern. How pleasant it must be to rise above us all, to live always looking down . . . but not down your *nose*, of course, because that would be rude, wouldn't it? You would never think of doing *that!*" Jacob was slurring, and the whites of his eyes were an awful red.

"Matthew!" I spoke sharply, but he would not look at me. His brother blocked my view even further by moving his head and shoulders.

"I'm afraid my dear brother is *indisposed.*"

"Where are you going?"

"We *were* going to fetch our last bottle of Balmenach single-malt whisky from its hiding place in our booth, but once we heard the thunder of your pursuit, we thought we might extend our expedition to the street instead, in the hope of avoiding any company."

As he spoke, Jacob turned toward me and I saw that Matthew's head lolled chin-to-chest. Jacob had tied his brother's wrist to the waistband of their trousers with a silken scarf. Matthew's shoulder drooped forward; Jacob was working hard to keep both of them steady on his own. I lunged forward and grabbed Jacob's arm.

"Don't touch me," he hissed. But he could not free himself.

"What's wrong with him?"

For a moment, I thought Matthew was unconscious from alcohol or some violence, but when I lifted his chin, against Jacob's whining protest, his skin was cold and my own skin prickled. His face had no color at all. It looked as if Jacob had tried to disguise Matthew's state by coloring his lips a garish red — I recalled the moment after Maud flung open the door to their room, the brothers in their dance, Matthew's slender arm bedecked in jewels — but now his open eyes undid any attempt to hide the fact that Matthew was dead, or as close to dead as he could be in that shared body.

Under my hand, Jacob's shoulder shuddered. He was laughing, silently, his eyes glazed and red.

"What will happen now?" he asked me breathlessly. "What in this cursed world is going to happen now?" He continued to laugh, his frame shaking, surrounded by dozens of portraits whose ghostly faces watched us, unmoved. I backed away.

If they need to die, they will do it. My sentiment, so knowingly articulated, now stung with ruthless complacence. I had known something terrible would happen. Certainly if the conflicting wills within me were given physical form, they would mutilate one another. And here it had been done.

"You are a vile thing," I said. He only laughed.

I hurried away, across the gallery and down the marble stairway. I found one of the night watchmen on the street just outside the main doors.

"Come quickly to the portrait gallery, and bring two more men."

"What is it? What happened?"

"Just hurry."

The twins had not moved and Jacob was no longer laughing. I stood just close enough that I could grab them if I needed to, but we did not speak in the minutes it took for the watchmen to arrive. For a few seconds these three men, all dressed in dark blue uniforms, just stared, their faces in shifting configurations of shock. Fear probably followed, but before they let that show on their faces they ricocheted back to the safety of their assigned jobs. They dragged the twins away.

"Take them somewhere safe," I called, knowing that no such place existed. A hospital? What butchery would follow? A crime had been committed, but one unknown to the laws of ordinary man. My breath constricted in my lungs. I walked to my booth and sat down on the stool. Jacob should have finished the job here while he could, and quickly. But instead he had relinquished the power to end it himself, the only thing left to him. Now he would meet his end somewhere in the crowded city, alone for the first time in his life.

I imagined the watchmen returning to their homes after this night. I watched them enter their small apartments, places as bewildering to me as the museum was to them. They stroke the cheeks of their sleeping children and listen to the even breathing of their wives. They look out their windows over their domain and thank God for their sweet, simple life.

Sixty-two

Of all the fifth-floor residents, only the albino children and Tai Shan had been asked to join the torchlight parade. I suppose the rest of us were not considered eligible for an Ethnological Congress. Our draw was exoticism, but of a more local flavor.

The parade would begin at nine o'clock. For the hour leading up to it, I sat in Maud's parlor draping the children with scarves and bangles from Maud's supply. Clarissa hovered over them, scolding and brushing their colorless silken hair until it stood up in its own electrical storm. Through the thin walls came the sounds of a hundred newcomers also preparing for the parade.

Tai Shan came in wearing a dazzling robe of bright red silk embroidered with serpentine dragons in green, purple, and black. From his days at the Imperial court, he said.

"I would die for a gown made from that," breathed Maud, fingering the fabric.

"I'll ask my uncle where to find it here. Are the children ready?"

"Thank you for looking after them," Clarissa said. "I wouldn't trust them with just anybody out there."

"I won't let them out of my sight," Tai Shan said. The children twirled in front of us, two white dervishes. We applauded politely.

After they left, Maud, Clarissa, and I finished our tea, listening to the fading sounds of the Congress as people filed

431

down the stairwell to the bottom of the museum and out to Ann Street to begin the parade a few blocks north of us. When it was time, we headed for the balcony. The only light still burning in the apartments of the Wonderful was coming from the tribesman's room.

"Shouldn't he be in the parade?" whispered Maud.

We heard him singing inside the room, the song punctuated by clapping.

"Apparently not," said Clarissa. "That little fellow seems to do what he pleases. I know for a fact he hasn't performed a single time since he came here."

"Like the beluga," I said as we emerged into the fifth-floor gallery.

"But the beluga is next," Clarissa continued. "After the Congress, Barnum will open up this gallery." We strolled to the beluga tank and climbed the steps to the viewing platform. "It's about time this whale started earning its keep."

The creature hovered motionless in the middle of its tank, its knobby back like a small white island.

"It surely must miss the sea," Maud said.

The whale sighed through its blowhole and floated nearer, but it did not raise its head.

"Perhaps it prefers a finite world," I said, though I didn't believe it. I would miss the whale once it was surrounded by a crowd, once it was no longer just ours.

"Come on, the parade is about to start."

Barnum's employees crowded the balcony. I spied a group of ushers and automatically searched for Beebe's face among the red caps and jackets. Stupidly, I also looked for Thomas at his usual place; of course he was not there. But the harpsichord was, having weathered several rain showers on the balcony since Thomas' departure. Now two men sat on its smooth wooden back. I wondered that the instrument did not cave in. Maud and Clarissa shoved their way to the railing, but my line of sight was clear so I stayed at the back.

Broadway was a sea of tightly packed bodies, faces like fields of nodding sunflowers along both sidewalks. Boys had climbed the lampposts, as they will in times like these. Figures leaned from the windows of every building as far up and down the street as I could see.

Barnum must have paid the lamplighters to ignore Broadway tonight. Twilight's mauve web spread the perfect atmosphere, a dimming, anticipatory pre-show lull. Light breezes came off the harbor, refreshing but not strong enough to snuff the candles people lit below, a hundred fireflies blinking into their short lives. I shut my eyes for a minute, sensing the crowd shifting around me. How often had I been among an audience? Usually on display myself, I tended to watch the museum patrons as a spectacle unto themselves.

The sound of drums reached us first, a faint pulse felt before sight is possible. With my eyes still closed, the percussion emerged beyond the clumsy sounds of the people on the street, the clattering noise of each isolated life. Without eyes, I perceived with a strange clarity. The drums, two of them, emitted a unifying rhythm, connecting those lives on the street with the life of the cosmos. Then the drummers lost synchronicity by half a second and the planet tilted, all imperfection, sin, cruelty, and death suddenly apparent. Uniting again, they regained symmetry and the invisible mathematic of the universe coalesced into the movement forward, always forward, of time. Then the crowd saw something and their reaction was a hiss slithering toward us, gaining volume and energy as it approached the balcony, and when it was upon me I opened my eyes.

Two behemoths rounded the corner and ambled heavily, trunks swaying, backlit by a dozen torches. Their great domed heads moved side to side, the mirrors and gilt of their headdresses glinting. Ears flapping like sails and pierced with thick gold loops, the elephants approached on painted legs, riderless, impenetrable creatures of daunting grace. As they passed I smelled a hot, grassy scent and heard their footfalls echo between the buildings. I watched their tasseled tails disappear with a sharp feeling caught in my chest.

Phineas T. Barnum appeared in a lacquered black carriage driven by a masked figure wearing a black cloak. He waved and shouted. "If you have ears to hear, then listen! *Mandatum nuovo,* a new commandment I give unto you!" They were grand words, but his voice was barely audible; he'd been dwarfed by his creation.

Next came the five Haitian women in jewels and bright swaths of cotton, walking straight-backed, tall as alders, their expressions obscured by the flickering shadows cast by the torches they carried. The Esquimaux family followed, wearing costumes of sealskin and feathers. Their patriarch lunged and turned circles while his women struck small leather drums, chanting and tossing their hair, their children running along beside them. Here came the pale twins, tripping along holding hands and waving at their admirers, ushered by Tai Shan, elegant as ever. Some groups were lit brightly, smiling and addressing the crowd, while others came and went in the shadows. The gipsies appeared, wearing layered skirts embroidered with bells. Behind them came a lone Indian dressed in bark and wearing a huge wooden mask, lunging and dancing. One by one, region by region, Barnum's Grand Ethnological Congress ceremonially passed and the crowd was unable to contain itself, shouting, clapping, shrieking, gasping. And on the balcony, for once we were no different.

Four bearded torchbearers dressed in deerskin presented Grizzly Adams. He stood atop the bare back of a sorrel mare with his arms folded across his chest. The mare walked slowly, pulling a high, planked cart that bore Adams' now uncovered cage.

"Behold Orthrus!"

Unlike Barnum's, Adams' voice reached the balcony with force. "Behold the Geryon Dogs!"

"Orthrus!" echoed the torchbearers in a fierce chorus.

Inside the cage, bracing itself against the motion of the cart with four splayed legs, a great white wolf glared at the horde. The beast swung its head to reveal a second, twin face; another jaw with bared teeth came into view, another pair of black eyes reflected fire. Sprung from the same body, another skull filled with menace. The creature used both pairs of eyes to regard spectators on either side of the street, and both sets of twitching ears to listen.

What kind of entertainment was this? Released from the realm of nightmare, the creature's claws scraped against the flimsiest barrier, threatening to burst through our notion of what is possible. I shivered, transfixed by its splendor. For a moment, the only sound I heard was a child crying somewhere below. But Barnum's wonders overtook one another in quick succession, and by the time the cage disappeared into the shadows the next spectacle had already taken its place in the glittering lamplight and the crowd roared with pleasure.

Sixty-three

The Japanese Yamabushi was an ageless man with a long, thin beard growing from the point of his chin. His face had weathered many seasons outside, although his shoulders were narrow and his torso, made half visible by his loosely draped white robe, was soft and frail. He wore a coarse rope belt and from it hung a whorled conch, spiny and white with an obscenely flesh-like pink interior. He stood with his walking stick firmly planted in front of him, perched in a spot of bright sunshine atop one of the stone benches along the aviary path. Visitors moved past him, but he stood motionless, smiling up at the branches. Some people craned their necks to see what he was looking at, but they could not see what it was. I opened the registry and noted the Yamabushi's location next to his name.

I had seen the museum crowded before, of course, but nothing like this. In the morning after the parade, people walked shoulder-to-shoulder through the tented aviary and a line had formed at its entrance. Visitors were pressed together at each gallery door; I had already witnessed two scuffles between men shoving their way in. Barnum had outdone himself. It was only ten o'clock and already the museum was at capacity and it was the hottest day yet of the year. People fanned themselves with hats and handkerchiefs and the air was already sticky and stagnant.

In every gallery a demonstration was in progress. I found the Esquimaux at one end of the portrait gallery with an audience of fifty, holding up first a delicate coat made of salmon skins stitched together, and then a thick suit of wrinkled walrus to wear while out to sea. On the other side of the gallery were the Roumanians, teaching the New York masses a complicated jig while their ancient grandfather kept time, playing a rough-hewn fiddle with violent passion. In one gallery three Laplanders exhibited their native costumes, in the next, a group of Africans carved small throwing spears. In the theater Professor Stokes introduced the Great Chiefs of the Plains Tribes. The Congress had even reached the Cosmorama salon, where a single Asiatic monk sat motionless on a cushion chanting strange syllables in the half-light.

Incredibly, all members of the Congress were accounted for. I reviewed each page twice, but every group was in its assigned place. I could not help but feel delighted that I had a part, maybe even an important part, in this success. I wandered the galleries as an overseer. It took me fifteen minutes to make my way from the Cosmorama salon to the second floor. I waited as patiently as I could while families shuttled themselves forward, children carrying their jackets in front of them, pushed along by flushed mothers with bonnets flapping against their backs by the ribbons. Friends called out to one another, and people jostled forward, some stopping for lemonade or sarsaparilla sold in conical paper cups. Among the visitors, I was startled to see Oswald La Rue, his back to me, watching the Haitian sisters clapping and shuffling, dancing on a rickety stage. I waded through the crowd to him.

"Shouldn't you be working?" I whispered, tapping his shoulder.

"I should think not!" The irritated man who faced me was not Oswald at all, but another Living Skeleton. "This is my day off," he snapped, shaking his head and stalking off on his spider legs.

The Haitian sisters were singing an odd, reedy tune in nasal voices as they danced, faces sweating and their bodies dipping low, revealing glimpses of smooth skin below the loose necklines of their light dresses. Around me, visitors rolled up their sleeves. One woman even lifted her skirt well above her ankle and fanned cooler air underneath with her hem.

I returned to my booth, enjoying the breeze coming from the open balcony doors. I heard the faint sounds of the picketers outside. Mayor Harper had officially sanctioned a boycott of the museum. I could hear shouts and heckles from below and imagined Miss Crawford fuming prettily with Beebe perhaps beside her. But the Congress swept on, gaining momentum. Its voices ricocheted off every wall and its different rhythms blended and rose, lifting upward. I didn't see how the mayor could stop it.

Without warning, the chandelier above me swung in a wide arc. Its light swerved crazily around the gallery and bits of ceiling plaster fell to the floor. Dancers. Above us. Museum patrons ran from my gallery laughing and shrieking until only the South American Pigmy warrior remained on the stage opposite me. We watched the ceiling. I perceived the museum quaking, bursting at the seams, not just here but in every gallery and salon. It creaked like the Ark itself, slowly lifted by the rising flood. I imagined Barnum standing at the helm in those first seconds: *Will it hold? Will it burst? Where are we headed?* But this ark carries a stranger menagerie. You again, Mother. You come, laughing with sad eyes, standing on a stool to wipe away my tears. *The fish do not know the ark, Ana. Remember? The fish swim where they will. Always.*

Sixty-four

In the beluga's gallery, tattooed men wrestled each other to the floor. Near them the Roumanian grandfather played his fiddle while a dozen anomalous pairs of dancers swung wildly. Maud wore a frilled red Spanish gown and danced with the Esquimaux patriarch. In his robe of silk dragons, Tai Shan twirled a reedlike Haitian sister. Groups of torches cast changing light across the dancers; shadow was full dark since the moon was just a sliver. I sat cross-legged in my nightgown near the Sioux camp. This carnival had woken me; I hadn't bothered to dress, but a giantess in her sleeping clothes aroused no attention here.

I had encountered this before, in almost all the traveling shows where I'd worked and lived. A single night buoyed up by some charged current, an unexpected exuberance among the performers that carried us crackling and sparking through the night. On these occasions some would fight. Some would succumb to passions that normally lay dormant. Someone would sing more beautifully than she ever had, bringing someone else, who hadn't cried for decades, to tears. Some would turn from the lamplight and walk away, never to return. A carnival loosened us from the calendar's stricture. Tonight, among the Congress, was such a night. No costumes here and no stage tricks. It was neither show nor celebration, but a simple pouring forth, a departure from the ordinary bounds. A carnival, indeed. *Carne vale. O flesh, farewell.*

The wrestling match ended in a roar of laughter. The

defeated man lay on the floor with his heaving, blue-inked chest to the ceiling. His adversary helped him up and handed him a bottle. Four children scampered out of the darkness, their faces greased in black-and-white geometric patterns, transformed into grinning skulls of the dead. They brandished sticks, coming straight at me. One of them screamed and leapt into my lap for protection. The others stampeded away.

I felt no urge to dance, sing, or even stand. I felt strangely light, and that was enough celebration. No longer a lone fortress towering above, I sat comfortably like one of the children, eagerly looking instead of being looked upon. The bright blood on the fighters' knuckles. The shouts of the dancers. The drops of sweat glistening on the back of the child in my lap. My vision became elemental. I was aware that this carnival articulated a joy unknown by most people. It is a necessary mechanism, this joy, for without it none of us could persist in our public and, more important, in our private lives. The shifting orange flames of a hundred lamps blurred the delineations of the Congress itself; all Representatives of the Wonderful had dissolved into one grinning, spinning population. And I was anonymous, hidden from view, small. I remained as still as possible, not even daring to reassure the wild-eyed child on my lap.

On the other side of the gallery someone fired a gun. It might have been Grizzly Adams, who I knew was over there, or it could have been someone else. A group of people, including one figure wearing a huge wooden mask painted to resemble a bird or a dragon, ran over to the wall and plugged the bullet hole with a cork, cackling and shouting. Music never ceased, but changed hands often. Oswald La Rue danced a jig to the bells and metallic notes of an African instrument.

Near me, two figures emerged from the Sioux camp, where I knew They Are Afraid of Her's body still lay wrapped in blankets, now with several woven storage baskets set atop her. One figure was the Sioux grandfather, wearing his usual top hat and dark vest. The other's face was in shadow but my heart jumped because I thought it was Barnum. When he turned, I still wasn't sure because his face was painted like the face of the child in my lap, with black and white grease. He leaned down to speak into the Sioux grandfather's ear. It *was* Barnum, or was it? He turned from the grandfather and disappeared into the crowd. The Sioux shook his head and stepped out onto the gallery floor. A younger man hurried after him holding an uncovered oil lamp and a wooden crate. He set the crate on the floor, and the grandfather stepped up to face the Congress.

"Babylon the great is fallen!" the grandfather shouted. "It is fallen and is become the habitation of devils, and the hold of every foul spirit, and a cage for every unclean and hateful bird! Come out of her, my people, that ye be not partakers of her sins, and that ye receive not of her plagues."

No one appeared to be listening. After a moment of looking around, the grandfather shrugged. He pulled a small glass vial from his pocket. He unstopped it and appeared to drink. He took the lamp from the hands of the younger man and blew the alcohol across the flame in a whooshing cloud of fire. People whooped and clapped.

"Babylon is fallen," the grandfather said more softly. "Seal not these sayings, for the time is at hand."

The younger man helped the grandfather down from the crate. Suddenly the small child leapt from my lap and ran away. Another song started up and a roar from the men across the gallery flowed over us.

I was sorry to hear someone call my name. I did not want to rise up. *Ana!* I did not recognize the voice. *Where is she? She must be here.* I was hidden. What a blessed, blessed thing to be. I relished it for whole minutes. I savored each moment until they found me.

"We need you." It was the Esquimaux, or maybe it was the Yamabushi. I could not tell but I rose up and glided behind the man as he hurried between dancers, across the gallery floor to the beluga tank.

The whale's viewing platform was crowded but they made room for me. Something was wrong. The whale was not singing.

The red-bearded voyageur stood at the edge of the platform. "It swallowed my bottle," he said softly. I could see in his eyes he did not mean for it to happen.

"A bottle," I repeated. The whale hung just under the surface of the water. I had never seen it motionless. It had always whistled and chirped in circles, endless circles.

"And it was a big bottle. And then it stopped swimming."

The whale rose to the surface, exposing its blowhole. A puff of droplets and air issued forth.

"The bottle's probably stuck in its throat," I said. The people on the platform nodded and looked up at me expectantly.

I thought the water would be putrid but it was not, just cold. It was also deeper than I expected; I could not reach the bottom and had to swim. The sounds of the carnival faded. My dress billowed out from my body as I pushed off from the wall. The tank felt much bigger now that I was in it. I remembered They Are Afraid of Her gliding in circles, one arm thrown over the creature's back. I drifted toward the whale. At first it backed slowly away from me. I slowed down, and I crooned to it in soft words. I even whistled.

The whale raised its head and turned so that it could see me with one of its small eyes. Someone lit another torch on the viewing platform. The whale blinked and lowered its bulbous, milk-white face. When I came close again, it did not move away. I reached out an arm and stroked the silk-smooth skin of its back. I positioned myself in front of it and gave both of us a few seconds to get used to our proximity. The whale had many small scars across its forehead. I did not want to wait too long. I put my hands on either side of its head. A firm touch would ease its nervousness, I hoped. I was not rough. I told the creature I would do it no harm and then I pried open its mouth. It must have let me inside, because I know it could have thrashed me away with one quick motion. It must have braced itself against the side of the tank, then, because when I slipped my arm into its mouth it held steady so I could do my work.

I reached inside, past its rough tongue and the corrugations of its upper throat. By the time my elbow was at the threshold of its mouth, my fingers had reached a taut, ribbed chamber. Another few inches and they pushed into a soft cavity. I explored, feeling the pillowy flesh pulse and quiver. I felt the bottle's neck just as the whale's teeth brushed my shoulder. I tried to grasp it, but it slipped away. I found the bottle again and thrust one finger into it to hold it. I tugged. The whale breathed shallowly through its blowhole, but I held my breath. I pulled the bottle gently up. The whale's body constricted around it, I felt the creature gagging but it did not dart away. I pulled the glass free. It was covered in foul-smelling bile and it took some strength to disengage it from my finger. The whale remained with me, again raising its head to look at the terrestrial world.

I shivered, filled with sudden happiness as the beluga gently swam around me and began to trill.

The Titans were put on the earth to fight the Olympian gods. The words from the old book came back to me from Pictou. They were put on the earth to fight, but I had never had a purpose here, so the whole world became my adversary, until some opportunity for good work, like this, arose. The realization did not upset me as I bobbed in the water. On the contrary, I felt a great burden sloughing away. It was a pure, fleeting sensation and I could recall no other like it. The whale swam. It whistled. It resumed its circles. When I turned back to the people on the platform, they saw something radiant on my face. I could tell it was something they'd never seen before. Among them was Tai Shan. When I reached out he pulled me from the water.

Tai Shan took off his dragon robe. Beneath it he wore loose white trousers and a white tunic. He draped the silk robe over my shoulders and gave me the sash. He waited until I had it tied and then he bowed to me, from the waist and with his palms together at his chest.

"Thank you, Ana." He held this posture for a few more moments and then he went, ghostlike in his pure white, away from me among the revelers. I watched him walk across the whole gallery and disappear through the door to the stairs that led out of our world.

The tribesman looks out the window of his room and sees lanterns swinging from carriages. He hears hooves and the murmurs of invisible drivers on their way to or from some nocturnal errand. Music and shouts from the fifth-floor gallery reach his ears in waves. Occasionally he hears a splash from the whale in its tank.

It is because of the keeper that the tribesman is here, standing in this building, in a night that is just about to fade to morning. The keeper strayed from his duty; his heart strayed from the heart of the people. For the tribesman, this moment at the window is the betrayal's terrible consequence.

The tribesman's nostrils fill with stinging salt air and his ears fill with the suffocating sound of waves hissing over the sand. He was back there, at the end of the journey. He was finally climbing over slick tangles of mangrove roots, up to his thighs in water that felt as if it were erasing his legs. He would not look at this water as he walked. He pushed his way through the dense branches, his brother's lean figure disappearing ahead of him and then reappearing. His brother called out: Higher ground. They reached a sandbar and stopped. His brother pointed. A black ship lay at anchor in the distance. And then the tribesman saw five men sitting in the shade of the mangroves near them on the sand. The men were resting, some lying on the ground near a campfire. Their small vessel lay in the shallows. In a moment, they rose and came toward the brothers, speaking in a hollow, high-pitched language that raised the tribesman's hackles like the voice of an owl. Immediately the men killed the keeper using a blast from a stick and smoke. That stopped the song.

The first thing the tribesman did as the men walked toward him across the white sand was disentangle the bundled mulga root from his brother's body. He strapped it to himself and then the men were there, foul-smelling and dirty. He kept his arm over the bundle while the men chained him by the neck and wrists. Even if he died in a moment, at least he would have done everything he could to protect the hollow root and its contents. But he survived, first the men, then the ocean's terrible expanse. He had emerged in an ominous country and followed an angry man through crowds, walking upon unnatural stone surfaces and seeing people dressed in strange garments all walking the same direction. Now he had not-quite-lived in this place for countless days, and finally the song had consumed him. It was only through this song that he remained with the people, no matter how far away they were from him. He knew when they made camp in the stone country and when the floodwaters dried, and when, finally, it was the season for fires.

He turned from the window. He became the keeper. He had absorbed the song into his body and finally understood what it had been showing him. It was his. There was no fear in his mind anymore, no doubt.

In the home place, the winds lifted dust from the floodplain and whipped it into whirling spirals. Any moisture on the ground had evaporated. The waters had disappeared and the geese flown away to the coast. The people made their way down from the cliffs holding cloths over their noses and mouths, heads bowed. They moved camp to the leeward side of the monolith that they had come to for centuries during Yegge, the season of wind.

In the evening, the men gathered to scrape red ocher from the rock. They stored this red dust until the next morning, when they rose before dawn to verify that the wind was right. They mixed the dust with spittle. They painted one another with it, drawing finger-wide vertical lines straight down their faces, forehead to chin. They hand-printed their chests and strapped their lighting-sticks to their backs. They asked the home place to understand their actions, to understand that their intention had always been and would always be to assist, to cleanse the land in preparation for Wurrgeng. The men walked in a single-file line away from the monolith, asking for guidance as they carried out their task.

The men stopped in a stand of pandanus palm and formed a circle. In the museum, every bone in the tribesman's body aches with longing to be with them during the cleansing time, a time when the people directly serve their home place. They serve as heralds of seasons, their actions helping the land to its most abundant flow. The men's voices are low reverberations of sound. They sing in layers of vibration that the tribesman hears clearly from the dim room above the museum. Now one man kneels in the center of the circle, with flint and a hearthboard. He shaves bark into a nest and spins alight an ember, blowing deep breaths into the bark nest until flame comes and the men raise their voices. They each dip their lighting-stick into the flame and move slowly away from one another to light the land on fire.

The tribesman walks to the door, his eyes wide open and the song suspended in his mouth. He hears whooping and music from the others and he does not know if the sounds come from his people or the beings inhabiting the museum. He does not know why these creatures would celebrate, but he smiles, already smelling the euca-lyptine smoke of the home place.

Sixty-five

Was that the wind or shouting? Was it the last of the revelers? Slowly, I spiraled up from sleep, considering these
sounds from a great distance. Were they fighting? Bidding
each other farewell? The sounds became urgent; they seemed
to be pulling me toward a foreign country that existed outside these museum walls. Surfacing now, emerging into my
room and the waking life, I was delivered into the knowledge that something terrible was happening. Someone ran
down the corridor outside my door in heavy shoes. Opening
my eyes I could tell by the quality of the darkness that dawn
was coming.

"Bring buckets!" It was a voice I did not recognize. Who
was that? I sat up. Close by, I smelled smoke.

Black clouds seethed from the windows below mine and
drifted up, fragrant and sinister. I peered down but the
ground wasn't visible. I heard more shouting, the sounds of
a crowd, of horses snorting, people hurrying and moving
things. I turned from the window and saw the distant, appalling reflection of my disheveled self across the room in
the mirror. A pale face above a tapestry of dragons. *I'm so
tired of this, Mother. I will need a new booth, a new Life History. A
new body. This one is finished. Nothing lasts.* Only ten more years,
and I die. *I see death in every shadow, behind every door.* What
had Tai Shan said? *It's the same with the sages. That's what gives
them a sense of humor.* Who needs a sense of humor, though,
when your life is the joke?

"If we don't get down there, we can't get out!" It was Maud. She was running. My body followed her voice, dumbly, like an animal. In the corridor I saw the ruffled hem of her dress disappear around the corner into the gallery.

I hadn't run in years and it rattled every bone as if the whole blasted thing would come flying apart, a pile of sticks. Fuel. The gallery was filling with stinging smoke. People emerged from the haze, changed directions uncertainly, and disappeared. I passed the beluga tank where people were crowded on the platform, dipping ceramic pitchers while the whale trilled and splashed. There were voices all around me but I recognized no one.

"Get to the third floor!" someone shouted. "The whole museum's going up!" I heard a dozen sets of feet change direction.

"Maud?" I shouted. I wanted to say good-bye before this scattering. But it was the tribesman who emerged from the haze. He wore a wool jacket buttoned all the way up to his neck and a strange knapsack of bundled rags and rope. He walked swiftly past me, looking straight ahead, his eye on some distant, invisible target. He was singing and maybe smiling. He disappeared. I reached the stairwell and descended into the heat.

On the fourth floor, people were running in all directions, some screaming, some silent, some dragging others by the hand. Most were making their way toward the stairway and I descended among them.

Along the Broadway side of the third floor, people were climbing out the windows into the arms of men standing on the ends of ladders. The heat was intense, and the sounds of roiling fire menaced us from below, and yet the crowd was orderly around these windows. The people knew they would get out. I moved away from them.

I heard a woman wailing. Unlike the others, she had gone to the east side of the building. Maybe she had not seen the windows, the easier escape. I followed her voice and found a black-haired girl, one of the Esquimaux, perhaps. She was howling and jumping up toward a very high window, where

I could see the outstretched arms of a fireman. He could not reach her.

"Here." I offered her my arms and lifted her to the man.

"Do not try to go to the lower floors," the fireman shouted as he enfolded the girl. "It's too hot."

Below me, another child appeared, his arms reaching up. When the fireman reappeared I lifted this one, too. "Here. Come."

More appeared. Another child, then the Haitian sisters, each a delicate crane in my arms. Others arrived, more and more. My body creaked and heaved, doing the kind of work it was made for. I took in their different hefts and scents, all the world's people made into children in my arms. Then Maud was standing below me.

I smiled. "Here," I told her. "Come on."

She shook her head.

"Don't be ridiculous, come on." I bent my knees and lifted her by the waist.

She clung to my neck for a moment. "You are magnificent," she whispered. "How will you get out?"

I shook my head as I lifted her higher. "I don't need to."

I handed her to the fireman and watched the trailing hem of her Spanish dress slip over the threshold.

There was no one else in the room with me. The fireman shouted something after me but I would not hear.

I went to the roof, emerging into the lightening layers of dawn and soft columns of smoke pouring upward. The restaurant chairs were tucked in tight to the clothless tables and I passed silently among them. I heard the squeals of the Happy Family and went to the cage, bending the flimsy bars easily. Whether they would escape the flames was not my burden. As I walked toward the edge of the roof, I examined my arms. Whether I lived to eat a thousand more meals, or whether I had eaten my last did not matter. My legs moved mechanically, but not without pain. Whether I walked a hundred miles before I die, or twenty feet, there is no difference.

I can see you, Mother, even from this great distance. You

come to my bedside when you think I am asleep. You cover my legs, which have outgrown these flimsy beds. You cover me and then you sit by the window and cry. When you muffle your face with your hands I open my eyes and see you mourning for my life. I always thought you were crying because of my body, but you wept for this moment. You knew one day it would come to this, that I would either live obsessed by death, or choose to die. I am not angry, Mother. I can see the brightening lines of dawn. Here are flags whipping in the wind, and rows of daffodils only just starting to scum with smoke.

But at the edge of the roof I looked down onto a sea of upturned faces and the wrongness of it pushed me back. A crowd, no different from standing in my booth or walking in the galleries. Would I give them the biggest spectacle of all? Would I give them this gift? For a moment I felt myself dangling by a filament: Would I falter? Would I leave no trace that I had ever been? It was the vain clinging of the polar explorer that reminded me of the True Life History on my desk, its pages already starting to curl and blacken. I whirled around and ran toward the stairs.

In my room one edge of the curtain had caught fire. Everything else was perfectly intact. A dent in the pillow where I'd lain, the quilt mussed from my rising. Look at my ill-fitting bed, still ridiculously propped on its crates. I gave it a kick. It wobbled. I kicked it again and the whole thing fell to the floor. I pushed it to the center of the room, quilt and all. The headboard snapped away from the frame under my hands and I threw it down. I went to the window and ripped the curtain from its rod and threw it on the pile. The edge of the quilt began to curl and smoke. Not the first bed I've burned, Mother. I can still hear you, your words coming out in a rush, crowded by laughing. *Use it for kindling!*

At my desk, I turned the pages of the True Life History until I reached the end of the scrawl. From the drawer I lifted my pencil. While the bed burned in the burning building, I made an entry: The fighters' bright blood. The children's faces the skulls of the dead. Grizzly Adams' arms folded across his chest in the torchlight, standing on the smooth back of his mare. The beluga eyeing me as I reached down its throat. I wrote until the smoke stung my eyes to tears. Then I took up the History in my arms.

I heard a voice in the gallery near the beluga's tank and I walked there with one arm extended in front of me and my eyes half closed against the smoke.

From the whale's platform a creature with long red hair blinked down at me. Its slender black hand shielded its nose. It clung to a man who leaned over the edge of the whale tank and appeared to be speaking to the whale. The taxidermist.

"Will you take this?" I ventured.

He coughed. He held the orang-outang like a child on his hip. Under his other arm was a purple, hen-like bird with a strange knobby face. The bird clucked nervously.

"Mr. Guillaudeu."

"There's nothing we can do for the whale," he said, not looking at me.

"True."

"The octopus is already dead." His eyes followed the circling whale. "And the seahorses. Most of the birds have escaped, but the ravens don't seem to mind the flames, somehow. I —"

"I want you to take this." I held out my True Life History. "Please look at me." I gently shook his shoulder. He finally turned. "Take it."

"All right." He adjusted the bird and the ape so he could hold my History, too. He was looking at the whale again. I heard it whistle uncertainly.

"Mr. Guillaudeu, it's time to go."

"And which would be the best way to proceed from here?" He looked up at the high windows. "If one wanted to reach the ground."

"You need to go to the third floor right away. They're on the Broadway side of the building. They can reach you if you go there, but you've got to go now."

"I did the best I could," he said.

"I know you did," I said. "Please go now."

"All right."

I lifted him and his various cargo down from the platform and pointed them in what I hoped was the direction of the stairwell. The smoke quickly took him. "Hurry," I murmured.

The gallery, not yet engulfed, was poised on the brink of its own destruction. The air was electrified against my face. The beluga screamed. I covered my ears and started back toward my apartment. The whale whistled hopelessly, splashing in its interminable circles, and I turned back to ease its passage.

It was easier than I thought to undo the carpentry of the tank. The metal bands holding the planks together were hot, but I slammed my body into the tank as hard as I could. I felt the wood tremble, but it held. I slammed again. The hot metal burned me, but what did that matter? On the third try one plank popped loose, then two more. By the fifth hit, water was gushing from the tank and a metal stave had sprung loose from one end. I stepped aside just as the whale leapt free, hurdling the jagged wall I'd broken. It sailed silently across the gallery toward the apartments and hit the wet floor sliding. It broke easily through the partition wall and into hall of the Wonderful, and then it was lost in the smoke. I heard a tremendous crash, then nothing. The creature left a steaming trail and I followed it.

The heat was so intense in my room I could step only a few feet inside. The flames already glowed blue at the center of the blaze that had been my bed. The wood popped and crackled and sparks spilled up in a dazzling firmament until the floor gave way and sucked the burning bed down. Wisps of quilt were flung upward like the surprised arms of a human being before plummeting, and then all that was left was a ragged hole. I leaned toward it and felt a column of heat so intense I jumped back. The remaining floor creaked and I felt a lurch. Flames licked up through the hole, burning with devouring energy. My heart told me to relinquish this shell but I paused. I looked back, but the way was blocked. The fire had moved in behind me, had eaten up the hallway, the museum, the world.

Sweat fell in rivulets and evaporated. My hair was a hot, wet coil against my neck. Heat climbed each finger of my left hand and covered my right, which was curled into a fist. I saw my wooden booth and heard Thomas playing Separation Waltz on the balcony. I felt fire in the creases of my face and moved quickly to the edge of the hole. It was only a moment before my body's weight did the rest.

I rode the back of an old elephant for the rest of the way. We swayed through a furnace of skin-splitting heat. We rode through the worst of it, across the cracked earth of a desert, where I could smell my flesh burning. We reached a narrow canyon passageway and entered it. Buzzards circled, closing in. I leaned all the way forward, resting my head against the great dome of the elephant's skull. It carried me on toward the place where all giants' bones must lie.

Sixty-six

Guillaudeu stood in the wings, perspiring. *You would think I'd get over these ridiculous nerves, considering how many times I've done this,* he thought. He mopped his face with a handkerchief and scolded the merciless butterflies in his stomach. To help ease his mind he focused on the clear, familiar voice coming from the other side of the curtain.

He had been surprised by how easy it was to leave New York. His home was already almost bare and it was no trouble to arrange for his remaining things to be sold and the proceeds forwarded. When he left the apartment for the last time he carried just the satchel he'd taken on his walk in the wilds of New York Island. A small trunk of clothes would be delivered later.

He stood in the crowd at the edge of the still-smoking ruins of Barnum's museum and verified with his own eyes what he'd already heard shouted by the paperboys for the past three days: It had been completely destroyed. Barely visible among the ashes, he saw the blackened outline of the marble staircase and also the jutting remains of the second-floor balcony, which had crashed to the ground at an angle reminiscent of a sinking ship. And his life's work? Gone, of course. But when he imagined his specimens consumed in flames, from the smallest songbird to the cameleopard, and their orderly taxonomies and dioramas burned away, he did not feel pain or despair, but relief. An echo of Cuvier drifted to mind: *Out of the rubble of the old age will arise entirely new creatures to crawl and fly across the globe.* He walked swiftly away.

Across Broadway he climbed aboard an omnibus and from that vantage point observed for the last time the clatter of people intersecting, outstripping, meeting, and avoiding one another on the street, seeing it all as if through the glass of a swaying aquarium. He disembarked at the southern terminus and strolled through the Battery, enjoying the brisk air, children playing on the grass, rows of oyster vendors peddling wares, and the simple sensation of being among the living.

At Whitehall Slip, the Royal Mail Ship *Acadia* lay at anchor with colored flags waving from all three masts and her crew swarming the decks. Without pausing, Guillaudeu presented the attendant with his ticket, climbed the gangway, and proceeded to his modest cabin. He spent the three hours until the ship's departure writing letters, to Edie and then to John Scudder, to the Lyceum, and even one to Barnum. He paid another attendant to mail them right away. He stood at the small cabin window staring out at the city, the only home he'd ever known, and he did not feel much at all. He wondered if the fire had made a shell of him, if he would soon fall to charred pieces. Only after he felt the ship lurch into motion, and he had sprung up on deck and stood at the railing until the great mouth of New York Harbor slid backward over the horizon, did he thrill eastward, toward London.

He waited until the *Acadia* was far out to sea and then he read what she'd given him. After he'd followed her, page after page, through black and then indigo ink, through hurried scrawl and careful, beautiful script, through the last twenty pages of pencil that had been applied with force that at times buckled or ripped the page, he was breathless. So thoroughly astonished was he by these intimacies, her histories and fantasies, recollections, speculations, and especially her delicate hopes, that afterward, when he went up on deck to take in the sea air, he beheld all the other passengers as vessels for their own such wonders, and he was humbled to the core. He then understood the gift she had bestowed.

Before saying a word, before the astonishment had left her eyes or he could truly believe he was there, he put the bundled pages into Lilian Kipp's hands. "She saved my life."

Her eyes searched his, and she almost asked questions, but she saw a sad and wondrous expression in him that settled her after some moments. She beckoned him inside and closed the door behind them.

All afternoon in her sitting room, Guillaudeu rested while Lilian read Ana Swift's life history. At first she sat at a small lacquer desk and Guillaudeu watched her from an upholstered chair. After a while he dozed off and when he woke she had moved across to the window seat, where she was curled like a girl with the charred and flaking pages in her lap, gazing out the window. It was an image he carried with him from then on.

"Hello," he said.

She regarded him. "Hello."

Ana Swift was a sensation in the few days between the fire and his departure. There had been dozens of articles in the papers about Barnum's Giantess, Her Heroism in the Flames, Her Giant Sacrifice, and so on. The press put the number of lives she'd saved at thirty-one, and there was talk of erecting a bronze statue in her likeness at the site of the museum. Guillaudeu was sure Barnum's men would be looking for her bones among the ruins, but the heat had been so fierce, the fire so annihilating, he knew that nothing, not her bones nor the bones of his life's work, remained.

Guillaudeu watched Lilian in the fading afternoon light. Framed by the window behind her, she traced patterns on the final page of Ana Swift's life story. She read it aloud.

"There is just one direction for me to go now, and I am comforted even in the midst of my destruction, because I am choosing it, just as it has chosen me. It is a painful, and a beautiful, embrace. What was once a dark mystery lurking in a corner of my mind is now utterly clear. But whether I am the last of my kind, if now the world's only giantess bids her leave, remains to be seen by you, whoever you are. And if another

like me steps into the world's sights, will you see her? Will you truly see her?"

Lilian carefully lay the pages down. She got up, brushed the burned flakes of paper from her skirt, and came to stand in front of Guillaudeu.

"It looks like we have our work cut out for us." She put both her hands on his shoulders and kissed his cheek. "I know people who can help us get started. You stay right there. I'll make some tea and then you'll tell me everything."

That had been six months ago. Now, still nervous, Guillaudeu listened to Lilian's voice on stage. It was almost time.

"We all have read narratives of foreign lands, diaries of voyages and accounts of new geographies and species," she said to the audience. "In our time, hundreds of lives have been honorably lost in the name of exploration. But the prism of life you are about to look through will flash with an entirely different light, one new to the world. It is the life of one who walked among us, but she walked apart, and that distance, though measurable in feet, was often as great as any ocean. Her vantage point at times may seem foreign, but far more often you will recognize her in yourself. And now, to present you with more on the life and death of this re-markable woman, and to introduce you to her True Life History, which you are encouraged to purchase after the lecture, is Mr. Emile Guillaudeu, formerly a curator and taxidermist in Barnum's doomed museum, who was there on the night of the fire."

The book already had sold so many copies that there had been a second printing. After news of it had reached New York they'd received several letters from Barnum's lawyers, who claimed that Barnum owned the rights. Lilian shrugged this off and continued to plan the lecture tour of America that would come early the following year.

Holding tightly to the leather-bound volume, Guillaudeu emerged from the wings into the bright light of the stage.

Acknowledgments

I wish to thank Valerie Martin for her invaluable guidance during the initial drafts of this book and beyond. Many thanks also to Joshua Henkin, Peter Cameron, Stephen Dobyns, Karen Rader, Elise Proulx, and Rebecca Brown for their insight and tutelage.

The Djerassi Resident Artists Program and the Gerlach Artists Residency each gave me the gift of time to write, for which I am very grateful. The wonderful staff of the Somers Museum of the Early American Circus, as well as the librarians and archivists at the American Museum of Natural History, the New-York Historical Society, and the main branch of the New York Public Library graciously lent their expertise to my endeavors. Among the many books that informed this novel, I am especially grateful for Edwin G. Burrows and Mike Wallace's *Gotham*, Bluford Adams' *E Pluribus Barnum*, and James W. Cook's *The Arts of Deception*.

Heartfelt thanks to Chip Fleischer, Roland Pease, Helga Schmidt, John Gall, and everyone at Steerforth Press. Kate Garrick, your passion and advocacy is a special gift. Thank you.

To my parents, Stan and Sue Carlson, your encouragement and support over the years has been an invaluable anchor. And finally, Jason, your unwavering love and steady presence during the book's (and my) journey has made all the difference.

Reading Group Guide for *Among The Wonderful* by Stacy Carlson

Note: Before your group begins discussing Among the Wonderful, invite each member to take one minute to present his or her general impression of the book, without interruption or comments from the other members. This preamble to group discussion provides an opportunity for everyone to voice their opinion, and does not hinder the discussion that follows.

1. In many ways, Ana Swift and Emile Guillaudeu are very different characters. But what are some preoccupations or themes that they share?

2. How would you describe Ana Swift at the beginning of the novel? What does she hope will be different for her now that she works at Barnum's Museum? As she settles into a routine there, does her outlook change? How?

3. Over the course of the book, what changes in Guillaudeu's character surprised you?

4. Guillaudeu goes on a journey into the still undeveloped regions of upper Manhattan. Discuss this journey's importance to the plot overall. How successfully did the author portray this landscape?

5. There are many texts within the book, related to both Emile Guillaudeu and Ana Swift's stories. How do the works of Georges Cuvier and Linnaeus, as well as Ana's True Life History and Quincy Kipp's Epistemonicon, help to build the world of the book? What does each text reveal about the time period of the novel?

6. Among the Wonderful explores a particular place and time through the lens of Barnum's museum – the book is full of displays, spectacles, and the blurred line between fact and fancy. What similarities do you see between the world of Barnum's museum and the present day?

7. How would you describe PT Barnum's character in the book? Is he a villain? A prophet? Just a businessman?

8. How do Barnum's Representatives of the Wonderful treat one another? Are they as isolated as they think they are? Do they form a real community?

9. Why do none of the residents of the fifth floor intervene when the relationship between the conjoined twins, Matthew and Jacob, becomes violent?

10. Contrast Ana Swift's relationships with Mr. Ramsay and Beebe. What can you distill about her longing for love in her life?

11. Why does Ana despise other giants? How do her feelings change as she gets to know Tai Shan?

12. Barnum's business practices are still taught in business schools today. How would you describe his showmanship, and why do you think his strategies persist?

13. How would you describe the Australian tribesman? What role does he, as well as the American Indians, play in the book? How does the depiction of indigenous culture function in the book?

14. Metamorphosis, or transformation, is a central theme of the book. Which characters undergo transformations? What about the museum itself?

15. Among the Wonderful is set in antebellum New York City. How would you describe the language of the book? Does it draw you into the time period, or keep you at a distance?

16. Which historical details in the book surprised you? What cultural aspects of Barnum's world do you find familiar in our culture today?

17. What narrative techniques does the author employ to tell the story of Ana Swift's life?

18. How do Guillaudeu and Ana Swift's stories intertwine at the book's conclusion, and how does this cast each of their lives in a different, new light?

19. What is Barnum trying to prove with his Grand Ethnological Congress of Nations? How is Ana's perception of the event different from Barnum's? Guillaudeu's? How would such a congress be met today?

20. Consider the intersecting and meandering themes of class, gender, and minority that wend their way through the book. How does the mid-nineteenth century social and cultural environment surrounding these issues contrast with today's milieu? Which characters or events could easily happen in today's America without raising eyebrows?